Debra Webb is the award-winning USA Today bestselling author of more than one hundred novels, including those in reader-favourite series Faces of Evil, the Colby Agency and Shades of Death. With more than four million books sold in numerous languages and countries, Debra has a love of storytelling that goes back to her childhood on a farm in Alabama. Visit Debra at debrawebb.com

Carla Cassidy is an award-winning, *New York Times* bestselling author who has written over 170 books, including 150 for Mills & Boon. She has won the Centennial Award from Romance Writers of America. Most recently she won the 2019 Write Touch Readers' Award for her Mills & Boon Heroes title *Desperate Strangers*. Carla believes the only thing better than curling up with a good book is sitting down at the computer with a good story to write.

Discover more at millsandboon.co.uk

A PLACE TO HIDE

DEBRA WEBB

WETLANDS INVESTIGATION

CARLA CASSIDY

MILLS & BOON

All rights reserved including the right of reproduction in whole or in part in any form. This edition is published by arrangement with Harlequin Enterprises ULC.

This is a work of fiction. Names, characters, places, locations and incidents are purely fictional and bear no relationship to any real life individuals, living or dead, or to any actual places, business establishments, locations, events or incidents. Any resemblance is entirely coincidental.

This book is sold subject to the condition that it shall not, by way of trade or otherwise, be lent, resold, hired out or otherwise circulated without the prior consent of the publisher in any form of binding or cover other than that in which it is published and without a similar condition including this condition being imposed on the subsequent purchaser.

® and ™ are trademarks owned and used by the trademark owner and/or its licensee. Trademarks marked with ® are registered with the United Kingdom Patent Office and/or the Office for Harmonisation in the Internal Market and in other countries.

First Published in Great Britain 2024
by Mills & Boon, an imprint of HarperCollins*Publishers* Ltd
1 London Bridge Street, London, SE1 9GF

www.harpercollins.co.uk

HarperCollins*Publishers*
Macken House, 39/40 Mayor Street Upper,
Dublin 1, D01 C9W8, Ireland

A Place to Hide © 2024 Debra Webb
Wetlands Investigation © 2024 Carla Bracale

ISBN: 978-0-263-32216-3

0224

MIX
Paper | Supporting responsible forestry
FSC™ C007454

This book contains FSC™ certified paper and other controlled sources to ensure responsible forest management.

For more information visit: www.harpercollins.co.uk/green

Printed and Bound in the UK using 100% Renewable Electricity at CPI Group (UK) Ltd, Croydon, CR0 4YY

A PLACE TO HIDE

DEBRA WEBB

Chapter One

The Lookout Inn
Mockingbird Lane
Lookout Mountain, Tennessee
Sunday, February 18, 5:00 p.m.

The last guest had checked out and the inn was quiet.

Grace Myers wandered through the lobby. Despite having every reason not to ever smile again, she smiled. She loved this place. She crossed to the French doors that led onto the terrace. Never in a million years had she expected to be this happy again. Not ever.

She walked out into the crisp winter air and inhaled deeply.

But she was okay now. Really okay.

How long had it been since she'd really smiled? Smiled and felt it all the way to her bones?

Two years and ten months. One thousand thirty-two days.

Every single one of those days had been painful and terrifying, but the intensity had begun to lessen since Christmas. A part of her had started to get comfortable. Now, *this* felt like home. Her life felt like her own.

Another deep breath and she hugged herself against the cold. She hadn't bothered with a jacket. Grace had wanted to feel the cold. To stand out here staring at that amazing view of the valley below, feeling the icy air penetrating her sweatshirt and jeans. It was a welcome reminder that she was alive. More important, her precious little boy was alive. And they were free of the threat that had almost killed them both. They had not only survived—they had thrived.

Grace shivered at those old painful memories before slamming a mental door, banishing them to a rarely visited place. She gazed out over the views from her mountaintop perch one last time before going back inside. Liam would be waking up from his nap soon. He would be frightened if he woke up alone. Though his fear was natural at his age, she couldn't say as much for her own. She wasn't sure how long it would take for her to overcome the panic of being more than a few steps away from him.

She closed and secured the door. Then she moved around the lobby and ensured the others were as well. Usually she didn't lock the main entrance until midnight, but her guests had all checked out and she wasn't expecting anyone else until tomorrow. There was the rare occasion when an unexpected guest arrived, but he or she could press the doorbell.

An evening of solitude with her favorite little man would be a nice change of pace. The inn had been for the most part solidly booked through the Christmas and New Year season, and busy all the way to Valentine's Day. At least ten of the twenty guest rooms had been occupied all that time until today. It was a great winter season, and she was genuinely grateful. Just maybe this was a sign of things to come.

Good things.

Honestly, it was still difficult to grasp the idea that this place was hers. She stalled, gazed around the large space that served as the lobby. Hundred-and-fifty-year-old shiplap walls soared some thirty feet to a beamed and vaulted ceiling that still took her breath away. The vintage chandeliers and numerous windows and sets of French doors filled the space with light. The stone on the floor was the same stone that covered the exterior facade and climbed the better part of the far wall in the lobby where a massive fireplace added a homey feeling. It was more beautiful than any home or business she could ever have hoped to own.

When she'd bought it, the inn had been empty for years. The former owners had retired to Florida with the idea of perhaps leasing out the property. The couple hadn't been able to adjust to the idea of someone else running the inn. Eventually they'd had no choice but to sell in order to prevent the property from falling into disrepair. A vacant home—or inn—lost its soul when empty of people and slowly fell apart. Grace had taken one look at the place and known this was the dream she wanted for herself and her son. She and Liam had gone to Florida and spoken to the elderly owners. Forty-eight hours later, the property was theirs. As triumphant as she had felt at that moment, that had only been the beginning.

Months and months of hard work were required to bring the inn back to life—to infuse vibrancy into it once more. Lucky for Grace the bones had all been there; she'd only needed to tweak the mechanics like the electrical and the heating and cooling systems and then spruce up the rest cosmetically. Finding the perfect furnishings for their private quarters had been the most difficult. The previous owners had taken their personal furnishings with them to Florida. Months of frequenting vintage shops and perusing online dealers had paid off. Luckily the French drapes tailor-made for the many large windows had only required cleaning. The same went for the numerous Persian rugs. The furnishings in the common areas and the guest rooms had been perfect and only in need of polishing.

It had all come together beautifully. The ridiculously happy smile slid across her face once more. She wasn't sure she would ever stop smiling again. A good thing, she decided.

Before returning to the registration desk to tidy up, she placed a couple more logs on the fire. Sparks flared and a hint of oaky smoke stirred. Until she'd started this new life, she hadn't realized there was such a variety of scents when it came to firewood. For the most part she bought hickory. The scent was classic, very traditional. But cherry was her favorite by far. She used the cherry for special occasions, like Christmas.

She dusted her hands together and moved on to the registration desk, where she locked the drawers and ensured all was as it should be. A few taps and the computer system went dark and silent. From there she moved through the dining room. The tables had been cleared and prepped for the next meal, which wouldn't be until lunch tomorrow, when her guests were due.

She paused, rested her hands on the back of a chair. More lovely sets of French doors in the dining room provided access to the terrace that flanked both sides of the structure where it overlooked the valley below. The view was simply incredible. She wandered there, gazed out for few moments before testing the locks. Once those doors were checked she continued to the large kitchen. Her chest squeezed the tiniest bit. How she loved this kitchen. Vintage in every way save the appliances.

The back-door lock was secure. This was a nightly ritual for her. A desperate need time would never assuage. Though she had an alarm system, it wasn't the best. Later she hoped to upgrade, but that was one expense that would have to wait.

With all as it should be, she sneaked quietly into their private suite. Liam slept like a precious little lamb. Generally he was up well before now, but his usual one o'clock nap hadn't happened until past three. He lay in the middle of the big bed. He had his own small room right next to hers, but she hadn't been able to move him there just yet. She wanted him with her at night. Some would scold her for the decision, but they had not lived through what she had survived.

Their suite included a small parlor and a kitchenette as well as a nice-sized bathroom. It really was all quite small compared to the size of the inn, but it was everything they needed and she loved it. It felt cozy and comfortable. Of the twenty guest quarters, there were ten rooms with en suites upstairs as well as ten more small cottages that had been added to the property fifty or so years ago. The additions formed a semicircle on either side of the rear gardens. Each cottage had an enviable view of the valley below.

Grace climbed carefully onto the bed with her child. She had never been one to take afternoon naps, but she had been working really hard for months and it was starting to catch up with her. She needed a break. A little getaway.

She almost laughed at the idea. Maybe by summer's end,

late August perhaps, she would be able to afford a shor
time away. Certainly, that would be low season. Maybe sh
would take Liam to his favorite theme park. Every time h
saw a commercial about the place, he jumped up and dow
and shouted in delight.

His blond hair was just a tad curly and brushed his shoul
ders. There were moments when she chastised herself fc
not giving him his first haircut yet. Whenever they droppe
in at any of the local shops, most people they encountere
thought he was a little girl, but frankly, she was glad. Bein
seen with a little girl was less likely to put her on anyone'
radar since the one person who—if given the chance—
might ever look for her would be looking for a woman with
little boy. She swallowed hard against the thought. Her littl
boy's eyes were closed, but she knew them by heart. He ha
the most vivid blue eyes. Like the sky on a frosty morning

Grace closed her eyes and thought of the last time sh
had seen her father and how amazed he had been by hi
grandson. William Reinhart had adored his namesake. Thei
time together had been far too short. The memory ache
deep in her chest.

Her father's sudden death was her fault. She shouldn'
have taken her problems to his door, but she'd had no plac
else to go. Even now—if he were alive and despite wha
had happened—her father would insist that she had mad
the right decision. Of course he would. But she should hav
taken care of herself—after all, it was her fault she'd ende
up in trouble. Ultimately, her choices had been limited be
cause it hadn't been just about her. She'd had to protec
Liam, and to do that, she had needed help. Desperation ha
dictated her decisions.

Maybe her father wouldn't have suffered that massive heart attack if she and Liam had run in a different direction. Didn't that make his death her fault?

Before her mind could come up with an acceptable rebuttal, sleep dragged her into its tumultuous depths.

HE SCREAMED HER NAME.

The sound echoed through her, sending terror through her veins. The knowledge that she was dead if he caught her shuddered through her very soul.

You're dreaming. Wake up!

But she couldn't. She was in too deep.

She had to run faster. But it was so cold… The snow was deep and dragging at her feet; the woods were dense and foreboding. She was lost in the darkness. It was only that damned snow catching the light of the moon that prevented her from running headlong into a tree or over a cliff.

Keep going.

Don't stop.

The bare trees loomed over her like shadowy creatures backlit by that big moon. A hint of familiarity had hope fizzing through her. Was she almost to the highway? A new burst of adrenaline fired in her blood. Maybe just a little farther now. If she reached the main highway, someone might come along and stop for her. She could get to help then.

All she had to do was make it to the highway.

Another pain deep in her belly forced her to a stop, made her cry out.

The baby was coming.

Dear God, she had to keep going…had to hurry. Her

feet began to move again. She stumbled forward. Panted for breath.

Please, please let her get out of these woods and to help before the baby was born. She blinked back the burn of tears and rushed forward a little faster, staggering and lurching. She was so, so cold now. Her feet felt like leaden weights, her legs stiff and unresponsive.

Don't stop.

She pushed onward. Almost there.

The sound of a car's engine humming along in the distance gave her hope, sparked her determination not to give up. She could do this! She could make it. All she had to do was keep going.

Grace broke through the tree line. The inky black highway cut a winding path for miles through the trees, snow and ice lining the shoulders and ditches on both sides. She scrambled down and then up from the ditch and staggered onto the slick pavement.

Air sawed in and out of her lungs as she gasped for breath. Had the car passed this point already?

Please, please let another one come along.

She winced as she tightened her fingers into fists, the bones feeling as if they were breaking, her skin numb from the cold. There had been no time for gloves, no time for anything but to run.

He'd shown up unexpectedly, and she'd had no other choice except to get out of there. She'd had to abandon everything. Every. Single. Thing.

The only thing that really mattered was still inside her... the *baby*.

She prayed he wouldn't find her before another car came along.

The distant sound of something—a vehicle, she hoped—brushed against her senses.

She started in that direction, barely maintaining her balance on the slippery asphalt.

The sound came closer and closer. Finally, she saw the headlights. Grace braced herself to keep her balance and started to wave her arms.

"Help me," she cried out, her voice weak and not nearly loud enough. "Help!"

The gush of warmth that flowed down her legs warned her that her water had broken. She grabbed at herself. "Oh, God."

The car started to slow. She waved one arm, held her belly with the other. "Please! Please!"

The car stopped and she reached for the door handle, her fingers so cold she couldn't make them work. The door suddenly popped open as if the driver had understood and leaned over and opened it.

"Thank you." She pulled the door open wider and collapsed into the seat. "My baby is coming." She turned to the driver. "I need—"

It was him.

The man who had the same blond hair and blue eyes as her son smiled at her. And she knew her fate.

She was dead.

GRACE BOLTED UPRIGHT, her eyes searching the darkness.

A dream. It had only been a dream.

She pressed a hand to her chest and forced her breathing

to slow. She reached her free hand to the lamp and turned on the light. What time was it? Six p.m. flashed on the digital clock. She'd slept for well over an hour.

"Liam." He should be awake by now.

She reached for her son, but beside her the bed was empty…and cold.

Fear slammed into her chest. She jumped from the bed and looked around the room. "Liam!"

She never went to sleep like that. And even if she did, any move or sound he made generally woke her.

She searched the room. Hurried to the parlor. No Liam.

He wasn't anywhere in their private space.

Her gaze landed on the door. It was ajar. As she rushed across the room and through that door, she reminded herself that her little boy, who was not yet three, could not unlock the entry doors. He would be somewhere in the house. The realization should have calmed her but it did not.

"Liam!" She moved from room to room, the kitchen, the dining room, calling his name.

Then she spotted him.

He stood in the lobby staring out the window nearest the fireplace. She rushed to him.

"Liam." She dropped to her knees and turned him toward her, visually examining him from head to toe. "Are you all right?"

He nodded his curly blond head. "I watching the man in the snow."

Grace frowned and stared out the window. It had snowed. Not so much really, just a thin coat of white. She shuddered. She'd been dreaming about running through the snow. The memory had left a bitter taste in her mouth and a cold stone in her gut.

She scanned the landscape as best she could with nothing but the moonlight and a few exterior lights that weren't nearly bright enough, she decided. "I don't see anyone."

"Gone. Gone," her little boy said with a giggle.

Had he been dreaming and only imagined a figure in the darkness?

Grace's gaze searched the snow once more…and her heart stalled.

There, in the newly fallen blanket of snow where the cobblestones led to the front entrance, were tracks. Too large to be any sort of animal. Too well formed to be anything other than boots or shoes.

Liam was right. Someone had been here.

She rose to her feet and surveyed the yard and the steps. She could see where the prints seemed to come from the thick line of shrubbery and crossed the yard, then came up the steps to disappear since there was no snow on the covered porch.

"Me want it."

Grace shook herself. She knelt back down to her little boy. "I'm sorry, sweetie. What did you say?"

"Me want it." Liam pointed to the window.

Grace followed his chubby finger to the porch, but there was nothing there. "Mommy doesn't see anything."

"Down there!" he urged.

She leaned closer to the glass and stared at the stone floor of the porch. The small silver object glinted in the light from the window and had her heart pitching to a near stop.

A heart-shaped locket on a chain.

She didn't have to touch it or even to see it more clearly to know it would be vintage and blood would be smeared on the chain and maybe inside the locket.

Grace grabbed Liam and ran back to their private space. She closed the door, sat Liam on the floor and engaged the security bar she had ordered just for a moment like this. She backed away, tugging Liam with her.

She had to call the police.

Entering the digits, she collapsed on the floor and pulled Liam into her lap. When the dispatcher answered, she said, "We've had an intruder on the property at the Lookout Inn on Mockingbird Lane. Can you please send someone?"

She had wanted to sound calm but her voice had been thin and hollow. Liam stared at her, his face ready to pucker into tears. He was frightened. She should have been more careful not to upset him.

When she'd answered all the dispatcher's questions and had the promise that a cruiser was en route, Grace ended the call. She held tightly on to the cell phone while hugging Liam to her chest.

"What's wrong, Mommy?"

"Everything's okay, buddy." She rocked back and forth as much for her own benefit as for her child's.

She told herself it couldn't have been him. He was in police custody awaiting trial.

He would never be free again after what he'd done. There was no reason for her to be afraid…none.

But what if she was wrong? She had been wrong before.

A MERE FIFTEEN minutes later, the police had arrived and begun the search of the property outside the inn. Before the deputies had started roving the landscape, she, with Liam on her hip, had slipped onto the porch and picked up the locket. She'd done so using a plastic sandwich baggie so as not to touch it. She'd opened it using the bag to protect her fingers. A bloodstained picture of her had been trimmed down to fit inside. She'd closed it instantly. Then she'd taken it to the kitchen and hidden it under the sink. She'd distracted Liam with two chocolate coins. The child loved the gold-wrapped goodies—pirate booty, he would say. The kind in his favorite animated movie. She hated using sweets to bribe him, but sometimes there was just no other option.

The entire search by the police took an hour since the deputies felt it best to have a look around inside as well. Grace didn't have a problem with that. She wanted to be certain whoever had been out there was gone. She told herself again that it couldn't be him.

Impossible.

If she really believed this, why was she hiding the locket from the deputies?

Grace dismissed the thought. It had to be a coincidence. Some local yahoo who was reliving Halloween. Or a true crime fanatic who liked playing games. Her nightmare had dominated the headlines and online news feeds for months. The bastard who'd created that nightmare had quickly gained a bizarre cult following. The first Halloween after she escaped him, some manufacturer had even created and sold a mask of his face. How sick was that?

She shivered. This had to be some serial killer buff playing games. Couldn't be anything else.

But was her certainty only wishful thinking?

Finally, one of the deputies—Scott Reynolds—came into the main parlor to announce they were finished.

"Beyond the tracks, we didn't find anything," he explained. "You said your son saw someone."

Grace looked over at her child, playing with a puzzle at the coffee table that sat between two sofas. "I woke up and he'd climbed out of the bed. I found him in the lobby staring out a window. He said he'd been watching a man in the snow. That's when I noticed the tracks."

Reynolds glanced at Liam. "He said a man."

Grace nodded. "The tracks came up the steps, so I'm guessing the intruder came onto the porch and maybe all the way to the window where Liam was watching." Her stomach tied into a thousand screaming knots at the idea.

Reynolds lowered into a chair. He glanced at his notepad. "Ma'am, I'm not meaning to pry, but I have to ask—where is his father?" He nodded toward Liam.

Folks in the area knew Grace was a single mother. She'd been here almost two years. She and Liam had fit fairly well into the community, though she had been careful not to get too close to anyone. Keeping a certain distance was essential. Getting close to anyone required a willingness to share history, to be open. She couldn't do that. At least, not yet.

"He—" she cleared her throat and lowered her voice "—passed away before we moved here."

Reynolds nodded. "Sorry to hear that." He made a note on his pad. "If you don't mind, I'd like to ask Liam a few questions to see if he remembers anything about the man."

Worry that Liam would mention the object the man left on the porch tore at her. "We could try. He's more likely to respond to me." Her child was on the shy side when it came to talking to anyone he hadn't met before.

Reynolds nodded his understanding. "Just ask him general description questions. Big? Small? Dark? Light?"

Grace nodded. "Okay."

The deputy prepared to jot down any responses onto his notepad.

"Liam." He looked up and Grace motioned for him to come to her. "Deputy Reynolds and I have some questions about the man."

Liam eyed Reynolds speculatively, then walked over to climb into his mother's lap.

"'Kay." His fingers went to his mouth. He did that when he was nervous.

"Was the man you saw big?" She nodded to Reynolds. "Tall like the deputy or shorter like Mommy?"

Liam pointed to Reynolds with his free hand.

"So tall like Deputy Reynolds?"

Liam nodded.

"Did you see his hair?"

Liam moved his head side to side. "Hat." He patted the top of his head.

Reynolds nodded. "Did he wear a hat like mine?" He picked up the baseball-style cap he'd placed on his knee when he sat down.

Liam scooted out of his mother's lap and ran toward their private quarters.

Reynolds made a face. "You think I scared him off?"

Grace stood. "Give me a moment and I'll see if he will come back."

As if her words had summoned him, Liam ran back into the room. He held one of his favorite beanies.

"Like dis." He held up the beanie.

Reynolds grinned. "All right. Good job, little man." He jotted down the information. "What about his eyes?" He looked to Liam once more. "Did you see what color his eyes were?"

Liam had warmed up to the deputy now. He touched his own eyes. "Mine."

Grace's heart dropped to her feet. "He had blue eyes?"

Liam nodded. "Mine."

Grace lowered back into her chair for fear her knees would buckle any second.

"Great job!" Reynolds praised the boy. "Was he wearing blue jeans like your mom?"

Liam shook his head. "Like Batman."

Grace found her voice again. "So black. All over like Batman? Pants and shirt?"

Liam nodded.

"And gloves too?" Grace lifted her hand.

Once more Liam nodded.

"Thank you, Liam," the deputy said. "You've been very helpful." He closed his notepad and stood. "Ms. Myers, I'll let you know if we figure anything out, although I have to say we don't have much to go on. We did take photos of the boot prints and we are questioning neighbors. But considering the gloves, we're not likely to find prints."

"I understand." She stood. "I just appreciate you coming."

When the deputies were gone, she made Liam a sandwich, poured him a glass of milk and settled him in front of the television. She went to the main kitchen and retrieved the plastic bag from beneath the sink.

She opened it and peered inside. Her gut clenched.

It was the same type of locket the bastard had left behind with his murder victims. Blood smears and all. But why was her picture inside?

Because he wanted her to be his next victim.

With a chill dancing down her spine, she wadded the bag around the damned thing, her eyes closing in defeat.

How could this be? He couldn't know where she was. But he must. It was the only way to explain this. She wanted to believe that, worst-case scenario, he had located them somehow and sent some paid thug or crazed fan to drop off the locket. But Liam said the man had his eyes. Would he have specifically sought out the help of a man with pale blue eyes? Or had the eyes been colored contacts?

Maybe. The bastard was evil to the core.

He would do anything to terrify her.

Would he send the creep back for another visit? Or worse, to hurt them?

She steadied herself. First, she had to make sure he was still in custody. He had to be. He'd been charged with murder and he'd tried to kill her. Bail had been denied.

If Adam Locke, the infamous Sweetheart Killer, was out, wouldn't she have heard?

Of course not. She'd given no one her new address or her new name. How could anyone contact her? Her goal had been to disappear.

Since she hadn't bothered to see what was happening with his trial in a long while, she had no idea if it had even begun. Just hearing his name made her feel ill. Seeing photos of him was more than she could bear.

But now she had no choice.

She had spent the past two years building Liam a safe home here on Lookout Mountain. She had ensured that no one from their old life knew where they were, and no one here knew their true identities.

Was her decision two years ago to disappear—avoiding witness protection or any other support—a mistake? Was keeping her identity here a secret—especially now in light of what had just happened—yet another misstep?

No. She had made the right choices. The only way to protect Liam was for no one anywhere to know their location. As for the locket, until she could be certain this was not some prankster, she wasn't sharing that detail with anyone.

But then…if Adam had found them and had sent this person, how would she ever keep Liam safe?

Chapter Two

Robert Vaughn shuffled through the messages on his desk. How had he received so many calls on a Sunday evening? The last time he'd gotten that many calls in one stretch was on his birthday. The Mountain was generally far too quiet for this much excitement.

Didn't matter. He couldn't have answered any of them while transporting a violent criminal. His cell phone had stayed in the console of the SUV he'd been driving—on silent. He'd dropped the prisoner off in Knoxville and headed back, not rolling into his own driveway until four this morning.

The two hours' sleep he'd gotten before being called to an accident at seven this morning was not enough sleep to have his brain operating on full power, but he hadn't wanted to take the day off.

More coffee. He needed another shot of caffeine if he was going to survive the morning.

Leaving his closet-sized office, he headed for the break room, which was really just a niche in the corridor leading to the lobby. He refilled his mug and wandered into the small lobby. There was a bench and a coatrack but no room for much else. Beyond this space was another, slightly larger office that was shared by the four other deputies assigned to this substation. Rob was the deputy in charge. The only other space was a storeroom, which served as a multipurpose area. The tight squeeze was all temporary while the new substation for the community was being built. Just more growing pains. The Mountain was expanding.

Rob liked the assignment even with the expansion. He'd been on the mountain for a year, and it still surprised him that he felt completely satisfied here. He'd always considered himself a city boy. So when the opportunity to serve as the deputy in charge of a small community substation had come up, he'd expected to turn it down. But then he'd shocked himself by saying yes.

So maybe it hadn't been such a shock considering he'd been single for nearly a year and he'd needed change. Having the woman he'd expected to marry take off with a deputy from a neighboring community had proved just a little unsettling. Truth was, he'd felt as if they were drifting apart months before she actually split. Still, his ego had been bruised and he'd moped around for a while. The move had come at a good time.

No regrets to this point. He'd even sold his condo in Chattanooga and rented a small studio apartment only a couple of miles from the substation. When he needed total solitude, he spent a few days at his cabin in the woods, perched on the Tennessee River. He'd changed from a sports car to an

SUV. Made sense, anyway. The old truck he'd inherited from his father that stayed at the cabin on the river was not four-wheel drive, and sometimes he needed the extra muscle to get up the mountain.

He spent his time in jeans and muck boots when not on duty. He chuckled and shook his head. Maybe there was something about approaching forty that had changed him. Not that thirty-seven was over the hill, but he damned sure wasn't getting any younger. If he was totally honest with himself, starting a family was something he'd hoped to do by now, and that hadn't worked out either.

Banishing that line of thinking, he walked back to his office. Those calls weren't going to answer themselves.

The first two were easy. Follow-ups on a couple of small burglary cases. Both recently solved. He scheduled a date and time for his range qualifications test. He'd put it off longer than he should have already. Not that he was worried about the test; he was an excellent marksman. It was just carving out the time from his schedule.

A rap on his open door was followed by "Morning, boss." Deputy Scott Reynolds stood in his doorway.

"Morning, Reynolds."

"You hear about the excitement over at the inn last evening?"

Rob straightened, going instantly on a higher state of alert. "What excitement?"

"Somebody was creeping around the place, peeking in windows apparently."

The last of the messages forgotten, Rob pushed to his feet. "Everyone okay?" The image of Grace and her little boy formed in his mind, sending him further on edge.

"Yeah, yeah," Reynolds assured him. "Whoever was poking around was long gone when we arrived. Ms. Myers was pretty upset."

"What about the kid?" Rob forced his heart rate to slow. "He okay?" Liam was a cute kid, really cute, and he'd stolen Rob's heart on day one. He really liked that kid. Liked his mom too, but she kept her distance. Rob respected her wishes. Whatever had broken her trust in relationships, he wasn't going to push for answers. If she was interested, she would let him know when she felt comfortable doing so. He could be patient. He'd decided very quickly that she was the sort of woman worth waiting for.

Reynolds nodded. "Apparently he saw the guy. The boy was able to tell us he was tall, wore a beanie and had blue eyes."

Good to know but not particularly helpful when searching for an unknown perp. "No indication the guy tried to break in or took anything?"

Reynolds shook his head. "His footprints showed he moved around to a few windows and came up on the porch. Nothing seemed to have been tampered with. Nothing taken that Ms. Myers noticed." He shrugged. "I asked her about the boy's father. Since nothing was taken, that was my first thought. Maybe the kid's dad showed up unexpectedly, but she said he passed away."

Rob wanted to ask why he hadn't been called, particularly since he was in charge of the security of this community, but he knew the answer. He'd been on the road transporting a violent criminal. He'd volunteered for the job to prevent one of his less experienced deputies from having to do it.

"I should do a follow-up," he announced, feeling the need to see for himself that all was well. "Have a second look around."

Reynolds shrugged. "I parked on the street and hung around until the chef, Diane Franks, arrived. Everything was all quiet, but if you think there's reason for a second look, I can do that now."

Rob grabbed his cap. "Thanks, but I've got it."

He felt bad for not knowing about this already. That traffic situation had caused him to miss the staff meeting. Generally, he would have passed off the call to someone else in order to be at that meeting, but one of the drivers involved had been a friend who had called him directly. That was the other thing about small communities: everyone knew everyone else.

He headed out to his SUV, thankful the windshield was still clear. He'd had a hell of a time removing the crusted ice this morning. Last night's forecast of two inches of snow had turned into four, with a layer of ice mixed in. The roads had been cleared early this morning, but there would still be side streets and roads that were icy. This time of year, sudden winter storms were to be expected but only appreciated by the kids who got a day home from school.

The Lookout Inn, 10:40 a.m.

THE RENTAL LICENSE plates on the vehicles parked in the lot suggested there were guests. Grace had told him she'd had more bookings than expected all year so far. A number of folks who'd lived in this community for the better part of their lives were impressed with what Grace had done with the inn. When she'd bought it two years ago, it had been closed for nearly a decade. No one really expected it to be brought back to life quite so easily or so well. Grace had come in, renovated the place and put it back on the map in record time.

Folks liked her. She was quiet and reserved, but she tirelessly supported the other businesses and worked hard to keep the inn innovative.

He exhaled a big breath, fogging the air, and headed for the front entrance. Rob had asked her out on three occasions, and she'd turned him down. In a nice way, of course. She was always too busy or Liam was not feeling well.

After the last time, Rob had decided to settle for being friends until she was ready for more—which might be never. He hadn't exactly given up on persuading her to give him a shot, but he had opted to continue being patient. She was a really nice person. Didn't hurt that she was pretty gorgeous too and had an adorable kid to boot. He knew nothing about her past relationships, not even about her deceased husband. But he recognized when a history was bad. She would tell him her story when she felt ready. Something else he could wait for.

When Angela, his former fiancée, had left him, he'd rushed back into the dating scene in an effort, he supposed, to prove something. But that had grown old real quick. From there he'd decided to just take his time and see where life took him.

Then he'd met Grace.

He'd had zero interest anywhere else since.

Rob paused at the entrance to the inn's lobby, squared his shoulders, opened the door and walked in. His gaze instantly locked in on the woman behind the registration desk. Long brown hair so light it was almost blonde. She kept it in a braid, and he'd had plenty of fantasies about deconstructing it. Gray eyes and a smile that stole his breath every single time. The fact that she was a looker was great, but it was her gentle spirit and kind heart that really got to him.

Whoever had hurt this woman had been a fool.

"Mr. Pierce, this is your key." Grace smiled as she passed the actual key—not a card—to the new guest. "You are in cabin 10." She gestured toward the dining room. "Take the French doors out onto the terrace and you'll see the cabins."

"Thank you." He glanced at Rob as he moved closer.

"Morning," Rob said.

The older man gave him a nod. "Good morning to you—" he considered Rob's uniform "—Deputy."

"If you need anything," Grace said to the new arrival, "don't hesitate to let me know."

"Will do." Pierce headed for the dining room. At the door, he glanced back, noted that Rob was still watching and gave another nod before continuing on.

Uniforms made some folks uneasy.

Rob turned his attention to the woman watching him expectantly.

"Good morning," she said, her smile not quite as bright as usual.

"Good morning." He leaned against the counter. "I wish you had called me last night." He didn't bother telling her he was miles away and couldn't have helped, because he wanted her to call him in the future—no matter the circumstances. It was selfish of him, he understood that glaring fact, but he wanted her to feel comfortable coming to him with any issue.

She looked away, busied herself with decluttering after checking in her guest. "I honestly wasn't sure what the situation was." Her gaze finally landed on his once more. "Frankly, I was terrified, and my first thought was to call 911."

"I understand. You had every right to be afraid." Except she had never once mentioned—in the year he had known her—being afraid. She'd had a mountain lion lumber into her backyard, more than her share of woodland varmints. Even a bear once. She'd called for whatever help was required and calmly gone about her business. But he supposed none compared to having a man attempting to look inside your home. Humans could be the most dangerous of predators.

"I should see about the lunch menu." She flashed him another visibly lackluster smile.

"Mind if I tag along?" He wasn't walking away that easily.

She hesitated, then shrugged. "Sure. I just need to let Cara know to keep an eye on the desk."

Rob waited where he stood as she headed for her private residence. Cara Gunter was the new assistant Grace had hired. Well, *new* wasn't exactly right. She'd been here three months already. Nice lady. Hailed from Chattanooga originally, with an elderly grandmother here on the mountain. She'd been in Memphis for years until her grandmother grew too feeble to take care of herself and Cara had moved back. Early thirties, like Grace, and very blunt and focused. But Liam really liked her, which was more than half the battle, Grace had insisted when she hired Cara. With a toddler in the mix, running an inn without an assistant would be impossible. The first assistant Grace hired had died in an automobile accident. Both Grace and Liam had been devastated. These mountain roads could be treacherous.

There was also Karl Wilborn, the gardener, and his wife, Paula, the housekeeper. The couple were lifetime residents of the Mountain. Good folks. Diane Franks was a newcomer. She'd run her own catering business in New York before retiring and relocating to Tennessee, and taking the chef job at the inn. She too was a widow, but rumor was she and the new principal at the middle school were getting serious.

When Grace waved at him from the hall beyond the lobby, he headed in that direction, followed her through the massive dining room. The coffee bar had him wishing for another cup. Grace was brilliant with coffee. She mixed blends and added ingredients that made for some seriously good coffee. Her baking skills were nothing to scoff at either. He'd never been a pastry man, but he dropped by a couple of times a week for Grace's coffee and pastries... and maybe just to say hello.

"Try the new wake-you-up breakfast blend." She gestured to one of the silver coffee urns. "I think it's my best yet."

"I'm always happy to be a taste tester." He picked up one of the dainty china cups and filled it with the steaming brew. "If you ever start your own coffee company, I'm ready to join your staff." He lifted the cup to his lips. The robust but creamy taste burst on his tongue. "Very good."

She smiled. "Thank you."

The aroma of baked scones and muffins lingered in the kitchen. The baskets covered with tea towels he noticed at the coffee bar had likely been loaded with both. His gut rumbled, warning that he should have grabbed breakfast this morning. Wouldn't have mattered, he imagined. Even if he'd already eaten, he would've been lured by Grace's creations.

He'd been invited to Sunday lunch or dinner more than once. Funny, he'd thought those invitations were leading them in the right direction, but so far that was where things stalled.

"Grab a scone," she suggested, her smile a real one this time. "There's cranberry-orange and cherry."

"They smell great," he said. He set the cup he'd emptied on the counter and went for a cherry scone. He bit off a piece and groaned in satisfaction. "Wow. This is great." He leaned against the counter and, before going for another bite, said, "Tell me about last night."

"It was the end of a busy four-day weekend," she said as she picked up her iPad and checked the screen.

He had learned that Grace kept her menus and other inn-related activities electronically. Made sense, he supposed. But he suspected she studied it now to avoid his gaze. That was off somehow. She'd seemed to trust him well enough. Was comfortable with him as long as he wasn't asking her on a date. Maybe last night had unnerved her more than usual.

"By the time the last guests checked out, I was exhausted." She held her iPad against her chest like a shield now. "Liam had already fallen asleep for a late nap, so I decided to lie down next to him just for a few minutes. I hadn't really meant to drift off, but I did. I woke up an hour or so later, and he was gone from the bed. The house was dark by then, so I went through the house turning on lights and calling his name." She shivered. "The more I called without getting an answer, the more terrified I grew."

He could see how that was a lot scarier than a mountain lion. "I'm glad you found him and he was okay."

She nodded. "He was in the lobby staring out one of the windows. It was…" She shrugged. "A bit creepy."

He could understand that. "Did Liam say anything?" Rob resisted the urge to reach out and touch her, maybe comfort her. But she wouldn't want him feeling protective. Grace Myers was far too independent.

"He said he was watching the man in the snow." She closed her eyes a moment as if the memory pained her. "The snow had started to fall after I went to sleep, I guess. There was enough by the time I woke up to see the footprints the guy left. I guess the part that really got to me was the idea that anything could have happened to Liam while I was sleeping. I shouldn't have allowed myself to fall asleep like that."

Rob straightened away from the counter. Again, he resisted the urge to reach out. "Have you noticed anyone hanging around or maybe driving by regularly? Since nothing was taken last night, this could be someone casing the place. It's a nice inn. He may believe you keep cash on the premises, and with the inn relatively secluded, it would make for an easy target."

She turned her attention back to the iPad. "No. I haven't noticed anyone hanging around or driving by. Honestly, I'm hoping it was just some person who…" She shrugged. "Who got disoriented in the snow and made a mistake."

It happened, he'd give her that, but the idea was a stretch. "If you think of anything or anyone we should look into, let me know and I'll see that it gets done."

Again, she hugged her iPad. "I will, of course."

She was nervous, but this was more than just the jitters. Talking about what had happened got under her skin. This was a new reaction. One he hadn't seen in Grace before. Maybe it was only because she'd felt Liam had been at risk.

Rob opted to change the subject. "You have more guests coming in this week?"

"The two today and no one else before Friday." She visibly relaxed with the subject change. "I'm very pleased with how the winter business has panned out so far. If the spring and summer carry through with no mechanical breakdowns or bizarre accidents, I think I can safely say we've survived the typical restart costs."

The chamber of commerce had already presented Grace with the best new business award. He expected that was only the first of many honors for her hard work and commitment to the community.

"I've always thought you were going to do well. You're good at the online reach. That's really important for an independent inn like this one."

"I try," she agreed.

The few seconds of silence that lapsed warned that she was ready for him to be on his way. She didn't generally give off that vibe. Obviously she really was rattled.

"If you need me to talk to Liam or anything else, all you have to do is say the word."

She nodded. "And I appreciate that more than you can know."

Another few seconds of silence. Definitely his cue to go. "All right, then. If you don't mind, I'll have a quick look around outside before I head out."

"Sure. That would be great. An extra pair of eyes is always appreciated."

"If I find anything, I'll check back in with you before I go."

She kept a smile in place as she nodded her understanding, but again, it didn't make the usual cut.

He left through the back door.

Maybe her chilly response to him wasn't about what had happened. Could be something else going on. Had she met someone? Had she decided she didn't want to be friends anymore?

Kicking aside the ridiculous and immature ideas, he focused on what he'd promised to do. Taking his time, he walked the shrub border that outlined the perimeter of the backyard. He had a look under the larger shrubs and inside the one good-sized storage shed out back. The door was unlocked, and he'd have to suggest that she keep the building locked going forward. He found nothing unexpected among the yard and gardening tools neatly stored there. Wilborn likely was in and out of the building more than Grace. He'd mention it to the older man as well.

Heading back around front, he spotted Liam at the window. The boy waved. Rob smiled and waved back. He should have insisted on speaking to the boy. Maybe he'd come by later and broach the idea.

Cara, Grace's assistant, appeared behind Liam, gave Rob a wave and then ushered Liam from the window.

All appeared to be good to go. Except he had a gut feeling that something was off with Grace.

He just had no clue what.

Chapter Three

Grace watched from a front window as Rob Vaughn drove away. Her heart reacted with a heavy thud to the idea that she should have been truthful with him. Maybe it was time she told someone the whole story. Particularly after last night.

But if she did, she risked her identity and location getting out. She could not—would not—risk Liam's safety by allowing anyone to know the truth.

Not even the man she had come to trust...had come to have feelings for.

So not smart, Grace.

She shivered, hugged her arms around herself. She should have learned her lesson three years ago.

Didn't matter. Rob Vaughn would never know how she felt. He would—could—never know her secrets. How could she possibly ever have any sort of deeper relationship with anyone while keeping the kind of secrets she could never ever share?

She couldn't.

"Diane says lunch is ready if you'd like to join us."

Cara's voice startled Grace. She ushered her thoughts

back to the present and smiled at her assistant. "Thank you, Cara. I'll be right there."

Cara nodded and walked away. Grace wasn't sure what she would do without the woman. She'd felt torn about the need for an assistant when she'd hired Cara. Kendall Walls had been with her from the time she moved to the Mountain. Kendall was the daughter of the assistant who had worked with the former owners back when the inn was in operation. The previous owners had highly recommended her. Grace and Liam had adored her. The accident and losing her still hurt. It wasn't until nearly two months later that Grace had been forced to break down and hire someone else. She just hadn't been able to handle everything alone and take care of Liam.

The holiday season had blasted off, and Liam was getting so independent. He wasn't always agreeable to following Mommy around and entertaining himself with his toys. Neither of which was a bad thing, except she couldn't watch him as closely as she preferred.

Plus Grace so loved baking. Without help, she couldn't possibly do much of her own baking. So, she'd started the interviewing process and found Cara. With her housekeeper and gardener and the wondrous chef, Diane Franks, they had made it through the holiday season without a glitch.

Grace added more logs to the fire. She adored the inglenook-style fireplace. She was so grateful that it hadn't been closed in or altered during the numerous renovations that had come before. Most of the inn was heated by a modern gas system, including a neat little fireplace in each guest room. But this large one in the lobby was completely original.

The sound of her little boy's voice had her smiling as she

moved toward the dining room. Liam was already entertaining whoever had decided to pop in for lunch. All the way from Seattle was Henry Brower, sixtyish, with salt-and-pepper hair and kind eyes, who sat at the far end of the table. He was laughing at something Liam had said or done. Cara sat next to Liam. Their other guest, Joe Pierce, from Los Angeles, had not come inside, yet Grace hoped he would put in an appearance. She enjoyed chatting with her guests. To Grace, part of the draw of inns and bed-and-breakfasts was the gathering for meals. She had altered her appearance enough to do so without worry of being recognized. That too was something she had worried about in the beginning. But in two years no one had recognized her, so she'd begun to relax…until last night.

Henry smiled in Grace's direction when she picked up a plate at the serving buffet. With effort, she returned the smile before surveying the lovely meal Diane had prepared. An array of sandwiches and a very tasty-looking salad. Grace had baked a variety of cookies. Chocolate with walnuts and drizzled with white icing, cherry almond with sprinkles, and lemon with white chocolate. Diane had arranged them beautifully on a vintage tray. Grace was thankful for the vintage dinnerware and serving pieces. It felt important to the atmosphere she wanted to create—something she and the previous owners shared. Guests frequently complimented the choices.

Funny how a small compliment could go so far after all she'd been through these past few years. In her old life, she had been an accountant. She'd worked for a large firm with an enviable salary and great benefits. But the environment had been cold and austere. It had been nothing like owning and operating an inn.

Grace moved to the table and sat down beside her little boy. He was busy telling Mr. Brower all about last night's excitement. Grace bit back the urge to hush him. It was too late anyway.

"Was this a ghost you saw?" Brower asked, his eyes big with feigned concern.

Liam moved his head somberly from side to side. "No. It was a scary man."

Grace patted Liam on the back. "But he's gone now," she assured him.

Liam nodded and took another bite of his peanut butter and jelly sandwich. He pointed a finger at Brower. "Mommy says he's *neber* coming back."

"I am so glad to hear that," Brower affirmed.

Cara looked to Grace. She kept a smile in place for her assistant. Cara had seemed inordinately worried about Grace when they talked this morning. Cara often voiced her concerns about Grace and Liam being here alone at night when there were no guests. The closest neighbors were nearly a mile down the lane. But Grace hadn't worried—at least, not until last night. Still, she wasn't sharing that worry with Cara.

The memory of Liam describing the man's eyes as being like his had her quivering deep inside where no one could see.

Liam had his father's eyes.

Grace pushed away the thought.

"Mr. Brower, what brings you to our mountain?" Cara asked.

Brower sipped his iced tea. "I'm here for a mini conference in Chattanooga. I prefer the peace and quiet of a small community like this rather than staying downtown amid the hustle and bustle."

"We appreciate your choosing our inn," Grace said.

The middle set of French doors that led onto the terrace opened and Mr. Pierce appeared, aiming straight for the serving buffet. He was perhaps midfifties, with a shaved head that contrasted sharply with his long beard. He'd arrived this morning. Grace was always unsettled when a guest from California arrived. She wasn't sure she would ever get past worrying if that person had seen her ex-husband in person…or perhaps had seen Grace. She'd gone to great lengths to avoid being recognized. She wore her hair longer now, and darker. She worked diligently to keep her blond roots covered.

Changing hers and Liam's names had been the most difficult part. Finding the right sort of help—someone who did foolproof work—to pull off new IDs wasn't as easy as the movies made it seem. When she'd started her business here at the inn, she had taken the sole proprietorship route—far less complicated. Thankfully, her son had been only an infant when they'd had to disappear. With her father's death, there was no one left behind to consider. Her few close friends and old acquaintances likely no longer missed her. He had ensured she'd distanced herself from basically everyone during those final months together. She'd had no idea how much he'd controlled her life until it was too late.

Sadly, that had been a mistake, as was every other decision she had made after meeting Adam Locke.

She glanced down at her precious son. Except for sweet

Liam. She could never regret him or the nightmare she had survived to have him.

"I should get back to work." Cara rose from her chair, plate and glass in hand, and hurried from the dining room.

"Mr. Pierce," Grace said, acknowledging the new arrival despite her reservations, "I hope your cabin is satisfactory."

He settled at the table, directly across from her. "It's great. Everything is great." He said the last with a lingering glance at Liam.

"This is my son," she said, "Liam." She smiled when Liam looked up. "Liam, this is Mr. Pierce."

Liam gave a salute. This was something new he'd picked up from his most beloved cartoon.

Pierce gave an indifferent nod before turning his attention to his salad.

When Liam had lost interest in the remainder of his lunch, Grace ushered him from the table, gathering their plates and glasses.

"Have a nice afternoon, gentlemen," she offered. "Please let me know if you need anything."

Liam skipped along beside her until they reached the kitchen. Diane had left already since she also taught an afternoon yoga class. She would be back in time to take care of dinner. Judging by the delicious scent filling the room, Grace suspected there was a roast in the oven. No one made a better or more tender roast than Diane.

While Liam created a Lego tower on the rug, Grace inventoried the pantry and refrigerator. She added the items that needed to be restocked to the list Diane had made for the upcoming week's meals. Grace placed the order online, and Diane would pick it up on her way back to the inn this evening. Now that the guests had left the dining room, Grace cleared the lunch service and settled the glass dome back over the cookies. Those would stay handy in the event a guest needed a snack.

Once Grace had loaded the dishwasher, she and Liam retired to their space for his nap. She generally used the time for catching up on paperwork. As she settled on the sofa, she heard the vacuum running in the lobby. Paula Wilborn, the housekeeper, had arrived. She'd needed the morning off for an appointment. With Paula here, her husband would be about, clearing pathways or raking leaves. The couple was very good at their work and needed no direction, something Grace was grateful for.

Liam took a few extra minutes to settle. Last night's excitement still had him wound up. When he'd finally fallen asleep, Grace dared to start the search she'd been dreading. She'd resisted the idea last night, this morning as well. It was easy to pretend she was too busy to take a moment. But the truth was, she was terrified at what she would find.

Stop. Adam was in jail. His trial had started at the beginning of the month. Or at least that was the last information she'd found. Trial dates were subject to numerous sorts of changes. The original trial date had been set only months after his arrest—two years ago. But then there had been countless delays. Scheduling issues with attorneys. There was discovery and depositions and much preparation that led to many requests for continuances. On and on it had gone. Once the trial actually started, it was expected to take several weeks, perhaps a couple of months, just because of the sheer number of witnesses and the mountain of evidence.

Grace's statement had been videotaped. She did not have to testify again. At least, that was the promise. Didn't matter now. After her father's sudden death, she had made the decision to disappear. No one knew where she was or how to contact her. She might not have made the decision if not for the fact that her testimony was barely a sliver of what the DA had against the bastard. If for some unforeseeable reason they wanted her to make an appearance and couldn't reach her, it wouldn't make or break the case.

The evidence actually spoke for itself.

Nothing could change Adam's destiny now.

She stalled, fingers poised on the keyboard. Every time she thought about him and about the trial, she found herself back in that crazy loop of fear and self-loathing. How had she lived in that house for all those months and not known what Adam had in his secret basement room?

The hot, sour taste that rose in her mouth had her lunch threatening to make a reappearance. She closed her eyes, swallowed back the bitterness and forced herself to calm. She was away from him now. He would never see his son... would never touch his son.

But what if the blue-eyed man from last night had been him?

No. No. No. It couldn't have been. There had to be a reasonable explanation.

Gathering her resolve, she opened her eyes and forced herself to type the name.

Adam Locke.

Grace held her breath while the search results populated her screen.

Locke Case Thrown Out on Technicality...police must start from scratch...

For several seconds her brain refused to absorb the meaning behind the words.

She swallowed back the lump in her throat and compelled herself to continue reading.

The San Francisco District Attorney's Office had been hiding a secret—the warrant used to obtain the majority of the evidence against the Sweetheart Killer, Adam Locke, contained a fatal flaw. The warrant authorizing lead investigator Detective Lance Gibbons to search the suspect's home was not obtained until after the forced entry into the Locke residence. Since exigent circumstances could not be proved, the search of the Locke property was unlawful. The judge's decision suppresses all evidence found in the unlawful search of the home.

Ice filling her veins, Grace's gaze zoomed back up to the top of the article to see when it was released.

Friday.

Which meant Adam could have been here last night.

Fear tightened her chest, wrapped around her throat like bony fingers.

This couldn't be right. No. Not possible.

Okay, okay. He was out. There was no denying this. The words were right in front of her. Still, wouldn't the investigation resume? Wouldn't he be under house arrest or something like that under the circumstances? The man was definitely a flight risk.

And even if for some reason he had ditched the house arrest ankle bracelet or whatever, how would he have known where to find her?

The same way you escaped with a new, fake ID.

Anything was possible if a person was willing to pay the price.

Hands shaking, Grace closed the search box. No, she refused to live in fear again. He couldn't possibly know where she was. Finding her wouldn't have been that easy. But he had... To deny it was ridiculous. Still, how had he managed the feat in less than forty-eight hours?

Unless he'd had someone looking for her all this time.

She shook her head. Stood on shaky legs. She'd been too careful. So, so careful.

Grace hurried, her feet tripping over each other, to the bedroom to see her son. He slept like an angel in the middle of the big down comforter. Her heart ached at the idea that her child would never be free if that bastard was out there.

Her heart stumbled, flailed like a wounded bird. Adam would do all in his power to kill her. She was the reason he had been caught. She was the one who'd told Detective Gibbons about the room in the basement. She was the one to release his final victim, and still the woman had somehow managed to get murdered. If that last victim had lived, she could have testified about what Adam had done.

Grace should have done more...should have found a way to save her.

She lowered herself onto the side of the bed. She hadn't witnessed her husband kidnapping or harming anyone. He'd been so charming, so good to her. She would never have known about any of it if she hadn't found that room.

How had she not sensed the evil in him?

After what she'd found, she had gone straight to her father in Lake Tahoe. Together they had come up with a plan that would best protect Grace and the child she carried. She had called the hotline for the Sweetheart Killer. Instantly she had been connected with the lead detective—Lance Gibbons. She'd told him everything she knew. All the police had to do was go to Adam's place of employment and take him in for questioning, obtain a search warrant for their home, and voilà—he would spend the rest of his life in prison because of what he'd done.

Adam Locke—her husband, her son's father—had been a serial killer.

Grace inhaled a deep breath, then another to slow her runaway heart. She had to think clearly—something she hadn't done then.

Her husband had come home that evening and discovered his house had been invaded by the San Francisco Police Department, so he'd driven right on by and gone straight to her father's house. The bastard had known that if the police had found him there was only one person to blame. And he'd known exactly where she'd gone.

He had driven the two hundred miles from San Francisco to Lake Tahoe. She and her father had no idea the police had not taken him into custody. No one bothered to call with the warning. This, she now realized, was where the detectives had jumped the gun. Rather than going to Adam's workplace and arresting him, they'd gone to the house and burst through the door to get their hands on the evidence first. They had claimed she told them there could be a victim in jeopardy in the basement. And she had, sort of. She'd released the victim she'd found, but certainly her husband could have brought in another as soon as Grace left. It wasn't like she had set out to mislead the police. How was she supposed to have known what his schedule was like? She hadn't even known he was a killer. Damn it.

Not to mention she had been confused and terrified... out of her mind, really.

But she hadn't claimed with any certainty that there was another victim in the basement and some ambitious clerk had zeroed in on that discrepancy in her statement during the latest deep dig into the evidence. After all those months of preparation for trial, it was all for naught because of one five-letter word.

Might.

In her answer to the question of whether or not there may have been yet another victim stashed somewhere in the house, she had stated there *might* be. Because like everyone else in the tristate area, she'd been aware that another woman fitting the profile of his victims had recently gone missing. Bella Watts. To Grace's knowledge, she was never found.

While the police had conducted what was now considered an illegal search and seizure, Adam had broken into her father's home to get to her. He'd left her father unconscious on the floor and chased her through the snowy woods behind the family cabin. Her water had broken during the chase, and she'd thought for certain both she and her baby were dead. After he'd found her waving for help on the side of the road, she rushed back into the woods and he'd abandoned the car and followed. He'd had her on the ground, choking her, when her hand found that rock. She'd slammed it into his head. When he toppled off her, she scrambled up and ran. She had hoped the blow killed him. Later, at the hospital, after Liam was born, she and her father had learned that his body had not been found.

Adam Locke was gone.

Two days later, sitting in a chair next to her hospital bed, her father had suffered a fatal heart attack in his sleep.

She'd named her son after him, William James. Weeks later, with her husband finally arrested in an attempt to get to her and Liam, she had made up her mind that the police would never be able to keep her safe. She'd taken her father's insurance money and savings and disappeared.

She hadn't cared if the police believed her dead—that was all the better. Adam Locke had not just fans but followers, Gibbons had told her, who looked up to him. Any one of them would have loved to see her dead. She suspected he had told her this to keep her pliable, but all he'd done was make her more determined and given her all the more reason to disappear.

Grace forced the horrible memories away. She checked the windows before leaving the room but didn't close the door. If a sound came from where her son lay sleeping, she wanted to know.

Her fingers itched to pick up the phone and call Detective Gibbons. He could tell her what was really happening. But she couldn't risk her call being traced. He would want her to return to San Francisco. Though he had her videotaped testimony, he would no doubt feel that an in-person statement would serve the case better.

She couldn't do it. Not and risk Liam's life. Not for anything.

The best thing to do was to stay calm. No one here knew she was Gianna Locke. Liam's California birth certificate carried the name Aidan Reinhart Locke—the name she and Adam had chosen. She had only used that name in an attempt to prevent him from ever knowing the real name she intended to give her son, William James Myers. She had gone way back in her mother's family history to find the name Myers. Grace was an easy decision since it was no doubt by the grace of God that she and Liam had escaped the bastard.

A rap on the door of their private quarters had her hurrying there. She needed Liam's nap to last long enough for her to consider what steps she might need to take.

She opened the door to find Cara.

"I'm sorry, but I need to leave early today. Is that a problem?"

"Go ahead." Grace took a deep breath. "I can monitor the lobby from here until Liam wakes up." Her door had a direct view into the lobby.

Cara smiled. "Thanks. I appreciate it. My grandmother has an appointment with her heart specialist, and she failed to tell me until a few minutes ago."

"No worries. You take care of your grandmother. We'll be fine here."

Grace left the door open and watched as Cara exited through the main entrance. She wondered if the woman had any idea how lucky she was to still have family alive. Grace had Liam and she cherished him beyond measure, but she missed her father so desperately. Her mother had died when Grace was only five years old, and since Grace had been an only child, there was no other family. Her parents had no siblings either, so she truly was alone except for Liam. She had always told herself she would never have an only child for just that reason, but now she couldn't see herself ever trusting anyone enough to go down that path again.

The image of Rob Vaughn slipped into her mind, but she dismissed it. He was a very nice man, but no matter how much she liked him, and he appeared to like her, his opinion of her would change dramatically when he learned the truth. Considering what she had just discovered, she wasn't sure how long her dark secret would stay hidden.

Rob had family. He would never dream of bringing someone with her past into that tight, loving group. It was foolish even to consider such an idea. He deserved someone without the sort of baggage she carried.

The front entrance opened, and Grace's heart stopped. Why hadn't she locked it after Cara left?

Because she had guests. She couldn't lock the door until tonight.

Cara. It was Cara coming back. Grace managed to breathe again.

"Did you forget something?"

"The mail." She placed it on the desk. "See you tomorrow." She waved and disappeared out the door once more.

Grace steadied herself. She had to pull herself together. She had a son who needed her, and she had guests. She couldn't fret about this a minute longer. She had to do something. If she worked at the desk, at least that would put her between the front door and Liam. First, she popped into the kitchen and ensured the back door was locked. Diane had a key. No need to leave it unlocked.

The inn was quiet with only two guests and Liam having a nap. The only sound was the big old grandfather clock ticking. There were many vintage clocks throughout the inn, but the grandfather clock in the lobby was her favorite. The sound soothed her just a little.

At the desk, she checked her email. Worked hard to keep her mind off events in California. Then she picked up the bundle of mail and picked through it.

The utility bill sat on top. She opened it, reviewed the charges, then set it aside. She would take it to her desk later. Then she smiled when she counted three postcards from previous guests who wanted to thank her again for a lovely stay. She appreciated the online reviews, but to receive a handwritten note was particularly heartwarming.

A copy of the *Lookout Mountain Monitor*. She set it aside as well to review later with a cup of tea. It was her favorite late-afternoon appointment with herself. Lots of junk mail, which she tossed into the recycle bin beneath the desk. A six-by-nine-inch white envelope with no markings. A frown tugged at her brow. Probably went with the junk mail, but she checked to see what was inside just in case.

A photograph…the kind printed from a computer onto plain white paper.

She froze, then started to shake as her heart bumped back into rhythm and then began to pound frantically.

Liam…standing at that window last evening. His curly blond hair sleep tousled.

Someone had taken the picture from outside the window. The man Liam had seen in the snow.

The man with blue eyes like Liam's.

"Oh my God."

He was here.

Grace didn't have to wonder. Adam had signed the bottom of the photograph the way he always signed notes to her.

XOXO

Chapter Four

Bluebird Trail, 1:30 p.m.

"Mrs. Sells, you're certain about the timing?"

Rob watched the elderly woman consider the question. She'd called to say someone had been staying in her garage. From the looks of the place, someone had indeed fashioned a makeshift bed by throwing together a couple of moving quilts in one corner.

"Well, I was out here Sunday around lunchtime. I parked my car in the garage after church, so I think I would have seen this mess then."

Rob nodded. "But you haven't been out here since then?"

"Not until lunch today," she explained. "Mattie England and I have lunch together every Monday. I didn't notice anything out of place until I came back, of course. When the garage door opened I could see straight in here and there it was." She shook her head. "Now, I don't mind anyone trying to stay warm by whatever means is handy, but it would be nice to be warned."

Rob gave the lady a nod. "Mrs. Sells, if someone you don't know shows up at your house needing a warm place to stay, you send them on over to the shelter on Bennett Street. There's always plenty of room there. Never let a stranger into your house."

"Well, now, Deputy," she argued, "he didn't knock on my door."

Okay, now Rob was really worried. "Did you see this man?"

The ninety-year-old lady frowned. "Well, no, but I did see a young fella walking down the trail just before dark on Sunday. He wasn't from around here, so I suspect he's the culprit who did this." She gestured to the mound in front of her vintage Ford sedan. "No one who lives in the neighborhood would do this and then not bother to fold the quilts up and put them away like he found them. He could have at least done that."

"What was this man wearing?" Rob asked, pulling out his notepad to jot down anything she remembered. Under other circumstances the lady's opinion might have been amusing, but these days nothing about an intruder should be minimized.

"A black coat and one of those beanie things." She patted her head. "It was black too."

The man Liam had seen had been wearing a beanie. Considering Bluebird Trail was the next street over from Mockingbird Lane, there was a reasonable possibility it was the same guy.

"Could you see any details of his face? Was he Caucasian?"

"Oh, yes, yes, he was. I couldn't make out any real details like the size of his nose or anything like that, but it was clear that he was white."

Rob surveyed the garage again. "Have you noticed anything missing? Tools? Anything at all?"

"Well, no." She too glanced around. "But I never really kept up with what Harvey had in here. The garage was his domain."

Harvey was her late husband. He'd passed away last year.

"Do you mind if I have a look around?"

"You go right ahead, Deputy." She shivered. "I'm going in the house. It's cold out here with that overhead door open."

"Yes, ma'am, you do that. I'll close the door and check in with you before I leave."

When the lady had gone back into the house, Rob started on one side of the garage and surveyed the shelves. Tools lined most of them. Tools for working on automobiles and tools for gardening. Since Mrs. Sells rarely came into the garage, he hoped anything recently taken or moved would be noticeable due to the fine layer of dust that coated the shelves. He moved slowly along one side, then progressed to the other. Nothing jumped out at him. He retraced his steps, studying the concrete floor where a few items were stored beneath the shelves. In the corner, sawhorses had been tucked away. A creeper for sliding beneath cars. None of which appeared to have been moved.

So far, it seemed that whoever had found his way into the Sells garage had only been looking for a place to sleep. Still, this was not safe, particularly for an elderly person like Mrs. Sells.

Rob closed up the garage and walked to the back door of the Sells home. He knocked and then waited for the lady to answer.

She opened the door. "Did you find anything?"

"No, ma'am, nothing more than you did." He made a face. "I'm not happy with the idea of someone creeping about on your property. I need you to be sure to keep your doors locked at all times. Tonight, around six, I or another deputy will come by and check your garage. We'll do it again at midnight. If you have no objections, we'll do this for a couple of days just to be sure he's gone for good. If your trespasser notices this, he may find someplace new to hang out."

"Sounds like a good plan," she agreed.

"But I do need you to call it in if you see any strangers in the area. Even if they're just on the street. If someone you don't recognize is walking by, I want to hear about it." This was a dead-end street with little or no traffic. Strangers stood out.

"I sure will," she promised.

"All right, then. I'll be on my way."

Rob had just backed out of the Sells drive when his cell sounded off.

Grace Myers.

His pulse rate sped up as he accepted the call. "Hey, Grace. Everything okay?"

"There was something in my mail," she said, her tone more than a little reluctant. "Do you mind dropping by and having a look?"

"I'll be right there."

Mockingbird Lane, 2:10 p.m.

WHILE LIAM RAN around the room chasing the multicolored balls that had escaped his portable ball pit, his mom stood by nervously watching Rob study the photograph and envelope she'd discovered in her mailbox.

Since there was no address and no postage mark, obviously the envelope had been placed in her mailbox by someone unaffiliated with the postal service. Also, obviously, it was the person who had walked through the snow and stood on her porch staring through a window at her son.

He hated to ask the question he couldn't avoid any longer. It would sound like an accusation, and he didn't want that. But there was no way around it. "And you don't have any idea who may have left this for you to find?"

It was the lengthy hesitation before she summoned a response that told him all he needed to know.

"I—I just can't imagine why anyone would do this." She gestured to the photo. "It makes no sense."

Rob glanced at Liam to ensure he was occupied with his attempts to get all the balls back into the pit before saying what he could no longer put off. "Think carefully about your answer, Grace. This person could be dangerous. You shouldn't have any hesitation talking to me about this. The *XOXO* at the bottom feels personal."

Tears welled in her eyes, and she blinked rapidly to hold them back. "Give me a minute."

She hurried into the hall outside her private parlor and called for Mrs. Wilborn. A moment later the housekeeper appeared, and Grace asked her to stay with Liam for a bit. Evidently, whatever Grace had to talk about, she didn't want Liam overhearing.

Mrs. Wilborn smiled as she breezed into the small parlor. "Afternoon, Deputy Vaughn."

"Afternoon, Mrs. Wilborn. How's Mr. Wilborn?"

She harrumphed. "Complaining as always but managing to stay out of trouble."

Rob laughed. "Planning that big garden already, I imagine."

"He is." She settled on the floor with Liam. "What's happening here, Mr. Liam?"

Grace waited in the doorway. "We can talk in the kitchen."

Rob gave her a nod and followed her in that direction.

In the kitchen, he waited while Grace opened one cabinet door after the other. He had no idea what she was searching for or why, so he settled on a stool at the island and waited patiently.

"Finally," she said, withdrawing something from the last cupboard she searched. She set a fifth of bourbon on the counter, then went to another cupboard and grabbed two glasses. She placed them next to the bottle, opened it and poured a generous serving in each glass.

She looked to him. Blinked. "Sorry, I didn't think to ask if you cared to join me. I just assumed." She passed a glass to him, then raised her own and drank deeply.

His eyebrows reared up in surprise. This was going to be interesting. He'd never seen Grace drink wine or beer, much less anything stronger. Rather than explain how he was on duty, he simply set the glass down and waited for her to spill whatever was troubling her. The quickest way to slow the momentum of someone who wanted to talk was to make some unrelated comment.

Her glass landed on the counter once more and the look of pain on her face told him he was right to assume she wasn't much of a drinker. When she finally managed to swallow the strong liquid, she cleared her throat, coughed, cleared her throat again and managed a breath.

"Better now?" he asked.

She shuddered a little. "We'll see."

He felt confident this was no time to laugh, but he couldn't resist a soft chuckle. "Want to tell me what this is all about?"

GRACE CONSIDERED POURING another deep shot of bourbon but figured she should stop while she was ahead. Otherwise she might not be able to stay standing. She couldn't take that risk no matter how much she would love to drown out the world for a little while. Keeping Liam safe was all that mattered. Not her feelings. Not her own safety—only his.

Which was why she had to do this. There was no pretending it would all be okay. Not anymore. Her reprieve from the nightmare was over.

For more than two years she had promised herself that no one would ever know the truth about her past. No one would ever hear the awful story and associate Liam or her with it. But she had no choice now.

Clearly the legal system had failed Liam. Failed her. Failed all those victims.

She squared her shoulders, stared Rob Vaughn straight in the eyes and said what she needed to say. "I'm not who you think I am."

There. She'd said it. She allowed herself to breathe again. The burn in her throat and stomach had settled, and she felt the beginnings of another sort of warmth seeping through her system.

"Can you be a bit more specific?"

He frowned, his brown eyes clouding with questions. He had the nicest brown eyes and thick black hair.

She blinked. *Focus, Grace.*

When she failed to find the words to continue in a timely manner, he said, "I can see this is serious." He nodded to her. "You're serious."

"Yes. Very serious. My real name is Gianna Reinhart Locke. You may have heard of my…" *Take a deep breath and just say it.* "My ex-husband is Adam Locke."

He didn't have to say a word. The look on his face told her that he knew who she meant. The whole world knew.

She closed her eyes and forced away the memories that attempted to intrude.

"Okay."

The single word caused her lids to flutter open. She studied his face. She had come to trust this man on some level. Something she had thought she would never again do. She liked him. Was attracted to him. And he felt the same way about her. But now, the way he looked at her put a new fracture in her already damaged heart. He didn't look at her with suspicion but with something far too similar, and it hurt. It hurt because she had worked so hard to build a new life here. She had struggled and fought to make it the best life possible for her and her son.

Now it was all crashing down.

"I barely got away from him after…" She forced her mind to allow the past back in. She had kept it at bay for so long that her brain resisted the intrusion now. "That day…" The memory of that day—the hours that bled into night. "I discovered the basement room that morning. He'd left extra early for work. He was supposed to be on vacation, but an emergency had come up and he'd had to go into the office."

The man she had married—the man she had thought she knew better than herself—had been a savvy businessman. He'd traveled frequently. But twice a year he had taken a week off. Grace hadn't known then what the timing was all about. Most people she knew took a vacation once a year. But not Adam. Every six months he took a week off. He stayed home and worked on his projects.

She, like a good wife, had believed him. Just as she had believed his projects were the handmade furniture he crafted for their home and as gifts for special friends. His little semiannual vacations were always spent on his *projects*. The two of them never actually went on a vacation. This hadn't bothered her at the time because they'd only been married a few months before she'd gotten pregnant, and then they'd both wanted to stay near home.

"He was angry," she continued, her voice sounding hollow. She hugged her arms around herself as the memories and the cold that accompanied them filled her. "It was some sort of emergency with an account, and he was livid that he had to go into the office on his time off." She vividly recalled how furious he'd been. "The baby was due in a short two weeks, and his big surprise was not finished." Her mouth struggled with forming the words she had to say. "He warned me not to go into the basement. He said I might fall and he didn't want me to see his surprise until it was finished."

She hadn't meant to break her promise. She really hadn't. "I never went into the basement. It was his domain. I thought it was a bit odd that he pressed me on the issue that morning." She fell silent for a moment. "But not long after he left I started to understand."

She looked around the kitchen she loved so much. Nothing would ever be the same now. "At first I thought I left the television on in the bedroom. But I hadn't and then I heard the sound again. A banging or thudding from the basement somewhere."

When she didn't continue, he prodded, "What did you do next?"

She blinked, drew back from the memory. If she allowed herself to be too fully immersed, she would never get this told. "I got up and checked the house. The doors and windows were locked. There was no one in the house except me. No one in the yard. I even considered that I'd imagined it or maybe that a bird had somehow gotten trapped in the attic. Then the sound grew louder, more frantic, and I realized it wasn't in the attic."

She moistened her lips. "I took a hammer from the drawer in the kitchen where we kept miscellaneous items." She shrugged. "We all have one of those drawers." She thought of the one by the back door in this very kitchen. "I unlocked the basement door." She frowned, considered that the locked door needed additional explanation. "The door to the basement was in the hall, and Adam had insisted on keeping it locked. Since the stairs led right up to the door, I figured he didn't want a guest—not that we actually had people over—to think they were walking into a bathroom and fall down the stairs. It made sense to me at the time."

Rob nodded. "I can see that."

She tried to smile, couldn't. "I turned on the hall light and started down the stairs. The banging was so much louder down there." She recalled how her heart had started to pound in time with the banging. Fear had pumped through her veins.

"I told myself that maybe there was an animal trapped down there…but even then I had started to realize something was very, very wrong." When she reached the bottom of the stairs, she flipped the switch turning on the overhead fixture. "When I turned on the light the banging stopped. Almost like whatever it was knew someone was there and was afraid of who it might be."

The quaking started deep inside her as if she were there now, standing in the middle of that basement with the knowledge that something was terribly wrong welling inside her. It had been the strongest, most crushing sensation—a knowing that whatever came next was going to change everything.

"The cradle in the center of the room, amid his tools, stole my attention for a moment." Pride and happiness had swelled inside her. So that was his surprise. A cradle for the baby. She hadn't known. "For just a moment I was so happy." The ache in her chest was fierce, as if the memory were only yesterday. "Then the banging started again. This time there was grunting…some sort of muffled sound."

Grace had moved to the wall where the sound appeared to be coming from. The banging was so loud there it had made her jump.

"At that point, I think I was in a sort of shock. I said, 'Hello? Is someone there?'"

The grunting and nonverbal sounds clearly coming from a person had become so loud that she stumbled back.

Someone was on the other side of that wall.

She had stared at the narrow basement window on each

side of the room. The windows were up high near the ceiling and very small. She had closed her eyes a moment and mentally calculated where this first set—in the foundation, one on each side of the house—were located. She had realized then that the wall she stared at was about the center of the house. There could be more basement space beyond it.

"I knew I had to get beyond that wall...because someone was there. I pulled and tugged at the shelving units lining the wall. Things fell off the shelves but I ignored them. I couldn't stop. I had to know...to fix whatever this was." Her pulse bumped into a faster rhythm.

Behind the unit crowded with the most items was a frameless door painted the same color as the wall so that it almost blended in.

"I almost didn't see the door. I remember reaching out... my fingers wrapping around the handle." She made a face. "Even the handle was painted like the wall. I kept thinking how strange it was."

But the door was locked.

"I turned the handle again, and the sounds on the other side grew more frantic. No matter how I tugged and twisted on the handle, it wouldn't open. I said out loud that I was going to find the key. I searched and searched for a key. Every drawer. Every shelf. The whole time questions were pounding in my brain. Why was someone locked in some sort of room in our basement? What if it was some bad person? Should I call the police?"

She clasped her hands together, pressed them to her lips for a moment before she could go on. "I couldn't find the key. I wrapped my arms protectively around my belly, thinking how I had to be careful because of the baby and wondering what I should do."

If she called the police…

Foolishly, the idea of her husband being taken away had torn at her heart. She had tried to rationalize the situation. If someone was locked in the basement, Adam must have some sort of compelling reason…

No, that made no sense.

"Then I took a deep breath and I knew what I had to do. I wanted to demand answers before I opened that door, but obviously whoever was locked in there couldn't answer since he or she was gagged or something." She shrugged. "I kept thinking that I trusted my husband completely…but this…" She braced her arms on the counter and went on. "I walked over to the door and I said that it sounded as if you've been gagged and you can't speak. The answering sounds were clearly a yes, even though the word wasn't stated. I said I would ask a question and I wanted one bang on the wall for no and two for yes. I asked if that was okay. I got one bang and then another."

Whatever Rob was thinking, he kept his face reasonably neutral. But he watched her so closely…so intently. She could only imagine what he was thinking.

"I first asked if the person was a man. There was one bang, so this was a woman. Then I asked if she was injured. One bang and then another." Even now, Grace's heart pounded even harder with the memories. "Then I asked if a man had put her in there. Two bangs. Still wanting to believe my husband had to be innocent, I asked about his hair color and eye color. By the time I made myself stop, I knew beyond any doubt that Adam was responsible. It took a moment for me to gather my wits, and then I told her I was going to find a way to get her out. I looked around the basement, searching for something usable, and I spotted an axe. I grabbed it and walked back to the door. I told her to stand back."

Grace squeezed her eyes shut at the memory of swinging that axe with all her might.

"When you got her out, did you take her to the hospital or the police?"

The sound of Rob's voice forced her eyes open. "She didn't give me the chance. As soon as I had untied her and removed the gag, she ran out of the house and down the street. I couldn't run after her. I was nine months pregnant. By the time I got the car keys and tried to follow her, she was gone. Then I just started driving. I didn't stop until I reached my father's house in Lake Tahoe."

From there everything had gone downhill.

By the time Grace had told Rob the rest of what had happened that day and then about what she'd learned on the internet, Diane had arrived to prepare the evening meal. He waited patiently while she and Diane chatted for a moment, then followed her to her private quarters. Mrs. Wilborn hurried back to finish her chores and Liam had fallen asleep during the movie he'd begged to watch.

"I can make some calls," he said. "It's possible Adam was released on bail pending other charges. We can't be sure what actually happened until I speak to the detectives there. What we read in the press is not always completely accurate."

"If Adam's not here," she said, her heart flopping helplessly behind her breastbone, "then someone he sent is here. Either way, my son is not safe. And just like that woman who ran away from my house—Alicia Holder—the police won't be able to protect us. Believe that if you believe nothing else I've told you. He is the worst kind of monster. You have no idea."

Rob nodded. "I have some idea. I followed the story."

Grace felt confident he didn't really understand. He was in law enforcement and had likely seen and heard bad things, but no one save someone who had survived that kind of evil could really understand. Either way, she needed his help. If she could have gotten through this alone, she would never have told him this awful truth. She remembered the locket she'd hidden under the sink... She should turn that over to him. It was evidence, after all. But somehow with all the secrets she'd kept from him already, she just couldn't bring herself to share one more ugly piece of this nightmare. Especially since she hadn't given it to the deputy who'd come last night. Now she just felt ridiculous for not doing so.

"I have to get my son to safety." She braced herself for a battle. "If I simply notify the detectives on his case, then they'll want me to stay put. I can't take that risk."

"What is it you want to do?"

As much as she wanted to trust this man, she wasn't sure she should. He was a cop. He had an obligation to the badge he wore. "All I'm asking is that you let me get my son to someplace safe. If you can't or won't help me, I'm doing it alone. I don't want to risk my son's safety, so I'm begging you, please help me hide him."

He held her gaze for a long moment. "I should say no. I mean, you could have told me this a long time ago. I could have been helping you from day one."

She bit her lips together and prayed he wouldn't allow pride or anger or anything else to sway him.

"But the answer is yes, I'll help you get Liam to safety before I do anything else."

"Thank you." Such relief washed through her she wanted to weep.

"Don't thank me yet. I haven't told you my conditions."

Chapter Five

Rob wasn't entirely confident he'd made the right decision, but more important than anything, he needed her to trust him. For that, he had to at least give her instinct to hide the benefit of the doubt. Protecting her child was top priority—for them both.

No time like the present to jump in.

"First," he said, "I decide the place."

"And then?" she asked, clearly skeptical.

"Then, if we agree on the first step, we move on to the next."

She seemed surprised or unsettled that he had agreed to consider her plan. The way he saw it, there weren't a lot of options just now. He would deal with the official side of this mess as soon as Grace and Liam were someplace safe, and he knew just the place.

"Okay." She took a big breath. "Where do you have in mind?"

"I have a place kind of off the grid. It's isolated and difficult to find."

She nodded. "Sounds good. I have a bag with some extra cash and new IDs. Everything we need to…"

As if she'd realized that it sounded exactly like she planned to disappear, her voice trailed off.

"I get it." He shrugged. "You're prepared to run if necessary. You will gladly give up everything to keep Liam safe."

She squeezed her eyes shut for a moment before meeting his gaze once more. "I would. Including my life."

"That's not going to happen," he shot back. "I will not let that happen."

She took a deep breath. "Thank you."

His cell vibrated on his utility belt. He checked the screen. *Reynolds.* "I have to take this."

"I should check on Liam."

He gave her a nod as he accepted the call. "Hey, Reynolds, what's up?"

"Damn, boss, we've got ourselves a body," he said, his voice humming with excitement. "That's what's up. You should get over here to the Cashion place. This is bad. Really bad."

A new line of tension threaded through Rob. "A homicide?"

"Definitely. This guy has been stabbed like a couple dozen times. There's blood everywhere."

Well, hell. "Okay, stay out of the blood. Don't touch anything and see if we can get Snelling over there."

"Will do."

Sergeant David Snelling was top-notch. He led an excellent team of forensic analysts.

"I'll be there in five."

The Cashion place was only a couple of miles away. Rob couldn't help thinking of the intruder who'd been sleeping in the garage at the Sells home. The Cashion home was only blocks from there. He made a call to Deputy Lyle Carter to get him over to the inn. He was close by already and would arrive in the next couple of minutes. Then he went in search of Grace. He found her talking with Diane.

To Grace he said, "There's something I need to check on, but I'll be right back. Deputy Carter will be here, right outside, if you need anything before I'm back. Do not go anywhere without me."

"I'll be here," Grace assured him.

"Now, that sounds intriguing," Diane said with a wink in Rob's direction.

He only smiled and gave the two a nod. "Ladies." On second thought, he added, "And Liam."

Liam was too busy shoving cookies into his mouth to do anything but grin.

Rob pulled on his cap as he headed for his SUV. After Carter arrived, he gave the deputy his instructions before loading up. The drive to the Cashion home took less than five minutes.

If Snelling was not already tied up with another scene, it would take him maybe half an hour to arrive. The second cruiser on-site told Rob that Reynolds had called in Donnie Prater. The youngest and newest of the deputies assigned to this substation was already knocking on the doors of neighbors. Reynolds was rolling out the crime scene tape around the Cashions' detached garage.

Rob pulled to the side of the street and climbed out of his vehicle. He walked to the garage, where the overhead door remained closed. The walk-through door on the side stood open. No sign of the homeowners. Danny Cashion was a lifelong Mountain resident. His wife, Tasha, was a transplant from Knoxville. The couple's two sons were in college.

Reynolds waited for Rob to get close enough to talk in lowered voices.

"Snelling is on his way. The Cashions are in the house. I've interviewed them already. They were on a mini vacation for the weekend and just got back to find…this."

"Let's have a look." They didn't get homicides around here very often. Not the way they did downtown. The lack of violence and trouble overall was one of the reasons most residents had chosen the Mountain.

The family's minivan was parked in the garage, but it was a double-car garage and a good-sized one at that, so moving around the vehicle was no problem. The victim lay on the floor in the vacant bay. Like Reynolds had said, he'd been stabbed repeatedly. Probably a dozen or more times.

"This guy must have really pissed someone off."

"Looks that way," Reynolds agreed. "The ME is on his way."

"Did you find any ID?"

"That's the really weird part," Reynolds said as he pulled out his phone. "This guy is from California."

A warning sounded in Rob's brain. He instantly noted the guy's blond hair and sightless pale blue eyes staring at the ceiling. He judged the victim to be midthirties. Oh, damn.

Reynolds showed him the image of a driver's license on his phone. "Adam Locke. He was just released from—"

"Did you run his license?" Something cold and dark stirred in Rob's gut. Of course he had. It was straight out of the training manual.

"I did. Got a hit ASAP. A Detective Lance Gibbons called

me, like, instantly. Said he's getting on a plane right now and that he'd be here tonight."

As much as Rob hated that a homicide had occurred in his jurisdiction, this could potentially be a huge relief for Grace Myers. He took out his own cell and zoomed in on the victim's face. He snapped a pic. Then he pulled a pair of gloves from his coat pocket and crouched down. He checked the victim's finger, then an arm, to judge the path of rigor mortis. He'd been here a little while. He was in full rigor.

"Okay, as long as you have things under control here, I need to…" Rob pushed to his feet. How the hell did he explain what he had to do? "I have to finish up at the inn. As soon as you hear from Gibbons, let me know."

Rob felt bad about leaving Reynolds with this mess, but it was only until he had Grace settled at the cabin. Then he'd be back.

"Don't worry about me," Reynolds assured him with possibly a little too much bravado. "I've got this."

Rob had a last look at the dead guy before returning to his SUV. He struggled to drive slowly away from the new crime scene. He really wanted to believe this was a good thing. If this victim actually was Adam Locke, then Grace was free of him and the world was a safer place.

The trouble lay in who murdered him and the connection to Grace and her son.

Lookout Inn, 3:30 p.m.

GRACE TRIED TO focus on anything else for the half hour or so that Rob was gone, but she couldn't. Her mind kept going back to the last time she'd seen Adam. He'd insisted on talking to her. He'd promised the police that if they allowed him to see her he would confess to all his victims—even the ones they didn't know about.

Of course, he hadn't. After the meeting he'd only laughed and said he was innocent.

Fury rushed through her when she thought of how he'd used her, how he'd treated her like another of his puppets. She supposed she should be thankful that he hadn't killed her. In that short meeting Gibbons had pressured her into, Adam had insisted that he would never have hurt her. He'd claimed to be just as surprised by what she'd found in the basement as she was and that he'd chased her through those woods at her father's cabin to try to warn her that she might not be safe. Everything that had come out of his mouth was a lie.

He'd promised her they would be together again someday, and until then she was to take good care of his son.

His son. Not their son.

More of that fury boiled up inside her. How the hell had he found her? What did he expect to accomplish by coming here? She was never going to allow him anywhere near Liam. No judge in this country would ever give him any sort of visitation rights—even if he did somehow manage to escape charges for all that he had done.

But he wouldn't. She wouldn't allow him to escape justice.

She had found that woman in the basement. Alicia Holder had said a man with blond hair and blue eyes had put her there. To Grace's knowledge, no other prints were found beyond Adam's. He had claimed that the perpetrator had likely used gloves. Since Alicia—as well as all his other victims—was dead, she couldn't testify. Without the evidence in that basement room, all Gibbons had was Grace's account of how she had found the woman.

But then Grace had run away when she couldn't catch up with the woman. And why wouldn't she? She may have been in shock but she wasn't stupid. She had known that when Adam came home and discovered what she had done he would kill her. The same way he likely killed that poor woman. She'd been found in an alley. As it turned out, she'd been homeless. Many of his victims had been. Young women who'd made the mistake of deciding they would be happier on their own or who had drug issues and had been cast out by their families. Prostitutes. People society sometimes ignored. Each one was found wearing nothing but the heart-shaped locket with their photo inside wrapped around their cold, dead fingers. This was the one thing he always left behind. After endless torture, he'd stabbed each victim directly in the heart—as if he'd studied the organ and knew exactly how to slide the blade into precisely the right place. Then he stabbed them over and over as if he'd suddenly lost control.

There had been three in a two-year period. Then he'd stopped. Gibbons and his profiler had speculated that after Adam married Grace he'd stopped for a while. The woman in the basement was the only other known victim.

Grace supposed it was possible he had tried to stop, but as the pressure of fatherhood closed in on him, perhaps he broke and sought out the pleasure he got from taking a victim.

She rolled her eyes. She was not giving that bastard one iota of slack. He had brutalized and murdered at least four women. He didn't deserve to keep breathing, but he would.

The best she could hope for was that he would spend the rest of his life in prison.

"You okay, Grace?"

Grace snapped back to the present and realized Diane was right beside her. "Sorry. I was deep in the past."

"I should get started setting up the dining room," Diane suggested. "I'm not sure Liam will hold a bite of supper after eating all those cookies."

Somehow Grace managed a soft chuckle. "Well, a few extra cookies now and then won't hurt."

Diane grinned. "You should never say that around a yoga instructor."

Grace laughed outright this time. "Sorry. You're right. Bad mommy."

As if Liam realized they were talking about him, he rushed over to Diane and tugged at her apron. "I can take the *nackins*."

"You can," Diane assured him. She handed him the basket that held the freshly laundered and folded cloth napkins. "Mom can do the silverware."

Grace gave her a salute. "Aye aye, captain."

As they worked to ready the table for their guests, Grace wasn't sure she could eat a thing either. The idea that her ex-husband was out there somewhere a free man wouldn't let go of her. She couldn't possibly eat.

Adam hadn't actually ever agreed to the divorce, but under the circumstances, Grace was able to push it through without his agreement. Would that change now that the murder charge against him might very well be dropped completely in the end?

God, she hadn't thought of that until just now.

She supposed it didn't matter. She would never be that woman again.

But it would matter if he mounted a legal battle.

The sound of the front door opening and then closing had Grace hurrying into the parlor. The weary look on Rob's face tightened the band around her chest. Had something more happened related to her situation?

Stop, Grace. She was overreacting. Rob had an entire community to worry about. She wasn't the only person with problems. Hers were just more twisted and complicated than most.

"We should talk privately."

Oh, dear God. It was about her situation. She nodded. "I'll let Diane know."

Grace hurried to the dining room. "Diane, do you mind seeing after Liam for a while? Deputy Vaughn is back and…"

Diane nodded. "Got it." She smiled at Liam. "Little man and I have dinner under control." She waved Grace off. "Shoo."

"Shoo, Mommy," Liam repeated with a giggle.

Grace managed a laugh and left them to it. Rob wasn't in the parlor anymore, so she walked quickly toward her private quarters and found him waiting there. This must be bad, she decided, to warrant this level of privacy.

She closed the door behind her and steeled herself.

"There was a murder just a couple of miles from here."

Her breath caught. A murder? "What happened?"

He moved toward her and she suddenly wished she hadn't asked. Wished she didn't need to know.

He withdrew his cell phone and tapped the screen. "Do you know this man?"

Grace stared at the image, a close-up of a face she knew as well as her own. Her brain froze up for a second. She blinked. Told herself to look again.

"It's him. It's Adam." Something hot rushed through her body, followed immediately by an icy cold. She swayed. Rob's hand reached out and steadied her.

"You're certain?" he prodded.

"Yes. It's him. What happened?" The question popped out all on its own, even though she really didn't care. Judging by the pallor of his skin, he appeared to be dead, and some part of her was jumping up and down and shouting that she was free. Free!

"Stabbed multiple times."

She stared at him, reminded herself to breathe. "Like his victims."

"Looks that way."

"How long…?" She drew in another desperate burst of air. "Do you have any idea when this happened?"

"The Cashions were away for the weekend. When they came home this afternoon, they found him, so we really can't be sure just yet. I'm guessing early this morning. Maybe the middle of the night. The medical examiner will give us more on time of death after he's had a chance to examine the victim. Obviously only hours after he was here."

Grace made her way to the closest chair and dropped into it. "I'm certain I should be feeling something, but I only feel numb."

Rob took a seat on the sofa directly across from her. "The

emotions will come later when your mind has been able to absorb the reality of what's happened."

She understood this from before, but still… Adam was dead. She didn't have to worry about him coming after her. She could live her life any way she chose. She could—

A new question bobbed to the surface of the haze currently shrouding her. "Who killed him?"

"That's the problem." Rob turned the navy cap that matched his uniform around and around in his hands. "Like you said, he was stabbed in a manner consistent with that of his victims. No one here except you knew him—I'm assuming—so that can only mean one thing."

The reality of what he was saying slammed into her. Her heart dropped into her belly, and she wanted to rush into the kitchen and grab Liam. Hold him tight. "Someone followed him here…or came with him. One of his followers."

"It's the only logical explanation."

Adam had followers. Before his identity was even known, there were those who praised the work of the Sweetheart Killer. Like all criminals who rose to notoriety, there were fans. After his arrest, the fan letters had poured in. The fact that Adam had been a handsome man—a charismatic man—had garnered him a huge audience.

The fans had flocked to the home she and Adam had shared. The place had to be guarded to prevent them from going inside. His office in the business district and her father's cabin in Lake Tahoe had both become shrines to Adam Locke.

Well before that, Grace and baby Liam had gone into hiding.

"I have to leave." She rocketed to her feet. "I have to get

Liam to safety." Adam was dead, but if one of his fanatical followers was here, they wouldn't be safe. All manner of threats had been made against her two years ago by those obsessed with Adam Locke.

"Grace," he said softly, too softly, "I know I promised you that I'd help you do that, but this has changed everything."

"How?" She shook her head. "I don't understand. We could be in danger. We can't stay here."

"Detective Gibbons is on his way."

If he'd wielded a physical blow, he could not have shaken her more violently. "What does his coming have to do with me?" That fluctuation between hot and cold started again. She couldn't stop it.

"We have to do this the right way. Locke came here after you. Gibbons will want to talk to you. He'll want to go over what happened on Sunday evening."

"None of this…" Fury tightened her lips. "Not his murder… Nothing is more important than my son's safety. I don't care what Gibbons wants."

"If you take off before this is finished, then Locke will still be haunting you, because you'll look guilty. If you hold on just long enough to get through this, then you can put it behind you once and for all."

He was right. She recognized he was, but that didn't make her like it one little bit.

"I just need to be sure my son is protected."

"I'm going to ensure that the two deputies on shift tonight drive by every hour or so, and I'm checking into the inn and staying right here on this sofa."

"You…" She searched his face. "You would do that for us?"

"I will do whatever it takes to keep the two of you safe. You have my word on that."

"Thank you." She blinked to hold back the burn of tears. "There hasn't been anyone since my father died. It's just been Liam and me."

"That's not the case anymore, Grace. You have me and a whole community of people who admire and respect you. You are not alone."

She wanted desperately to cling to that hope, but what this man didn't understand just yet was that although Adam Locke was dead, his followers were not. By the time they finished or were caught, this whole community would rue the day Grace Myers arrived in their midst.

Chapter Six

Grace could only imagine the lengths to which Detective Lance Gibbons had gone to find a flight leaving San Francisco for Chattanooga as soon as he heard the news. The strings he must have pulled to get on that flight. The minute he had landed, he'd gone straight to the morgue to view the body. Now he was headed here. Based on the call Rob had received from the man, Gibbons should be here in the next fifteen minutes.

The memory of the way he had hammered her for answers during those first few days in the hospital after having Liam assailed her. He'd been ruthless, pushing her as if she were the criminal. The manhunt for Adam had been ongoing with no results. No one had called in to say they had seen him. Not even the usual crazies. It was as if Adam had put out the word for radio silence and the world had obeyed.

But Gibbons had had a plan even then. Like Grace, he had known that Adam would want to see his son. She had begged for police protection in the hospital, but Gibbons had put a single guard on her room and left it at that. Her father had remained at her side until his heart attack. She hadn't even been able to make his funeral arrangements for days after his death because she was still in the hospital. The doctor kept saying she couldn't be released just yet.

Later Grace had learned that Gibbons had seen to it that she stayed in the hospital three extra days. His long shot had paid off. Two days after her father's death, Adam had stolen a doctor's ID badge and scrubs and entered the hospital. Gibbons had been waiting.

The pressure lowered on Grace for a while after that. She'd been able to leave the hospital and prepare for her father's funeral. It was at his graveside service that she'd learned about Adam's followers. A trio had shown up and attempted to abduct Liam. The two policemen assigned to watch her had done the best they could to hold them off. The funeral director had managed to get her and Liam away from the cemetery. A similar attack had occurred days later as she was leaving the pediatrician's office. That was when she had known she had to disappear.

Disturbed by the memories, she went to the bedroom to check on Liam. He had fallen asleep a little later than usual since Rob was here. The fact that Diane had stayed so late and Cara had returned had unsettled him. He was accustomed to there being only the two of them and the guests after eight in the evening. Generally, they only saw the guests passing through the lobby on the way to their rooms after dinner or an evening out.

Tonight everyone had rallied around Grace. Even the Wilborns had returned for a short time to see if their help was needed. Both Cara and Diane had been stunned by her story and promised to do whatever was necessary to help her keep Liam safe.

Grace sat down on the bedside now and swiped the hair from her sweet child's eyes. Would they feel the same way if someone they knew and cared about lost their lives to one of her ex-husband's followers?

She hoped that did not happen. Enough lives had been lost to Adam Locke's evil deeds, but there was no way to know when the other shoe would drop. If a follower had for whatever reason murdered Adam, she or he was likely far more deranged than the average fan. It was possible Adam had rebuked him or her for some reason. Or perhaps the killer wanted to prove he or she was better.

At the soft knock Grace opened the parlor door expecting to find Rob, but it was Cara and Diane.

First one and then the other hugged Grace tightly. "That detective from San Fran is here," Diane explained.

"We can stay with Liam if you'd like to see him," Cara offered. "He says he doesn't need to interview either of us just yet."

Diane made a face. "I don't like him."

The two women could not be more different. With dark spiky hair and dark eyes, Diane was thin but well toned thanks to her dedication to yoga. Every one of her fifty years showed in the lines on her face, but she didn't care. Never wore makeup. What you saw was what you got. Cara was more reserved. Her long blond hair was silky smooth, and she took great care with her makeup and dress. Though thin like Diane, she was more into running than yoga. Both were good friends to Grace. Better friends than she'd ever had in her adult life.

"I don't like him much either," she admitted.

"He wants to speak with you if you're ready," Cara said.

Grace would never be ready, but she had no choice. "Thank you."

Diane urged, "We will get through this."

"I really appreciate the two of you being here." Grace looked from one to the other and then did what she understood she must. She walked out, closed the door to their private quarters behind her and went to the kitchen. Since additional security was needed in light of the murder, Rob had ensured the new police presence was not overwhelming. Both deputies on duty for the night were dressed in plain clothes. Rob had spoken to the inn's two guests and explained the situation. Both had been far calmer about the situation than Grace had expected, and she greatly appreciated their understanding. This was not the sort of thing she wanted to see in a Yelp review.

For support, her gaze locked on Rob as she entered the kitchen. In her peripheral vision she noted that Gibbons stood at the island, his back to her. Grace walked wide around his position and straight to Rob's side. With heavy reluctance she faced the man who had added to her nightmares for weeks after finding that woman in the basement.

"Gia," Gibbons said with a nod.

"It's Grace," she corrected him. He certainly knew that by now, but he no doubt wanted to show he knew her for who she really was.

"Grace," he amended.

Though it had been just over two years since she had seen this man, he looked at least a decade older. She hadn't fared much better, she supposed. The sort of evil she had survived tended to age a person. Gibbons's suit was travel rumpled, and an evening shadow had darkened his jaw. His bloodshot eyes told her he still didn't sleep well. During the investigation, he'd told her he hadn't had a good night's sleep since earning his detective's shield. He was a homicide detective in a major city. The Locke case was just one of many nightmare cases he'd investigated. A good night's sleep likely wasn't a perk of the job for any investigator.

Gibbons was a good man. A husband, a father. Grace had wanted to like him, but she'd experienced firsthand the ugly side of his need to get the job done at all costs. It was not pleasant, even though her only crime had been falling in love with the wrong man. Add to that the need to protect her child, and she was basically a hostile witness, in the detective's opinion.

"Detective Gibbons and I have discussed how this is going to go," Rob said. "He has assured me you don't need an attorney present." Rob eyed the man with open suspicion. "But I don't know that I agree."

She had a feeling their earlier conversation hadn't gone as Rob expected. She wasn't surprised. Gibbons never bothered to hide his opinion that Grace hadn't told him everything. But she had. She had told him all that she knew about Adam. How they'd met…all of it.

"Why would I need an attorney?" She looked from Rob to Gibbons. Though she asked the question, the answer was simple. The victim was a serial killer. Her ex-husband. The father of her child. The one she had turned over to the police. Of course she was a suspect.

It didn't matter that Rob would insist this wasn't the case.

She had been down this road before. Everyone knew when a person was murdered the spouse or ex-spouse was the primary suspect. She had more reason than the average ex to want Adam Locke dead. Last time around she had been a person of interest as well. No one had believed that she could live in a house where a victim was imprisoned and not know it was happening. But she hadn't. Adam had kept his victims bound and gagged as well as drugged. He'd expected to be finishing off his latest victim that day when he got the unexpected call from work. He'd anticipated being back before her last dose of sedative wore off. Except it hadn't worked out the way he'd anticipated.

Apparently, his journey here to find her hadn't either.

That was the only upside in all this. She was so damned glad he was dead. It was as if a steel cage had been removed from around her...except a glimmer of danger still lingered close by. It was impossible to fully understand the threat until the person who killed Adam was found.

"I'm certain you don't need an attorney," Gibbons said, drawing her back to the moment. "It is your right, however."

"Let's move on," Grace suggested. It was late, and she had no desire to drag this out any longer than necessary. "I would ask you to sit down, but I'm hoping this won't take that long."

"You've been here for two years," he said. "The deputy confirmed as much. On the plane I googled the inn and you, but oddly I found no photos of you or your son."

"I've been careful about that." She was only too happy for photos of the inn to be snapped but never with her or Liam in the frame. Even when she'd been given awards by the community leaders, she had been careful not to be in a photo.

She had learned the hard way that the internet was forever.

"Where were you before coming here?" Gibbons asked.

"If you want to know if Adam's been in contact with me, just ask." She refused to go into detail about where she was before finding this inn and starting her new life. "Where I've been is irrelevant to your investigation, I believe."

"I agree," Rob said. "The murder occurred here. I can't see how where she was prior to two years ago would have any bearing on the murder."

Grace pressed her lips together to hold back a smile. It was really nice to have someone on her side this time. Last time her father had just died, and all the people she'd thought were friends were suddenly gone. Busy. Unavailable. Not that she blamed a single one of them.

Bottom line, she had been on her own.

"Was he in contact with you at any time since you left California?" Gibbons asked. He watched her carefully over the top of his glasses as he waited for her to respond.

The glasses were new. She didn't recall seeing him with glasses last time. Looking at him more closely now, she noticed the light scattering of gray in his hair and in the stubble on his jaw.

"No. I was very careful. No one from my old life had any idea where I was or where I was going. After my father's death, there was nothing left in California for me."

"You had no reason to believe he was aware of your whereabouts now?"

"None at all." She thought of the visit to her porch. She

felt confident Rob had already told him about this. "The first inkling I had that he might be in the area was when my son discovered a man walking around the house the other night. The man came onto the porch and looked into the window. I had no idea who he was, but my son said he had blue eyes. I have to admit that rattled me. But I assumed Adam was still in jail. It wasn't until the next day that I googled him and learned he'd been released."

"I would have warned you," Gibbons said, "had I known how to reach you."

Anger stirred deep in her belly. "You're well aware why you didn't know my location."

He glared at her, his own anger making an appearance. "We did what we thought was right."

"I'm sure you did," Grace replied. "But you did so with no care about the cost to me and my child."

"He was already on to us," Gibbons argued. "When we reached his office, he was gone—as you well know. Obviously he'd gotten a heads-up somehow."

On some level she understood that the police—Gibbons in particular—had thought that perhaps she had gotten cold feet and warned her husband they were coming. But that could not be farther from the truth. "He was on vacation. The call into work was an emergency. Did it not occur to you that he might return home before the end of his usual workday?" She shook her head. "Whatever you were thinking, rather than warn me that he was on the run or come to where I was—which was the most likely place he would go—you went into the house without a proper warrant."

"We had exigent circumstances since we believed you

might be in danger," he argued. "Or that there could be a victim hidden in another secret room of the house."

Grace laughed. "Except I wasn't there and you knew I wasn't there. As for another victim, I never said there was another one." Thinking about the risk he took with her life and her son's infuriated her even now.

He shrugged. "We couldn't be sure of anything—not even your statement."

"Let's get this over with," she suggested. "Do your interview and then do your job. My son's life is at stake, and just like last time, I'm not going to stand around here and wait for you to provide the protection he needs."

Gibbons stared at the floor a moment before lifting his gaze back to hers. "We did what we thought was right."

"You said that already," she reminded him.

"I won't let you down this time, Gi—Grace," he promised.

"I'll be taking care of Grace and Liam's security," Rob countered.

Grace would never be able to thank this man enough.

"I do not want her leaving this property," Gibbons warned. "We lost track of her last time, and I don't want that to happen again until we finish this."

"No promises," Rob argued. "This could take weeks or months to sort out on your end. We will do whatever is best for our citizens on this end."

For the first time since she was a kid growing up in the woods well beyond the tourist setting of Lake Tahoe, Grace felt as if she belonged. She would never be able to thank Rob enough.

"The medical examiner provided me with a preliminary

time of death," Gibbons was saying. "Between midnight and six this morning."

That would mean he'd been murdered only six to twelve hours *after* coming here and looking at Liam through the window. Her heart shuddered. Had someone been with him or following him even then? She shuddered at the idea.

"He'll be able to pinpoint the time more closely as soon as he's completed the autopsy," Rob added.

Gibbons nodded. "I'm familiar with the routine." He shifted his attention to Grace. "Can you verify where you were during that time frame?"

She had expected the question. "I was here. Asleep with my son until about five and then I got up and started baking. My chef can confirm that I was in the kitchen elbow deep in dough when she arrived at five thirty."

No matter that she understood his questions were necessary, it still angered her that she was considered a suspect. Not that she hadn't dreamed of killing the bastard. It was the only way her son would ever be free. But she couldn't risk him losing his mother. She was no murderer, and the odds that she wouldn't get caught were not in her favor.

"Can anyone confirm you were here prior to Ms. Franks's arrival?"

She thought about that for a moment. There hadn't been any guests and Liam had been asleep. "No. I suppose not."

"Actually," Rob said, "I can vouch for her. A deputy was stationed outside the inn until Diane Franks arrived. Grace never left."

Grace stared up at him in a kind of shock. Why would he cover for her? He had to know Gibbons would attempt to confirm his statement. Whatever the case, she appreciated the effort.

"You had eyes on her vehicle all night?"

"Her SUV was in the garage and it never left."

"But she could have walked. It's less than two miles to the Cashion residence, where the murder occurred."

Now he was reaching.

"I would not have left my son alone," she argued.

"It was snowing," Rob stated. "And it was about twenty degrees. So no, that's not feasible."

"But you suspected Adam was here," Gibbons countered, his point directed at her. "How could you sleep knowing it was possible?"

"I couldn't be certain." This was not entirely true. She had found the necklace. She'd known that at the very least one of his followers was close by.

She should have given the damned locket to Rob… She shouldn't have pretended it didn't matter. Now if she told Gibbons about it, Rob would see it as her having hidden a perhaps important piece of evidence from him.

She really, really had to get her head on straight here.

Cutting herself some slack, she had sort of talked herself into believing it could be someone else. She'd come up with all sorts of other scenarios. The truth was, she hadn't been sure until she'd done that Google search the next day. "You can check my computer. Why would I have looked for information about him online if I'd known he was here and I had already killed him?"

"I suppose you wouldn't have," Gibbons admitted, "unless you'd done it to strengthen your alibi."

"Enough," Rob warned.

Grace jumped at his tone. Though he'd startled her, she was grateful he'd intervened.

"You are here—in my jurisdiction—and this is getting us nowhere," Rob warned him. "Unless you plan to carry out some sort of constructive investigation, then you should be on your way and allow us to do our jobs."

Gibbons held his glare with one of his own for a beat or two. Then his eyes pierced Grace. "He came here for a reason," he charged. "He wanted you back or he wanted his son and you dead. Whatever it was, if he brought help along, for some reason that helper turned on him. We need to know why that happened."

"I'm glad he's dead," Grace confessed. "I'm not going to lie. But I didn't kill him, and like you said, if he brought someone with him who did, then what's the motive? Does this other person want my son—his son—or just revenge for someone else?"

"So far," Rob pointed out, "you've talked about Locke having maybe brought a follower or a friend with him. Maybe this was a family member of one of his victims who's been posing as a follower, waiting for the right opportunity to take his revenge. Or one who learned of his impending release and then followed him here. He or she may be long gone now that the job is done."

Grace hadn't considered that option, but Rob was right. It was possible.

"We need to find whatever vehicle they were using," Gibbons suggested. "We started trying to track Locke as soon as he was released. He vanished before we could come up with other charges against him—at least to hold him until the original investigation was reopened. He didn't use public transportation, which would mean he likely drove or the person with him drove."

"So we're looking for a new arrival in town," Rob said. "One who came from the West Coast."

Grace thought of the two guests currently registered right here at the inn. One from California, the other from Seattle.

Rob's gaze collided with hers. "We're going to need to wake up your guests."

That was the last thing she wanted to do. Involving her guests was the worst possible scenario, but Rob was right—they fit the profile, so to speak. "I'll talk to them," Grace said. "In the morning. I will not disturb them tonight."

"I can't risk one or both disappearing when the police presence here tonight is gone," Gibbons countered.

"The police presence isn't going anywhere," Rob assured him. "I and one of my deputies will be here all night."

Gibbons straightened. "Well, I suppose under the circumstances I'll need to take a room as well. I'm not booked anywhere else." He turned to Grace. "I would think the multijurisdictional police presence would give you comfort."

How could she debate the statement? Gibbons knew Adam Locke better than anyone—maybe better than Grace.

Though she didn't find his presence here the least bit comforting, if his being on hand was in any way helpful in keeping Liam safe, she could deal with it.

Her son's safety was all that mattered.

"All right. Follow me and I'll get you registered."

He followed her to the registration desk, where she selected a key to one of the cabins. She could tolerate his presence but some distance was necessary.

"You're in cabin 15." She placed the key on the counter.

"I'll fill in the necessary information. Your stay will be on the house. We appreciate all that law enforcement does to keep the community safe."

He picked up the key, his gaze searching hers for a moment. "Very well."

"I'll show you the way to the cabins," Rob suggested, saving Grace the trouble.

She'd have to remember to thank him later.

"I'll see you in the morning, Grace," Gibbons said before turning away.

She would see him. Only because she had no other choice.

Chapter Seven

It was well past midnight when Grace returned to her room. She found Diane and Cara pacing the floor. She peeked in on Liam, who remained fast asleep. Grace closed the door quietly and joined the others in her small parlor.

Rob had said he would check in with her once he'd walked the perimeter of the property and updated Reynolds. Grace felt immensely better with those two close by. She couldn't name what she felt with Gibbons in one of her cabins. She felt…uneasy. Restless. Like she needed to run as far and as fast as she could.

Stay calm. Focus on the necessary steps.

"This is insane," Diane insisted. "This guy cannot believe you killed that—that—"

"Monster," Cara said. She settled on the sofa and pulled her knees to her chest. "You saw the things we found on the internet," she said to Diane. Her attention shifted to Grace then. "I don't know how you survived."

Flashes of scrambling through the snow with him right behind her zoomed through her brain.

"I was lucky."

"You're also strong," Diane said. "Only someone with

incredible courage could have gone through what you did and still be standing." She dropped into a chair. "My God, look at what you've accomplished here. You've built a great new life for you and Liam. It's amazing what you've done."

"Thank you." Grace dredged up a smile. "I'll just be thankful if we get through this and then move on with the rest of our lives."

She had to keep reminding herself that Adam was dead. It didn't feel real. No one was more grateful than her that he was gone, but it hadn't completely sunk in yet. She kept asking herself how she would deal with him, only to abruptly remember that she never had to deal with him again.

He was dead. Done. Gone. He was never coming back.

Except he'd likely brought someone with him, and that person could still be here. That person could be watching from a distance at this very moment.

She had an obligation to warn her employees. Just one more nightmare to add to the mix.

"There's a strong possibility he didn't come here alone."

"I read about him having followers," Cara said. "Does the detective from San Francisco feel someone like that may have come with him?"

"He does. Worse, there's a strong possibility that person may be a killer as well. May have killed Adam." At least, that was how Grace felt. "Until we know more, it's really important that both of you be very careful. I'll be having this same conversation with Paula and Karl."

"What about the guests?" Diane asked. "Are they in danger?"

Grace felt sick with the burden of this unholy mess. "The

best way to look at this is that anyone close to me could be in danger."

Cara's eyes went wide. "Oh, no. Liam." She shook her head, her face a study in worry. "You should let me take him to my grandmother's cabin. We'd be safe there. Trust me, no one would ever find that cabin."

The offer gave Grace pause. "You know, I might have to take you up on that."

"The kid certainly adores Cara," Diane pointed out. "It could work."

The thought of not having Liam close was nearly more than Grace could bear. They had never been apart. Never separated by anything other than a wall. But this time there might not be a choice. His safety had to be her absolute top priority. No matter how painful to her mothering instincts.

Grace looked from one woman to the other. "Thank you. Both of you. I am so glad to have you in my life. Liam and I would be lost right now without you."

"I'm just sorry you didn't feel you could share this with us before," Cara said, the sadness in her tone tugging at Grace.

"You really can trust us," Diane chimed in.

"I know and I'm sorry," Grace confessed. "I thought I was doing the right thing."

"Anyway," Diane said with a shake of her head, "we're here and so is Rob. The man obviously has a serious crush on you."

Grace laughed off the suggestion. "He's a very nice man but—"

"Don't even go there," Cara interrupted. "The guy likes you and you should give him a chance. A little time for just the two of you would be a good thing. All the more reason to let me take Liam to the cabin."

"You could be right," Grace acknowledged. "And I promise to keep your offer in mind."

A soft rap at the door had Grace's heart rising into her throat. Rob opened the door and stepped in. "Ladies, if you're ready to go home, Deputy Reynolds will follow you and make sure you get inside safely. You live the nearest, Diane, so they'll go to your place first."

She hopped up. "Sounds good." She flashed Rob a big smile. "I always appreciate a man showing his gentlemanly side."

"I second that," Cara said as she joined Diane.

Grace hugged one and then the other. "See you in the morning."

Rob said, "I'll be back in a bit."

Had he and Detective Gibbons discussed the situation in greater detail? She hoped Gibbons was being entirely straight with them. If he was holding anything back, it could put Liam in danger. She really hoped he understood and cared about their safety.

She glanced at the clock. It was really late. She was exhausted. But obviously Rob wanted to talk, so she busied herself picking up Liam's toys and tidying the room. The idea of getting up at five to bake the day's sweets suddenly held no appeal.

Resentment tightened in her throat. How dare that monster come here and damage the carefully constructed life she and Liam had built. This was their home and they were happy here. It was the only place Liam remembered as home. She did not want anything to take that away from him. From her.

Another tap on the door and Rob was back.

She resisted the urge to sigh. She was so tired. "Can I get you anything, Rob? More coffee? A sandwich?" It wasn't until then that she realized they hadn't bothered with dinner. Diane had seen that the guests and Liam were taken care of, but Grace and Rob hadn't stopped long enough to think about food, much less to eat. "I just realized you worked through dinner."

"I'm fine. Thanks." He closed the door behind him. "Let's go over the situation with Gibbons without him around. That okay?"

"Sure. Although you might not want to hear my thoughts on the man."

Rob smiled, the expression a little dim considering he had to be as exhausted as she was. "I'm certain you've given him every benefit of the doubt."

Grace sat down on the sofa. She was too tired to keep standing. Rob had apparently been waiting for her cue, because he sat down in the chair facing her.

"Before," she said, thinking back though she would rather walk over hot coals than do so, "I was naive. I'd never been involved with any sort of trouble and certainly not with a criminal." Twenty-nine seemed so far away, although she was only thirty-two now. It felt like a lifetime ago. "I had no idea how to handle the situation. On top of that, I had pregnancy brain—it was focused on other things rather than what my husband was up to."

"I can only imagine," he offered, "how frightening the whole situation was."

"It was surreal." She thought about the word. "It didn't feel real at the time. It was as if it were happening to someone else and I was only watching."

"You don't recall any friends or colleagues he had who might have been involved with what he was doing? No one he had the occasional beer with? Took a fishing trip with or whatever California guys do?"

She had to laugh at the last. "No. No one. But keep in mind that we started dating and less than a year later we were married and I was expecting a baby any second. We went straight from an accidental date to being parents."

"Accidental date?"

"I was supposed to have dinner with my first ever dating-app guy, but he didn't show. Adam's client had gotten ill and had to leave the restaurant before their food even arrived. He'd noticed me and saw that I was leaving before placing an order and figured things out. He suggested I have dinner with him if I wasn't opposed to salmon. We hit it off instantly. He was an executive at an advertising firm, and I did website work for clients. We shared a lot of the same interests and..." Her throat felt suddenly dry. "Then I made the mistake of my life."

Except she shouldn't say that since she wouldn't have Liam if not for having met Adam Locke.

"But there was no one he ever mentioned as a friend?"

"Sorry. No. He spent all his time talking about us and the baby. Occasionally he'd mention his work. But nothing about family. He'd said they were all dead and he didn't like talking about them."

"I'm confident Gibbons looked into the possibility of family."

"He did. He didn't take my word for anything, and I suppose he shouldn't have. My judgment was not what it should've been, obviously."

The memory of forgetting where she'd left Liam...of frantically searching for him...poked through the exhaustion. She blinked the memory away. The breakdown wasn't because something had been wrong with her. It was about her mind not being able to handle any more. Postpartum depression wasn't rare. It happened. Pile on top of that learning her husband was a serial killer and the abrupt death of her father, and her breakdown hadn't been surprising at all. Her mind had simply done what was necessary to preserve her sanity.

But this was an aspect of the past she would never share with anyone. Especially not with this man—a man she had started to think she might be able to develop feelings for. Who was she kidding? She already had. Frankly, she'd never expected to have those feelings for anyone again. This was a good thing. Really. It meant she was moving fully back toward normal.

Given her current circumstances, she wasn't so sure it was the right move. Her life was too damaged. Her past too haunted.

"Are you okay with having Gibbons here? He doesn't have to stay here. There are other places on the Mountain."

"No, it's okay. I suppose I should be grateful for his presence. I certainly am glad you and Deputy Reynolds are here." She made a face. "I am really sorry for all the trouble, Rob. This is a nightmare for you and your deputies."

"No trouble," he assured her. "A lady over on Bluebird Trail discovered someone had been sleeping in her garage. Then, after finding the body in the Cashion garage, I thought maybe it might have been Locke. But I'm wondering now if that's right considering he obviously had a vehicle of some sort. Why stay in some lady's garage? Is that the kind of thing he would do based on what you know about him?"

Grace thought about the question for a moment. Adam had always had a plan. Had always been a smooth operator. "I can't imagine him not having a plan—even a backup plan in place. He was very good at juggling things at work. He used to tell me how he kept management impressed. Since his employer and colleagues seemed as stunned by who he really was as anyone else, I suppose it was true. If you're asking me if I can see him staying in a garage..." She shrugged. "Maybe. If he was desperate enough. Otherwise, no. But whoever came with him or followed him may have much lower standards."

"Since he was released and could come and go as he pleased," Rob said, "I'm not feeling the idea that he'd take up residence in a garage. The Cashion place maybe. They were out of town. He may have picked an empty house at random. Noticed the pile of mail in the box and decided they were away. The place is close enough to have easy access to the inn."

A new thread of tension slid through her. "But if he was free to do as he pleased, why didn't he confront me face-to-face? Just walk through the door during business hours and make his presence known?"

This was the first time she'd considered the idea.

"And why hasn't Gibbons asked that question?" Rob added, considering the idea.

Grace felt the air escape her lungs. "Because he had a

plan and no one was supposed to know." Her gaze latched on to Rob's. "Except he wanted me to know he was coming. That's why he came to the window and left that photo in my mailbox. He wanted me to be afraid. Gibbons probably suspects as much. He's well versed in the MO. There were always indications that the Sweetheart Killer selected his victims in advance. They were never random, although his selection pool was—mostly homeless people. Runaways. Women working the streets. Those who knew the victims would talk about gifts they had received just days before going missing. Chocolates. Flowers. The sort of things a man gives a woman when he's trying to woo her."

The doorbell rang and Grace jumped. At night, when she locked up, the only way to access the inn was to have a key or to ring the bell, which sounded only in her private quarters.

By the time she was on her feet, Rob was already across the room. "You expecting anyone?"

"No. Could it be Deputy Reynolds?" She followed him into the lobby.

"He'd call my cell."

Her heart was pounding by the time they reached the front entrance. Rob checked the security viewfinder. He frowned and turned to Grace. "Did you order pizza?"

"No. Maybe one of the guests. There are flyers from the local restaurants that deliver in all the rooms and cabins."

Rob opened the door. "Evening," he said to the delivery guy. "You have a name on that order?"

The deliveryman looked from Rob to Grace and back. "Grace Myers."

Grace shook her head. "I didn't order pizza."

The delivery guy dug out his cell phone. "Says here the call was made by Grace Myers." He rattled off the phone number.

The number was hers, but she hadn't called anyone.

"How much?" Rob asked.

"Twenty-eight fifty."

Rob paid the man and took the pizza. He closed the door and locked it. Then to Grace he said, "Check your cell."

She hurried back to her parlor, Rob right on her heels. She scanned the room for her phone. She couldn't remember when she'd had it last. Then she spotted it on the counter.

Scrolling through her recent calls, she saw there was only one she didn't recognize, and it wasn't one of her contacts. She pressed the number and waited through two rings.

"All Night Pizza."

"Sorry," she said and disconnected the call. Her gaze lifted to Rob's. "The call came from my phone."

She couldn't have made the call and forgotten. There had to be a mistake. Right? Or had she ordered pizza for Rob and Deputy Reynolds and forgotten?

"Maybe Diane or Cara placed the order and then forgot to tell you," Rob suggested.

"Maybe." In spite of everything, her appetite stirred with the scent of pizza filling the room. "Whatever the case, we shouldn't let good pizza go to waste." She produced a smile. "I could eat a slice."

He nodded. "Same here. I'll take some out to Reynolds too.

"I was thinking," he said while she rounded up plates and napkins, "I might park myself on the sofa in the lobby.

The one by the fireplace. I'll have a direct view of the front entrance as well as your door."

She nodded. "Sure. Do you plan to spend more than just tonight? I'm happy to give you a room."

He didn't hesitate. "Yeah. I'd like to, as long as you don't have an issue with me being here."

"Absolutely not." She may have said that a little too quickly, but it was true. Particularly now that this unexplained delivery had arrived. "I'm glad you're here."

His smile made her heart feel just a little lighter. "Circumstances notwithstanding, I'm glad I'm here too."

She felt the urge to tell him about the breakdown and how every time something like this pizza delivery happened, she felt terrified that she was losing her grip again…but she wouldn't. It was bad enough he knew the deepest, darkest of her secrets. Having him know anything else negative was just too much. She really had expected to spend the rest of her life alone, except for her son. Since moving here and becoming so entrenched in the community, then becoming friends with Rob, she found herself thinking maybe she could let someone else in. Whenever the idea popped into her head, she dismissed it immediately because she was afraid to hope.

She would not feel that way now. No matter that her world had turned a little upside down in the past twenty-four hours, she refused to give up on a brighter future. She wanted a future with someone like Rob in it. No, not *like* Rob. With Rob himself, she amended.

Maybe that was wishful thinking, but there was no harm in wishing.

"Thank you, by the way," she offered, "for covering for me with Gibbons."

He shrugged. "It was true. Deputy Reynolds was concerned about the call, so he hung around until Diane arrived."

Grace shook her head. "I had no idea, but I'm certainly grateful."

"Just part of the job," he insisted.

In Grace's opinion, it was above and beyond.

"Tell me about your family, Rob." She bit into a slice of pizza and her taste buds screamed in delight. She was starving and hadn't realized it. "I know you have a brother in the military and a sister, but not much else."

Listening to stories about someone else's life would be a refreshing change.

"That's right. My younger brother is in the army, stationed in Colorado. My sister lives in Nashville. Her husband is a sound engineer at one of the labels there, and she's an interior designer to the celebrities. They're talking about starting a family. My mom is überexcited since she has no grandchildren yet. My father died a few years ago, and I think she's a little lonely. She lives in Chattanooga in the home where we grew up. She wants nothing more, she insists, than to have it filled with the laughter of grandchildren."

"You're the oldest?" Grace had gotten that idea somewhere.

"I am." He tore off a bite of pizza and hummed his appreciation. "This is good. Whoever ordered it, I'm glad they did."

Grace opted not to think about it. "Why aren't you married and having grandchildren for your mother?"

There, she'd done it. Asked the most personal of questions. Something she never ever did for fear of having the same asked of her. Then again, he knew most of her personal information.

He laughed. Swallowed. Then laughed again. "Actually, about a year ago I thought I was on my way. But my fiancée changed her mind. She married someone else, and now they're a few weeks away from having their first kid together."

"Oh, wow. That…" She wasn't sure what to say.

"Sucks?" he suggested.

"Yeah." Grace glanced around. "I should get us something to drink." She got up and went to the refrigerator. It was smaller than average, kitchenette size, but it worked. She opened the door and reached for a couple of bottles of water.

She stalled, her hand midreach. On the glass shelf was the big ring of the dozens of keys to the inn and its many locks. The metal keys were coated with moisture from sitting so long in the fridge.

Questions zoomed through her mind, and it literally hurt not to make a sound of surprise. Instead, she removed the keys and placed them on the counter, careful that Rob didn't notice. Then she grabbed the bottles of water and elbowed the door closed.

Everything was fine. She was fine.

This had just been a crazy day. Liam may have put the keys in the fridge. Cara or Diane may have ordered the pizza and forgotten.

None of this meant she was losing her grip again.

She was fine. Everything was fine.

The man who'd destroyed her life and pushed her father into an early grave was dead.

How could it not be fine?

Chapter Eight

Tuesday, February 20, 6:00 a.m.

Grace washed her hands thoroughly. The baking hadn't provided the mindless relaxation it usually did. There were a
couple of reasons for that, she admitted as she reached for
a towel.

One, she'd come into the kitchen at five to get started and
her favorite rolling pin had been in the oven. It was a miracle she spotted it as she turned on the oven to preheat. She
considered the possibility that Liam had tucked it into the
oven as he had the keys in the fridge in their little kitchenette. But she couldn't be sure he'd done either. She planned
to ask him when he was up.

But did she really want to know?

Wasn't it easier just to assume...to pretend?

The alternative was the very real possibility she was on
her way to a new breakdown. She'd certainly been there before. Grace pressed her fingers to her lips to stop their trembling. Maybe she was just growing more absent-minded. Or
perhaps all the fear and drama of the past twenty-four hours

had triggered that anxiety she kept hidden so carefully. Anxiety could lead to other issues. No one knew better than her.

It would be so easy to pretend the anxiety and panic that too often crept its way in didn't exist, which was what she generally did. The panic attacks and generalized anxiety had appeared after finding the woman in the basement and then having to run for her life, not to mention losing her father. The one doctor she had dared to discuss the situation with had explained that when the stress of life became too much, a person's mind could simply shut down completely or do so intermittently. It was a way to reduce the level of anxiety. Panic attacks were not unusual in a situation such as the one she had survived. She was only human, after all.

The symptoms were easy to recognize once you had been down that path. Rapid heart rate. Constant lingering fear that something terrible was about to happen and there was nothing you could do to stop it. Forgetfulness. Confusion.

The crash had come suddenly and with extreme ferocity that first time. Typical, the doctor had explained. Her mind and body hadn't known what to expect, so the reaction was magnified. Her father's longtime house manager had taken Grace in. Valentina Hicks, an old hippie who lived mostly off the grid near the community where Grace had grown up, had known all the right things to do. She claimed to have helped many of her flower-child friends through their breakdowns in the seventies. Whatever she was or had done, Val had kept Grace and Liam safe for months. Long enough for Grace to figure out a plan.

She'd been wrong before when she said there was no other family. Val was family, even if Grace hadn't seen her or spoken to her in more than two years. Val had insisted that Grace not look back when she left. No calls. No letters. Nothing that could leave a trail. During their stay with her, Val had taught her about taking care of herself when the burdens around her grew too large.

Sadly, with cops everywhere and a nearly three-year-old running around, not to mention an inn to manage, it wasn't like she could slip away for a couple of hours of meditation or a nice long run. At this point she doubted even that would work.

Adam Locke, the man who had devastated her life, was dead.

She'd lain in bed last night and tried to think of anyone she remembered being a friend to him when they were married. Anyone he'd ever mentioned. But there was no one. Not a single person she could recall in their twelve months together. Grace hadn't really spent a lot of time when they were together wondering about his lack of friends. They were young, in love and expecting a baby. Then, after all hell broke loose, she'd been too busy trying to survive and set up a whole new life for her and Liam. But now, the idea that someone had murdered Adam left her no choice. She forced herself to think.

Obviously the person could have been someone else he'd harmed. There were at least four victims left in his wake. Maybe a family member of one of those victims had been following his case and decided to see justice served on his or her own terms. Particularly after the abrupt release on a damned technicality.

If that were the case, she and Liam likely had nothing to fear from the person who had murdered Adam.

Unless—and this was the part that had taken root during

the wee hours of this morning—this same person saw Liam as a future threat. Some would believe that being the son of a killer meant Liam would be a killer as well.

But that wasn't true. Liam was an innocent child who knew nothing of his evil father. If Grace had her way, he would never know anything about the man.

It was the only way she knew to protect him.

Was that the right thing to do? She had no idea. Babies didn't come with an instruction manual. Although there was plenty written about the best ways to raise a child, the truth was, most people learned by trial and error.

In any event, this was Grace's error to make. Liam would never hear about Adam Locke from her.

The timer sounded, and Grace shook off the worrisome thoughts. She went to the stove and shut off the timer, then removed the muffins from the oven. A batch of chocolate chip cookies was already cooling on the counter.

"Smells great in here," Rob said as he entered the kitchen. He surveyed the cookies on the counter. "You do this every morning?"

"I do." Grace dumped the muffins onto another cooling rack. She quickly placed them in a basket and covered them. She passed the basket to Rob. "Would you put that on the buffet next to the toaster?"

"Sure."

He accepted the basket and headed for the door.

"While you're at it, make yourself a plate. All guests of the inn get breakfast."

"You don't have to tell me twice," he said before pushing through the swinging door that separated the kitchen from the dining room.

Grace smiled, especially grateful for even the small things this morning. She removed her oven mitts and left the kitchen, using the door that led into the hall and heading for their private quarters. Once inside, she turned off the app on her phone and walked into the bedroom where Liam still slept. The baby monitor was the best invention since sliced bread, in her opinion. It allowed her to be in the kitchen while Liam still slept. Though she was only a few yards away, she preferred being able to hear and see him. The app she had downloaded onto her phone prevented the need for carrying around a second device. It was perfect for her needs.

"Good morning, little guy," she said to her sleeping child.

His eyes fluttered open, and her heart stumbled before she could clear away the memory of Adam's.

"I 'mell cookies." Liam grinned sleepily.

"You do, but first you need to have breakfast with Deputy Rob. He's already in the dining room."

Liam tossed off the covers. "Yay!"

Their morning routine went far more quickly since Liam couldn't wait to have breakfast with Rob. His affection for the man gave her a warm feeling. Whether there was ever to be more than friendship between her and Rob, she was grateful for his presence in her son's life.

She and Liam joined Rob in the dining room. Mr. Pierce and Mr. Brower were already seated, their plates loaded with Diane's fabulous breakfast offerings.

"Did you invite Deputy Reynolds in?" she asked Rob, remembering belatedly that he'd had outside surveillance duty last night.

"I sent him home around two this morning," Rob explained.

"Good." Grace was glad to hear the deputy hadn't spent a cold night in his vehicle.

"Any news on the *m-u-r-d-e-r*—" Henry Brower glanced at Liam and made a face "—that occurred not far from here?" he asked. His brow furrowed in concern. "I'm not complaining, but there's been a little more excitement than I expected."

"We're usually very quiet around here," Grace assured him, grateful he'd spelled out the word. Liam remained focused on his muffin. "Hopefully we've seen the last of the unusual excitement." She didn't like making promises she couldn't keep, but she certainly didn't want her guests thinking this sort of activity was the norm.

"The crime rate in the area is very low," Rob assured him. "We're about seventy-odd percent below the national average, but things do happen occasionally."

Brower nodded as he reached for his coffee. "That's certainly good to hear."

Grace smiled. "It is one of the reasons I chose the area and brought this inn back to life. It's a lovely community."

If Mr. Pierce had any thoughts on the activities since his arrival, he kept them to himself. Coming from LA, he would no doubt recall the Sweetheart Killer case. He couldn't possibly have missed it. As soon as the name of the victim was released, he would know that an infamous San Francisco serial killer had been murdered on the Mountain. Then he would notice the cops hanging around the inn, and before long he would put two and two together and he would recognize Grace.

There was no way to stop it.

Her appetite vanished and she thought of Cara's offer. Maybe Liam would be safer away from all this.

"Mr. Brower," Rob said, "your company is thinking of opening a division in Chattanooga?"

Grace looked from Rob to her guest. Evidently, Rob had done some research. She hoped his questions wouldn't upset the guests, but then again, it was necessary. As much as she despised the idea, it was the only way to ensure this nightmare ended without harm to Grace and her son—or anyone else, for that matter.

"We are," the older man said. "Chattanooga is currently an up-and-comer. We thought long and hard about whether to go with Nashville or Chattanooga, and ultimately we believe we'll find a better home here versus in Music City."

"Nashville is a busy place," Rob agreed. "For now, it's easier to gain an identity in Chattanooga."

"Exactly our thoughts," Brower agreed. He studied Rob a moment. "You're the deputy in charge of this small community, isn't that right?"

Rob nodded. "I am."

Brower looked from Rob to Grace. "Should we be concerned that you're here at the inn in light of the other situation?"

Grace had hoped they were beyond that subject.

"You shouldn't be concerned at all." Rob flashed his trademark charming smile. "My reason for being at the inn is personal."

Grace felt her face flush. Their guests glanced at her, which didn't help, but she supposed this was a better option than the truth.

As if fate had decided to ramp up her already rising anxiety, Pierce stared a good deal longer at her. Just when Grace felt he might finally look away, he said, "Maybe you knew the *v-i-c-t-i-m*."

If he hadn't continued to stare at her, as if he were daring her to deny his suggestion, she might have considered his comment innocent. But the glimmer of certainty, of challenge, in his eyes told her he was dead serious and that he knew he was right.

"Well," Grace replied, opting to sidestep his obvious jab, "I'm certain that, whoever he was, Deputy Vaughn will see that the investigation is conducted carefully and thoroughly."

"Count on it." Rob seconded her assertion.

To add fuel to the fire of her uneasiness, Detective Gibbons appeared, wearing the same rumpled suit and still in need of a shave.

Grace pushed back from the table. She picked up her son's plate. "Liam, let's see how things are going in the kitchen." He scooted out of his chair and followed her, nibbling on his muffin as he went.

She hurried through the swinging door while Gibbons was still poking around the coffee urn. She helped Liam onto a stool at the island and placed his plate in front of him.

"You f'got mine juice," her little boy said, staring up at her.

"I'll pour you some more." She went to the refrigerator and grabbed the orange juice.

Diane watched her. "You okay?" She kept her voice low.

Grace managed a nod. "The man from LA may have figured out…" She glanced at Liam. "Things."

"Maybe Cara's offer was the right thing," Diane said. She shook her head. "I'm all for standing your ground, but this may get hairy."

Unfortunately, her friend was right. Grace had to consider Liam's safety and well-being above all else.

ROB WAS NOT happy this Pierce guy had upset Grace. But he let it go for her sake. She would not want him going off on one of her guests.

"Morning," Gibbons said as he placed his coffee on the table. He turned back to the buffet and reached for a plate.

"Morning," Rob said.

Brower did the same.

Pierce seemed to still have that itch he couldn't ignore. He stared at Rob. "That's why you're hanging around, isn't it? Because she knew the murdered guy?"

Brower shot him a squeamish look.

Gibbons tossed the man a glance as well.

Rob decided there was no help for what he had to do. "Mr. Pierce, you're a guest in this inn, so I'm going to be as nice about this as I can. What you're referring to is an official police investigation. I am not going to discuss it with you, and neither is anyone else employed at the inn. If you're interested in headlines for that paper you work for, I'll give you one."

Joe Pierce's stare turned triumphant. "That would be helpful."

"Here goes," Rob said, pressing the other man with his gaze. "How does a freelance reporter from LA know to come to a remote Tennessee community just in time for an infamous serial killer's murder? That's an article I would read for sure."

"Me too." Gibbons plopped his plate on the table and eyed Pierce. "Why don't you explain how that happened?"

Pierce's glare was back. "And who the hell are you?"

"Detective Lance Gibbons, SFPD."

Pierce's attention shifted back to his half-eaten breakfast. "I had this reservation last week."

"All the more reason to wonder why," Gibbons said.

Rob picked up a slice of bacon and tore off a bite. Maybe he did like Gibbons after all.

When Pierce said nothing, Rob said, "We're all listening, Pierce."

"I have a friend," the reporter said, "who told me the warrant was under review before it was public knowledge."

Gibbons shrugged. "How did that lead you to making a reservation in Chattanooga, Tennessee? Not a logical leap under any circumstances I can fathom."

Except one, Rob understood. This guy had a source.

Pierce grinned. "I guess you've got me on that one. I got a note, delivered to my office. The note said the story was here. In the Chattanooga area at this inn. I had no idea what that meant until I arrived."

"How did you know to arrive when you did?" Rob asked. "There was no body at that point."

"I was told there would be big news here this week, and that if I was smart I'd be at this inn to hear it." He shrugged. "I wasn't taking any chances, so I came on Monday."

Brower stood. "I'm confident this discussion will get even more titillating, but I certainly have nothing to add."

Rob agreed with the guy's conclusion. "Have a nice day, Mr. Brower."

Brower gave him a nod and exited the dining room.

"Any ideas on who sent the note?" Gibbons demanded of the remaining guest.

Pierce shook his head. "And even if I did know, I wouldn't tell you."

Gibbons shrugged. "Nothing on the note that might prove useful to my investigation?"

"Our investigation," Rob pointed out.

Gibbons made a nod of acquiescence.

"Not a single thing. No name. No address. No postmark. Just a plain white six-by-nine envelope."

The same plain white envelope in which the printed photo had come to Grace, Rob realized. He withdrew his cell and pulled up the pic he'd taken. He showed it to Pierce. "An envelope like this one?"

Pierce nodded. "Exactly like that."

Rob showed the pic to Gibbons. "Whoever this guy's source is, he was already here."

There was always the possibility that more than one person was involved with Locke and his murder. That person or persons could also know Grace's identity because of their connection to Locke. The real question was how Locke had known. Grace had gone to great lengths to disappear and start a new life.

"Mr. Pierce," Gibbons said, "would you be willing to submit your fingerprints for the purpose of being ruled out of this investigation? I'm sure you're aware that the timing of your arrival and the information you have just provided makes you a person of interest."

Pierce looked from Gibbons to Rob and back. "I'll make the two of you a deal. You allow me the exclusive on this story—however it plays out—and I'll give you my fingerprints, DNA, whatever you need."

"You have a deal, Mr. Pierce," Rob said before Gibbons could. "I'll call my CSI guy right now."

Gibbons nodded. "Works for me."

"Just one other question," Rob countered. "Have you reached any conclusions as to why your source sent you to this inn? There's lots of other lodging options in Chattanooga."

"You're here," he pointed out. "I'm guessing it has something to do with the owner. The timing of her purchase is within the past three years. She has a child the right age. It's an easy leap to the conclusion that she's the victim's former wife."

That he knew so much made Rob sick. He stood. "Excuse me, gentlemen. I'll make that call and get right back with you."

He needed to talk to Grace.

"I'm right, aren't I?" Pierce demanded.

Rob didn't bother with an answer. That was one for Grace and Grace alone.

In the kitchen, Liam was finishing his breakfast and watching cartoons on the small television that sat on the counter next to the refrigerator. Diane was busy cleaning up after her breakfast prep. Grace hovered near her son, looking as distraught as Rob imagined she felt.

Her gaze connected with his, and he didn't mince words. "Pierce is a freelance reporter from LA. I ran a background check on him last night."

Something like horror claimed her face. "How did he know to come?"

"He received a note in an envelope just like the one your photo arrived in. Delivered in a similar manner."

Her face paled. "So he *knows*."

Rob nodded. "He knows."

Chapter Nine

Grace's knees felt weak, and yet somehow, she managed to remain vertical.

If the man was a reporter and he knew her former identity—she refused to consider the past her true identity—then it was only a matter of time before the whole world would know.

"I—I can't…" Her gaze settled on her precious son. "I have to get him someplace safe until this is…"

Rob held up his hands to slow her down. "He's made a deal that we give him the exclusive and he cooperates. For now, this is under control."

Diane moved next to Grace. "How can you be sure?"

Grace was thankful someone had the presence of mind to ask the question.

"He's here for a story. An exclusive. This is important to him," Rob said. "We can control the narrative because we have the story."

Made sense, she supposed. "What about Mr. Brower?"

"He's here with a company planning an expansion into the Chattanooga area. He wants no part of this business."

Grace nodded. "My God, the man must be mortified at the idea of what's happening here."

"I think he's okay." Rob took a step closer. "Right now, my primary concern is for you and Liam."

"We appreciate that." Grace worked up a grateful smile.

"Deputy Reynolds is coming over for a couple of hours while I go home for clothes. Sergeant Snelling will be coming to take Mr. Pierce's prints. Gibbons wants to rule him out as a suspect in Locke's murder."

"If he's ruled out," Grace said, "which I suspect he will be, that means we're still looking for…"

Rob nodded. There was no need for her to go on with Liam in the room.

She felt an overwhelming urge to tell him and Diane about the keys in the refrigerator and the rolling pin in the oven. She'd already asked Diane about the pizza and she hadn't ordered it. The events were not unlike the breakdown Grace suffered after her father's death. But she couldn't bring it up…especially not now. Not with that reporter on the premises.

Diane patted her on the arm. "I'm canceling my yoga class today." She walked over to Liam. "Come on, buddy. You and I are having a party at your place."

"Yay! Can we play in the snow?"

"Maybe later, but not this morning," Grace answered for Diane.

"But we can build a Lego castle to the sky!" Diane teased as she grabbed him and headed for the door.

Grace had no idea how she would ever thank Diane enough. Or Rob. Her gaze shifted to him. "You don't know how much I appreciate all you're doing."

He held up his hands again. "No thanks necessary." He dropped his arms to his sides. "I have a couple of calls to make. Then I should confirm Gibbons and I are on the same page. You okay for a few minutes?"

"I am." She nodded. Forced a smile. "Thanks."

When he'd disappeared through that swinging door, Grace hugged herself. How would she ever feel comfortable in this life she'd carved out once everyone knew the truth? It wasn't that she felt she wouldn't be safe once Adam's killer was found. It was more about how this would affect Liam in the future. She hadn't wanted him to know this horrible truth. How could she protect him if everyone around them knew?

She drew in a big breath and gathered her resolve around her. For the moment, her choices were limited. Their immediate safety was paramount.

A knock at the back door made her jump. Her gaze landed on a face in the door's window, and Grace breathed a sigh of relief. Cara. Forcing a steadiness she did not feel, she walked to the door, unlocked and opened it.

"Sorry," Cara said. "I forgot my key."

"It's okay. I'm just a little jumpy this morning."

Cara hung her coat on one of the remaining hooks in the corner drop zone. Then she grabbed Grace in a hug. "Of course you are. I am so sorry all this is happening to you." She drew back. "Any news this morning?"

Where did Grace begin? "You mean besides the fact that Mr. Pierce is a reporter from LA who received a note telling him to come here?" Grace shivered, hugged her arms around herself again. "A note in an envelope exactly like the one that photo was in—the one someone had tucked into the mailbox."

"Oh my word, have they arrested him?" Cara hung her purse on the hook with her coat. "He could be the killer."

Grace shook her head. "At this point they think he was lured here by the killer." She drew in a big breath. "Or maybe Adam lured him here and then something went wrong."

Cara grabbed a mug and went to the coffeepot. "That's what I'm saying. Reporters can be pretty ruthless. Who knows why he came or what he's done since he got here."

"I'll ask Rob what he thinks when he gets back."

"Where's Liam?" Cara sipped her coffee.

"Diane took him to our space to play. It was getting a little tense in here." Grace frowned. "Did you order pizza for us last night?"

Cara made a face. "Pizza?"

Grace explained the delivery, and, like Diane, Cara had no idea who could have placed the order.

Another load of dread sagged Grace's shoulders. How could she order a pizza delivery and not remember? Her cell vibrated in her hip pocket, drawing her from the worry. She checked the screen. Paula. "Good morning, Paula. Is everything okay?"

Paula and Karl were usually here by now. Grace had been so caught up in the news about Pierce she hadn't noticed their absence.

"I'm headed to the urgent care with Karl. He woke up with a fever and a horrible headache this morning. I'm worried it's the flu."

"Oh, no. Please keep us posted and take care of yourselves. We'll be fine here."

The call ended, and Grace considered all that she would need to do with Paula not coming in. Maybe for a few days if they actually had the flu.

"Everything okay?"

Grace blinked. She really had to get her head on straight. She'd forgotten Cara was in the room. "Karl is sick. Paula thinks it may be the flu."

"All right, then." Cara finished off her coffee and put her cup in the sink. "That means I'm Paula today. You just let me know if you need anything."

Grace shook her head. "I can do Paula's work if you want to man the desk."

"No way," Cara said as she backed toward the door. "I'm the assistant. You're the boss."

Rather than argue, Grace finished the cleanup in the kitchen and then did the same in the dining room. She tidied the buffet, leaving the muffins and cookies. She loved the array of glass domes the former owners had collected. All shapes and sizes, making for the best displays.

She ran the sweeper over the dining room carpet before moving on to the registration desk. She wasn't expecting any new arrivals today, but there was always some sort of paperwork to be done. Or bills to pay.

On her way to the desk, she checked in on Liam. As promised, the Legos were climbing ever higher. She caught Diane up on the Wilborns and how Cara had volunteered to pick up the slack.

"I'll be at the desk whenever you're ready to send Liam my way."

Later, as she worked on some bills, Mr. Brower waved goodbye and hurried through the lobby, heading out for today's conference session. Grace was grateful to see he wasn't carrying his luggage. After the events of the past twenty-four hours, frankly, she was surprised he wasn't abandoning ship.

"Have a nice day," Grace called after him.

The temperature was higher today, which meant the snow would likely all melt away. It was too warm at this point for any ice on the roads. Good news on both counts, as far as Grace was concerned. She loved snow around Christmas, but she was over it well before February rolled around.

The bell over the front door rang, drawing her attention there. Deputy Reynolds walked in, looking far more chipper than a man who'd had surveillance duty until 2:00 a.m. should.

"Good morning," Grace said. "Thank you so much for your late stay last night."

"No problem." He glanced around the lobby. "I just wanted you to know that I'm here. Deputy Vaughn had to run home for a bit, but I'll be here until he returns."

"I appreciate that. There are fresh-baked muffins and cookies as well as coffee in the dining room."

Reynolds grinned. "You talked me into it."

The muffins had turned out especially well this morning. At least something had gone right.

The bell tinkled again. Grace propped a smile in place, expecting it to be Sergeant Snelling. Rob had said he would be stopping by.

Not Snelling.

The man in the jeans and puffer jacket strolled up to the desk. "Good morning. I'm Russell Ames. I have a reservation."

Grace tapped back her surprise. She hadn't taken any reservations for today. "One moment, Mr. Ames." She clicked the keys on her keyboard and scrolled the registry.

"Are you Ms. Myers?"

She looked up. "Yes. Grace Myers. Please call me Grace."

"Well, you were right, Grace. This mountain of yours is beautiful. The views from the inn are magnificent."

Grace bit back the words that rushed to the tip of her tongue. She had not spoken to this man. Had not taken his reservation. Her gaze slid back down to the screen and there it was—the reservation. Her initials were there as well.

No. This couldn't be right.

"Is everything okay?" Mr. Ames asked.

She nodded quickly. "Yes."

Struggling to keep her hands from shaking, she completed the check-in. "Almost all done. I'll just need your credit card."

When he provided the card, she tucked it into the machine and waited for it to process. With that out of the way, she assigned him a room and handed him the key.

"You may park anywhere you like," she said, barely keeping a smile pinned in place. "Breakfast and dinner are provided with your stay. Lunch is optional. Your key fits your room as well as the front door. We do lock up by midnight."

"Great." He hitched a thumb toward the door. "I'll grab my suitcase."

She watched him go, thankful he wasn't from California too.

How could she have made a reservation, chatted with the

man, and not remember it? Did she have to ask? She vividly recalled those moments the last time when she slowly began to realize something was very wrong. The worst moment had been when she'd started into town and realized the baby wasn't with her. She'd left him at home, sleeping.

What kind of mother left her baby at home alone in his crib while she drove away?

A mother who had gone over the edge from all the stress.

Was she hovering on that ledge again?

She finished up with the paperwork and decided she needed to check on Liam. When she walked into the room, Diane was straightening the mess Liam had created with his big build.

"He passed out." Diane cocked her head toward the sofa.

Liam was asleep there. He rarely took morning naps anymore. He must have tuckered himself out playing, and besides, he had gotten to bed late last night.

"Thank you," she said to her friend. "I really appreciate everything."

"Not a problem at all. In fact," she said as she stood, "I think if you're good here, I'll run to the market and pick up those pork chops I ordered. Remember they were out when I went the other day?"

"Are we having pork chops tonight?" Grace felt a new twinge of worry that she didn't remember Diane mentioning the market being out.

"We are," she said. "I have a new recipe I think will be the best ever."

"Your recipes are all the best ever," Grace assured her.

"See you in half an hour or so."

She was off. Grace draped a thin blanket over her boy and

walked back to the desk, leaving the door open and turning on the app on her phone.

The front entrance warned of a new arrival as she entered the lobby. This time it was Sergeant Snelling.

"Morning, Grace," he said.

Snelling was a tall, broad-shouldered man who stood at least six-three or -four. A little gray peppered his dark hair. His smile was as wide as his shoulders, and he was very kind. She'd only met him once at a big community picnic for July Fourth. Rob had made sure she was introduced around that day. Like everyone else Grace had met since moving here, Snelling was a very nice man.

"Good morning. Deputy Reynolds is here grabbing a coffee and fresh-baked muffin. Would you like to join him in the dining room?"

"I surely would."

Grace led him to the dining room and gave the two the cabin number for Mr. Pierce. They would be seeing him after their coffee and muffins.

A chill had penetrated the lobby, she noted as she returned to the desk. Though it was supposed to be warmer today, it was still plenty cool enough to keep a fire going. This was something she generally started as soon as she got up each morning. Likewise, she made sure it was out for the night when she went to bed.

She added a few logs, stirred the embers to get the flames going. This was a part of the job she would never dread. Her father had kept a fire going all winter when she was growing up. Maybe it was the scent of wood burning or the warmth or maybe just the ambience. But it reminded her of her father and her childhood. She wanted Liam to have those kinds of memories. The hard part appeared to be keeping all the ugliness at bay. Making that happen was getting harder every minute.

She thought of the reporter and what he would no doubt write about her and her son. Whatever it was, it was not going to bode well for their future.

Unable to help herself, she checked in once more to see that Liam was still sleeping.

The blanket lay on the floor and the spot where he'd been lying was empty.

Grace's heart rushed into her throat. "Liam?"

She hurried into her bedroom. No Liam. Then she ran to his room and to the bathroom. No Liam. She called his name over and over. Checked under and behind every single thing.

Where was he?

Something in the yard beyond the window caught her attention.

Her breath caught. There he was…playing in the last of the melting snow.

"Liam!"

She rushed to the kitchen and out the back door. "Liam!"

Her beautiful little boy looked up at her. He wore his boots and his jacket but not his gloves or his hat.

"What're you doing out here?"

She reached for him, drew him into her arms. He was cold. His hands and boots were muddy from the melting snow.

"You told me I play in the snow."

"No, Liam," she said, heading back toward the door. "I did not tell you it was okay to come outside alone and play in the snow."

He nodded firmly, tears welling in his eyes. "Did too."

Her own tears burning her eyes, she opted not to argue with him. All that mattered was that he was okay.

"Come on. We'll get some fresh clothes and warm up."

She carried him close to her chest and didn't put him down until they were in his room. She fished out clean sweatpants with a dinosaur sweatshirt, and fresh socks. As he shed his boots and wet clothes, she barely suppressed the need to scream in frustration.

He had to have misunderstood when he'd asked her earlier, in the kitchen, about playing in the snow.

"Liam, remember when you were watching television and you asked me about playing in the snow and I said maybe later but not this morning?"

"Yep. Yep."

"When I said *maybe later*, it didn't mean *yes*."

He peered up at her, his eyes big. "You waked me up on the couch and said go outside play."

Disbelief slammed into her chest. "What?"

"You said go outside, Liam. Play in snow!"

Okay. It was possible he'd dreamed this. "How about next time you wait for Mommy to go with you? Is that a good idea?"

"Yep." He nodded enthusiastically.

When he was dressed and his soiled clothes were in the hamper, Grace selected a new sweater for herself. Though her jeans had survived without getting muddy or wet, her sweater hadn't. She brushed her hair, decided she was too tired to do her usual braid. Over the past two years it had become her trademark style. Not fancy or even trendy, but it worked. Just like her normal jeans and a sweater during the cool months and a simple blouse in the warm ones.

Grace would never be accused of being stylish, and that was okay with her.

The sound of someone coming through the main entrance had her heading in that direction. Liam had resumed his Lego creation, so she left the door open and confirmed the app was still on. She really should have heard him leave the room before. And she surely would have heard someone speaking to him, because it certainly wasn't her. Why hadn't she?

But could she be certain? The dread tightened her throat.

The idea occurred to her that the back door should have been locked in any event. Had Diane forgotten to lock it when she left?

In the lobby, Rob waited for her.

His hair was still a little damp from his shower, his jaw shaved clean, his uniform fresh. "Snelling is here already?"

"He and Reynolds went to cabin 10 to see Mr. Pierce. Maybe fifteen minutes ago."

She hesitated, wondered if she should tell him the things she appeared to be forgetting. Probably she should tell him everything about her breakdown and how she was feeling a little—maybe a lot—like that again.

The French doors that led onto the back of the property and the guest cabins suddenly burst open. Reynolds rushed in, nearly running in his hurry.

"Pierce is gone."

Rob frowned. "But there are two rentals in the lot. I saw them when I came in."

"We have a new guest," Grace said. "He's driving a rental."

"Well, damn." To Reynolds, Rob said, "Get the license plate from Grace and put out an APB. Where's Snelling?"

"Still at Pierce's cabin." Reynolds looked from Rob to Grace and back. "The door was standing open."

Grace wanted to yell or kick something. What the hell? Adam was dead. And now the Los Angeles reporter who had also received an anonymous message was missing.

What was next?

Or better yet, *who* was next?

"I have to check on Liam." She ran back to her room. Found her son right where she'd left him.

Grace collapsed on the sofa, the tears spilling past her lashes however hard she tried to hold them back.

It felt like she was back there, two years and eight months ago. Falling apart and wholly dependent on the one and only person left to take care of her and her child.

"Grace."

She turned to the door where Deputy Reynolds lingered. Oh, God, she'd forgotten he needed the license plate number.

"I'm sorry." She stood, swiped at the damned tears. "Can you stay here with Liam while I get that for you?"

"Course I can." Reynolds walked over to where Liam worked and crouched down. "Wow, that's the most amazing Lego tower I've ever seen."

Grace went to the desk, opened the registration software and pulled up the information on Pierce. But his rental car information was missing.

"Wait." She closed the software and reopened it. There was no way she would have failed to enter the information. A license plate was required to register.

Still, the space was filled with zeros. Empty boxes would

not have allowed the program to save and close, but the zeros did the trick.

Shaking her head, she closed it out and stormed back to her parlor, where Reynolds waited. "The information is missing."

He pushed to his feet. "Missing?"

She explained what she meant. "It had to have been deleted."

At hearing the shift in his mother's tone, Liam looked up, worry shadowing his sweet face.

Grace drew in a deep breath and reached for calm. "Could you let Deputy Vaughn know I need to speak with him?"

Reynolds nodded. "Sure thing. I'll go tell him now."

She had made a promise to herself that she would never tell anyone about those horrible, horrible weeks that had turned into months after her father's death…after the police had harassed her relentlessly. She had fallen completely apart. If not for the help of Val, she would surely have lost her son and maybe her life. The media had already printed accusations that any woman who lived with a murderer and claimed not to recognize what he was wasn't operating on all cylinders, or maybe she was just as evil as he was.

But she hadn't been crazy or evil. She had been naive. She had believed the man she loved.

She had made a mistake. And that mistake had cost her everything she cared about, except her son.

She could not lose her son.

Chapter Ten

Joe Pierce had split or he'd been abducted. Either option was bad.

Fury cut through Rob, and he wanted to punch something.

What the hell was the guy up to? He'd admitted he received a note that told him to come here, had agreed to be fingerprinted, and now he'd just disappeared?

It didn't look good for Pierce.

"No sign of foul play other than the door being open," Gibbons said, surveying the room. "His bags are still here." He nodded to the suitcase and carry-on bag on the bench at the foot of the bed.

"We've put out a BOLO." Since Grace hadn't been able to pull up the info on his rental car, they hadn't been able to provide a description of the vehicle just yet. "I'm hoping we'll get a quick response from anyone who's seen him."

"I say," Gibbons suggested, "we lift some prints from this room to compare with any you've collected at the Cashion scene."

"Already in the works," Rob assured him. "Sergeant Snelling called in another of his investigators."

Maybe Gibbons thought a small town wouldn't be able

to keep up with his big-city way of doing things, but he would be wrong.

"We're in your jurisdiction," Gibbons said. "You could call in the FBI if you felt you needed the assist."

"You didn't call them in when you were working on the Locke case the first time," Rob countered.

"I did call them. But the support I got was minimal. The only things we knew back then," Gibbons said, "was that three women had gone missing in the span of two years, and all three ended up dead with a heart-shaped locket on a chain wrapped around their left hands. Same manner of death—tortured, stabbed in the heart, and then over and over for whatever reason. We found no matching cases in the databases we checked. The Bureau gave us a profile that turned out to be pretty accurate, but that was about the extent of what we got. We just didn't have enough to tie what we'd found to anyone or any trail left behind in any other case. It was a dead end."

"Until," Rob said, "Locke's wife found a woman in the basement of their home."

Rob had done his research. The details of the case had sickened him. All three victims, four including the one Grace had freed from the basement and who was later found murdered, fit a particular profile. Blond hair, pale eyes—either blue or gray—and petite. He hadn't realized until he'd done his research that Grace fit the profile as well. She obviously kept her hair dyed brown for that reason. He hadn't known it wasn't her natural color until he saw the images of her from the news during Locke's arrest nearly three years ago.

He couldn't even conceive how those memories haunted

her. That part of her life had been a nightmare—the things horror flicks were made of.

Gibbons walked to the window. "At least he got what was coming to him in the end. I'm just sorry I wasn't here to witness it."

Rob's gaze narrowed. "This case is personal for you."

"He has that handful of followers—fans," Gibbons said, his attention fixed on the backyard. "They harassed my family for all those months as the case built toward trial. Killed our dog." He exhaled a big breath. "You have no idea how badly I wish I could have caught the son of a bitch who did that. And then, just as we're finally going to trial, Locke gets to walk. Like nothing happened."

Rob felt for the guy. "Like you said, he got his. It's the follower or followers we have to worry about now. Do you think Pierce is one of his followers? He wasn't on your radar during the initial arrest or more recently as the trial was about to start?"

Gibbons turned to face him. "I've never seen him before. Never heard of him. Doesn't mean he isn't one of them."

"Locke had that many followers?" Rob would never understand how people could become obsessed with killers, but it happened. More often than not.

A shrug lifted the older detective's shoulders. "Not so many, really. Maybe a half dozen who showed up in person to protest outside the courthouse when he was arraigned. But there was someone who was involved with him or worked closely with him. All the indicators were there, but we were never able to pinpoint anyone."

Rob got it now. "You thought it was Grace."

"His wife, yes. She was with him all that time. They were

expecting a child together. I assumed she was protecting her family in a twisted sort of way."

No way would Grace ever do anything like that. "But you were wrong."

Gibbons hesitated, then nodded slowly. "I suppose I was."

It annoyed Rob immensely that the man didn't sound entirely convinced.

"In the end, what really killed the case was my mistake," Gibbons admitted. "I wanted solid evidence—the foolproof kind. I knew the only way to ensure we got it was to go into that house before Locke or whoever was helping him could get back in there and maybe destroy evidence. Bella Watts, another woman who fit the Locke profile, had gone missing just days before, so I used the possibility that she could be in that house for exigent circumstances. When Watts was found, a couple weeks after Locke's arrest, I knew that damned search would come back to haunt us. Nothing I could do about it then."

"So Watts wasn't one of his victims?" Rob had been curious about how a seasoned detective could make such a mistake regarding the search.

Gibbons considered the question for a moment. "I'll always believe she was—she fit his MO perfectly. But her throat was slit, her body dumped unceremoniously in an alley."

"Damn." Rob could understand the man's pain.

Reynolds appeared at the door. "Ms. Myers needs to see you," he said to Rob.

"We have someone from Snelling's team headed this way," Rob said, before exiting. "Make sure he understands we need a comparison with the prints taken from the Cashion place ASAP."

"You got it," Reynolds assured him.

Rob was grateful for an excuse to get back to Grace. He really tried to see Gibbons's side of things, but considering most of his conclusions put Grace on the wrong side of the issues, Rob was having trouble with the idea.

Grace was staring out a window in the lobby—the same one where Liam had seen the man looking in at him. The laughter coming from down the hall told him Cara was with the boy. A clatter of pans from farther down the hall suggested Diane was in the kitchen, maybe prepping for dinner or just putting together lunch. No sign of the newest guest to arrive.

Rob joined Grace at the window.

"Did you find Pierce?" she asked.

"He's not in his cabin, but his bags are still there. All we know for the moment is that he's MIA."

She shook her head. "I don't want my son touched by all this, and I have no idea how to stop it."

He reached for her hand, gave it a squeeze before letting go. She stared up at him, her eyes full of worry. "I'm sorry this has come here—to this community. I really thought I'd outrun my past."

"Locke's gone," Rob reminded her. "He will never bother you again. Once we pinpoint whoever was helping him or following him, it'll be over."

"I need to tell you what happened to me after he was arrested. After I'd made my statement and gone home to settle my father's affairs."

Rob glanced around. "Why don't we go into your office."

She looked confused, then nodded as if she'd realized what he meant. She was badly shaken, no question about that.

She led the way to the small office behind the registration desk. The room had originally been a coat closet since at one time the inn had hosted enormous dinners. He leaned against the doorframe so he could see any comings and goings in the lobby.

Grace stood in the center of the small room as if she couldn't decide whether to sit or to pace.

Finally, she said, "I had a breakdown. Liam was only three months old and I fell apart. My father's longtime house manager, a member of the family, really—Valentina Hicks— was like my surrogate mother after my mom died. She took care of everything, including me, all my life, while my father was at work and then later, when I fell apart. She took me to her home near Truckee. She cared for me until I was well enough to get away and start over."

The story gripped his chest like a vise. "If anyone ever had a reason to fall apart," he offered, "you certainly did."

She folded her arms over her chest. "You don't understand. I mean I fell apart completely. I couldn't remember anything. I kept misplacing things—even my baby. I stopped eating. Taking care of myself. I was a mess."

"I get it. It was bad. I still say you had every right."

"I suppose so." She looked away. "But I think it's happening again now."

He considered the ramifications of her admission for a moment. "How so?"

"I had no idea I'd made a reservation for Mr. Ames. I've put my keys in the refrigerator—my rolling pin in the oven.

Pizza was ordered using my cell phone. Mr. Pierce's license plate number was left off his reservation or removed later. And the real heart-stopper—I woke Liam up from a nap this morning and told him he could go outside and play."

Worry twisted his gut. "You found him outside playing?"

She nodded. "I asked why he went outside, and he said I woke him up and told him he could."

"Maybe he dreamed it." Damn. No wonder she was upset.

"I thought the same thing, but when you consider all the other little things, I'm…" She drew in a breath. "I'm terrified. I need to know that my son is safe, and now I'm worried I can't trust myself to make that happen."

"I'll be here," he promised.

"You were here today," she argued.

"But I didn't know you needed me in that way. I do now."

"No matter what else happens," she urged, "I need to know Liam is safe."

"You have my word, Grace."

"Thank you." She crossed the narrow space that stood between them and hugged him. "You have no idea how much that means to me."

The warmth her touch sent coursing through him had him wanting to do more than comfort her. But he resisted. Instead, he put his arms around her and hugged her back. "We've got this."

She drew back and smiled, though it was impossible to miss the emotion shining in her eyes. "Liam and I have felt at home here, and I don't want to lose that."

"There's something you should know, Grace."

Her smile faded and the worry that filled her eyes told him she expected the worst.

"It's not about all this," he assured her. "It's about me."

Her expression shifted to an expectant one. "Is something going on I should know about?"

"I've been meaning to ask you out to dinner or a movie again—" he shrugged "—something simple, for weeks now, but I kept putting it off. You didn't seem interested."

She grinned. "Well, you're wrong, Deputy Vaughn. I'm very interested, and if the idea still holds appeal for you, let's revisit the possibility as soon as all this is over."

"Deal." He leaned down and brushed his lips across hers in the briefest of kisses before drawing away.

She pressed her forehead to his chin. "That was very nice."

He resisted the urge to do it again. "I should get back to work."

She stepped back. "Me too."

When they exited the office, Gibbons was coming from the kitchen, his expression grim.

"We need to talk," Gibbons said.

GRACE'S HEART SANK. The warmth generated by Rob's words and that quick kiss vanished. She was afraid to ask what had happened now. "I should check on Liam."

"You'll need to join us once you're done," Gibbons said to her.

Grace nodded and went on her way. In the parlor, Cara and Liam were watching a movie. Cara glanced up and smiled. "Everything okay?"

Grace wasn't sure everything would ever be okay again. Rather than say as much, she plastered on a smile and gave a nod. "You two having fun?"

"Shh," Liam whispered. "We missing best part."

Grace smiled and motioned to her lips as if she were zipping them. From there she went to the kitchen.

Diane held out a tray with sandwiches and veggie chips. "I thought everyone could use some food."

"I can take it to the dining room. Deputy Vaughn and Detective Gibbons are meeting there. I've been asked to join them."

"Did they find him—that Pierce guy?"

"He's not in his cabin and his car is gone. But his luggage is still here. He just disappeared despite knowing that he was supposed to meet with Rob this morning for fingerprints. Add to that the fact that his door was standing open, and it doesn't look good."

"Maybe he left the door open to make it look like foul play when really he had something to hide and didn't want to be fingerprinted." Diane shook her head, gave a shrug. "This just keeps getting better."

"For sure," Grace agreed.

Diane reached out and gave Grace's arm a squeeze. "We'll get through this."

Grace managed a smile. "Hope so."

Diane turned back to the recipe book she held.

"Did you find everything you needed at the market?"

"I did." She tapped the page she'd opened the book to. "We'll see how it turns out. This is a new entrée for me."

"I'm sure it will be amazing." She hitched her thumb toward the door. "I should get in there."

Dread making each step a burden, Grace carried the laden tray to the dining room. Rob immediately rushed over to take it from her.

"Diane made lunch," she announced.

After Grace offered drinks, she joined the two lawmen, choosing the chair closest to Rob.

"I made a few calls about this Joe Pierce," Gibbons said. "Turns out he got himself into some trouble about ten years ago. He was an *LA Times* reporter back then. He was working on a story—the Hollywood Hills Hunter."

Grace remembered that one. A serial killer had been stalking young women during early-morning runs. He'd killed four before he was caught. "I was a senior at UCLA then."

Gibbons nodded as if he'd already known exactly where she was at the time. He probably did. He'd investigated every part of her life when Adam was arrested. It was as if she had been the criminal.

"There was a young woman, also a senior at a local university," Gibbons went on. "Pierce hired her to run a particular route every morning in hopes of luring this killer. She wound up almost getting killed and Pierce was fired from the *Times*. He wasn't heard from for quite a while, which I suppose is why he started the freelance gig. No reputable paper was going to hire him after pulling a stunt like that."

Grace didn't recall any of those details. She must have been too caught up in exams. "Does this have something to do with the Locke case?"

"I hoped you could answer that for me."

Grace looked from Gibbons to Rob and back. "I don't know what you mean."

"Did you know Pierce back then? The LA detective I spoke with says there was another woman working with Pierce to lure the Hollywood Hills Hunter."

"No." Grace drew back as if he'd thrown something at her. "I've never met the man before. Never even heard of him."

"What exactly are you accusing Grace of?" Rob demanded, his tone just shy of heated.

"I'm not accusing her of anything," Gibbons argued. "I'm only trying to establish a connection. Pierce shows up here—apparently invited by the same person who left a note for you. It feels like there should have been a connection to you."

"Well, you're wrong," Grace said flatly. "I've never met him."

Reynolds appeared at the door. "Vaughn, can I speak with you a moment?"

"Give me a minute." Rob stood and glanced at Grace. "Don't answer any other questions until I'm back."

She nodded her understanding. Clearly Gibbons was determined to connect all of this to her one way or another.

Gibbons waited until Rob and Deputy Reynolds were out of earshot. "I'm not trying to accuse you of anything, Gia."

"Grace," she reminded him. "And it sounds as if that's exactly what you're doing."

"No," he argued. "I only want to get to the truth. Locke is dead, and I, for one, am glad. But whoever came here with him—whoever killed him—I want that person too. As I'm sure you do as well. You must know you're not safe as long as his killer is out there doing God knows what."

There was nothing to say. Unquestionably she understood the situation. The fact that he insisted he felt the same way she did didn't make her trust him.

Rob came back into the dining room. Right behind him was Deputy Reynolds and Diane.

Grace sat up straighter. Why had Diane been drawn into this uncomfortable situation? That she wouldn't look at Grace had a cold knot forming in her belly.

Rob looked to Grace. "There's been a development, but Diane has asked to tell you about it herself."

Grace clutched her hands together, hoped this wasn't going to be even worse news. "Diane, are you all right?"

Diane nodded. "Before I lived in New York," she began, "I lived in Los Angeles. I was a copy editor for the *LA Times*."

Grace tensed. The idea of where this was going made her want to run from the room before Diane could say another word.

"My boyfriend was an up-and-coming reporter hell-bent on making a name for himself." She closed her eyes a moment. "Joe Pierce."

Grace's hand went to her mouth. *No.*

"He was a jerk." She shrugged, still not looking at Grace. "And when I found out he'd hired this college kid to help him try to lure a killer, I was furious. I dumped him. But the worst part is, the girl was someone I'd introduced him to. She'd spent a few weeks interning with me. Anyway, I left and never looked back. And I never heard from him again. Apparently, he'd been following my blog the past few years and realized I was in this area. When he received that anonymous note, he thought I'd sent it to him. He caught me at the market this morning, and we had a terrible argument in the parking lot. I accused him of trying to use me again to get to a story. But he swears he only came because of the note and because he thought I was the one who sent it."

Maybe Grace was a fool twice over, but she believed Diane. "Thank you for telling me. I know you would never do anything to hurt Liam or me. I'm certain this is just as you said."

"Diane," Rob said, his attention focused on Gibbons, "has been living in the area for a year now. There have been zero complaints about her."

"I was already living in New York when the Locke case happened," she hastened to add. She turned to Grace then. "And you're right. I would never do anything to harm you or Liam. That's why Pierce and I argued at the market. I wanted to know what the hell he was doing here and what his intentions were. He only said he'd been invited."

Grace suppressed a shudder and somehow managed to work up a smile for her friend. "Thank you for trying to protect us."

"I believe," Gibbons said then, "that it would be best if you, Diane, and the other employees of the inn remained here until this situation is straightened out. At this point we don't know who or what we're dealing with. It will be easier to see that everyone is protected if we're all here together."

"I agree," Grace said. "If that's all right with you," she added, looking to Diane.

Diane nodded. "Whatever I need to do."

Grace made a face. "Wait. That may be a problem for Cara. She sees after her elderly grandmother." Grace remembered the call from Paula. "And the Wilborns are home with the flu, so they'll need to stay put."

"Very well." Gibbons stood. "We'll talk again when we have more information."

"We're awaiting fingerprint analysis from the crime scene where Locke's body was found," Rob explained.

Gibbons looked from Grace to Diane and then to Rob. "I'm sure you will all be happy to provide your prints for comparison."

The silence in the room was deafening.

Chapter Eleven

6:00 p.m.

The guests—except for Pierce—had wandered into the dining room. Grace had insisted that Rob tell his deputies to stop by as they were able and have dinner. They were all working overtime because of her. It was the least she could do.

Gibbons had left after Sergeant Snelling collected Grace's, Cara's and Diane's prints. Rob had told him not to bother the Wilborns under the circumstances. The couple had lived in the area for decades. To ask for their prints in this situation was ludicrous.

Grace watched Liam ride the tricycle he'd only just learned to pedal around the lobby. He'd gotten very good at avoiding the furniture. Her heart lifted watching him play as if the world weren't crumbling around them. She was so thankful for his innocent bliss.

The blaze of the fire on the far side of the room somehow gave her comfort. She remembered seeing that massive stone fireplace for the first time and how it had reminded her so much of the one at her father's home in Lake Tahoe.

She had known then that this was the place she and Liam would call home.

How had everything fallen apart so fast?

Because of Adam. Anger, hatred and frustration roared inside her. Even in death he tormented her.

She pushed the thought away and focused on the upcoming weekend's calendar. Two more guests were arriving on Friday. She sure hoped this was over by then, but she had a terrible feeling it wouldn't be.

The phone rang and she answered with the usual greeting. "The Lookout Inn."

"Hello. Grace Myers, please," the male voice said.

Grace braced for trouble, no matter that she received calls like this all the time. "This is she."

"Hello, this is Allen Warren of Warren Hardscapes. I'm calling to confirm our start date of Monday, the twenty-sixth, for your project. I'll need to stop by tomorrow and pick up your deposit."

Grace went stone still. "I'm sorry—who is this again?"

"Allen Warren," he repeated. "I did an estimate a few weeks ago for a backyard redo at your inn. You agreed to the estimate and we scheduled the start date—the twenty-sixth."

"I—I'm sorry. I have no idea about this. Are you sure it was me you spoke with?"

"Ms. Myers," he said, his tone going firm, "I don't know what's going on, but I've scheduled my entire team on your job for five days. I have other customers who are waiting."

"I'm really sorry, Mr. Warren." Her heart was pounding now. "If you can just give me some time to sort this out… Perhaps you can move one of your other customers up and then we can discuss this further. Right now, there's an official police investigation at the inn."

She hated, hated, to resort to using a murder investigation as an excuse, but she didn't know what else to do.

The dead air on the other end had her tension escalating.

"All right. I'll contact you next week to reschedule. Meanwhile, I suggest you review your contract. Good evening, Ms. Myers."

The call ended.

Grace placed the handset back in its cradle and quickly searched her computer for anything related to Warren Hardscapes. Her heart dropped when she discovered a string of emails, including a digitally signed contract for more than twenty thousand dollars in exterior work.

Her fingers numb, she closed out of the emails and shut off the computer. It would be nice to update the rear patio areas, that was true, but she hadn't anticipated doing it this year. She could scratch up the necessary payment. It would drain her working capital, but there was a contract. She had little choice. Unless she could prove there had been a mistake.Moving on autopilot, she stepped from behind the desk and walked over to where Liam had stopped riding and was pretending to work on his tricycle. The little plastic tools he kept in the basket made her smile. He so loved watching Karl Wilborn work on the lawn mower. For two years now, Grace had felt comfortable and safe here. She'd thought nothing of allowing anyone on her staff to see after Liam. Now, suddenly everyone around her was a suspect. Not in her eyes—not really, she insisted—but in the eyes of the law.

Would this nightmare ever be over?

The bell tinkled, heralding an arrival. Grace turned to

see who'd walked in. There were no new guests scheduled, as far as she recalled, which wasn't saying much.

Detective Gibbons.

He was back.

She'd expected he would return eventually, but a part of her had hoped never to see him again. Ha ha. Like that was going to happen anytime soon.

"We need a private meeting, *Ms. Myers*," he said without preamble, his expression more smug than usual. "Is Deputy Vaughn here?"

Grace swallowed at the lump that rose in her throat. She wanted to ask what now, but she wasn't sure she wanted to know. Whatever it was, it couldn't be good. Nothing associated with this man and her past was good

"He's in the kitchen talking to his deputies." She reached for Liam. "Come along, sweetie. We need to find Miss Diane or Miss Cara."

Gibbons walked quickly toward the kitchen. Grace watched him go; her heart had already started to pound. The way he'd called her Ms. Myers and the knowing look on his face spelled trouble for her.

She and Liam found Diane in the reading parlor. She was putting books back on shelves and tidying magazines.

"Is it okay if Liam stays with you for a bit?" Grace felt terrible having to constantly put her son off on others, but she was reasonably certain that nothing Gibbons had to say would be good for Liam to hear.

"Of course." Diane held out her hand. "Come along, my little friend, and we'll find that book you love so much."

Liam's eyes lit up. "Berry tales!"

"That's right." Diane grinned. "Fairy tales."

Close enough, Grace thought. Her son was never at a loss for answers or words, even if he had to make them up.

Grace closed the double pocket doors as she exited the parlor. She hurried to the main hall and then to the kitchen. The deputies were all gone, except Rob and, of course, Gibbons. Cara was loading the dishwasher.

Grace was so thankful for these women. They were true friends.

Rob smiled and gave her a nod. To Gibbons he said, "Grace and I need a moment."

Gibbons waved his hand as if to approve the request.

Anger stirred inside her, pushing aside some of the other emotions tugging at her.

Rob touched her elbow, guiding her from the room. He didn't stop until they had reached her private quarters. Inside, door closed, she said, "I'm almost afraid to ask what's happened now."

"Let's sit down," Rob offered.

The fear was back with force. She shook her head. "Just tell me, Rob."

"The fingerprint comparisons came back with one match."

She held her breath. Prayed that the people she adored—the people she trusted—were not somehow caught up in the bastard's murder.

"You."

Grace blinked. "What?"

"Your prints were found at the Cashion crime scene."

No. "That's impossible. I don't even know where they live beyond what you told me. How could I have been there?" This was crazy!

"That's exactly what I said," Rob said. "There were only three prints belonging to you. I've asked Snelling to further analyze them to determine if they were forged."

This was too much. "What does that mean? Forged?"

"There are techniques a person can use to lift prints from a surface and then to transfer them to another. It's not that difficult. The difficulty lies in making them look authentic. Some people and some techniques are better than others. These, according to Gibbons, are very good."

Hope flared. "Then he knows my prints were, as you say, forged. I wasn't at the crime scene."

"He knows that's a possibility because I told him your being there was impossible." He exhaled a breath, shook his head. "Until Snelling gets back to us with a call one way or the other, Gibbons can act on what he has. He's gone over my head and requested a search warrant for the inn and the grounds."

"Can he do that?"

Rob nodded slowly. "I spoke to the sheriff a few minutes ago. She called me right before Gibbons arrived to warn me about what was going down. I told him you would be more than happy to cooperate with a search."

"Of course." She shook her head. "It's the prints I can't get past. I was not there."

"I know you weren't. But the quickest way to defuse this is to cooperate. You have nothing to hide."

Grace felt suddenly sick. "Something else happened." God, she hated to tell him this. He believed in her. She wanted to believe in herself, but that confidence was slipping. Through the tightness in her throat, she told him about the call from Warren Hardscapes. "I found the contract in my email. It looks as if I made the deal and scheduled the work."

"Did you talk about possibly doing landscape work with anyone?"

"Sure." She shrugged. "I've talked all about the things around here I'd like to do to anyone who'd listen." Everything was crashing down around her. "I don't know what to think anymore." She fixed her gaze on his. "At what point do I admit that maybe I've already lost control and I'm having blackouts or something like that?" Her heart sank with the words.

His strong fingers closed gently around her arms. "We take this one step at a time, one issue at a time. Right now, the search and your prints are the most pressing ones. This other stuff will have to wait its turn. Like I told you, I'm here. I'm not going to let you down."

She wondered how long it would be before he understood what an error he had made trusting her.

She took a deep breath. "Okay. I've put Mr. Warren off for now."

"Good. Let's deal with Gibbons. He and two of my deputies will conduct the search, and then we'll see what happens next. Snelling will get back to me as soon as he's confirmed the prints were forged."

He stated it all so confidently.

Grace hoped he was right.

9:00 p.m.

ROB STATIONED REYNOLDS in the kitchen with Grace and Cara. Diane was with Liam watching television. Rob followed every step Gibbons made. He ensured every single thing touched was put back exactly as it had been found.

The only rooms or cabins off-limits were those currently occupied—except for Pierce's. He remained AWOL, so his room was fair game.

Thankfully, by the time they returned to the lobby to start the search of the common areas, the other two guests were either in their room for the night or out for the evening.

The lobby went relatively fast, as did the reading parlor and the office. Grace's quarters took some time. Liam and Diane had moved to the reading parlor to play hide-and-seek. It was past the kid's bedtime, but until they were finished with the private quarters, Diane would need to keep him occupied.

Rob had to grit his teeth when the search through Grace's closet and dresser drawers went down. He didn't like anyone—not even his deputies—touching her private things. He'd wanted to offer to search her quarters, but he'd known Gibbons would never let him. He had figured out Rob had a soft spot for Grace. What he had was a lot more than that, but it was none of the man's business.

A deep breath was impossible until they were out of Grace's bedroom. By the time they'd exited her private space, he was ready to go off on Gibbons. The man had to see that Grace was innocent. Why was he making this harder on her than necessary? He should be glad Locke was dead.

Except Rob knew what he was after. He was still stinging from the idea that someone had given Locke help before his arrest as well as after. He believed that someone was Grace, but there was no way that was true.

Rob trusted her. He believed in her. Whatever she had missed before Locke's arrest, she would not have helped him after. There was no way she'd put Liam's future at risk. No way.

They moved to the dining room and finally to the kitchen.

"I'd like the deputies to get started out back," Gibbons said. "I'll finish up in here."

Rob gave Reynolds and Carter a nod and the two headed out the back door. The outside space wouldn't take that long. There was an old shed but it wasn't that large. The rest was mostly open space with flower beds and seating areas, then the bluff that overlooked the valley below. An iron fence crossed the property at the bluff line.

It was well past dark, so seeing anything beyond that six-foot iron fence would be impossible.

Grace and Cara stood at the island, arms crossed over their chests, and watched as Gibbons checked each cupboard and drawer, the appliances...every damned thing.

When he'd stopped searching and stood surveying the room at large, Rob asked, "Seen enough?"

Gibbons made a face, then turned back to the sink. He crouched down and opened the doors beneath it. He'd already dug around under there once.

Cara shook her head. "This is ridiculous."

Grace looked horrified.

Rob wished he could save her from all this nonsense.

Gibbons stood, a box of cleaning pads in his gloved hand. He placed the box on the island and peered inside the open flaps. He looked up at Grace, something almost sinister in his expression.

Then he reached inside and pulled out a plastic bag.

The bag was dark… No… Rob's heart skipped a beat. It was rust colored.

Bloody.

Gibbons placed the bag on the counter. Rob moved closer. Inside the gallon-sized locking storage bag was a fixed blade knife.

With a bloodied handle and bloodied blade.

"What's this, Ms. Myers?" Gibbons asked, his narrowed gaze focused on his prey.

Rob felt sick. This was not good.

"I have no idea," Grace said, her head moving from side to side.

The back door burst open and Reynolds stood in the doorway. "Rob, you need to come outside."

The look of dread on his deputy's face, combined with the fact that he'd called him Rob, warned that there was something really bad outside as well.

Gibbons whirled on Reynolds. "What did you find?"

Reynolds glanced at Grace and Cara. "It's the missing guy. Pierce. He's in the shed. He's been stabbed multiple times." He glanced at Grace again before lighting his gaze on Rob once more. "Like the other victim."

"Call Snelling," Rob said, his voice far steadier than he'd expected. "And the ME. I'll be right there."

Reynolds gave a nod and went back outside, closing the door behind him.

"Well, Deputy Vaughn," Gibbons said, "I think we have ourselves a dilemma here." He set his attention on Grace. "Are we going to find your prints on this knife and with this dead man?"

"The shed is on her property," Rob said, his fury building

once more. "Of course her prints—real ones—will likely be there."

Gibbons shook his head. "I know you don't want to see this, but how do you explain what I suspect is the murder weapon being under the sink?"

"I have no idea how it got there," Grace fairly shouted at the man. "I've never seen that knife before."

"Even though you apparently used it on your ex-husband?" Gibbons demanded.

"No!" Grace fell back a step as if his words had pushed her.

"Grace," Rob warned. "Don't say anything else."

She stared at him as if he'd landed a blow as well. "Please," he added. "He'll just use it against you."

"Grace couldn't have killed him," Cara argued. "I was with her. We were here working."

"You worked all night?" Gibbons asked smugly.

Cara didn't hesitate. "I've worked overnight on projects with Grace numerous times. Yes, I was here. She never left her room that night."

"You do understand, Ms. Gunter," Gibbons cautioned, "that perjury carries a very stiff penalty."

She put an arm around Grace's shoulders. "It's the truth."

Judging by the shock Grace hadn't quite been able to conceal from her expression, Rob wasn't buying it. He understood Cara wanted to help, but she was likely only making things worse.

Gibbons chuckled as if he too saw right through the ruse. "We'll see, ladies. Maybe the two of you worked together that night. The question is, did your joint efforts result in murder?"

Chapter Twelve

It was almost midnight.

Grace paced the parlor in her private quarters. Thank God Liam was asleep.

What the hell was she going to do?

She hugged herself, rubbed her arms in hopes of warding off the chill that was coming from deep inside.

Adam was dead. Some part of her considered that she should be at least a little sad because he was Liam's father. But it was difficult to feel anything other than relief when put into perspective with who and what he had been. A killer. One who'd murdered at least four women. Why would she feel anything for his loss?

The world was a better place without him.

And what about Joe Pierce? He—a guest—had been murdered on her property. She closed her eyes and rode out the new wave of defeat. She wasn't sure the inn could survive all that was no doubt coming. The media would flock to the inn like buzzards to roadkill as soon as the news was out. The world would learn the truth about who she was and her troubled past.

No one in this little community would look at her the same. She would never be trusted again. And how could she blame them? She had basically lied by omission to every person she'd come to know since her arrival. Not one person had known the truth about her and Liam.

Now she would have to face the repercussions of that somewhat self-serving decision. Protecting Liam had been her primary concern, but she couldn't deny wanting to protect herself as well.

Diane, Cara, the Wilborns—they had all believed in her, trusted her.

Grace slowed in her pacing. Cara had lied to protect her. She and Grace hadn't had the opportunity to talk privately since the unexpected announcement. The CSI team had arrived and then the medical examiner's van. This end of Mockingbird Lane was lit up like a Christmas scene from a horror movie. She had been exiled to her quarters. Diane and Cara were ordered to separate rooms in which they would be staying until this was sorted out.

Her fingers went to her lips to stop the trembling there. Where had the knife come from? The only thing she had put under the sink was the locket she'd found on the porch. But instead of finding a locket, Gibbons had found a knife. The same one that may have been used on Adam and possibly Mr. Pierce. Grace didn't have to wonder if that would be the case. Of course it would be. The knife wouldn't have been under her sink otherwise.

How did this happen? Who had taken the locket?

Whoever did this, it wasn't her. She could not have killed anyone.

Her fingers formed a fist and she pressed it hard against her lips to hold back the scream building in her throat.

Rob was still standing by her. Nothing Gibbons had thrown on the table had seemed to give him pause. Grace was very thankful for his loyalty, but she didn't deserve it. She had lied to him as well.

How foolish she had been to think that perhaps in time they might be able to have some kind of relationship beyond friendship.

"So much for that," she grumbled under her breath. She paused at the window and stared out over the backyard. The entire area was lit up like an airport runway. Sergeant Snelling's team of forensic investigators was swarming every inch of the property. Spotlights had been brought into the shed and placed around the yard in strategic places. Beyond all that was the sheer darkness that spanned out over the cliff. There were no stars to see tonight. The sky was a blanket of black with a mere sliver of a moon barely visible.

Her chest tightened with the loss she understood was coming. Loss of business for certain and loss of friendships no doubt.

She supposed she could sell the place and take Liam somewhere new to start over again. But it would be more difficult this time. He wasn't an infant anymore. He would be sad…and so would she.

A soft rap on the door had her hurrying in that direction. She hoped it was Rob and that there was news of who had done this latest awful thing.

She swung the door open, but it wasn't Rob.

"Cara." Grace glanced beyond her. "Gibbons won't be happy if he finds us talking."

Cara walked in, causing Grace to step back. She quickly closed the door, then hurried to the window and closed the shutters. Cara wandered to the fireplace, stood there staring into the flames.

Grace joined her, feeling a sudden need for a glass of something strong. She rarely drank alcohol at all, but if there was ever a time, this was it.

"Why did you lie to Gibbons about our being together?" she asked her friend.

Cara looked taken aback. "Lie?" She shook her head. "I didn't lie. Don't you remember? You called me right after the police left. You were so upset about someone coming onto the porch. You were horrified that Liam had gotten up without you knowing it and saw the person."

No. Grace wouldn't have forgotten that...

"Oh." She nodded. "Of course. I—I remember." *Liar.*

"We sat right here for hours. Had some sherry. You were so upset." Cara shook her head again. "I felt so bad for you. You finally fell asleep on the sofa about two thirty and I left."

Grace's heart sank to her feet. Cara must be right. She had fallen asleep on the sofa. Cara couldn't have known that if she hadn't been here. "You shouldn't worry so much about us, but I do appreciate being able to count on you at even the worst of times."

Cara put an arm around her shoulders. "We're family. And I meant what I said about Liam. If you want me to take care of him at my grandmother's cabin until this is finished, you know I would be happy to do so."

Maybe she should have taken Cara up on this offer already. How selfish to want to keep her child close with all that was going on.

"You're right. I'll talk to Rob and Gibbons and see if the two of you can leave in the morning. Liam doesn't need to be here with all this."

How did she protect her child from the rising insanity? From her own dance on the edge of reality?

Send him away from it. It was the only logical step.

"Sounds good." Cara hugged her. "Would you like me to prepare some hot chocolate for you? You might sleep better. Or I could pour us some sherry. We'd both sleep well then."

"Thanks, but it's late. You go on. I'll be fine."

Another knock at the door drew both Grace's and Cara's attention there. They stared at each other for a moment, and then Grace hurried to the door. She hoped no other bodies had been discovered.

It was a miracle both remaining guests hadn't requested to check out already.

Grace opened the door to Diane, who stood there clad in her pajamas and wringing her hands.

"I couldn't sleep. I saw the light under your door and figured you couldn't either."

Grace opened the door wider. "That seems to be the trend tonight."

Diane came in and Grace closed the door.

Cara waved. "Same here."

Diane hugged her arms around herself and joined Cara at the fire. "What a mess."

Grace wandered to the double windows that overlooked the backyard. She cracked open the shutter just enough to see. "Maybe we'll hear soon what they've found out there." Besides Pierce's body, she kept to herself.

"I'm still reeling," Diane confessed. "I mean, I hated Joe for what he did. Frankly, I never expected to see him again. But to have him murdered—right here where I work—it's beyond bizarre."

"I get that," Grace admitted. She left the window and joined the others in front of the flames. She stretched out her hands, feeling chilled to the bone. "I thought Adam was going to prison for the rest of his life. I never thought I'd have to see him again or have him invade my life."

"How—" Cara snapped her mouth shut as if she'd thought better of what she'd intended to ask.

"What?" Grace searched her face.

"It's nothing," Cara assured her.

Grace hated that she felt annoyed by her friend's response, but she did. Maybe only because she was on the edge already. "Ask whatever's on your mind. Please."

Cara searched her face for a moment. "You never noticed anything off about him? Nothing that made you the least bit uneasy?"

Grace had gotten that question before. So many times. She stared into the flames. "I wish I had. But the truth is, he seemed perfectly normal. He was funny, charming, thoughtful. I know it sounds crazy, but he acted as if he really wanted to take care of me. Especially after he found out about the baby. It was like he'd been waiting for that moment his whole life. He fussed over me continuously."

She couldn't say more. The words she'd said already had her insides wrenched too tight. She wished none of it were true. She wished she had never felt anything at all for him. That she'd never known him…but then she wouldn't have Liam.

How did one put that in perspective and voice it to another person?

"You didn't know," Diane said. "My situation was nothing on the caliber of yours, but I believed in Joe. I trusted him completely. I had no idea he would go so far to get the story. It was like nothing else mattered, especially not another person's life or my feelings." She looked to Cara. "Have you ever had anyone betray you that way?"

Cara laughed. "Only once. But then, once is enough, isn't it?"

"More than enough," Grace agreed.

"So true," Diane murmured.

"You two should get some sleep," Grace suggested, feeling the need to be alone. She was confident she wouldn't sleep, but she needed to think. To figure out where she went from here.

Diane hugged her. "See you in the morning."

Grace hugged her back, then did the same with Cara. "Thanks." She drew back, looked from one to the other. "Both of you. This would have been far harder without you."

When Grace had closed the door behind them, she checked on Liam. He'd insisted on sleeping in his own bed tonight. She sat down on the edge and brushed the hair from his eyes. How she loved this child. She hoped so hard that she could keep him safe and somehow protect him in the future from this nightmare.

She kissed his cheek and turned out the light on his bedside table. She wandered back to the parlor and stared out the window at the scene taking place. Maybe it would be better if she checked her guests out in the morning and closed down the inn for a while.

She wasn't so sure the inn would survive anyway, so what was a few bad reviews for sending guests away? No doubt both her current guests would be posting about the murder, and she didn't blame them.

She crossed her arms over her chest and thought about how she couldn't remember calling Cara on Sunday night after the police had gone. Why couldn't she remember something so important? Forgetting about registering a guest and misplacing her keys weren't such huge deals. But to forget calling over a friend after the police had searched your property for a would-be intruder?

Who was she kidding? It had happened before. However, she wanted to rationalize it or doubt she would have made such a mistake. She had.

This was real and it was happening. Again.

Grace reminded herself of all that she'd learned the last go-round. This would pass. She would make it through to the other side.

As long as whoever had murdered Adam and Joe Pierce was found and stopped.

She searched her memories for any discussion of associates Adam had before. Any friends who had visited their home. But there was no one. She and Adam never went out with other couples. He never had friends over. He rarely talked about work or his past. He had no family—at least, that was what he'd claimed. He'd told her his parents died when he was a baby and he'd been adopted. His adopted parents were older and had no other children. They had died when he was in college. To Grace's knowledge, there was no one else in Adam's life, and she felt sure Gibbons would have mentioned if he had discovered any differently.

For months after his arrest and before her breakdown, she had followed the investigation very closely. Gibbons had checked in with her at least weekly. There had been no contacts or connections to Adam found. His employer only knew what Adam presented to him. Hard worker. Top earner. He had been friendly and charming to everyone on a very superficial level. No friendships. No hanging out. No luncheons. He only attended the work functions required of him.

And he was the only employee who took two vacations at precise intervals without exception. He requested those days off every year. Though he'd been with the company for four years when he and Grace met, none of his coworkers knew anything at all about his life. Only his wife's name. Not that they were expecting a child or anything else.

Why had he kept secret the fact that he was going to be a father?

Their whole life together had been one lie after the other, all built on a make-believe existence.

A knock on the door had her turning toward it. Had Diane or Cara decided to come back? Was one of the guests leaving now for fear that he would be the next victim?

Grace pushed the awful thoughts away and went to the door. She drew in a big breath and opened it.

Rob.

The fatigue and worry on his face, in the set of his shoulders, had her pulse racing with a new rush of adrenaline.

"Please tell me nothing else has happened."

He stepped in, prompting her to step back. He closed the

door, then gestured to the sofa. "Let's sit and go over what we know so far."

She nodded, unable to find her voice to respond. Grace made her way to the sofa and sat. She reminded herself to breathe while Rob took the seat across from her. Her hands wrung together. This was the nightmare that didn't want to end. She didn't see how things could get worse, but deep inside she understood they could. Much worse.

"Your prints were found in the shed," Rob said, finally. "But that was to be expected since you live here and it's your shed."

She nodded, knowing that was just the easy part. "What about the knife?"

"Your prints were on the knife handle too."

She wanted to rant, to get up and stamp her feet. She had not touched that knife. It took every ounce of restraint she possessed to remain seated. "I didn't put that knife under the sink. I have never seen that knife before."

"I know. Snelling is working on that. He believes the prints at the Cashion crime scene were planted. He's getting confirmation on that. It'll be tomorrow sometime before he can make an official confirmation. He believes the ones on the knife will be forged as well."

Relief swam through her veins. "Thank God."

"Grace." Rob braced his elbows on his knees, his hands clasped between them. "We know you didn't do this. It's important that you understand this."

She managed a bumpy nod. "I hope so."

"You don't have to hope. It's a fact. No one believes you did this. Not even Gibbons. He just has to be sure before he admits as much."

"I'm not surprised. He was the same way before. Determined to prove I knew something I didn't."

"I think," Rob said, "giving him maybe more credit than he deserves at this point, that what he's really trying to do is prove you don't know anything. His methods leave something to be desired, but he's worked some pretty nasty cases. Stuff like that changes a guy."

She supposed she could understand how that would happen. She nodded. "Thank you for telling me. I'll keep that in mind going forward." She stared at her hands, wished she didn't have to share the next part. But Rob had been too kind and helpful to her for her to leave him in the dark. "Cara said that I called her over that night—Sunday—after the police left. She says she stayed with me for several hours, which is why she told Gibbons I couldn't have killed Adam."

Rob nodded, waited for her to go on.

"I thought she was lying for me. I don't remember calling her or her being here."

Rob rubbed a hand over his shadowed jaw. "Does she have any proof that you called her? Do you have any that you didn't?"

She straightened, a thought occurring to her. "I can check my cell." She dug it from her pocket and scanned the recent calls. There were no calls beyond today's. She frowned. "Apparently I cleared my call log."

"Do you remember clearing it?" he asked gently.

She shook her head. "I don't." She exhaled a big breath and went for broke. It was time she came completely clean with this too-kind man. "What I do remember is putting a locket in a plastic bag and hiding it under the sink because I was terrified. My picture was inside. That's what I found on the porch after Adam was here. I didn't tell any-one because I was afraid. Now, what? Forty-eight hours later there's no locket but there is a knife? A bloody knife with my prints on it."

"You didn't tell me," he pointed out, his voice soft, gentle. Not accusing or angry as she would have expected—as she deserved.

"I was in denial. I didn't want it to be true and I thought maybe if I..." She shook her head. "I don't know what I thought. Apparently, I don't even know what I actually did."

"Have you considered that someone wants you to feel as if you're losing your mind? To doubt yourself?"

She searched his face, not daring to say how desperately she wanted that to be true. "But how could Adam or his follower know about my breakdown? No one knew. I was with Val and then I came here after. I've never discussed it with anyone until I told you."

"Have you been in contact with the woman—this Val?"

"No. She said we should never have contact of any kind. To prevent anyone from using her to find me."

"Smart lady." He took a breath. "We should have Gibbons request a welfare check. Maybe have a detective in the area interview her. See if she's been visited by anyone asking questions. She's older. She may have inadvertently mentioned you."

He was right. Val would be seventy-five or eighty. She could be in a nursing home by now with dementia. Grace had no idea.

"All right."

"My advice at this point," he said, "would be for you and Liam to go someplace safe until this is done. Cara and Diane can take care of things here. I've called Sheriff Norwood, and she's sending me four additional deputies. One will be here at the inn at all times."

She had been thinking the same thing. "Cara offered her grandmother's cabin. She said she'd take Liam there and keep him hidden until this was over."

"Gibbons wants you to stay here as a lure to whoever is behind all this. He hasn't said this, but I'm beginning to see how his mind works."

Grace shook her head. "If I have no choice, I can stay, but not Liam. I want him away from this."

"You do have a choice," Rob said. "This is my jurisdiction and I have the final say. I'm taking you and Liam to my cabin, and I'm staying with you until Gibbons and Reynolds find whoever is acting on Locke's behalf or whatever the hell he's doing."

She held his gaze. "Are you going with us because that's likely the only way Gibbons will allow us to leave?"

Rob held her gaze for a long moment. "I'm going because I'm not letting you or Liam out of my sight until I know it's safe."

Grace wanted to feel good about his words, but it was impossible, all things considered. "We might never be safe."

He managed a sad smile. "Then I guess it's a good thing I don't have a problem with however long it takes."

The warmth his words elicited almost chased away the cold leaching into her bones. Almost.

The one thing that prevented her from feeling happy about his words was the idea that Adam Locke had destroyed everything she'd loved once before. Though he was dead now, apparently that wasn't going to stop him from doing it again.

Chapter Thirteen

Wednesday, February 21, 8:00 a.m.

Rob walked the perimeter of the property. Things were quiet now save the half-dozen news vans parked along Mockingbird Lane. Anytime now they would gather around the gate and start watching for some sign of Grace or anyone else who might provide a sound bite. Rob had given a statement. He'd simply said there had been two murders. The perpetrator remained unknown, and folks should be on the lookout for anything at all out of the ordinary. They should lock their doors and check on shut-ins. Vigilance was required until they had this case under control.

About two this morning the ME had taken Pierce's body to the morgue. His next of kin, a younger brother, had been notified. The CSI folks had finished up by four and packed it in. Rob had sent Reynolds home for some sleep. Two of the deputies Norwood had sent were on scene, one stationed out front, one in back. After lunch Reynolds would be back. Rob wanted him here at the inn once he left with Grace and Liam. Reynolds would be his eyes and ears until it was safe for Rob to bring them back.

First thing this morning he'd told Grace they would be leaving shortly after noon. The next few hours should give her plenty of time to prepare for leaving the inn with Cara and Diane in charge. One of his deputies was stopping in to check on the Wilborns this morning. Grace was worried. She hadn't heard from the couple since early on Tuesday. She had a right to be worried with one of her guests dead and her ex trekking all the way here only to end up murdered.

Rob hoped Grace had managed at least a couple of hours of sleep last night—this morning, actually. He couldn't deny being concerned about the things she appeared to have forgotten, but he also recognized there was room for someone else to be behind the problems. It was too soon to make a call one way or the other, but his money was on Grace being gaslighted, particularly if someone knew about Grace's past breakdown. Gibbons had a detective friend in the Lake Tahoe area who would be paying a visit to Valentina Hicks this morning. If she'd spoken to anyone about Grace lately, that might provide a lead. At this point, Rob would take anything.

There had already been two bodies. He didn't want to uncover any more.

He'd asked Reynolds if he'd noted Cara's arrival at the inn after the search on Sunday night, but the deputy hadn't seen her. He had driven around the block a couple of times, so it was possible Cara had arrived during one of those occasions. With her compact car, she could easily have parked it near the garage and Reynolds hadn't noticed.

Rob stepped onto the terrace that ran across the back of the inn and knocked on the back door. He wanted all doors kept locked until further notice. An assistant who worked in the sheriff's office was running a background check on the remaining guests, Russell Ames and Henry Brower, as well as Diane and Cara. Since he'd already done a preliminary check on the two women, the new look was a deeper dig. Cara Gunter had roots here. Her grandmother was a lifelong resident. Rob had interviewed both women personally, but it never hurt to ask around town. Information was power. The lack of information was the road to defeat.

The turn of the locks and then the door opening brought him face-to-face with Diane. "I have a fresh pot of coffee brewed," she said. "Breakfast is on the sideboard in the dining room. Detective Gibbons is already in there."

Gibbons had turned in around four thirty. Rob doubted the man had gotten any more sleep than he had. Sleeping when there was a killer breathing down their necks was not easy.

"Thanks, Diane."

Liam sat on a stool at the island. He held up a slice of bacon. "Eat!"

Rob grinned. "Looks yummy, buddy."

When Grace walked in, she tried to smile and failed. "Did you talk to the reporters?"

He nodded. "I did. But they'll try to talk to you or anyone else who shows her or his face outside, so keep that in mind."

"They'll follow us when we leave," she said, obviously weary.

"They would, but I have a plan for that."

"Good. Okay." She smiled at her son. "As soon as Liam is finished up, we'll go get packed up."

"Woad twip!" Liam grinned and reached for a biscuit.

Rob smiled. "That's right, buddy. We're taking a road trip."

He poured himself a fresh mug of coffee and headed for the dining room to catch up with Gibbons.

The older detective was just finishing his breakfast when Rob joined him at the table. The two guests were finished already and moving toward the lobby.

"My deputy," Rob said, slowing their departure, "will see that the reporters don't give you any trouble."

Both men nodded. Neither looked excited about the idea of wading through a flock of reporters.

"You talked to the press already?" Gibbons asked as Rob picked up a plate from the buffet.

"I did." He gave him the details as he filled his plate. "After lunch I'll move Grace and Liam."

"I had some reservations about that," Gibbons admitted, "but after the phone call I just received, I'm more convinced than ever that whoever is behind this is here for Grace and her son."

Rob's instincts alerted. "Did you hear from your friend in Lake Tahoe?"

Gibbons gave a nod. "He's retired, so he spends a lot of time fishing. Gets out early to beat the crowds, so he popped in at the Hicks place before sunrise this morning. He's got the local authorities there now."

Oh, hell. "The old woman's dead?"

Gibbons nodded. "House was ransacked. Whoever killed her was looking for information. We both know it was for anything that could be found on Grace."

Damn, he hated to give this news to Grace. "I don't suppose he left us any clues."

Gibbons shrugged. "Too soon to tell, but there is one kicker."

Rob's gaze narrowed. "That is…?"

"Hicks has been dead for at least a year. That's based on her calendar being open to February and the expiration date on the milk container in her fridge. My friend is no medical examiner, but he's guessing, based on the condition of the body, that the time frame is reasonably accurate."

"So our killer has been putting this plan together for a long time." Damn. No wonder he'd left no evidence except what he wanted them to find.

"Looks that way." Gibbons pushed his plate away. "If he's had that much time, then he has the lay of the land here. He could be living here, for all we know. Maybe knows who is who in the community. You should watch out, Vaughn. If that's the case, he likely knows you have a personal interest in his target."

Rob pushed his plate away as well. He'd lost his appetite. "I'll be watching," Rob promised. "I won't go down so easy."

Gibbons nodded. "I'm guessing he's figured that out already too."

"Do you know how long you'll be gone?"

Grace considered Diane's question. "Not long, I hope. The sooner this is over, the better." She finger-combed her son's hair. "Every minute that we live like this terrifies me."

"I can't even begin to imagine." Diane visibly shivered.

"Can't imagine what?" Cara pushed through the swinging door, a load of plates in her hands.

"Deputy Vaughn is moving Liam and me to a safe house until they find the source of the trouble."

For a moment Cara looked surprised.

"It's the only way Gibbons would agree to our leaving," Grace explained quickly in hopes of assuaging any offense Cara might take about Grace not accepting her offer.

Cara nodded knowingly. "I think that's the best plan." She winked at Diane. "Does this mean you and I are in charge?"

Diane grinned. "We are."

"Will we have any security?" Cara asked, opening the dishwasher.

"Deputy Reynolds and at least one other deputy will be here with you."

Cara made an agreeable sound. "Okay, I can live with that."

Diane moved to Grace and put an arm around her shoulders. "We will take very good care of everything until you're back."

"It's about time you took a vacation," Cara chimed in. "You work too hard."

"'Cation!" Liam said triumphantly.

Grace relaxed a little. "For a little while," she promised her son.

Now that she thought about it, she and Liam had never been on a vacation. When this was over, she intended to remedy that sad condition.

She helped Cara and Diane clean up the kitchen and dining room before heading to the registration desk to take care of a few things there. Cara took Liam to their quarters to play. Liam adored Cara. He'd loved the inn's former assistant too. Kendall's death was such a shame.

Grace scrolled through her calendar. So far, nothing she hadn't expected had occurred this morning. She certainly hoped things stayed that way. The next guests arrived on Friday, three couples. She'd called Mr. Warren and asked if they could postpone the exterior work until later in the spring. He'd been surprisingly agreeable in this conversation. Grace supposed he'd heard about the murders. Who wanted to send a crew of workers to a crime scene?

Grace made a few more calls before walking through the inn for a final look around. She didn't dare go outside for fear of running into a reporter. Upstairs, she walked from room to room. Checked the unoccupied ones, mostly so she could look out the windows and see what sort of crowd had gathered.

The half-dozen news vans Rob had mentioned earlier had been joined by four others. Mostly statewide channels. Nothing national yet. But they would come. The Sweetheart Killer murders hadn't gone unnoticed by the big networks. Adam's demise wouldn't go uncovered either.

As she walked back down the long, carpeted hall, she paused outside Mr. Ames's door. She still couldn't understand how she had made his reservation and not remembered. Like Pierce, he didn't look familiar to her. In fact, he'd mostly ignored her since his arrival. He had given her a look this morning after all the excitement of last night. But who wouldn't?

Grace moved on. She descended the stairs and went to the reading parlor. This room was one of her favorite places. Mostly because of the wall of shelves loaded with books. There was also a well-stocked bar.

She walked back into the hall, checked the powder room

under the stairs. She'd have to remind Cara to see that it was cleaned. She had no idea how long it would be before the Wilborns could return to work. All the common areas would need a good cleaning before Friday.

Grace took a long, deep breath. It felt good to think about something besides murder and mayhem.

She strolled through the dining room, checked the pastry trays. Her bear claws had gone over well with their guests. Focusing on her baking this morning had helped take her mind off the horror of last night.

Her father had told her many times growing up how much her mother had loved to bake. Sometimes when he would tell her stories of her mother, Grace had almost been able to smell the delicious scents his words conjured. Perhaps the smells were memories. Either way, Grace had loved listening to him talk about her mother. He would say a man could only love one woman the way he had loved her mother.

Grace didn't even bother wondering anymore if she would ever know a love like that. Her mind instantly summoned up the image of Rob. She didn't doubt that he was the sort of man who could make that kind of love happen. He liked her. She knew he did. But considering all that had happened the past few days, he might not want to take that risk with her, and she wouldn't blame him.

She sighed. This was the worst possible time for her mind to be wandering in that direction. She went to the lobby, checked out the windows and groaned at the growing crowd of reporters and what she suspected were curious residents.

Grace felt sad that the life she'd built here was now over. Wherever things went from here, they wouldn't be the same.

Depressed all over again, she checked the kitchen. Empty.

Maybe Diane had joined Cara and Liam. With her work done, there was no reason not to.

Grace made her way to their private quarters. Diane and Liam were sitting on the floor watching his favorite cartoon.

"I'm just going to pack a few things so Liam and I are ready when it's time to go."

Diane nodded. "Let me know if you need any help. Cara popped out to check on her grandmother since we may be here for a few days."

"That was a good idea." Grace felt bad for keeping her away from her grandmother. She hoped Cara had a friend who could check in on the elderly woman.

In the bedroom, Grace picked through her closet until she found the overnight bag she'd used when she fled California. She'd taken nothing but what she could fit into that small bag. This was much the same situation. She grabbed a few items, then went to Liam's room and packed his little backpack with clothes and his favorite stuffed animal.

After putting the two bags by the parlor door, she made her way to the lobby. The inn's landline rang, and she hurried to the desk to answer it. "Lookout Inn."

"Hi, Gia."

Grace froze. The voice was female. No one she recognized.

"If you walk back to the fireplace and look out the window on the right, you'll see me."

Grace walked to the window and stared out. A woman with red hair and dressed in a white parka waved to her with her free hand. Her other hand held the cell phone to her ear.

"Who is this?" Grace didn't recognize the woman. Not from this distance, anyway.

"This is Renae Keller from the *Bay Area News*. I'm sure you'll remember me if you think about it."

The name and face jogged no memories for Grace. The truth was, there had been so many back then, she only remembered the most cutthroat of the bunch. Evidently, this one hadn't risen to that level—or perhaps hadn't sunk to that level.

Grace's heart thudded with frustration and no small amount of anger. "What do you want?" She almost laughed at herself. The woman was a reporter. She wanted whatever she could get.

"Did you murder your ex-husband? Not that anyone would blame you if you did. In fact, you would be considered a hero by most."

Grace ended the call.

The reporter stared at her as she reached up and closed the window shutters. The phone in her hand rang again.

Grace realized this was the way it would be. The phone would ring constantly. She turned off the handset and returned it to its cradle. Then she walked around the downstairs area and closed the shutters on all the windows. She turned off the ringer on the other two handsets.

The back door opened and she froze, hoping it wouldn't be a reporter who had sneaked past the deputies serving as security.

She saw Rob and sighed with relief.

Thank goodness.

"Everything okay in here?" he asked, searching her face as if he noted the discomfort she felt.

"Fine." She produced what she hoped passed for a smile. "We're packed and ready to go whenever you are."

"We checked in with the Wilborns. They both officially have the flu, but they're doing pretty well and hope to be back to work sometime next week."

"That's a relief." At this point, Grace was worried about everyone close to her.

"Deputy Reynolds will be in charge of things here. He'll keep me posted at regular intervals, so you don't have to worry about anything once we're gone."

"Thank you. I worry about Diane and Cara being here, but I really do appreciate not having to shut down the inn entirely."

"They'll be in good hands and so will you and Liam."

Her smile was real this time. "Thank you."

Grace didn't see any reason to tell him about the reporter's call. She should have known they would start calling the inn's official phone number. If they had her cell number, it would be blowing up.

"We're moving back the reporters to the other end of the lane. As soon as they are blocked in, we'll go. I don't want to risk one following us. So be prepared. When Reynolds gives the word, we're out of here."

"We'll be ready."

Grace hurried back to her quarters. "We'll be leaving soon," she told Diane. Then to her little boy she said, "Liam, we should be prepared to go. Deputy Rob will be ready to take us on our adventure soon."

"I ready!" He executed an air punch for emphasis.

Grace loved that he was excited. She went to her room and found her favorite hiking boots and tugged them on. She found Liam's and helped him into them.

"We'll put on our coats when we're ready to go, okay?"

Liam nodded at her, his little smile melting her heart.

"I'll call you if anything comes up," Diane promised. "I don't want you to worry. Cara and I will take care of everything the same way you would."

"I know you will. Just stay inside and stay safe. If anything at all feels wrong, get Deputy Reynolds on it ASAP. Don't hesitate."

Diane gave her a salute. "Yes, ma'am."

The door opened and Rob poked his head in. "Time to go."

Grace picked up Liam and said goodbye to her friend.

She told herself again that this was the right thing to do. The only thing to do.

Chapter Fourteen

Chestnut Bridge Hollow, 2:30 p.m.

Rob's getaway was only twenty miles from the inn, but it seemed much farther considering the place was so far off the beaten path. This was where he spent his off time, he'd explained. The historic log cabin had been in his family for four generations. The part he hadn't mentioned was that the cabin sat on hundreds of acres that flowed right up to the Tennessee River. The driveway from the main road wound more than a mile into the woods before reaching the clearing where the cabin, a big old white barn and several sheds spread across acres of grass and enormous old trees. Beyond that were the majestic woods that went on seemingly forever, rising up the mountains all around.

It was perfect…incredibly picturesque.

The memory of all those reporters rushing toward his SUV had her even more grateful for this getaway. It would have been only a matter of time before one or more would have figured out a way to get into the inn. She so appreciated Rob bringing them here and was grateful that he'd made double sure they weren't followed.

"No wonder you love coming here," Grace said, the view taking her breath away. As much as she loved the mountaintop views from the inn, this was truly magnificent in its own right. But more important, it wasn't easy to find.

Rob was right. She and Liam would be safe here.

Grace relaxed for the first time in days.

Rob parked his SUV and shut off the engine. "This is the first time I've brought anyone here with me since… last year."

She understood. "I'm sorry it had to be under current circumstances." She hoped it wasn't a terrible inconvenience. She hated the idea of being such a bother. She'd brought him nothing but trouble lately.

"I'm glad you're here no matter the circumstances." He smiled and she relaxed again.

"Thank you."

"No thanks necessary." He climbed out and opened the back door. "Come on, buddy." Rob released Liam from his car seat. "There's something I want to show you."

He set Liam on the ground and grabbed their bags.

Grace followed the two toward the cabin. Liam, who insisted on carrying his backpack, kept pointing at different things—like the barn—and asking what was inside. She suspected he hoped for horses or cows. Maybe pigs.

"There are two horses," Rob explained. "They're in the pasture, so they may be down at the stream right now. We'll track them down later and maybe your mom will let me take you for a ride sometime."

Liam jumped up and down and shouted, "Please! Please! Please!"

Rob paused at the front door of the gorgeous cabin to unlock it. "Sorry, Grace. I should have asked you first."

"I think it's a great idea," she said, letting him off the hook. To her son, she offered, "How about we see how the weather is tomorrow? We should get settled now and rest up. How about it?"

"'Kay!" Excitement danced across his little face.

Inside was every bit as breathtaking as outside. When Rob had called the place a cabin, she'd anticipated three or four rooms. Rustic. It was a log cabin, all right, but this was huge. When they entered, what had likely once been the main room had been turned into a massive foyer with views straight through to a wall of windows that looked out over the river. Grace walked in that direction. A large addition had been built onto the back of the original cabin that included soaring vaulted ceilings cloaked in natural wood and windows that extended from the floor to that peak and provided incredible views all around.

"Wow."

"I added this part when my mom insisted on turning the place over to me. She said she wasn't interested in spending much time out here once Dad was gone. My sister is too busy with her career in Nashville to get out this way often. She preferred the beach house in Florida my parents thought they couldn't live without when they retired. Turned out my sister was the only one who really liked it."

Grace stood at the window staring at the river. It was so close, almost overpowering and at the same time alluring. "I don't know how you ever leave this place."

"Work." He grinned, ruffled Liam's curly hair. Her son

too was enthralled with the river view. "A man's gotta earn his keep."

Grace surveyed the room again. "I can just imagine how beautiful this place is at Christmas."

"Last year was the first time I'd put up a tree since my dad died. It didn't feel right, and then the renovation was going on. But this last time I went all out. It was great." He shrugged. "A little much for just me, but I enjoyed it. I invited a couple of my friends and their families over. It was fun."

How on earth was this man still single? Then she remembered him telling her about his former fiancée. Grace was certain the woman was a fool. But then, the heart knew what the heart wanted. Sometimes it made no sense to anyone else. Grace understood this better than most. No one could understand how she'd fallen in love with a monster. A killer. A liar. But she hadn't seen that side of him. Emotion had blinded her, she supposed.

"Let me show you around." Rob turned back to the older part of the house. "The kitchen is this way."

The newly remodeled kitchen took up most of the right side of the house. Whatever had been upstairs had been removed to make room for another soaring ceiling. It was modern and at the same time very country. Grace was impressed with his remodeling decisions.

"You did a great job." The dining area had a huge bay window facing that river view.

"My mother was impressed, but I can't claim all the credit. Most of the design decisions were based on input from my sister. She also wrangled me some killer discounts."

Grace was glad for that. She'd been certain he was going

to say the decisions had been made by his former fiancée, which left whoever he was involved with in the future to live in her design.

Though, admittedly, it was a really good one either way.

Back at the other end of the original part of the house was a powder room, an owner's suite and the staircase that led to the three bedrooms upstairs. All had been updated. All were impressively well done. If the place was hers, Grace wouldn't change a thing.

When the tour was over, Rob carried Grace's bag to the owner's suite. "You and Liam can have this room. I'll take the sofa where I can keep an eye on all the access points."

Grace started to argue but his reasoning was sound. He needed to be able to keep eyes on the doors. She was grateful for his vigilance.

Liam followed Rob back into the main room. The boy adored having Rob around. Grace had noticed this a couple of months ago. Every time Rob would drop by the inn for a meal or just to check on them, Liam was drawn to him. He was otherwise fairly shy with anyone outside their close circle. But not with Rob.

Grace had wrestled with the urge to make more of Rob's interest than there was. But then a part of her had given in and started looking forward to his calls and occasional visits.

She sighed and opened her bag. Probably not smart to make too much of this either. He was trying to protect them. This was not a romantic getaway.

A chill made her shiver. Was it just her or was this room colder than the others? She walked around the room, checked the windows. All secure. Then she moved on to the attached bath and saw the problem. The window over the claw-foot tub was open just a couple of inches. It was a large window, so even that little gap allowed the crisp winter air to slip in. She glanced around the room and over the ceiling and didn't spot an exhaust fan, which likely explained the window being open a bit. Although the claw-foot tub and the pedestal-style vanity were original looking, she'd wager the large shower was not. She imagined some seriously steamy air would come from the shower.

Before she could stop it, her mind conjured the image of Rob in that shower, the water slipping over his naked body. Steam rising around him.

"And that's about enough of that," she grumbled as she climbed into the tub and closed the window.

When she made her way back to the main room, Rob and Liam were on the deck, seated in two of the rocking chairs. Her heart squeezed. She so much wanted a happy life for her son. She wondered if she would ever be able to make that happen. She had thought she'd been mostly successful until Sunday night.

How had she ever believed for one minute she would be free of that monster as long as he was still breathing?

Even now that Adam was dead she had to worry about this partner or followers. Until now she hadn't allowed herself to consider what this person—the person who'd killed Adam and Pierce—wanted. Certainly he wasn't there to protect her and Liam.

The thing that terrified her more than any other thought was the idea that he wanted Liam—not just Grace or maybe not even Grace. Every instinct she possessed was screaming that this killer wanted Liam above all else. Either to hurt him or simply to have him. It was feasible this person who was clearly obsessed with Adam would be obsessed with this child. Maybe Adam had seen this too and attempted to be rid of him, and that person killed Adam.

Grace rolled her eyes. She refused to give Adam any benefit of the doubt. Whatever he had done or said that caused his death—assuming that was the case—it was not some heroic deed.

Her cell phone rang and Grace jumped. She pressed a hand to her chest and took a breath. Just thinking about Adam made her jumpy. She dug the phone from her pocket and smiled at the name on the screen.

Cara.

"Hey, was your grandmother okay?"

"She is," Cara said in her trademark perky tone. "I'm just calling to make sure you and Liam made it and to tell you that Diane and I have everything under control."

"We do!" Diane called out. The call was on speaker.

"Dinner is in the works, and surprisingly," Cara went on, "a good many of the reporters have peeled off. We're hoping they haven't tried to follow you to your secret destination."

Grace hoped not. "Several deputies blocked the end of the lane where they'd been pushed back to, so they couldn't get out until we were well on our way."

"Excellent," Diane said. "That Deputy Vaughn is pretty smart."

Grace wasn't getting into that conversation, even though her gaze was on the man at that very moment. She loved watching him with Liam.

"Any news from Detective Gibbons?"

"He and those CSI guys have been crawling all over the

inn," Cara answered. "Mr. Brower has returned from his conference, but we haven't seen Mr. Ames since he left this morning. He may show up later. We're preparing for dinner as if he'll be here."

"Be sure to make plates for the deputies as well," Grace reminded her.

"Will do," Diane promised. "I'll even see that Detective Gibbons gets what he deserves."

"Oh, no," Grace said with a laugh. "That sounds ominous."

"Just kidding," Diane joked.

"What about the news?" Grace hadn't checked any headlines on her phone, and they hadn't turned on a television since their arrival here. She doubted she would be happy about the details already discovered about hers and Liam's lives.

"We shut the televisions off," Cara said. "We're living it. We don't need to see it."

Which meant it was bad. "Thanks, but you didn't answer my question."

"Told you," Diane muttered to Cara.

"Fine. If you must know, they're speculating you killed him—Locke, I mean," Cara said. "Pierce too."

Grace closed her eyes and waited a moment for the frustration to pass. She shouldn't be surprised. Of course they would say she was the killer. She had the most to gain with the bastard's death. It didn't matter that she didn't know Pierce. The media would make what they would of it all.

"The people who know and care about you won't believe what they suggest," Diane insisted. "You know they won't."

What Grace knew was that people believed what was

shown to them over and over by the media. It had happened to her before, and it wouldn't be any different this time no matter how this played out.

"I appreciate the support," she said. "And I truly appreciate the two of you taking care of the inn until we're back. Watch out for each other."

"We always do," Diane said. "Be careful, Grace."

"Ditto," Cara chimed in.

Grace ended the call and decided to go to the kitchen to see what sort of supplies they had. Making dinner was the least she could do after all that Rob was doing for them.

The pantry was quite large. She wandered through, noted a good supply of dry and canned goods. Then she moved on to the refrigerator.

She checked the date on the carton of milk. It still had several days before expiring. There was a surprising array of fresh items. She could definitely work with this. She started to close the door, but something snagged her attention. She opened the door wider once more.

A thirty-two-ounce bottle of one of those sports drinks sat behind the milk and the orange juice. She reached toward it, noted that it was only half-full. So what? Lots of people drank sports drinks. No big deal.

Except this one had been Adam's favorite. This brand and this flavor. It was all he'd drunk besides the occasional beer or a glass of wine—both of which were rare. He'd insisted his body was a temple. He consumed very little sugar and never ever failed to have this sports drink in the refrigerator.

It was just a coincidence. It had to be.

Grace slammed the door shut.

It couldn't be anything else.

Except her instincts were screaming otherwise.

ROB STOOD, STRETCHED. "Little man, we should get inside and see what your mom is up to."

"Can we see the horses?"

"We'll go out to the barn and have a look around in a little while. Maybe your mom will come with us."

"'Kay."

Rob opened the French door that led inside. Grace stood at the windows. She'd been watching them.

"I think Liam likes it here," Rob offered. Her expression was hard to read, but he suspected she was feeling unsettled. With all that was going on, she had every right.

She smiled, but it didn't reach her eyes. "It's a very peaceful place."

Liam tugged at his hand. "See the horses now?"

Rob smiled. "If it's okay with your mom, we'll go to the barn and call them in for a special treat."

Liam tugged at his mom now, repeating, "Please, please, please!"

"Sure. It'd be nice to get outside."

He should have thought of that. Grace and Liam had been cooped up in the inn since Sunday. No wonder the kid wanted outside so badly.

As they stepped off the porch, Rob pointed beyond the barn. "The land goes to the top of that mountain." He pointed in the other direction. "And just over the top in that direction. There are dozens of trails through the woods. As kids, my sister and I walked all over these woods."

"It's really beautiful." Grace surveyed the woods. Then she smiled. "I see the horses."

"I see!" Liam jumped up and down, trying to see what his mom saw.

Rob picked him up and sat him on his shoulders. "See beyond the barn? The horses are in their pasture. It goes all the way to the tree line at the base of the mountain. They have plenty of room for roaming and grazing and their own year-round stream for water."

When they reached the barn, Rob set Liam on his feet once more. "We'll go to the corral at the back of the barn and call them in. They know when I call for them that they're in for a special treat."

He showed Liam how to climb up on the rails of the fence so he could watch the horses gallop in. Grace stood next to him. She seemed as enthralled as her son. He was glad. She needed to relax. Rob called to Lucky and Dolly and their heads came up. They surveyed the scene for a moment, then started galloping toward the open corral. Once the horses entered the corral and settled down near the fence, he picked Liam up and showed him how to pet the animals so he didn't spook them. Then he helped Liam add their feed to two buckets, and the two of them gave the horses their special treat.

"They too big," Liam said, his eyes huge.

Rob laughed. "They are big but they're gentle. They won't try to hurt you. With a good horse, the only time you have to worry about being hurt is if you do something you shouldn't."

Liam peered up at him. "Not me. I a good boy."

Rob laughed. Grace did as well. It was good to hear her laugh.

After they'd fed the horses and petted them until Liam had grown bored, Rob gave his guests a mini tour. The woods marched right up to the pasture's edge and then to the clearing where the house and other outbuildings stood.

"That one," he said to Liam as he pointed to one of the oldest buildings on the property, "is the smokehouse."

Liam frowned. "Smoking house?"

"It's where folks used to cure their meat before there were refrigerators and freezers."

Liam pointed to another shed. "What's that one?"

"The chicken house."

"You gots chickens?" Liam looked intrigued.

"Sadly, I do not, but maybe one of these days when I'm here more often."

"Mom wants chickens."

Grace laughed. "How do you remember that?" She shook her head. "I don't even remember when, but I did say once that I would love a chicken coop and chickens. I'm just not sure the guests would appreciate them."

Liam stopped and looked around. "You gots dogs?"

Rob had expected that question. "I had a dog. Bandit. He was a really good dog and I had him for a very long time. He loved coming out here with me."

Liam's face fell. "Did he run away?"

"No, buddy, I'm sorry to say he just got too old and died. I buried him over there by that grove of oak trees." He pointed to the copse of trees that stood in the center of the drive-way that circled the clearing. "Bandit used to lie there in the summer when it was hot. He could see everything happening around the house and barn from there."

Liam frowned. "You needa get another dog."

Rob smiled sadly. "I guess I do. Maybe you and I can go to the big animal shelter and find one to adopt."

"'Kay." Liam spotted the ancient swing set. "I wanna swing!"

He took off in that direction. Grace followed. "Be careful."

Rob caught up with her. "I'm sorry. I'm probably making way too many promises."

Grace shook her head. "I'm sure Liam would love all your suggestions." She winced as she watched her son scramble onto the lowest hanging swing.

"My married friends will tell you that I like spoiling kids."

She smiled then. "I can see that."

"Push me, Mommy!"

Grace gave Liam a small push. "Hang on tight."

Liam squealed with delight.

Grace gave him another gentle push. "Do you have friends over often?"

"No one since Christmas." Rob wished he had made the move to full-time living out here already. Soon, he hoped. He'd made a New Year's resolution to do that, but something always got in the way.

"I didn't think to suggest we stop at a market. I was glad to see there was milk in the fridge."

"Should be bottled water too." He made a face. "No soft drinks or juices. Sorry, I didn't think of that."

"Sports drinks are okay," she said.

"I've never cared for sports drinks. Mostly I stick with water or coffee. You?"

She flinched. "Water works for me."

He couldn't decide if the flinch was about something that had flown too near her face—nothing he'd seen—or something he'd said. Before he could ask, his cell vibrated. Rob pulled it from his pocket and checked the screen. *Reynolds*.

He flashed Grace a smile. "Excuse me."

He walked away from the swing as he accepted the call. "Hey, man, what's up?"

"Well, maybe nothing, but I can't seem to find Detective Gibbons."

Now, there was an update Rob hadn't been expecting. "Is his rental car there? I talked to him this morning."

"Yeah. That's the weird part. But I can't find him anywhere, and he is not answering his cell. I haven't heard from him since the two of you talked."

"Keep looking. Let me know the minute you find him." Rob ended the call and immediately put one through to Gibbons's cell number. The call went straight to voice mail.

Rob hoped like hell they didn't have another murder.

He glanced back at Grace and Liam. She was watching him. Was that suspicion he saw before she looked away? Seemed odd that she would be suspicious of him taking a call out of her earshot, but then if anyone had a right to be worried about every little thing, it was Grace.

The call from Reynolds had him worrying about the West Coast detective. Whatever had happened to Gibbons, the only thing Rob could do right now was protect Grace and Liam.

But if Gibbons was still breathing, where the hell would he be?

Had he taken a different vehicle and followed Rob here? Was he that hell-bent on keeping Grace and Liam in his sights?

Or maybe he was in this deeper than just as a detective. It was mighty damned convenient that he'd been able to get a flight from San Francisco to Chattanooga in such a timely manner.

What if Rob had been looking for the trouble in all the wrong places?

Chapter Fifteen

6:30 p.m.

Grace turned off the stove. Dinner was ready. She took the rolls out of the oven and set them on the stove top. There had been hamburger meat in the freezer, so she'd thawed it in the microwave and made a meat loaf. Instant potatoes and a can of green beans had to suffice as the sides. Not such a bad meal.

She set her hands on her hips and surveyed the room. As soon as Rob and Liam were in from seeing the horses, they could eat. Liam really enjoyed the time outside. As he got older, Grace had to make it a point to see that he had more of it.

Her cell chimed with a text, and she checked the screen. The number wasn't one in her contacts, but she recognized it. Detective Gibbons. Why was he contacting her? Rob had made it clear that the man was to go through him.

Grace rolled her eyes and opened the message.

This is Gibbons. You and Liam are not safe with Vaughn.

"What?" Grace mentally recoiled from the message. She typed a response and hit Send.

What are you talking about?

She waited, her frustration mounting as she watched the ellipses that confirmed he was typing a response.

Look around. See for yourself. I found evidence at his office.

This was insane. She sent another message.

Why were you at his office?

Reynolds found it...showed me. Get out of the house.

Grace didn't bother with a response. The man was playing some sort of game, and she was not going there. If she had to choose between trusting him or trusting Rob, she was going with Rob.

Still, she hesitated. There was the sports drink in the refrigerator. But he'd said he drank water mostly. So if it wasn't his, then whose was it?

She walked back to the refrigerator and opened the door. She moved the milk aside. It was still there—half a thirty-two-ounce bottle of red sports drink. She shivered and slammed the door. There had to be a reasonable explanation.

But Gibbons's words had dug in their claws. She opened drawer after drawer...cabinet door after cabinet door. Found nothing out of the ordinary. No hidden files or surveillance photos of the inn or of her and Liam. Nothing that made her suspicious as to why Rob would bring them here.

Then she went to the main room. Scanned the shelves, the side tables and their drawers. She checked the coat closet… the powder room. Grace moved into the owner's suite then. She rifled through the drawers. Nothing. The same in the closet. Under the bed.

She was losing her mind. Gibbons had done this on purpose to make her doubt Rob. That would give Gibbons control.

She stamped out of the room.

Did Rob have an office here? He hadn't mentioned one.

She rounded the staircase and followed the narrow hall between it and the front exterior wall of the cabin. Sure enough, at the end of that little hall was a small room with a desk and chair. A laptop sat on the desk. A bulletin board adorned one wall. There were a couple of photos of him and his deputies, but little else. She chewed her lip. The top of the desk was clear save the laptop. It wouldn't hurt to have a quick look in the drawers.

As she took a deep breath, she moved around the desk and sat down behind it. Rolling back in the chair, she started with the middle drawer. She pulled it open, expecting to see pens and pencils and other miscellaneous office supplies.

Instead, she found newspaper clippings.

Her heart stumbled. Her fingers trembled as she picked through the array of clipped articles and the printed images of *her*…of Adam.

She wanted to believe these were gathered after the trouble started at the inn, but that was impossible. The clippings were from articles published in newspapers right after Adam's arrest. Dozens of them from the months immediately after that. Her trembling hands pushed them aside, only to find recent photos of her and Liam around town.

Why would he have all this?

Then her fingers touched something cold. She pushed the printed images and clippings aside and her gaze homed in on a chain. Silver. Rusty. No, not rusty—crusted with dried blood. On that chain was a locket. As if they had a mind of their own, her fingers plucked it up and opened the locket.

The small cut-to-size photo of her stared back at her.

The locket that had gone missing after she'd hidden it under the sink at the inn.

"Oh my God."

The sound of the kitchen door slamming and Rob's voice as he answered whatever question Liam had asked had her dropping the locket and easing the drawer closed. She hurried out of the room and down that narrow hall.

Her heart pounded so hard she couldn't catch a breath.

Maybe Gibbons was right. She had to get out of here until she knew for sure it was safe.

No. That couldn't be right. She knew Rob...

She came to a dead stop before reaching the kitchen. For well over a year she had thought she knew Adam. And look how that turned out. Didn't matter either way. She couldn't take the risk. For now, she could not allow Rob to see that she was upset. She had to be calm. Had to act as if nothing had happened. And then she had to get out of here... somehow.

It would be dark soon, and though she had paid attention to the landscape as they'd driven here, she wasn't sure she could find her way out on foot.

If she could get her hands on his SUV fob…

The voices were coming nearer. Her sweet little boy's baby voice and Rob's deeper one.

Her cell chimed. She jumped and checked the screen.

I'm coming. I'll bring help.

Gibbons was coming. Okay. They could straighten this out when he arrived. If Rob— She halted that thought. It just wasn't possible. Gibbons had to be wrong.

Finding those newspaper clippings and photos was one thing…but the locket. Had he found it and hidden it to protect her?

Or was he the one who'd planted the knife under the sink at the inn?

No. That couldn't be right.

Stop. She had to stop. All she had to do was stay calm and get through this. There would be logical explanations. There had to be.

She shoved the phone into her back pocket and hurried to the other short hall that led to the powder room and owner's suite. She did an about-face and started forward as if she'd only just come from the bedroom.

"Mommy! Mommy! I sit on horse!"

Liam's eyes were big, and his little body was literally vibrating with excitement.

Rob wore a big grin as if putting Liam on the horse had been almost as exciting for him. "I'm going to have to take him riding tomorrow. He loves the horses." His grin fell. "You okay?"

He searched her face, no doubt noting her emotional state as if the fear and desperation were written across her skin.

"I'm good." She shrugged. "I made the mistake of checking the news feed." She shook her head. "I shouldn't have."

"The media can get ugly." He made a sad face. "But it will pass."

How could he be so kind and just down the hall have all those things hidden in his desk?

"I should get Liam cleaned up for dinner. It's ready." She picked up her son, thankful he had on his shoes and coat. She could sneak out the kitchen door and hide until Gibbons was here and they had all this sorted out.

Guilt piled on her shoulders for thinking badly of Rob. He had been so kind to her and to Liam. But she could not risk Liam's safety for anyone—no matter how much she wanted to believe in Rob.

Rob's expression shifted to one of concern as he gazed past her at something outside. "There's a vehicle coming. You and Liam go in the kitchen. Stay out of sight until I see who this is." He shook his head. "Reynolds would have warned me if he'd sent anyone out here. Whoever this is, they shouldn't be here."

"Be careful." Her pulse was hammering now. What if this was a trap and Gibbons intended to hurt Rob? But why? It made no sense. Had this case pushed him over the edge?

Rob moved closer to the window. "Whoever it is has stopped on the other side of those trees. Out of eyesight." He bent down and removed a small handgun from around his ankle. He turned to Grace and handed it to her. "Go out the back door and into the barn. Hide in the darkest corner you can find. If anyone comes out there besides me, shoot first and ask questions later."

"Rob, I—"

"Go," he insisted as he headed for the door.

"Mommy?"

Liam's voice was full of uncertainty. Grace gripped the gun, lowered it to her side. "It's okay. We're going to play hide-and-seek. Rob will look for us, but first we have to hide."

Maintaining her balance with Liam in her arms, she shoved first one foot and then the other into her boots. She didn't bother to track down her coat. She rushed to the back door and slipped out.

Her cell chimed. She bit back a swear word, tucked the handgun into the waistband beneath her sweater and reached for her cell. Another text message from Gibbons.

Come to the woodshed.

Rob had said go to the barn. He'd given her a gun. Why would he do that if he was working against her?

"Mommy," Liam said. "We gots to hide."

She would check the woodshed, and then she was going to the barn. She hurried along the end of the cabin and surveyed the treed area between the end of the house and the barn. She could get to the barn without being seen from the front of the house. Then she'd have to slip around the back of the barn and through the corral to get to the woodshed without anyone out front seeing her.

She could do that.

Grace held Liam pressed close to her chest. She moved

as quickly as she dared without risking a fall carrying him. She'd expected to hear Rob talking to someone by now. The good news was she hadn't heard any gunshots or other sounds of trouble.

She moved through the dark barn. The sun would be setting soon. She slipped out the back and through the corral. The horses at the water trough raised their heads and stared at her.

"Horsie, horsie," Liam said softly, his little voice muffled by her hair.

She held him tighter, tears burning her eyes. Her instincts were screaming at her. Something was wrong. *This* was wrong.

Finally she reached the woodshed. She paused to catch her breath, then reached for the door. The wood crossbar that secured it closed had already been removed, so all she had to do was pull it open.

The fading light filled the space beyond the door. Grace froze.

Detective Lance Gibbons lay on the floor. Blood soiled his shirtfront. He'd been stabbed over and over...just like Adam...just like Pierce.

"Grace!"

Rob shouted her name from the direction of the house. He was looking for her.

She opened her mouth to answer but snapped it shut.

She couldn't be sure of what was happening. Her best option was to hide until she could figure out who was telling the truth.

She ran for the woods.

"Mommy, we hide!"

"Shh," she urged. "Yes, but he'll find us if he hears us," she whispered.

It was dark in the woods. Grace slowed. She couldn't see well enough to move fast.

A gunshot, then another rang out. She stumbled, almost fell. She darted behind the nearest tree and hovered there. She made soft shushing sounds to keep Liam quiet.

"We hidin'?" he whispered as best as an almost three-year-old could.

"Yes," she whispered back.

Gibbons was dead. The realization slammed into her all over again. Had Rob been shooting at someone? Or had someone been shooting at him?

Fear twisted inside her. She couldn't just hover here. She needed to get to a better hiding place or to find help.

Like that was going to happen. She was in the middle of nowhere.

She should call for help.

She pulled out her phone and tapped the necessary digits. But the call failed. She bit back a curse. No service. But she'd had service before she came into the woods. At least for text messages.

There was no time to figure it out. She had to hide.

ROB HUNKERED DOWN behind the unknown vehicle. It looked familiar but he wasn't sure. It was getting dark, so it was difficult to make out all the details, but someone in the tree line had shot at him.

He'd shouted for Grace, and then the shots had rung out.

She had his handgun, but she hadn't been the one to shoot at him. She'd gone in the direction of the barn. No way could she have gotten to the trees on the other side of the vehicle that had shown up unannounced.

This was someone who'd come for Grace and Liam. His first thought was Gibbons. The trouble Rob had with that theory was why the detective would turn like that. Was he so thoroughly convinced that Grace was guilty too?

Rob's cell vibrated, and he scanned the tree line again before pulling it from his pocket. Reynolds.

"Listen carefully," he whispered before Reynolds could speak. "I'm under fire here at the cabin. I need backup."

"Heading that way." The sounds of Reynolds running and then a vehicle door closing punctuated his words.

"I'm going to move toward the last known location of the shooter," Rob explained, "to make sure he hasn't started toward the barn where I told Grace to hide with Liam. I need you and anyone else you can get ahold of here as soon as possible."

"You need to know something," Reynolds said as he started the engine of his vehicle. "Cara Gunter disappeared today. Just vanished."

What the hell? Grace would be devastated if someone had gotten to Cara. "How did that happen?"

"You got me, but it gets worse," Reynolds went on. "When Cara didn't answer her cell, I went to her grandmother's looking for her. I thought maybe she'd gotten sick and Cara had to go to her. But old lady Gunter is dead, Rob. Has been for months. I'm guessing four or five, anyway. There are other remains with her. I can't be positive about anything beyond the fact that the remains are a younger female with blond hair. I don't know what to make of it, but Cara Gunter has been lying about taking care of her grandmother."

The realization of what that meant hit Rob like a sucker punch. "Gotta go," he said. "Get me some backup out here."

He'd have to analyze the news about Cara Gunter when he had this situation under control. He had to keep the shooter away from Grace and Liam.

Rob braced himself and made a dash into the open.

"Hang on to me tight, Liam," Grace said as she prepared to leave the cover of the trees. "We need to hide better."

"There you are."

"Cara!" Liam started wiggling, trying to escape his mother's firm hold.

Grace turned around. Cara was walking toward them. A rush of relief made Grace's knees weak.

Then she saw the gun in her friend's hand.

Grace tightened her hold on Liam, ignored his protests. "Cara, what's going on?"

Cara didn't stop until she was only a few feet away. "I have to get you and Liam out of here, Grace."

Heart pounding, Grace glanced at the weapon in her hand. "Why do you have a gun?"

Cara smiled. "Don't worry. I know how to use it." She shrugged. "For protection." Her attention zeroed in on the child in Grace's arms. "Liam, come to me."

It was all Grace could do to keep her son with her. "Be still," she ordered, fear funneling through her. "Cara, answer me. Why do you have a gun?"

It was almost completely dark now but not quite, and maybe even if it had been Grace would have spotted some-

thing different about Cara's eyes. They virtually glittered—
the lightest, brightest shade of blue.

Like Adam's.

No, that was impossible. Cara had green eyes.

She laughed as if Grace had said the words out loud. "You
see me now, don't you? I have the same eyes as him." She
looked to Liam. "The same as his."

Grace stumbled back a step. Almost tripped over dead-
for-winter underbrush. "I don't know what you're doing—"

"I do." She took another step toward Grace…toward
Liam. "Do you have any idea how many fair-haired, pale-
eyed women he had to go through before he found one who
could give us what we wanted?"

Adam's victims—all with blond hair and pale eyes—
flashed one after the other in Grace's mind. Then her own
image stalled there.

"One couldn't get pregnant." She rolled her eyes. "She
lied about that. Then DNA showed all these issues with
the others. I suppose it had to do with the selection pool. I
warned him about going so low-rent, but he was worried
about taking someone who would be missed." She smiled.
"And then he found you. Completely by accident and you
were perfect. And Liam is perfect." She stared at the boy
Grace held tightly against her chest. "Come to me, Liam."

He tried to turn and see her. Tried to get loose from
Grace's grip. "Don't listen to her, Liam. She's pretending
so she can win the game. We still have to hide."

Cara's face twisted in a sneer as she stepped right up
to Grace and jammed the gun under her chin. "Put him
down. Now."

Grace slid her right hand between her and Liam. "You know you don't want to hurt him," she said, buying time.

"Of course not." Cara smiled. "He's mine. He was always going to be mine."

Fear and outrage rammed into Grace. She steadied herself. "Let me think," she pleaded.

Cara waved the gun in the air, but she remained toe-to-toe with Grace. "Put him down and we'll talk about how to handle this. I'm sure we can work something out."

"Okay. Okay. Just give me a moment." Grace glanced around as if uncertain, and then she hefted Liam higher with her left arm while snagging the handgun in her waistband with her right hand. She jammed the gun into Cara's body and pulled the trigger.

Nothing happened.

Cara stumbled back in surprise. Then she laughed. "Were you going to shoot me, Grace? You might remember to take it off safety next time."

Before Cara could stop laughing, Grace pivoted the thumb lever on the weapon and fired again. This time the bullet left the chamber and struck the other woman in the abdomen.

Cara lurched back a step.

Gun clutched in her hand, Grace wrapped both arms tightly around her son and turned to run. She bumped into someone.

Diane.

Grace froze. Her heart thumped against her sternum. Why was Diane here?

"You okay?" Diane asked, looking from Grace to Liam with concern.

Grace blinked.

Diane asked again, "Grace, are you okay? Is Liam okay?"

Tears flooded Grace's eyes. "Cara tried to—"

Liam started to whine.

"Shh, shh," Grace shushed him. "It's okay now."

"Really it's not," Diane said. She leveled a weapon at Grace. "Toss that little gun you're carrying and put my grandson down."

Grace felt the air leave her lungs. This could not be real. Maybe she truly had lost it and none of this was actually happening. Dear God, where was Rob?

The other woman's words reverberated in Grace's head. "Grandson?"

Diane smiled. "Adam was my son. Adele—Cara—is his twin sister. She wanted a baby so bad but she couldn't have one." Diane made a sad face. "So Adam promised her a baby." She motioned with her weapon. "Now toss the gun."

Grace allowed the handgun to fall to the ground.

"But," Cara announced as she joined the two of them, "Adam screwed it all up." One hand was pressed to her abdomen, blood seeping around her fingers. The other hand still held her weapon. "The bitch shot me." She glared at Diane. "Why haven't you killed her already?"

"Just shut up," Diane, or whatever her name was, growled before swinging her attention back to Grace. "Give Liam to me and we'll be done with this."

Grace understood that if she gave up Liam she was dead, and she could only imagine what would happen to her son then. Still, both these women had weapons, which meant running wasn't an option. Grace's heart twisted. Diane and Cara had been like family to her and she had never suspected a thing…because they were too good at hiding the truth and she had been desperate for a real family after losing her father.

An idea took shape. That was her only hope. *Family.*

"Why can't we share him?" Grace urged, her mind frantically grappling for a workable escape plan. "We've been like family all these months. We can make it work."

Where the hell was Rob?

Was he dead? Had one of them shot him? The memory of those gunshots echoing spiked terror in her veins. Her stomach dropped to her feet. *Please don't let him be dead or gravely injured.*

"She can't be serious," Cara—Adele said with disgust.

Diane threw her head back and laughed. When she'd pulled herself together again, she demanded, "Why on earth would we do that?"

Liam's little body had started to shake. Grace had to do something fast.

"All right." Grace took a breath. "At least let me carry him back to the house. Give him time to calm down." His whining had turned to sobs now, the sound breaking her heart.

"Fine. Start walking," Diane ordered. "And remember we'll be right behind you. You make a mistake, and I'll put one in the back of your head."

Grace summoned her fleeting courage. The way she saw it, she had maybe five minutes to come up with a better plan since the chances of being rescued looked pretty slim at this point. Her gut clenched again at the idea of what had likely happened to Rob.

If he was dead… No, she couldn't think about that.

"I liked you, Gia," Diane said. "I knew you were the one when Adam finally found you, but then he had to go and do something stupid like take someone else. I thought he'd broken that nasty habit since you were pregnant with Liam and his promise to Adele was fulfilled. Guess I was wrong."

"Ha," Adele snarled. "He liked that part. He was never going to stop. Once you get the taste for killing, there's no going back."

"Whatever his problems, you had no right to do what you did." Diane was the one snarling now. "He was *my* son."

"*He* is the reason," Adele fired back, "we're in this mess. If he hadn't decided he wanted to keep Liam for himself, none of this would have happened."

Grace took her chance while they were distracted. She lurched forward, pretended to trip and fall to her knees. She set her son on his feet. "Run, Liam," she whispered in his ear before pushing him forward.

Diane snagged her by the hair and tried to pull her up. "Get up."

"Run!" Grace screamed, urging her son to go with every part of her being.

Liam rocketed forward.

"Liam!" Diane shouted.

"I'll get him," Adele grumbled.

As Adele took off and Diane watched her disappearing grandson, Grace twisted just enough to kick her in the knees with every ounce of strength she possessed.

Diane pitched sideways.

The gun flew from her hand.

Grace scrambled for it.

Diane hurled herself on top of Grace. Grabbed her by the hair again and slammed her head against the ground.

Pain reverberated through her skull. Grace rode it out. With all her strength, she bucked and clawed at the other woman's eyes. Diane jerked her upward once more and banged her head against the ground. Grace balled the fingers of her right hand and punched her in the throat. As Diane grabbed at her throat, Grace bucked her off. She clambered away, got to her feet.

Diane made a keening sound and scrambled after Grace. "Don't move!"

At the sound of the deep voice, Grace froze, then whipped around.

Rob stood over Diane, the barrel of his weapon pressed against the back of her head.

She'd never been so happy to see anyone in her life. But her relief was short-lived. "Liam…" Grace surveyed the woods. Where was her baby? "Adele…" She turned back to Rob. "Cara is Adam's sister Adele. She's after Liam."

Rob cuffed Diane's hands behind her. He hitched his head toward the abandoned gun on the ground. "Watch her. I'll be back with Liam."

Grace grabbed the gun. "You watch her. I'm going after Liam."

She took off before he could argue. Her son would likely run to someplace he recognized…a place where he felt safe. He would reach the barn first… Maybe the horses were still there.

Grace ran through the darkness, straining to see the trees before she hit one. She wanted to scream for him but didn't dare. When she burst into the clearing by the barn, the exterior lights had flickered on, parting the darkness. Cara—Adele lay on the ground, her body writhing in pain. She'd dropped her weapon and was clutching at her belly with both hands. Blood had soaked into her blouse, rose up between her fingers.

The horses stood away from her, closer to the barn as if they knew the woman on the ground was trouble.

Grace kicked the wounded woman's gun aside the way she'd seen cops do in movies.

"I need an ambulance," Adele moaned.

Grace ignored her. "Where is Liam? Liam!" She could call for him now that Adele was no longer a threat. "Liam! It's Mommy. Everything is okay now."

"Mommy!"

Her heart rushed into her throat as she looked frantically from side to side. Where was he?

The horses stepped apart and Liam stood between them. Had they been hiding him?

He rushed toward her.

Grace grabbed her son and held him tight.

Sirens wailed and lights flashed as two county SUVs bounced along the long driveway.

Grace dropped to her knees, unable to take another step.

Thank God.

Help was here.

And maybe…just maybe it was over.

Chapter Sixteen

Grace sat in the office belonging to Sheriff Tara Norwood. Grace had not slept all night. How could she? Liam had crashed around midnight. Rob had helped her lay him across the small sofa in the private waiting room.

Caffeine and adrenaline were all that kept her eyes open and her mind working, however sluggishly.

Adele—aka Cara Gunter—was at Erlanger hospital in guarded condition. The shot Grace had managed to pull off had lodged in a precarious spot next to an artery. Then all the running and attempting to grab Liam had caused it to move, creating a small tear. The evil woman was lucky to still be alive.

Diane Franks, the mother of Adam and Adele, was in custody. The FBI had arrived late last night and she had immediately gone for a deal. She was now singing like the lead vocalist in an out-of-control rock band. Apparently, there was a lot more to the Locke family than anyone had known. Grace suspected even more would come out in time.

Diane claimed she had the twins when she was only sixteen, and she'd given them up for adoption—forced to do so by her parents. Later, she'd found them and taken them back after the adoptive parents had met with untimely deaths. She'd changed the twins' surname to Locke, her own as well. Then she'd married a man named Franks and gotten a job with the *LA Times*. By then the twins were adults and doing their own thing. But they always stayed together, oddly so. When they got into trouble, they ran to Mommy and she took care of them until the heat settled.

Adele had learned she couldn't have children, and Adam had decided to "make" one for her. After he was arrested, Adele had flipped out and was institutionalized. But her mother had promised that she would find her baby for her. It had taken Diane more than a year, but she'd finally found Grace. She'd made sure Liam grew attached to her, and then when her daughter was well enough to be released, they had found an identity for her to assume and inserted her into Grace's and Liam's lives by killing Kendall Walls and making it look like an accident.

Grace felt sick at the reality that Kendall had been murdered. On top of that, Diane had killed poor Mrs. Gunter and her daughter to give Adele a place in the community. Mrs. Gunter had been housebound and her daughter had moved away years ago, only visiting occasionally. So no one in the community realized that Adele wasn't her.

All the while, Adam had spent his time in custody deciding he wanted to keep his son for himself. He felt his mother and sister were ganging up on him. When he was suddenly released, he'd come to Lookout Mountain to change that situation.

Diane had lured Pierce to the inn to ensure there were plenty of suspects. Ultimately, she had hoped to see that Grace was charged with whatever had to be done—like murdering Pierce and Gibbons. Killing Adam wasn't part of Diane's plan. Adele had gone rogue with that one.

The FBI agent in charge had explained to Grace that she had nothing to worry about as far as Adam's followers. Any he had garnered eventually lost interest and moved on to newer and bigger headline grabbers. The others who wrote letters were just the typical jailhouse fangirls.

That part gave Grace some sense of relief. The rest, she thought as she stared at her sleeping child, was terrifying. She'd never wanted Liam to know about these people, but she wasn't sure how she could protect him from something this big. He had a grandmother and an aunt who were murderers.

Somehow she had to find a way to keep them from his life. Those people were responsible for her father's untimely death. They had murdered poor Val.

The sooner the two were extradited back to California, the happier Grace would be.

She had given her statement to Sheriff Norwood and the FBI, not holding anything back. Rob assured her she had nothing to worry about. She hadn't done anything wrong. She could take steps to legalize her name change and a good attorney could square things with the IRS related to her business operation the past few years.

Hopefully the community would see her side of all this and forgive her for all the secrets and lies. Sometimes a person just needed a place to hide and this little community had welcomed her with open arms. She didn't want to lose that.

The door opened slowly, and Rob peeked in before stepping into the room. She waved him in and he sat down in the chair next to hers. "I can take you home now."

Grace closed her eyes to hold back the tears that had been threatening for hours. When she could speak, she looked to Rob. "I honestly don't know where home is anymore. How can we go back to the inn with all those reminders of Cara and Diane? Will we ever feel safe there again?"

Rob took her hand in his. "You know you can trust me, right?"

Grace didn't doubt him. She'd shown him the clippings and the locket in his home office, and the sports drink in the refrigerator. They'd figured out that Cara/Adele had set him up as soon as she discovered that Grace and Liam were going there. The excuse that she needed to see about her grandmother was the perfect alibi for slipping out when no one was supposed to leave the inn. The open window in the bathroom at Rob's cabin should have clued Grace in.

"I trust you completely," she assured him.

"Liam saw nothing bad at the inn—other than the man in the snow. It makes sense that he would feel most at home there. How about we go back to the inn. I'll stay as a guest in one of the rooms for as long as you need me there."

Grace wanted badly to do that but… "Diane and Cara won't be there." This would be the hard part for Liam.

"He'll get used to them being gone, just as he did Kendall. Eventually you'll hire a new chef and a new assistant and things will settle down into a normal rhythm. I'll be there whenever you like."

As hard as she understood it would be, Rob was right.

She and Liam needed to go home and work through the loss. "You're right. We should try."

"If it doesn't work out, there's always my apartment. I'll gladly put the two of you up there for a while."

Grace should never have doubted him. He was such a good man. Liam adored him and that meant a great deal to her.

She smiled, the first real one in days. "All right. If you're sure that's what *you* want. This is a big undertaking."

"I have never wanted anything more in my life." He hugged her. "Let's get you home."

Home... She hoped she could still call this place home. And she desperately hoped this man would always be a part of it.

Chapter Seventeen

The Lookout Inn
Mockingbird Lane
Lookout Mountain, Tennessee
Thursday, February 29, 5:00 p.m.

Grace shut down the computer and glanced around the lobby. She was finished for the day.

As she rounded the end of the counter, Liam came zooming through with his new toy airplane, making, of course, engine sounds. He and Rob had put the plane together two days ago and it had been his favorite toy since.

Grace wandered to the kitchen with the intention of starting dinner. There were no guests at the inn tonight, but she was fully booked for the weekend. The insanity of the Locke family murders hadn't hurt business one little bit. But the best part of the past few days was the reaction of the community. Everyone who lived on this part of the mountain had personally visited Grace and praised her bravery and fortitude. It was amazing. She blinked back tears even now. She cried every time she thought about how the community had come together in support of her and Liam. She wasn't sure how she had been lucky enough to pick this place, but she was certainly glad that she had.

Next week she intended to start interviewing for a new staff. The Wilborns were well and had returned to work. Their presence had been good for Liam—something constant. Both had gone above and beyond to keep Liam distracted from looking back. Karl planned to have him help with a small vegetable garden. Paula had come up with a plan to build a little chicken coop and enclosed run on the other side of the shed. Liam was thrilled at the idea.

And Rob. There were not enough ways to convey how much Grace appreciated all he had done. His presence evening after evening had made all the difference.

The sound of Liam's excited voice told her Rob was home—here. This wasn't his home and she had to keep reminding herself not to get too used to him being a part of their daily lives.

Rob pushed through the door to the kitchen wearing a big grin. "Don't cook," he said. "We're going out to celebrate."

Grace smiled. "What are we celebrating?"

He spread his arms wide. "Seven days free of the past."

Grace laughed. "You're right. We should celebrate." The idea of what this might mean tugged at her. They were doing great. This was true. "Does this mean you're ready to move back to your place?"

She held her breath. He'd spent every single hour off duty here since they came home from the sheriff's office that night…seven days ago.

His face turned serious as he stepped closer. "Does that mean you want me to move back to my place?"

She dared to breathe and without hesitation told him the absolute truth. "No. I like...you...here."

He moved closer still. Lowered his head so that his face was close enough to hers to make her heart pound like crazy. "I like being here."

She looked up at him...at his lips...into his eyes. "So you'll stay."

That grin spread across his face again. "I will. But don't worry. I'm not trying to rush things. We can take this as slow as you want."

Grace thought about the idea for a moment. Then she shook her head. "Forget the slow part. I'm ready to start the rest of my life." She draped her arms around his neck and pulled him closer still, kissed him firmly on the mouth.

That grin of his widened, the feel of it against her lips making her heart skip. "Works for me," he murmured.

He kissed her long and deep, and Grace knew with complete certainty that she was really home now.

* * * * *

WETLANDS INVESTIGATION

CARLA CASSIDY

Chapter One

Private investigator Nick Cain drove slowly down the main street of the small town of Black Bayou, Louisiana. It was his first opportunity getting a look at the place where he'd be living and working for at least the next three months or longer if necessary.

His first impression was that the buildings all looked a bit old and tired. However, in the distance the swamp that nearly surrounded the town appeared to breathe with life and color. And it was in the swamp he believed he would do much of his investigation. At the very thought of going into the marshland, a wave of nervous energy tightened his stomach muscles.

He'd been hired by Chief of Police Thomas Gravois to assist in the investigation of four murdered woman. Apparently, a serial murderer was at play in the small town. He would work as an independent contractor and not as a member of the official law enforcement team.

Before he checked in with Chief Gravois, he needed to find the place he'd rented for his time here. It was Gravois who had turned him on to the room for rent in Irene Tompkin's home. Irene was a widow who rented out rooms in her house for extra money.

Once he turned on to Cypress Street, he looked for the correct address. He found it and pulled into the driveway. The widow Tompkin's home was a nice, large two-story painted beige with brown shutters and trim. An expansive wraparound porch held wicker furniture and a swing that invited a person to sit and enjoy. The neighborhood was nice with well-kept lawns and older homes.

He decided to introduce himself first before pulling out all his luggage so he got out of the car, walked up to the front door and knocked. The early September sun was hot on his back as he waited for somebody to answer.

A diminutive woman with a shock of white hair and bright blue eyes opened the door and her wrinkled face wreathed with a friendly smile. "Even though you're a very handsome young man, I'm sorry but I'm not buying anything today," she said.

"That's good because I'm not selling anything. My name is Nick…"

"Oh, Mr. Cain," she replied before he had even fully introduced himself. "I've been expecting you." She grabbed his hand and tugged him over the threshold. "I'm so glad you're here. It's such an honor for you to stay in my home and the town needs you desperately. Let me show you the room where you'll be staying." She continued to pull him toward the large staircase. "How was your trip here?"

"It was fine," he replied, and gently pulled his hand from hers as he followed her up to the second floor.

"Good…good. I baked some cookies earlier. I thought you might want a little snack before you get to your detective work." They reached the top of the stairs and walked down a short hall, and then she opened a door and gestured him to follow her inside.

The bedroom sported a king-size bed, a dresser and an en suite bathroom. The beige walls complemented the cool mint-green color scheme. There was also a small table with two chairs in front of the large window that looked out on the street and a door that led to an old iron fire escape staircase to the ground.

"Is this okay for your needs?" She turned to look at him, her blue eyes filled with obvious apprehension.

He smiled at her. "This is absolutely perfect." It was actually far better than he'd expected. His main requirement was that the place be clean, and this space screamed and smelled of cleanliness.

"Oh good, I'm so glad. Well, I'll just leave you to get settled in and then we can have a little chat?"

"Of course," he replied.

She scurried out of the room and he followed after her. At the foot of the stairs, she beelined into another area of the house and he went outside to retrieve his luggage.

Within thirty minutes he was unpacked. He went back downstairs and stood in the entry. "Mrs. Tompkin," he hollered.

She appeared in one of the doorways and offered him another bright smile. "Come," she said. "I've got some cookies for you and we can have a little chitchat about house rules and such."

The kitchen was large and airy with windows across one wall and a wooden table that sat six. She ushered him into one of the chairs. In the center of the table was a platter of what appeared to be chocolate chip cookies.

"Would you like a cup of coffee?" she asked.

"That sounds nice," he replied.

"It's so easy now to make a cup of coffee with this new-fangled coffee maker," she said as she popped a pod into the machine. She then reached on her tippy-toes and pulled a saucer from one of the cabinets and carried it over to the table.

"You have a very nice place here," Nick said.

She beamed at him as she placed three cookies on the saucer and then set it before him. "Thank you. Me and my husband, Henry, God rest his soul, were very happy here for a lot of years. He passed five years ago from colon cancer."

"I'm so sorry for your loss," he replied.

"It's okay now. I know he's up in heaven holding a spot for me. And that reminds me, there's no Mrs. Tompkin here. Everyone just calls me Nene."

"Then Nene it will be," he replied.

"I just thought we needed to chat about how things go around here. I have one other boarder. His name is Ralph Summerset. He's a nice man who mostly stays to himself. He's retired from the army and now works part-time at the post office. Cream or sugar?" she asked as she set the cup of coffee in front of him.

"Black is just fine," he replied.

She sat on the chair opposite him and smiled at him once again. Nick would guess her to be in her late seventies or early eighties, but she gave off much younger vibes and energy.

"Anyway, I provide breakfast anytime between six and

eight in the mornings and then I cook a nice meal at around five thirty each evening. If you're here, you can eat, but if you aren't here, I don't provide around-the-clock services."

"Understandable," he replied. Even though he wasn't a bit hungry at the moment, he bit into one of the cookies.

"I usually require my guests to be home by ten or so, but I'm making an exception for you." She reached into the pocket of the blue housedress she wore and pulled out a key. "I know with your line of work, your hours are going to be crazy, so take this and then you can come and go as you please. Just make sure when you come in you lock up the door behind you."

"Thank you, I appreciate that." He took the key from her and then finished the cookie and took a sip of his coffee. He was eager to get to the police station and find out just what he was dealing with, but he also knew it was important to build relationships with the locals. And that started here with Nene.

He picked up the second cookie. "These are really delicious," he said, making her beam a smile at him once again.

"I enjoy baking, so I hope you like sweets," she said.

"I definitely have a sweet tooth," he replied. "And I'm sorry, but two cookies are enough for me right now." He took another drink of his coffee.

"I hope you're good at detecting things because these murders that are taking place are frightening and something needs to be done to get the Honey Island Swamp Monster murderer behind bars."

"Honey Island Swamp Monster?" He gazed at her curiously, having not heard the term before.

"That's what everyone is calling the murderer," she replied.

"And who or what is the Honey Island Swamp Monster?"

She leaned forward in her chair, her eyes sparkling like those of a mischievous child. "Legend has it that he was an abandoned child raised by alligators. He's supposed to be over seven feet tall and weighs about four hundred pounds. He has long dirty gray hair and golden eyes, and he stinks to high heaven."

Nick looked at her in disbelief. "Surely nobody really believes that's what killed those women."

Nene leaned back in her chair and released a titter of laughter. "Of course not." The merriment left her face as she frowned at him. "The sad part is now you got town people thinking somebody from the swamp is responsible and the swamp people think somebody from town is responsible and our chief of police seems to be clueless about all of it."

She reached across the table and grabbed one of Nick's hands. "All that really matters is that there's somebody out there killing these poor young women and the rumors are the killings are horribly savage. I really hope you can help us, Mr. Cain." She released his hand.

"Please, make it Nick," he replied as he tried to digest everything she'd just told him. He'd learned over the years not to discount any piece of information he got about a particular crime. Even rumors and gossip had a place in a criminal investigation.

She smiled at him again. "Then Nick it is," she said. "Anyway, Nick, I read a lot of romance books and you look like the handsome stranger who comes to town and not only saves the day but also finds his one true love. Do you have a one true love, Nick? Is there somebody waiting for you back home?"

"No, I'm pretty much married to my job."

"Well, that's a darned shame," she replied. "Now don't make me stop believing in my romances."

"I'm sorry, but I'm definitely no romance hero," he replied. His ex-wife would certainly agree with his assessment of himself. Three years ago, Amy had divorced him because he wasn't her hero. At that time, he'd permanently written love out of his life.

His work was what he could depend on and thinking of that, he rose to his feet and grabbed the house key from the table. "If we're finished here, I really need to get to the police station and get to work."

"Of course, I didn't mean to hold you up as long as I have." She got out of her chair and walked with him to the front door. "I hope to see you for dinner, but I'll understand if you can't make it. I know you have important work to do so I won't delay you any longer."

They said their goodbyes and Nick got back in his car to head to the police station. As he drove toward Main Street, he thought about Nene and the conversation he'd just had with her.

His impression of his landlady was that she was a sweet older woman who was more than a bit lonely. He had a feeling if he would have continued to sit at the table, she would have been perfectly satisfied talking to him for the rest of the afternoon.

With his living space sorted out he could now focus on the reason he was here. When he'd seen the ad in the paper looking for help in solving a series of murders, he had definitely been intrigued.

He'd spent years working as a homicide detective in the

New Orleans Police Department. He'd won plenty of accolades and awards for his work and he'd labored hard on putting away as many murderers as possible. However, two years ago he'd decided to quit the department and open his own private investigation business, but that certainly hadn't meant he was done with killers.

When he'd reached out to Thomas Gravois, the man had told him about the four young women from the swamp who had been brutally murdered by the same killer, but he hadn't said anything about fighting between the swamp people and town people. In fact, Nene had given him more information about the crimes than Gravois had.

Still, that didn't matter. Gravois had hired him over a phone call after seeing all of Nick's credentials. Nick was now more intrigued than ever to get a look at the murder books and see where the investigations had gone so far and what kind of "monster" he was dealing with.

He didn't know if his fresh eyes and skills could solve these murders, but he'd give his all to see that four murdered women got the justice they deserved.

SARAH BEAUREGARD SAT at the dispatch/reception desk in the police office lobby and drummed her fingernails on the top as nervous energy bubbled around in the pit of her tummy.

She'd been working for the police department since she was twenty-one years old and for the past twelve years Chief Gravois had kept her either on desk duty or parked just off Main Street to hand out speeding tickets.

Over those years she'd begged him to allow her to work on any of the cases that had come up, but he'd refused. She had just turned twenty-one when her parents had been killed in a head-on collision with a drunk driver.

She'd been reeling with grief and loss and Gravois, who had been close friends with her father, had taken her under his wing and hired her on as a police officer. However, his protectiveness toward her on the job had long ago begun to feel like shackles meant to hold her back from growing as an officer.

Until now...once again butterflies of excitement flew around inside her. She stared at the front door, waiting for her new partner to walk in.

She frowned as fellow officer Ryan Staub walked up and planted a hip on her desk. "So, the little lady is finally going to get to play at being a real cop," he said.

"First of all, I'm not a 'little lady' and second of all you're just jealous because I got the plum assignment of working with the new guy on the swamp murders."

His blue eyes darkened in hue. "I can't believe Gravois is letting you work on that case. He must have lost his ever-loving mind."

"He's finally allowing me to work up to my potential," she replied firmly. "Besides, you already worked the cases and nothing was solved. And get your butt off my desk."

Ryan chuckled and stood. "Why don't you go out with me for drinks on Friday night?"

She looked up at the tall, handsome blond man. "How many times do I have to tell you I'm not going out with you? I've told you before, I find you impossibly arrogant and you're a womanizer and you just aren't my type."

He laughed again. "Oh, Sarah, I just love it when you sweet-talk me." He leaned down so he was eye level with her. "Do you want to know what I think? I think you have a secret crush on me and you're just playing hard to get."

Sarah swallowed against a groan of irritation. "Don't you have something better to do than bother me?"

He straightened up. "Yeah, I've got some things I need to get to."

"Feel free to go get to them," Sarah replied tersely. She released a sigh of relief as Ryan headed down the hallway toward the room where all the officers had their desks.

She and Ryan had known each other since they were kids, but it was just in the last month or so that he'd decided she should be his next conquest. And he'd already had plenty of conquests with the women in town.

At thirty-three years old, she had no interest in finding a special man. She'd thought she'd found him once and that romance had gone so wrong. Still, if she was looking, Ryan would be the very last man on earth she would date.

At that moment the front door whooshed open and a tall, handsome hunk of a man walked in. She knew in an instant that it was *him*…the man Gravois had hired to come in and help investigate the four murders that had taken place.

She'd read his credentials and knew he had been a highly respected homicide detective with the New Orleans Police Department. His black hair was short and neat and his features were well-defined. A black shirt stretched across his broad shoulders and his black slacks hugged his long, lean legs. Definitely a hunk, and her new partner.

He approached her desk and offered a brief smile. Not only were his twilight-gray-colored eyes absolutely beautiful, but he also had thick, long dark lashes. "Hi, I'm Nick Cain, and I'm here to see Chief Gravois."

"Of course, I'll just go let him know you're here." She got up from the desk and headed down the hall to Chief Gravois's office.

It really made no difference to her that Nick Cain was a very handsome man. What she was most eager about was diving into the murder cases and perhaps learning something from the far more experienced detective turned private investigator.

She knocked on the chief's door and heard his reply. She opened the door and peeked inside. "He's here."

Gravois was a tall, fit man with salt-and-pepper hair and sharp blue eyes. "Get Shanks to sit on the desk and you bring him back here so I can talk to both of you at the same time."

Once again, an excited energy swirled around in the pit of her stomach. She opened the door behind which all the officers on duty sat. There were only three men in house at the moment, Ryan and Officers Colby Shanks and Ian Brubaker, who was the deputy police chief. "Colby, Gravois wants you on dispatch right now."

The young officer jumped out of his seat. He was a new hire and very eager to learn about everything. "Sure. Is the new guy here?" he asked as he followed just behind her.

"He is," she replied.

"Cool, I hope he's as good as he sounds."

"Let's hope so," she said.

They returned to the reception area where Nick Cain stood by the desk. "Sorry for the wait, if you'll just follow me, I'll take you to Chief Gravois."

"Thank you," he replied.

As she led him down the hall, she could feel an energy

radiating from him. It was an attractive energy, one of confident male.

Suddenly Sarah wondered if her hair looked okay. Was the perfume she'd spritzed on that morning still holding up? She checked these thoughts, which had no place in her mind right now.

While she was working these cases with this man, she was a police officer, not a woman. Besides, one time around in the world of romance had been far more than enough for her.

She gave a quick knock on Gravois's door and then opened it. Nick followed her in and Gravois stood and offered his hand to him.

"Thomas Gravois," he said as they shook hands. "Please, both of you have a seat. It's good to have you here, Nick."

"Thank you, it's good to be here," Nick replied.

"Have you gotten all settled in at Irene's place yet?"

"I have," Nick replied.

"Okay then, first of all I want to introduce you to your new partner, Sarah Beauregard." Gravois pointed at her. "She will work side by side with you while you're here."

Nick nodded at her and Gravois continued. "Right now, you will be the only two working this investigation. If you need additional help then we can talk about that. I've set you two up in a small office that should have all you need. However, if there is something more that you want, please just let me know about it. In fact, I'll take you back there now and show you the setup."

The three of them stood and Gravois led the way down the hall to the office, which was really just an oversize storage area. A table had been set up in the center and a small filing cabinet hugged one of the corners. There was also a large whiteboard on one wall.

"I've put the murder books there in the center of the table, along with extra notepads for you to use. I'm sure you're eager to get started. I'm glad you're here, Nick. We need to get this guy off the streets as soon as possible."

"I hope I can help you with that," Nick replied.

"Later this afternoon I need to have a chat with you to finalize exactly how things are going to work," Gravois said. "I've also got some paperwork for you to sign."

"Whenever you're ready, sir," Nick replied.

"I'll just leave you to it and I'll check in with you later," Gravois said. He left the room and closed the door behind him.

Instantly the room felt too small. She could now smell the scent of Nick, a spicy intoxicating fragrance that she found very appealing. He gestured her toward a chair at the table and then he sat opposite her.

"Officer Beauregard," he began.

"Please make it Sarah," she said.

"Sarah, how long have you been with the police department?" he asked.

"I've been with the department for the past twelve years," she replied.

"Perhaps you have some insight into the murders?" He looked at her expectantly.

"Uh…to be honest, I haven't been involved in any of the investigations into the murders up to this point," she confessed.

He looked at her for a long moment and then released a heavy sigh. "So, what investigations have you been involved in during the last couple of years? I'm just trying to figure out here what I'm working with."

"You're working with a police officer whose sole desire and interest is to solve these four murders. I'm hardworking and tenacious and I'll have your back like a good partner should," she replied fervently.

His hard gaze on her continued. "I guess time will tell if you're really all that."

It was at that moment Sarah realized her new partner might just be a jerk.

Chapter Two

Nick walked back into Nene's house just before dinnertime. The house smelled of a delicious tomato-based sauce and freshly baked bread. He carried the four murder books up the stairs and placed them on the small table to look at later.

By the time he'd had a brief conversation with his partner, Gravois had called him back into his office for a lengthy discussion about how things would work with Nick hired on as a free agent within the department. There were several documents for him to sign as well.

Once their talk was finally over, Nick made the decision that he'd study the murder books tonight and then first thing in the morning he'd speak with Sarah about where to begin their investigation.

He went into the bathroom to wash up for dinner and as he did, thoughts of his new partner filled his head. She was no bigger than a minute. He would guess her at about five feet tall and no more than one hundred pounds soaking wet.

Her blond hair was short and curly and she could easily be dismissed as a piece of fluff, except for her bright blue eyes, which had shone with a hunger that he had immediately identified with.

He wasn't sure why she'd been partnered with him. The only reason he could think of was Gravois wanted two fresh sets of eyes on the case. And he didn't know why there weren't more officers assigned to the murder cases.

What irritated him as much as anything was the fact that he found his new partner extremely pretty, and the first time she'd smiled at him he'd felt a spark go off deep inside him, something he hadn't felt for a very long time and something he definitely intended to ignore.

He went back downstairs and into the kitchen. "Nick," Nene greeted him with a big smile. "I wasn't sure you'd make it for dinner tonight, but I'm so glad you did. Please, have a seat at the table."

He started to sit, but she quickly stopped him. "Oh, that's Ralph's seat. He's kind of a creature of habit and likes to sit in the same place every night."

"No problem, I'll just sit over here." Nick moved to the other place that was set for dinner. "Something smells really delicious."

"Swiss steak, I hope you like it. We didn't talk about your food likes and dislikes when we spoke earlier. Are there any allergies I need to worry about?" She pulled a large pan from the oven and set it on the countertop where a hot pad awaited it.

"None, and the only thing I really don't eat is brussels sprouts."

"That makes two of us," she replied with a tittering giggle. "To me no matter how you dress them up, they still taste like dirt."

"I totally agree," he replied.

At that moment a tall, fit man entered the room. He had

dark brown hair worn in a buzz cut and deep-set brown eyes. Nick rose from his chair and held out his hand. "You must be Ralph," he said. "I'm Nick."

Ralph's grip was firm. "Nice to meet you, Nick," he said as the handshake ended. The two men sat at the table. "I hear you're the man Gravois has brought in to solve these Honey Island Monster murders."

"That's the plan," Nick replied. "Do you have any theories about the murders?"

"Me? Nah, I didn't even know about them until just recently," Ralph replied.

How was that possible? How, in a town this size, did everyone not know about the murders? He could understand the first one not being talked about much, but when the second one had occurred, he would have thought everyone would be talking about them.

The dinner was delicious. The Swiss steak was nice and tender and there were also seasoned green beans, a gelatin salad and homemade rolls. Nene definitely knew how to cook.

Ralph did not attempt to engage Nick in any conversation while they ate; however, Nene filled what might have been awkward silences with chatter about the weather, the town and her plan to bake an apple coffee cake along with biscuits and gravy for breakfast the next morning.

"My biscuits and gravy are a favorite with Ralph, right?" she said as they were ending the meal.

"You know that's right," Ralph replied. "I could eat them every day for breakfast."

"Then I'm definitely eager to try them," Nick replied.

He was grateful that dinner went by quickly, as he was

keen to get upstairs and dig into the murder books. When they were all finished eating, he picked up his plate to carry it to the sink.

"Stop right there," Nene said. "I take care of all the cleanup around here."

"And don't even try to argue with her," Ralph said. "She's a very stubborn woman."

"Ha, that I am. Now put that plate down and go on your merry way," Nene replied.

"Then I'll just say thank you and dinner was delicious," Nick replied.

"If you want a little nibble later, I always leave chips and crackers and other snacky stuff on the table overnight for you to help yourself," she said.

"Thanks, Nene, and, Ralph, it was good meeting you." With that said, Nick left the kitchen. He probably should have looked at the murder books with Sarah, but he'd wanted to study the material on his own first.

Once he reached his room, he beelined toward the table. He first grabbed one of the fresh notebooks that Gravois had provided for them. He opened the notebook and made sure he had a pen.

While he read the files, he intended to make his own notes on the cases. He picked up the first murder book, surprised by how thin it was. In fact, he'd been surprised by how thin they all were when he'd picked them up to carry home.

The first thing he saw inside the first book were the crime scene photos. The victim, Babette Pitre, had been found in the back alley behind the post office and town hall. In the photos it appeared her throat had been ripped out and her face held wounds that looked like a wild animal had tried to claw her features off.

The autopsy also indicated that she'd been stabbed three times in the abdomen and it was probably some sort of claw gardening tool that had ripped out her throat and marred her face.

There was also an injection site in her upper arm. The tox screen had come back showing a heavy dose of Xanax in her system. The same was true in all the other victims. It was obviously the way the killer had knocked out his victims.

According to the records the people who had shown up at the crime scene were Gravois, Officers Ryan Staub and Ian Brubaker, the coroner, Douglas Cartwright, and his assistant, and somebody named Ed Martin.

Nick frowned as he set the photos aside and moved on to the actual investigation notes. There were only three interviews that had been conducted at the time, one with a Gator Broussard, another with Babette's mother and finally one with a man named Zeke Maloney. The interviews were short and contained nothing earth-shattering as far as information went.

He was shocked as he checked out the next three murder books and realized it appeared that very little had been done to actually investigate these killings. Why?

Was Gravois that incompetent? Lazy? What about the other officers in the department? Did they really believe enough had been done in an attempt to catch this killer? Nick couldn't believe how lacking the investigations had been.

He leaned back in his chair and stared out the window where darkness had fallen and the streetlights had come on.

He hadn't expected this. He hadn't expected the investigations that were done already to be so shoddy…so lacking. He had expected much better police work than this. He released a deep sigh.

Instantly a picture of his new partner filled his head once again. She'd already told him she knew very little about the murders. He also hadn't missed the fact that she hadn't answered him when he'd asked what kind of investigations she'd worked on before.

So, basically, he had crap in the murder files and a partner who he suspected was green as grass. It was a perfect recipe for failure.

However, he now had a vision of the four victims also in his head and they deserved justice, so failure wasn't an option. The way those women had been killed indicated that there really was a monster somewhere in Black Bayou. The length of time between the killings had shortened, so another one could occur any day.

He finally left the table and got ready for bed. He wanted to be sharp and refreshed in the morning. He'd told Sarah to meet him at seven thirty and they definitely had their work cut out for them.

Nick arrived at the police department just after seven the next morning. He was fueled by a good breakfast of the best biscuits and gravy he'd ever tasted and several cups of Nene's strong coffee.

He went directly to the room that had been assigned to them. He set the murder books back on the center of the table and then moved to the whiteboard, where he wrote the names of the four victims at the top.

He was pleasantly surprised when Sarah walked in at

seven fifteen. At least she was early rather than being late. "Good morning," she said with a bright smile.

She was definitely very pretty, and once again an electric spark shot off deep inside him. Despite the fact that it was hot and humid outside, she brought in the very pleasant scent of spring flowers. It irritated him that he even noticed her scent.

"Back at you," he said, apparently more gruffly than he intended as her smile instantly disappeared. "Feel free to start reading the murder books. I'll be interested to get your thoughts."

She sat at the table and picked up the first file. He watched her as she read it. To her credit, she flinched only a little bit as she saw the graphic photos of the victims. He also couldn't help but notice that her eyelashes were thick and long. Damn, what in the hell was going on with him?

She flipped through the interviews and then looked up at him with a delicate frown. "Is there more to this?"

"Apparently not, and the other three are just as thin." He joined her at the table.

"Surely there has to be more someplace," she replied with a look of confusion.

"I asked Gravois when I arrived a few minutes ago if there was more information on the murders and he told me what we have is all there is." He attempted to keep all the judgment from his tone, but some of it must have crept in.

Her cheeks turned a dusty pink. "Well, this is embarrassing." She shoved the murder book aside. "This should be an embarrassment to the whole department."

"I'm glad we agree about something. How do you feel about going into the swamp?"

"I don't have a problem with it. I ran in the swamp when I was young. What about you?"

"The same. My mother worked as an attorney in New Orleans and many of the people she represented were from the swamp. It wasn't uncommon for her to take me with her when she went to meet with some of her clients." The back of his throat threatened to close up at the very thought of the swamp. He swallowed hard against his rise of anxiety as he thought about going into the dark bayou.

"So, is that where we begin things? In the swamp?" she asked.

He nodded. "I think we should start by speaking to Lisa Choate's parents." Lisa had been the last woman killed.

"I think that makes sense. That murder is still fairly fresh," she replied.

"But before that, I'd like to take a look at the place where her body was found," he added.

"That was behind the bank. So, are we ready to go?" She gazed at him with big blue eyes that simmered with anticipation.

"Ready," he replied.

She stood. "I'll drive."

"Normally I drive," he said.

"It makes sense for me to since I'm sure I know my way around town better than you do." Her chin lifted as if ready to challenge him. It surprised him, the bit of sass she had in her.

"Okay, then you drive for today," he replied.

They left the room and headed toward the back door of the station, stopping only when another officer was coming their way.

He smiled at Nick. "Investigator Cain, I'm Officer Ryan Staub." He held out a hand and the two shook. "I just want to let you know that if you find Short-Stuff here to be lacking in any way, I'd be available to join your team and help you out."

"Jeez, Ryan, I definitely feel the bus wheels rolling over my back," Sarah replied drily.

"I'll keep that in mind, but I like my partner just fine," Nick said. "So far, I find her extremely intelligent and I know she's going to be a great asset to me going forward."

"Oh…okay," Ryan replied. "Well, let me know if you need more help."

"Will do," Nick replied, and then he and Sarah moved on down the hall and exited into the hot early-September morning.

"Thank you," Sarah said.

"Is he always such a jackass?" Nick asked.

She released a musical laugh that was quite pleasant on the ears. "Only on the days when he's not being a total jerk." She gestured toward a blue sedan parked in a space at the back of the building.

"Do your other officers often mention your…uh…small stature?" He'd been offended by Ryan on so many levels, especially as a fellow officer of hers calling her Short-Stuff.

"No, that's just Ryan," she replied. She unlocked her car doors with her key fob and he got into the passenger seat. The interior of the car smelled like her, that scent of fresh flowers he found so attractive.

What in the hell was wrong with him? It had been years since he'd noticed a woman's scent. Why now? And why his partner?

What he needed was to keep himself in check, solve these murders as quickly as possible and then get back to his life in New Orleans.

SARAH FELT UNACCOUNTABLY nervous as she took off from the parking lot and headed toward the bank. She'd initially written off her new partner as being a jerk, but then he had defended her to Ryan and now she wasn't so sure what to think about him.

He looked as hot today as he had the day before. Clad in black slacks and a short-sleeved gray shirt, and with his shoulder holster and gun in place, he exuded strong male energy.

Not that it mattered as long as they could work together well. More than anything else, Sarah wanted to prove herself to the rest of the department.

She wanted to show them all that she wasn't just a nothing who Gravois gave a job to because he felt sorry for her. She wanted to prove that she wasn't just good for answering the phone or giving out tickets. She was ready to earn her place as a valuable member of the team and this was finally her opportunity to do that. The last thing she wanted was to develop a crush on her partner and lose her focus.

It was a short drive to the bank, where she parked and they got out of the car. "Down this way," she said as she led him down the alley between the bank and Masy's dress shop. "She was found right around here." She pointed to the general area where the body had been discovered.

He stared at the ground and then gazed around the area. "No security cameras back here?"

"None, and there's also no lighting," she replied.

"So, the killer had to know this area well and was able to easily drop the body off and get out of the here fairly quickly without being seen."

"There aren't many people on the streets at two or three in the morning," she replied. "But the killer had to know that this was an ideal place to leave her because of the lack of surveillance and lights."

"You would think the bank would have security cameras all around it."

She smiled at him. "You're thinking like a man from the city. Bank robberies just don't happen in Black Bayou."

He nodded. "Point taken."

He looked around the area for several more minutes and then gazed at her once again. "Let's head to the swamp and at least get a first round of interviews done by the end of the day."

Minutes later they were back in her car and headed to Vincent's, a grocery store located just before the swamp took over the land. One thing the murder book held were directions to Lisa's parents' shanty.

"How was it that you ran the swamp when you were younger?" he asked.

"The house that I grew up in backed up to the swamp," she explained. "My parents worked full time and I was left alone a lot. When I was about eight or nine, I met a few kids who lived in the swamp, so I would go in to visit with them. I found it to be a magical place, but by the time I was a teenager I gave up the swamp for other after-school activities."

"And you were never afraid in the swamp?" he asked curiously.

"Never. My friends taught me a lot about the dangers

and I was probably too young and dumb to be afraid," she ended with a small laugh.

"So, what do you think? Is our killer from the swamp? Or is he somebody from town? Gravois seems to feel certain it's somebody from the swamp."

"I really don't have an opinion about it all right now. I don't have enough information to make an educated call," she replied.

"And that's good police work," he replied. "It's important that we both keep open minds going into all this."

His words warmed her. She hoped he wouldn't realize just how inexperienced she was, that she wouldn't show him what a neophyte she really was in actually working to solve crimes.

"What made you quit the police department and go out on your own as a private investigator?" she asked. "And I'm sorry if I'm being too nosy."

"Not at all," he replied. "In a word, it was burnout. I was working twelve-to fifteen-hour days for years and finally I decided it was time for me to slow down a bit. I now pick and choose the cases I work on."

"Is there somebody waiting for you back home? A wife or a girlfriend?" Sarah instantly wanted to kick herself in the behind for asking the personal question. But she was definitely curious.

"Neither, I've pretty much always been married to the job. What about you? Do you have a significant other?"

"No, and I'm glad. I want to stay laser focused on these cases without any outside distractions."

"Then we're definitely on the same page," he replied.

She pulled into the parking lot of the small grocery store,

where a trail leading into the vast swamp was nearby. A lot of the people who lived in the swamp parked their vehicles here, as the owner of Vincent's was very swamp friendly.

"This is it. According to the directions, Lisa Choate's parents live up this trail and to the right at the second fork," she said.

"Let's go and let's hope Abe and Emily Choate can give us some information about their daughter that will move the investigation along." He led the way as they entered the trail.

It had been years since Sarah had been in the swamp. As she followed behind Nick, she drew in the scents of mysterious flowers and fauna along with the underlying odor of decay. The heat that surrounded them seemed to magnify the scents.

Bugs buzzed around her head as little woodland creatures scurried away on either side of the trail. Spanish moss dripped down from the treetops in beautiful lacy patterns.

Despite the beauty, she was also well aware of the dangers of poisonous snakes and gator-infested pools of water and wild boar that roamed the area.

Thankfully, they encountered none of those things by the time they arrived at the Choates' shanty. Before they could cross the rickety bridge that led up to the front door, a man stepped outside the small, slightly listing home on stilts.

"Who are you?" he asked with obvious suspicion. "What do you want here?"

"Mr. Choate, I'm Sarah Beauregard with the Black Bayou Police Department and this is special agent Nick Cain. We'd like to come in and talk to you and your wife about Lisa."

The tall, shirtless man stood still for a long moment and

Sarah wondered if he was willing to speak to them at all. He finally nodded his head. "Come in then."

Nick and Sarah crossed the bridge and Lisa's father ushered them into the small shanty. "They're here to talk about Lisa," he said to the woman who sat on the end of the sofa. She stood as a slash of deep grief filled her features.

"Please, have a seat," she said as she stepped aside and gestured to the sofa. She twisted her hands before her. "Can I get you something to drink?"

"No thanks," Nick said. "And we're so very sorry for your loss."

He and Sarah sat side by side on the sofa and Emily sat in a chair facing them while Lisa's father remained standing by the door as if ready to kick them out at any moment.

"She was such a good girl," Emily said as her dark eyes filled with tears. "Always happy, always smiling." She swiped at her eyes. "She didn't deserve what was done to her."

"None of the victims deserved it," Sarah replied softly. "And we're going to work very hard to get justice for Lisa."

"Nobody else has been working too hard to catch this killer," Abe said in obvious disgust. "Four dead girls and still no answers."

"We're hoping to change that right now," Nick replied.

Nick took the lead in the questioning and Sarah made notes. For the next hour he asked questions about Lisa and her lifestyle. Her parents insisted that she wouldn't leave the swamp with just anyone, but somebody had led her out of the swamp and to her death.

It would help if they knew where the women had been killed. The place where their bodies were found had only been the dumping grounds. They had been killed elsewhere, but where?

Her parents didn't know of any town girls who had been friends with their daughter, but she did have a couple of close friends who lived nearby in the swamp. In fact, she had been coming home after having partied a bit with her friends when she had disappeared.

Sarah was impressed by her partner, who asked smart and pointed questions yet displayed a softness and compassion for the two grieving parents.

They finally got up to leave, but Abe stopped them at the door. "You better hope you find this killer afore I do," he said with dark narrowed eyes. "'Cause if I find him, I'll kill him and rip his throat out just like he done my baby girl."

"Understood," Nick replied.

They left the shanty but before heading away, they paused at the bottom of the bridge to talk about what they had just learned. "I didn't see any interviews of Lisa's friends in the file," Nick said.

"That's because there were none there," Sarah replied. Even as inexperienced as she was, she knew this was lousy police work. There should have been follow-up interviews with all of Lisa's friends.

She was completely embarrassed by the department. She was particularly embarrassed by the man who had given her a job so many years ago. She'd believed Gravois was better than this. She knew there were people in town who believed he was lazy.

Maybe he was or maybe as the chief of police in such a small town he really didn't know how to investigate serious criminal cases like these. Or had he not cared because the victims were from the swamp? All of these thoughts deeply troubled her.

"Shall we interview Hayley Duchamp while we're so close to where she lives?" she asked. Lisa's parents had given them directions to two of Lisa's closest friends' places.

"Sounds like a plan," he replied. "I'm honestly surprised the friends haven't been interviewed before now. They might have some information about Lisa that her parents didn't know." He started up the trail toward Hayley's family shanty.

There was a loud crack. A gunshot! Nick immediately took Sarah to the ground and covered her body with his. At the same time, she heard the path of the bullet as it whizzed through the leaves and slammed into the tree near where they'd been standing.

Chapter Three

Nick's heart pumped sheer adrenaline throughout his body as he quickly pulled his gun. He stared into the direction that the bullet had come from but he saw nobody. He'd already been on the very edge just being in the swamp and now this. What in the hell?

He looked down at Sarah, who was as still as a statue beneath him. "Are you okay?" he asked softly.

"I'm fine," she replied just as quietly, but he could feel the frantic beat of her heart against his and the tenseness of her entire body beneath him.

"Stay here and stay down," he said. He slowly rose up to a crouch and then raced forward, zigzagging among the trees and thicket toward the spot where he thought the shooter might be. He glanced over his shoulder and saw that Sarah had crouched up and had her gun out before her.

No other shots came and it was impossible to specifically locate exactly where the shooter might have been. Nick sensed the danger was over as nothing else happened, but he continued to crouch down as he made his way back to Sarah.

It was only when he reached her that they both finally

stood. "What the hell was that all about?" he asked. "Is it possible the people who live around here don't like law enforcement?"

"I guess that's possible, or it's also possible somebody just warned us off our investigation," she replied.

"Did it work? Do you want to be reassigned?"

"Heck no," she replied, her eyes lit with blue fire. "This just makes me more determined than ever to go forward."

He gazed at her for a long moment, looking for any cracks in her composure. That bullet aimed at them would have shaken up the most seasoned professional, but she appeared to have taken it in stride. Either she had a good poker face or she was utterly fearless.

While he could appreciate the first quality, the latter could be deadly. A cop had to function with a healthy amount of fear to stay alive. His partner was still such an unknown commodity to him.

What he did know was beneath her blue uniform and despite her slender frame, she had some definite feminine curves. In the brief moments he'd been on top of her, his traitorous brain had registered that fact.

"Is this something we should call in?" he asked.

"Call in to who?" she asked, and then continued, "It doesn't appear we need backup and we can't even be sure that bullet wasn't from somebody hunting in the area. Now that I really think about it, it's a bit too early for anyone to be that worried about what we're doing."

"The fact that there was only one shot and none following up makes me believe it was just some kind of a random thing. I say we go on to Hayley's place but we proceed with caution," he finally said.

Together they took off with their guns leading the way. They managed to interview not only Hayley, but also Lily Champueau, who was also a friend of Lisa's.

By that time, they decided to head back into the office and not only process what they'd learned that day, but also plan what they intended to do the next day.

Sarah now sat at the table while Nick wrote the names of Lisa's two friends on the whiteboard beneath Lisa's name. When he was finished, he joined her at the table.

"Both women agreed that Lisa had no boyfriends," he said.

"And that she would not just go off with a guy from town," Sarah added dispiritedly. "We didn't really learn anything new that helps us."

"No stone unturned," Nick replied. "Patience is the key here. This case isn't going to be solved overnight. I just really don't understand why more wasn't done on these cases at the time the murders occurred."

Sarah released a deep sigh. "It's probably because they were swamp women," she said. "I'll tell you a dirty little secret about this town. A lot of the people who live in town are very prejudiced against the people who live in the swamp. They believe the men there are all lazy and drunks, and the woman are all worthless sluts." Her cheeks dusted with color. "If it would have been four town women who had been murdered, I think the investigations would have been far more thorough."

"So, what's changed? Why was I brought in if they don't really care about solving these crimes?"

"Pressure from several influential businessmen who demanded answers about the murders and Gravois's fear of being recalled," she replied. "Things seem to be slowly changing with the newer generation. It's mostly the old guard who are still hanging on to the prejudices."

"Well, it's good if things are changing. If prejudice is what kept these murders from being solved that's a hate crime in and of itself." Nene had hinted at some of this when she'd first spoken to him, but she certainly hadn't laid it out in such stark terms. It ticked him off. All victims, no matter who they were or where they came from, deserved justice.

"I also think it's very possible that the officers involved in the case believe a swamp person is responsible and they've just been waiting for somebody to walk in and either confess to the murders or give up some information about the guilty person."

He frowned. "So instead of actively investigating, everybody has been just hanging around and waiting for the crimes to solve themselves."

"Nick, I swear I didn't know what had been done or not done as far as the investigations were concerned. I was kept away from all this. I'm seeing this all for the first time and it actually disgusts me." She looked so earnest as she held his gaze.

He released a deep sigh. "Okay, so we use what little information there is in the files and we forge ahead. I want to ask you about some of the people in the murder books."

"Okay, ask away," she replied. There was a small piece of green vegetation stuck in her golden strands of hair. He wasn't sure if he wanted to pick it out because it didn't belong there or if he just wanted to touch the hair that looked so silky and soft. Instead, he opened his notebook and tightly grabbed his pen.

"The first person is Ed Martin. According to the murder books, he was at each of the dumping grounds before the bodies were removed."

She frowned. "His father, Gustave, owns most of Main Street. Ed helps his father with his businesses and collects rent from all the store owners. He's married and he and his wife have one son who is around nineteen or twenty. But I can't imagine why he would be anywhere around the bodies or the crime scenes."

"And what about Gator Broussard? He was interviewed after the first murder, but the notes don't hold much of the conversation."

A small smile curved her lips, igniting that little flutter of something inside him. "Gator is about eighty years old and has lived in the swamp all his life. He is something of a character and he catches gators for a living."

"What would he know about the murders to warrant him being interviewed?" Nick asked.

"Gator knows most everyone who lives in the swamp and he usually has a handle on what's going on there," she replied.

"Definitely sounds like somebody we should reinterview," he said.

"I agree. If anybody knows anything at all about these murders it would be Gator."

"Then let's plan to talk to him in the morning. Finally, do you know Zeke Maloney? He was listed as a potential suspect because he was seen hanging out around Chastain's store the night Marchelle Savoie's body was found in the alley there."

Once again Sarah frowned. "Zeke is in his late thirties

or early forties. He lives in one of the rooms at the motel and I think he's a heavy drug user."

"Do you know what kinds of drugs he's into?" he asked.

"No, I'm sorry but I don't," she replied. "But if I was to make a guess, I'd say either cocaine or meth."

Nick leaned back in his chair. "So, tomorrow we'll plan on interviewing those three men... Ed Martin, Gator Broussard and Zeke Maloney. At some point later I want to talk to Gravois about the fact that we were shot at. Whether it was a stray bullet from a hunter or something else, he should be made aware of that fact."

"I agree," she replied. "Do you want me to go with you when you speak to him?"

"I don't think that's necessary." He closed his notebook and looked at his watch. It was just a few minutes after five. "Why don't we go ahead and call it a day and we can pick up fresh in the morning. I'm sure we are going to have some late nights going forward."

They both got up from the table. "Then I'll see you in the morning," she said. Once she left the room, he sank back down at the table.

He hoped like hell that she hadn't noticed how absolutely terrified he'd been the minute he'd stepped foot in the swamp. The swamp had haunted his nightmares for years, so going into the dark, mysterious marsh today had been a real challenge. It had been a terrifying journey for him.

He hoped his partner had seen none of his internal battle between duty and fear. The last thing he would want was to appear weak in anyone's eyes, but especially to his new partner.

He still didn't know what kind of a partner Sarah was

going to be, but already he found her damned distracting. Her beautiful smile felt like a gift each time she flashed it at him. Her eyes were the vivid color of sapphires and shone just as brilliantly.

She wore her uniform well. The light blue shirt emphasized the blue of her eyes and the navy slacks fit her like they'd been tailored to showcase her nice butt and slender legs. Her lips looked so soft and kissable.

Why didn't she have a boyfriend or a significant other? She was bright and pretty and he couldn't believe nobody in town would be interested in her.

And why in the hell was he sitting here speculating about her? He'd had many female partners through the years, but with none of them had he wanted to know anything about them outside of the job.

Something about Sarah was different and she had him more than a little bit out of his comfort zone. Starting tomorrow he had to get his head on straight where she was concerned.

SARAH JERKED AWAKE with her heart racing and adrenaline flooding through her veins. Frantically she looked around the room as she slowly came out of the nightmare that had awakened her in the first place.

She turned over and checked the time. Just a little past five. Instead of going back to sleep for another hour or so, she decided to go ahead and get up. She turned on the bedside lamp and got out of bed. She then went into the kitchen and fixed herself a cup of coffee.

As she sipped the hot brew, she thought about the nightmare that had jerked her awake. She'd been back in the swamp, tangled in the vines that held her captive while shadow people had been shooting at her. It was easy to figure out why she'd had the dream.

Being shot at the day before had scared the living hell out of her. She hoped her partner hadn't seen her abject fear and she'd played it off okay. The last thing she wanted to do was give him the impression she wasn't up to the job.

She stared out the nearby window where the morning sun was just beginning to peek over the horizon. She had bought this house four years ago after having lived in an apartment since her parents' deaths. It was a nice three-bedroom with a fenced-in yard.

She'd had such high hopes for a happy life at that time. She'd been engaged to Brent Williamson, a man she'd believed was her soulmate, and she was busy planning her wedding. That, along with all of her confidence as a woman, had been destroyed by a single image on his phone.

Instead of dwelling on thoughts of her past heartbreak, she finished her coffee and then headed for the shower. A half an hour later she was dressed, but it was still too early to go into the police station.

She made herself another cup of coffee and carried it into her living room and sank down on the sofa. While her bedroom was decorated in pink and white, this room was done in blacks and grays with bright yellow accents.

She also had a guest bedroom done in shades of blue and a room with a desk set aside as an office which she hoped to actually use now that she was officially investigating crimes.

As she sipped on her second cup, she couldn't help but think about Nick. She could usually figure out people fairly well, but she couldn't get a good read on him. She'd found him supportive yet standoffish. His gaze had alternated between a warm gray and a distant deep steel, all in the course of a single day.

He was a hot, handsome man who could become a total distraction if she allowed him to be. But she couldn't let that happen. All she wanted to do was prove herself to be a hardworking officer who could get the job done, somebody who had the respect of her coworkers.

And thinking about that, she realized it was time to go. Hopefully today they could find out something that would lead them closer to catching the killer.

The intense heat and humidity of the summer months had finally broken and today was supposed to be a more pleasant temperature in the low eighties.

Knowing they would be driving several places, today she parked in front of the police station and entered through the front door.

"Good morning," she said to Ian Brubaker, who sat at the reception/dispatcher desk.

"Morning, Sarah," he replied. "Your partner is already here."

"Thanks, then I'll just head on back. Have a good day, Ian." Her stomach knotted up a bit with anxious energy as she walked down the hallway and anticipated seeing her partner again.

"Her partner," that's how she had to think about him in her mind. She didn't want to think about him being Nick, because Nick was a man she was very attracted to.

She hadn't really dated much in the last couple of years and it ticked her off a little that the first man she found appealing on all levels was strictly off-limits.

She opened the door to their little office and walked in. Nick was seated at the table. "I'm just going over the people I think we need to talk to today," he said as a greeting. He gestured her toward the chair opposite him.

Instantly she smelled the scent of him, a mixture of soap and shaving cream and the spicy cologne. This morning he wore a gray polo that perfectly matched the color of his eyes, and his usual black slacks.

However, his eyes appeared distant, bordering on cold as he read off the list of people for questioning and then looked at her. "Anyone you want to add for today?"

"No, your list sounds good to me," she replied.

"Then let's get moving," he said, and stood.

She quickly got to her feet and followed him out of the office and down the hallway. "I'll drive today," he said once they were outside. "You can navigate from the passenger seat."

She wasn't about to argue with him, not in the mood he appeared to be in. He led her to a black sedan and after he unlocked the doors with his key fob, she slid into the passenger seat.

The interior smelled like him, a scent that instantly stirred her. She watched as he walked around the front of the car to get to the driver door.

Why couldn't he have a paunchy stomach and sloped shoulders? Why couldn't he smell like menthol rub and mothballs? That would have made it so much better, so much easier for her.

"I figured we'd start with Ed Martin this morning. I'm assuming he works out of an office?" He started his car.

"He does. His office is down a few blocks on Main Street," she replied.

"Any self-respecting businessman should be in his office by this time of the morning, right?"

"You would think so." She fastened her seat belt and they took off.

"Is there anything I should know about Mr. Martin before we go in to talk to him?"

"To be honest, I really don't know much about him other than what I already told you," she replied.

She couldn't help but notice that Nick's voice seemed brusquer today and she also couldn't help but wonder if she'd done something to somehow offend him. Or maybe he was just a moody person.

Just like she couldn't know whether the killer was from the swamp or from town because she didn't have enough information, the same was true about Nick. She just didn't have enough information about him to even hazard a guess as to what kind of a personality he might really have.

It took only minutes for them to pull up in front of Ed's office. The writing on the large window in the front announced the business to be Martin's Enterprises.

There was a small sign on the door that indicated the office was open. They got out of the car and Nick opened the door and ushered Sarah inside. A small bell tinkled overhead to announce their arrival.

There were several chairs in front of the window and Ed sat at a large desk. He rose as they walked in. He was a small man with jet-black hair. He had a neatly trimmed mustache and was dressed in a suit that was probably worth Sarah's salary for a month.

"Good morning," he said in greeting. He nodded at Sarah and then turned his attention to Nick. "Sir," he said as he held out his hand. "I don't believe we've met."

"Nick Cain," Nick replied, and the two men shook hands. "And I assume you know Officer Beauregard."

"Yes," Ed said with a nod to her. "Please, have a seat," Ed said, and gestured to the chairs right in front of his desk.

Sarah and Nick sat and Ed returned to his seat. "Now, what can I do for the two of you this morning?" Ed asked.

"We're in the process of investigating the murders of four women. In going over the files we noticed that you were present at each of the scenes where the bodies were found. Why were you there, Mr. Martin?" Nick asked bluntly.

Sarah would have sworn that Ed's face momentarily paled. He cleared his throat and leaned forward in his chair. "Mr. Cain, my father has invested heavily in the town of Black Bayou. He's now an elderly man who has health and mobility issues, and so I'm his ears and eyes out here on the streets. I told Chief Gravois that I wanted to be notified of anything that was happening in town."

"You realize your presence there was highly unusual," Nick replied. "You probably contaminated a crime scene just by being there."

"I stayed outside of the perimeter and was only there as an observer," Ed replied.

"It's still highly unusual and definitely not a good idea," Nick replied. "What's your son's name, Mr. Martin?" he asked.

Ed straightened in his chair. "Why? He has nothing to do with any of this. I know he has alibis for all the nights of all the murders."

"All I asked for was his name," Nick replied.

Even Sarah, as much as she was a beginner in all this, recognized that Ed's response had been strange and made her wonder about Ed's son.

"Gus…his name is Gus," Ed said reluctantly.

"Thank you," Nick replied. "We're just trying to keep our records clear. You'll be available should we need to speak with you again?"

"Of course," Ed said.

"We appreciate your time, Mr. Martin." Nick stood and Sarah did the same.

"I think he should be the first name on our suspect list," Sarah said the minute they got back in the car.

"He and his son," Nick replied as he started the engine.

"He definitely protested too much when you simply asked for his son's name. Is Daddy showing up at the scenes to make sure there is no evidence that might point to sonny boy's guilt?"

"Makes you wonder, right?" he replied. "Gus Martin is definitely somebody we need to speak to, and not with his father present. If he's over the age of eighteen then we can interview him without Daddy. Now, let's head on over to the motel and see what we can learn from Zeke Maloney. I know where the motel is. I passed it on the way into town."

"Okay, then navigation is officially off," she replied lightly.

They drove in silence for a couple of minutes. "Is there a big drug problem around here?" he asked, breaking the silence.

"Are there some people using here, yes. Is there a big drug problem here, definitely not," she replied.

"Have you ever wanted to try anything?" There was genuine curiosity in his question.

"Never." She hesitated a moment and then continued, "If I was ever going to use, it would have been in the weeks after my parents were killed. I was so grief-stricken in that time I could understand the need…the utter desire to numb the excruciating pain, but even then, I wanted nothing to do with drugs."

"How and when were your parents killed?"

"I had just turned twenty-one when they were killed in a head-on crash by a drunk driver," she replied. She was vaguely surprised that even after all this time, thoughts of her parents still brought up an edge of deep grief in her.

"I'm so sorry for your loss," he replied with a kindness in his tone that made her believe him.

"What about you? Have you ever used?"

"No, never had the desire to screw up my career, although there were several people on the force who I knew used."

It was as if the ice had been broken between them and any brusqueness that had been in his voice earlier was now gone.

"Were you close to your parents?" he asked.

"Very close. They were my best friends," she replied. "I still miss them very much." Sarah wanted to keep the conversation going, but at that time he pulled into the motel parking lot.

"Zeke lives in unit three," she told Nick.

The motel was a place of hopelessness and despair. The outside of the eight-unit structure was a dismal gray, made only worse by the intense weathering of heat and humidity.

There was a lot of history here. Years ago, in unit seven a young prostitute had been murdered in a crime that had shocked the town, especially when it was revealed that a highly respectable businessman had been responsible for the crime after an innocent man from the swamp had spent years in prison for the murder.

Beau Boudreau had returned to Black Bayou after his years in prison and had hooked up with his old girlfriend, Peyton LaCroix. Peyton was a criminal defense lawyer and together they had solved the crime and cleared Beau's name. Peyton was still working as a lawyer and Beau was making a name for himself in home construction and repair. They had rediscovered their love for each other and were now a happy couple.

Nick pulled up in front of unit three and parked. They got out of the car and Nick knocked on the door. "Yo...yeah... coming," a voice yelled out. A moment after that the door flew open to reveal Zeke.

He looked at both of them, then frowned. "Oh...uh... I was expecting somebody else."

Zeke might have been a good-looking man at one time, but now his cheeks were hollow and his teeth were rotten and an air of unhealthiness clung to his slender frame.

"Hi, Zeke, my name is Nick Cain, and this is Officer Beauregard. We were wondering if we could come in and ask you a few questions."

"Questions about what?" Zeke reached up and worried a scab on the side of his face. He dropped his hand to his side and shot a glance over his shoulder.

"We have a few questions about the murders that have occurred. We aren't interested in anything more than that," Nick replied pointedly. Sarah knew he was assuring Zeke that they weren't interested in his drug use…at least not for today.

Zeke stared at Nick for a long moment and then released a deep sigh and opened his door fully. Nick stepped in and Sarah followed right behind him.

The room was steeped in squalor. The blankets and sheets had been torn off the bed, displaying a dirty gray mattress. Used fast-food containers littered the floor and the top of the dresser. Flies sat on the old food wrappers, as if too full to fly.

"I'd invite you to sit, but there's really no place for you to do that," Zeke said. He bounced from one foot to the other. "I don't know what kinds of questions you want to ask because I don't know anything about the murders."

"What were you doing out on the streets on the night of June 23 around two in the morning?" Nick asked.

Zeke frowned and began to pick at his face once again. "I don't really remember that night in particular, but there are lots of nights when I just feel like getting out of this room. I like to wait to go at a time when there aren't any people around to look at me and judge me. So I often walk in the middle of the night, but I had nothing to do with those poor women."

"When you're out walking, do you ever see anyone else out and around?" Sarah asked. She did not intend to be a silent partner, and it was time she assert herself just a little bit.

Once again Zeke frowned. "I've seen Ed Martin a couple of times and Officer Ryan Staub and Chief Gravois out and about once or twice. I've also met up with Dwayne Carter a few times. He's a friend and we just hang out together."

"Is there a reason you hang out with your friend that

late at night?" Nick asked. Sarah knew the reason. Dwayne Carter was the local drug dealer.

"Uh…we're just both night owls, I guess."

"Did you see or hear anything that particular night that might have looked or sounded suspicious?" Sarah asked.

"No, not that I remember."

"Then you had no idea that Marchelle Savoie was dead in the alley next to where you and your friend were hanging out," Nick said.

"God no," Zeke replied. "I didn't find out about her murder until the next day. Look, I'll admit I'm a dope addict. I shoot and snort a lot of stuff, but I'm not a killer." He shook his head. "No way, nohow could I ever kill anyone."

"I think he's a dead end," Nick said minutes later when they were in his car and headed toward the swamp.

"I agree." She cast him a quick glance. "I hope I didn't irritate you by jumping in with some questions."

"Not at all. I want you to feel free to do that with anyone we interview. We're partners, right?" He cast her what appeared to be a genuine, warm smile.

"We are," she agreed. As he focused back on the road, she stared out her side window and again fought the wonderful warmth his smile had evoked inside her.

Nick seemed to have a split personality where she was concerned. One minute he was cool and distant and the next warm and engaged.

When he was warm and engaged, she found herself wanting to be his partner…his best friend and lover. She sat up straighter in her seat as the word…the very thought of *lover* whispered through her head. She hadn't been with anyone since Brent, hadn't even thought about a lover until now.

Nick had been nothing if not professional with her and she had absolutely no reason to believe he was into her in any kind of a sexual way. Still, she swore there was something between them, some snap in the air…a momentary absence of breath and a palpable energy she found very hard to ignore as it enticed and excited her.

She'd be a fool to allow these thoughts any more oxygen in her brain. Nick was here to do a job and not to play cozy with his partner, and it was in Sarah's best interest to remember that.

Chapter Four

Nick tried to keep his attention off Sarah as they drove to Vincent's, where he parked the car. "Do you know where this Gator lives?" he asked once they were out of the car.

"Not specifically, but from what I've been told he's most always around and all we really have to do is go in a little ways and holler for him," she replied.

He looked at her in open amusement. "If we go in there and yell Gator, I hope that isn't a wake-up call to all the alligators in the area."

She laughed, those same musical tones that he found so attractive. He'd tried to keep cool and aloof from her. He was sorry to learn about the tragedy of her parents' deaths. He hadn't wanted to know anything about her personal life. But now he did and despite any notion to the contrary, he found himself wanting to know more about her.

Surely it wouldn't hurt if they became friends as they worked together, he told himself. It was the thought of friends with benefits he didn't want…couldn't entertain.

They walked into the mouth of the marsh with their guns drawn as a precaution. As it had yesterday, his heart beat faster than normal as a wealth of anxiety knotted in his stomach and tightened his chest.

You'll be fine, he told himself. *You're an adult and you have a gun. The swamp can't hurt you.* He said the words over and over again like a mantra. It was his effort to still the irrational fear that pressed so tight against his chest.

They hadn't gone far when they came upon a large dead fallen tree trunk. They stopped there. "Gator Broussard," Sarah yelled in a surprisingly strong voice that sent birds flying from the tops of several nearby trees. They stood still and waited. After several moments had passed, she yelled for him again.

"I'm here, what's the damn fuss all about?" The old man seemed to magically appear from the thicket to their left.

Gator was clad in a pair of jeans held up at his slender waist by a piece of rope. A gray T-shirt stretched across his narrow shoulders. His hair was nearly white and his tanned face was weathered with wrinkles. He also leaned on a cane. But his eyes shone with not only a deep intelligence, but also a sparkling humor.

"Mr. Broussard, I'm Nick Cain." He held out his hand to the old man.

Gator gave it a firm shake. "Well, ain't you the fancy one shaking my hand and all." Gator looked at Sarah. "And look who it is…little Sarah Beauregard all grown up."

"Hi, Gator," Sarah said with a smile.

"Mr. Broussard, we'd like to ask you some questions," Nick said.

"Gator, son. Make it Gator, and what do you want to talk to me about?"

"Is it possible we could go to your house so we can discuss some things with you in private?" Nick asked.

He wanted to go to Gator's place because they were still hunting for the killing grounds. While there was no way he believed a man as old and as thin as Gator had killed those women and transported them into town, they would at least be able to positively exclude his place.

"I suppose I could take you home with me, but I gotta warn you, it ain't company-ready," Gator replied. Without saying another word, he turned and headed up the narrow trail.

Nick gestured for Sarah to go before him, and so she fell in just behind the old man and Nick brought up the rear. Despite the use of the cane, Gator scampered fairly nimbly through the thicket.

As they went deeper in, pools of dark water lined their way and the trail narrowed. Bugs buzzed around Nick's head and a slight edge of claustrophobia and apprehension tightened all the muscles in his entire body. The tree limbs pressed so tight into the trail and the thick underbrush seemed to be reaching out for him.

Suddenly he was five years old again and he was hopelessly lost in the dark and scary swamp. The waters were filled with huge gators that gnashed their jaws in the anticipation of eating him. The Spanish moss clung to his head and tried to blind and suffocate him. He wanted out. God, he needed to get out.

Thank God at that moment a small shanty appeared and snapped him out of his dark memories. He wasn't a little kid anymore and he had important work to do.

A rickety narrow bridge led up to the front door. Gator

raced across it and threw open the door and the two officers followed him inside.

It was a small structure with another single door that Nick assumed was his bathroom. A single cot obviously served as his bed and sofa and a potbellied stove looked dirty with use. There was only one other chair in the room, an old, broken recliner.

"I warned you it wasn't company-ready," Gator said. "Go ahead and have a seat." He gestured them toward the cot and then he sat in the recliner. "I suppose you're here about the murders."

"We are," Nick replied.

"What makes you think I know anything about them?"

"Gator, you know most all of the people who live here in the swamp. You know where they go and what they do. You would know if any of the men here are capable of committing such horrid crimes," Sarah said.

"I told Gravois when he first came around asking questions after the first murder that I didn't think a man from the swamp was the killer and nothing since then has changed my mind. My gut instinct tells me this is the work of somebody from town and my gut instinct rarely steers me wrong." His eyes darkened.

"What?" Nick asked. There seemed to be more that Gator wanted to say. "Gator, is there something else on your mind? Something you want to say?"

Gator frowned. "There is one man here in the swamp… name is James Noman. He lives in a shanty deep in and nobody knows much about him. Word is he's a bit touched in the head and folks steer clear of him."

"Sounds like somebody we should talk to," Nick replied. "Can you tell us how to find his shanty?"

"I don't think I can tell you, but I suppose I could show you," Gator said with a bit of reluctance in his tone.

"Can you show us now?" Sarah asked.

"We would really appreciate it if you could," Nick added.

Gator rose to his feet and she and Nick did the same. Could it be this easy? Was it possible this James Noman was the person they sought?

They left Gator's place and headed down a trail. Once again Gator moved quickly as they navigated over tubers and under branches. More water appeared on either side of them as the trail narrowed.

Nick lost track of time as he focused solely on staying on the trail, which had now nearly disappeared, and the direction that they were going in. The sunlight that had shone through the branches overhead earlier had faded. It was no longer feasible to see through the heavy canopy of leaves.

The air grew much cooler and a cacophony of sound filled his head. Fish jumped and slapped in the waters and strange birdcalls came from the trees.

He had never been this far into the swamp before and there was an air of deep mystery here that had him on edge. This was sheer torture for him. He had to keep reminding himself that he wasn't that lost little kid anymore. He was now an adult…with a gun and a desperate need to solve these murders.

Finally, Gator came to an abrupt stop. He pointed straight ahead where a shanty was almost hidden by the tupelo and cypress trees that surrounded it.

"That's Noman's place." Gator turned to look at them.

"And this is as far as I go." Nick could have sworn there was a touch of fear in the old man's eyes.

"Thanks, Gator. We'll take it from here," Nick said with forced confidence.

Gator stepped aside so she and Nick could go ahead of him. "If you get lost on the way out, just holler for me." He quickly turned and headed back the way they had come. Nick took the lead, with his gun held tight in his hand as they slowly approached the small shanty.

From the outside, the place appeared completely abandoned. There was nothing on the porch and one of the side windows was broken out. The bridge that led to the place was narrow and missing several of its old boards.

"Mr. Noman," Nick yelled when they reached the foot of the bridge. They waited and listened for a response. After several seconds had ticked by, Nick hollered again, but there was still no answer.

"He must not be home," Sarah said. Nick thought he heard a touch of trepidation in her voice. He felt more than a little uneasy as well.

They had no idea what they were getting into here. Gator had mentioned that Noman was touched in the head. What exactly did that mean? Dealing with somebody who had mental issues was always concerning and sometimes dangerous.

"Maybe we should go up and knock on his door," Nick said. And maybe they could get a peek in his windows and see what might be inside.

"Okay," Sarah replied.

He tucked his gun back into his holster to navigate the narrow, hazardous bridge. Once he was on the other side, he pulled his gun once again and watched as Sarah slowly came across.

Once she was by his side, he turned and knocked on the door. "Hello?" he called out. "Is anybody here? Mr. Noman? Are you there?"

There was a thick scent of decay around the small structure that instantly raised the hackles on the back of Nick's neck. It wasn't the smell of vegetation decay, but rather it was the odor of animal or human rot.

"Do you smell that?" Sarah asked softly.

"I do," Nick replied.

He walked up to the door and knocked. All of his muscles tensed. He had no idea what to expect, but the smell alone raised all his red flags.

As a homicide detective, he'd smelled this offensive odor far too many times in the past. So, what was going on around here? What was Noman doing in this isolated shanty?

He knocked once again on the door and still there was no response. "He's either not here or he's not answering." More than anything he wanted to just open up the door, but there were rules about things like that and working with a cop as his partner, he had to abide by the rules. Besides, if this was their killer, he didn't want to do anything that would mess up a prosecution.

Thankfully, at the moment his abject fear of the swamp was usurped by the desire to get some answers.

"So, what do we do now?" Sarah asked.

"I want to get a peek in the windows," Nick replied. He walked around on the narrow porch and reached the broken window. One glance inside showed him nobody was in the place.

There was a cot half-covered in a raggedy, torn quilt and a potbellied stove. Nick stared in shock at the walls, which were covered in bones. Large bones and smaller ones, Nick was unable to identify what kind of bones they were. Were any of them human?

His gaze caught and held on one corner of the room. Blood. Old blood and fresh blood, it spattered the walls and pooled on the floor.

Was this the killing place they'd been looking for?

SARAH AUDIBLY GASPED as she saw the bones and the blood inside the shanty. Without thinking, she tightly grabbed hold of Nick's forearm. "Is…is it possible this is the place where the women were all killed?"

"Anything is possible at this point," he replied. "I'd like to get inside and get a closer look at those bones and the blood."

She withdrew her hand from his arm, deep inside registering the warmth of his skin and the play of taut muscle beneath. "What now?" she asked.

"We head back and see if we can get a search warrant for this place." Frustration was rife in his tone. She had a feeling if she wasn't with him, he would have gone on inside. But that would screw up the prosecution who would want a clean, by-the-book investigation.

They each crossed back over the bridge. "Do you know how to go back or do we need to yell for Gator?" she asked. She certainly had no idea how to get them out of here. She'd been too focused on not falling off the narrow trail and into the gator-infested waters.

"I can get us back," Nick replied. "I paid special attention as to where we were going so I could get us back without Gator's help."

"Thank God," Sarah replied.

There was a sudden loud rustle coming out of the brush next to them. Sarah caught the flash of a slender, bare-chested man darting down the trail in front of them.

"James Noman," she yelled, and took off after him. He jumped over a pool of water and plunged into the thicket on the other side. She hesitated only a moment before leaping over the water, grateful to land on soggy marsh. "James, stop. We just want to talk to you."

She desperately wanted to catch him for questioning. She also desperately wanted to prove herself to Nick. Tree limbs tore at her as she ran by them as fast as she could to keep up with him. She was vaguely aware of Nick following close behind her.

Her heart pounded and her breaths came in deep gasps as she struggled to keep up with the man she knew was James Noman. He zigged and zagged through the brush and Sarah remained on is heels.

"James, please," she gasped out. "We just want to talk to you."

Like a gazelle, he leaped over another large pool of water.

This time she didn't hesitate and jumped after him. She didn't make it to the other side and instead plunged into the shoulder-deep water. She instantly tossed her gun to the trail and then gasped and flailed, momentarily shocked by the unexpected plunge.

Her heart exploded in fear as she thought of all the alligators that might be close to her. She tried to calm herself and then struggled to get out.

It wasn't until Nick offered her a helping hand that she was finally able to get her footing again and get out of the water.

By that time Noman had disappeared. "Damn," she exploded in sheer frustration. She wasn't mad only that they'd lost their suspect, but also by the fact that she now stood before Nick like a drowned rat. So much for impressing him with her prowess.

"We'll try to get him tomorrow," he said. "Let's get you back to the car. I have a towel in my trunk."

"Thanks," she replied, grateful that he took the lead so she could do her walk of utter shame behind him.

She shivered several times from being soaked in swamp water. Damn, why hadn't she judged the jump better? She felt like a total fool in front of the man she had most wanted to impress.

It seemed to take forever for them to finally get back to Nick's car in Vincent's parking lot. He opened his trunk and inside was not only a towel but there were also bottles of water, a box of energy bars and a kit for collecting evidence.

"You look like you're prepared for everything," she said.

"I'd like to tell you I was a Boy Scout in my youth, but the truth is I just like to try to make sure I have what I need to survive should I get stranded somewhere." He handed her the towel.

"Thanks." She ran the fluffy towel over her body, trying to get as dry as possible, and then placed the towel on the passenger seat and got into the car.

He closed the trunk and slid behind the steering wheel. "If you give me directions to your place, I'll take you there so you can change clothes."

"I appreciate it, and I'm really sorry, Nick." She felt so miserable about this. She should have judged the jump before leaping. Now they were having to take time out of their busy day for her stupid mistake.

"Don't beat yourself up about it," he replied. "I appreciate the effort you gave it."

"I'm just glad a gator didn't get me."

"Trust me, I wouldn't have let that happen. I've never lost a partner yet and I don't intend to start with you." He shot her a surprisingly warm smile. "So you're stuck with me."

"I'm surprised you want to be stuck with me," she replied. She released a deep and miserable sigh. "In case you haven't noticed yet, I'm totally inexperienced when it comes to investigations like this. I've been stuck on desk duty and handing out speeding tickets for the last twelve years of my career."

"To be honest, I kind of guessed as much," he said.

"I'll understand if you prefer to ask for another partner. Ryan has certainly indicated he'd like to work with you and Ryan is far more experienced than I am." She half held her breath for his reply.

"Nah, I'm good with you. On a positive note, I think you have really good instincts and besides, this way I can teach you how to conduct a murder investigation the proper way."

She released a dry laugh. "Then that will make me the only person in the department who can investigate properly. Turn left at the next street," she instructed him.

"Got it," he replied.

"All I can smell right now is nasty swamp." She plucked at her wet shirt. "At least I managed to keep my gun out of the water, but I hope your car doesn't smell bad once I get out of it."

He laughed. "That's the last thing I'm worried about."

A shiver raced up her spine. This time it wasn't from her damp clothes but rather because of the deep, delicious sound of his laughter.

"Make a right here," she said. For the second time, she felt like the ice had truly been broken between them. If all it took for him to share a laugh with her was for her to jump in the swamp, then she'd do it every day.

"My house is the fourth one on the left," she said.

He pulled up in her driveway. "Nice place," he observed.

She looked at the house that sported gray paint and black trim. The lawn was neatly trimmed and two wicker chairs sat on her front porch with bright red cushions. "Thanks. Are you waiting for me? My car is at the station."

"Sure, I'll wait," he agreed.

She turned in her seat to look at him. "Please, Nick, come on inside. I don't want you having to sit out here in the car when my sofa is pretty comfortable." She opened the car door, relieved when he opened his as well.

Together they approached the front door. She unlocked it and then gestured him inside. Nick was the first man to be in her house since her breakup with her fiancé. But he wasn't here for a visit, she reminded herself. He was here because of her own stupidity. God, she felt so dumb.

"Please, make yourself at home and I'll be out as quick as I can," she said, and then headed for her bedroom. Once there she stripped off her wet clothes and started the shower.

Within minutes she stood beneath the warm spray and

washed all the swamp off her, chasing the nasty smell away with her fresh-scented soap.

She was still confused about her feelings toward Nick. The more they spent time together, the stronger her physical attraction to him grew. Even when he'd grabbed her hand to pull her out of the water, an electric current of pleasure had raced through her at his touch.

Still, it was thoughts of Nick waiting for her that made her not dawdle. She got out of the shower, dressed in a clean uniform and then took a couple of minutes to blow-dry her hair. She spritzed on her favorite perfume and then left her bathroom.

When she returned to the living room Nick stood in front of her wall of photographs. There were pictures of her with her parents and her with Gravois. She also had photos of herself with two of her girlfriends, girlfriends she'd neglected for the past couple of weeks.

He turned when she came in the room and offered her a smile. "I'm assuming these are your parents," he said, and pointed to a picture that had been taken when she was twelve years old.

"You'd be assuming correctly," she replied. She stepped up next to him. "Are your parents still alive?"

"They are," he replied. "When I'm back home my mother insists I have dinner with them at least once a week."

"That's nice. And what about siblings? Do you have any?"

"I have a sister who is two years older than me and a brother who is two years younger," he replied.

"And are you all close?"

"We are," he replied. "What about you? Any siblings?"

"No, I've got no family." A hunger filled her, the hunger

that had been with her for a long time. It was the desire to have somebody in her life in a family kind of way. But at this point in her life, she wasn't really looking for anybody.

She'd thought she had found that with Brent, but that had ended up being nothing but a heartache and now she was reluctant to ever try romance again.

"There are days I'd gladly share my brother with you," Nick said with a touch of humor in his tone. "He teases me unmercifully and is a real pain."

She laughed. "I'd like to see that. Shall we go?"

"Yeah, I just realized it's almost six, which means I'm too late for dinner at Nene's place. I was wondering if you'd like to go to the café for a quick dinner. We can talk about things while we eat."

"Yeah, okay," she replied. She hadn't realized how late it had become and she was definitely surprised by his offer. It was nothing more than a business dinner, she told herself as she followed him back out to the car.

So why did she wish that it was something different? Why did she wish it was a real date?

Chapter Five

Once again Nick found himself fighting off a simmering desire for his partner. It had begun again the moment he had pulled her out of the water. Her wet uniform had clung to her body and shown off all her curves.

It wasn't just that. It had also been how quickly she'd responded to seeing the man on the trail and her bravery in taking the leap that had landed her in the water.

It had also broken his heart more than a little bit for her when he'd heard the haunting loneliness in her voice when she'd spoken of having no family at all. At that moment all he'd wanted to do was draw her into his arms and hold her tight.

Now in the small confines of his car, it was her scent that drove him half-dizzy with the desire to pull her close to him and taste the sweetness of her lips.

Jeez, what in the hell was wrong with him? He hadn't felt drawn to a woman in the last three years. Why now and for God's sake why her? Somehow, he was definitely going to have to try to keep himself in check.

"Have you eaten at the café before?" she asked.

"No, not yet. Is the food good there?"

"I think it's excellent," she replied. "How is Nene's food?"

"Very good. She'd an amazing cook. Do you cook or do you eat out a lot?" he asked.

"I rarely eat out. I like to cook, although there are nights when I'm too tired and I just throw something in the microwave. What about you?"

"Other than eating with my family one night a week, I cook for myself. My mom made sure all of us kids knew how to cook when we were teenagers."

"Smart woman," she replied.

"She told us it was a life skill that we all needed to know to survive on our own."

By that time, he had pulled into the parking space behind the café. He cut the engine and then the two of them got out of the car.

"Nice evening," he observed as they walked around to the front door of the place. The temperature was pleasant and the skies were clear with the sun slowly drifting down in the sky.

"It's beautiful out," she agreed.

He opened the front door and ushered her in before him. Once inside he looked around with interest. It was the usual setup for a café with booths along the two outer walls and a row of tables down the middle.

The walls were painted yellow, but two of them held what appeared to be really nice hand-painted murals. One was of Main Street and the other was of cypress trees dripping with Spanish moss.

The scents inside were positively wonderful. They were of simmering meats and savory sauces. There was also a sweetness in the air that made him think the desserts here might be terrific.

He was vaguely surprised by how many people were dining on a Thursday night, definitely a testament to how good the food must be. He spied an empty booth near the back and guided her there.

"Is this okay with you?" he asked.

"It's fine with me," she replied, and slid into the seat. He slid in across from her and picked up one of the menus that were propped up between the tall salt and pepper shakers.

It didn't take long for a waitress wearing the name tag of Heidi to come to wait on them. "Can I start you two off with something to drink?" she asked.

"I'll take a sweet tea," Sarah said.

"Make that two," he added.

"Are we ready to order some food? Or do we need more time?" Heidi asked.

"I'm ready to order. I'll have the bacon burger with fries," Sarah said as she placed the menu back in place.

"And I'll have the shrimp platter," he said.

"Okay, let me get those orders into the kitchen and I'll be back with your drinks."

As she moved away from their booth, he put his menu back in place and then leaned back in the seat. "Let's talk about today," he said. He needed this to be a business dinner, otherwise it would feel too much like a date and the last thing he wanted to do was to date his partner.

"Where do you want to start?" Sarah leaned forward, her beautiful blue eyes filled with that hunger to learn, a look he found incredibly sexy.

"Let's start with Zeke. Even though it's obvious the man

has a bad drug issue, that's one reason why I'm reluctant to pull him off the suspect list," he said.

"Who knows what kind of drug-induced delusions he might suffer and what might he do when in those delusions?"

"Exactly," he replied. He liked that she always seemed to know what was in his mind. "In my gut do I believe he's our guy? No, but I think we need to keep him on our suspect list until we interview him another time."

"I totally agree," she replied.

The conversation paused for a moment as Heidi delivered both their drinks and their food. His shrimp platter included both scampi style and fried shrimp. It also had slaw and garlic bread and it all looked and smelled delicious.

"Now let's talk about the elephant in the room," he continued.

"When you drop me off back at the office, I'll type up the paper requesting the search warrant for Noman's place. Hopefully we'll have it by sometime tomorrow afternoon."

"Good. I can't wait to get in there and check out both the bones and the blood. Have there been any missing women reported in the past?" he asked. If any of those bones belonged to women, then those women had to have come from somewhere.

"Not that I've heard about." She took a big bite of her burger. He appreciated the fact that she could eat while they talked about blood and bones. That was another mark of a good cop.

She chewed and then swallowed. "However, that doesn't mean girls haven't disappeared from the swamp and it just hasn't been reported."

He frowned. "I guess I don't have to ask why it wouldn't be reported."

"I'm sure the people from the swamp have lost all belief in the police department," she replied. "They have to recognize that little to nothing was done to investigate the murders of those young women."

For the next two hours they ate and talked about not only these particular crimes, but also some of the cases he had worked on in the past as a homicide detective.

She was an apt listener, stopping him only to ask questions. It was a new experience for him to talk with somebody who was actually interested in what he was saying. Amy had never wanted to hear about his work.

"I'll share with you one more story and then I'll shut up," he said as he realized he'd monopolized much of the conversation.

"Please, keep sharing," she replied. "I'm enjoying this and I'm learning so much."

"Let's order some dessert and coffee," he replied. Once he got Heidi's attention, he ordered a piece of caramel apple pie and Sarah got a piece of chocolate cream pie. They both got coffee and then he continued with the last story he intended to share with her.

"When I was a rookie cop, I got involved in a foot chase. We were after a guy who had committed the armed robbery of a convenience store. He'd already tossed his gun away so I knew he was unarmed. I really wanted to be the one to catch him, to prove myself worthy to the rest of the more seasoned officers that were with me."

"I know that feeling well," she replied with a rueful smile. God, she had a beautiful smile.

He took a drink of his coffee and then continued. "Anyway, I was running as fast as I could and he eventually darted into a clothing shop that had an open-air doorway. At least I thought it was completely open-air until I ran face-first into a pane of glass."

"Oh no," she gasped, her eyes wide.

He laughed. "Oh yes. I not only shattered the glass but I also broke my nose and my pride."

She laughed, that beautiful sound that reached in and somehow touched his soul. "I'm so sorry, I don't mean to laugh."

He grinned at her. "It's perfectly okay to laugh."

To his surprise she reached across the table and touched the back of his hand, shooting a rivulet of warmth through him. "Thank you so much for sharing that with me."

She pulled her hand back from his and picked up her fork and he immediately missed the warmth of her touch. As they ate their desserts, they talked about their plans for the next day.

"First thing in the morning we'll go back to the swamp and try to make contact with Noman again," he said.

"And after that?" she asked.

"I'd like to talk to Zeke once again and ask him about alibis for the nights of the murders. I'd like to see if we can either exclude him for sure from the suspect pool or keep him on."

"And maybe we need to catch up with Ed Martin's son and see if he has any alibis for the murders," she added.

"Absolutely," he agreed. "I find Ed Martin's reason for being at the crime scenes very sketchy. If he wants to stay up on what's happening in town, a simple phone call to or from Gravois would have sufficed. He didn't need to be at the scenes."

"I completely agree."

By that time, they had finished their desserts and coffee. "I guess we should get out of here," he said with a bit of reluctance. He'd enjoyed the food, but what he'd really enjoyed was the conversation and just looking at her across the table.

He motioned to Heidi for their bill. Sarah insisted she pay her own way and although he would have been perfectly fine to pay for them both, they wound up splitting the tab.

Night had completely fallen and the moon was nearly full in the sky. Now that they were out of the restaurant, he could smell the sweet flowering scent of her again. It tightened the muscles in his stomach, pulling forth a desire he desperately fought against.

She smiled up at him. "I hate to say this, but talking about murder sure gave me a big appetite."

He laughed. "That just means you're a good cop."

Her smile faltered as she held his gaze intently. "I'm not a good cop yet, but I'm definitely determined to become one."

They got into his car and he headed toward the police station where hers was parked. "I'm going to sleep good tonight," she said. "My tummy is so full, it's the end of the day and I'll definitely sleep well."

"That makes two of us," he agreed.

"My car is in the back parking lot," she said as he approached the station.

He pulled around back and her car was one of three in the dark lot. "I'm just going to head inside and get that paperwork done for our search warrant," she said as she unbuckled her seat belt.

"Do you need any help with that?" he asked.

"No, I think I've got it." She got out of the car and he did as well.

"I'll walk you to the door," he said, unsure what motivated him to do so.

"Okay," she agreed. "So, what time do we start in the morning?"

"Why don't we keep it at seven thirty," he said.

They reached the back door and she turned to face him. The moonlight caressed her pretty features. As she smiled up at him all he could think about was kissing her. Her lush lips seemed to call to his and he leaned forward.

It was only when he saw her eyes widen slightly that he snapped back in place, horrified by what he had been about to do. "Good night, partner. I'll see you in the morning." He turned quickly on his heels and walked back to his car.

SARAH WENT THROUGH the back door, her heart beating wildly in her chest. Had he been about to kiss her? She could swear she saw a flicker of desire in his eyes as he'd leaned toward her.

In that brief moment in time, she'd so wanted him to kiss her. She'd wanted to feel his lips against her own. She'd wanted him to pull her against his body and hold her tightly against him.

She headed to their workroom where her computer sat at the desk waiting for her. She had decided that morning to start bringing her computer with her each day, anticipating the time when something like a search warrant would come up. She'd also been keeping notes on it about the investigation.

She logged into her official account and searched to find the appropriate form. Once she found it, she began the process of filling it out.

Thankfully, about a year ago the department had paid to get things streamlined and online for the officers. Normally a search warrant would not be considered by a judge if it was without a senior officer on the application. However, she added Nick's name to the request and hoped Judge Harry Epstein would grant it.

She emailed the form to the judge and then closed down her computer and packed it up to carry home. Hopefully, they would hear something back on the warrant by tomorrow afternoon.

Minutes later as she walked back to her car, she thought about the evening that had just passed. There had been moments when it hadn't felt like a business dinner at all, but rather like a date.

She had loved hearing about his past cases and it had been especially kind of him to share the story of him running into the door and breaking his nose. She knew he'd told it to her in an effort to make her feel better about landing in the swamp waters.

She definitely was developing a mad crush on her partner and she couldn't stop thinking about that single breathless moment when she'd believed he was going to kiss her.

Did he feel it, too? That snap of electricity? That surge of warmth in the room whenever they were together? Had the desire she thought she'd seen in his eyes tonight just been a trick of the moonlight or had it been real? Only time would tell.

She got home, changed into her nightgown and immediately got into bed. She was utterly exhausted and almost instantly she fell asleep.

Her phone woke her, playing the rousing music of a popular song. She fumbled on her nightstand to find it and when she did, she saw that it was Nick calling her.

"What's up?" she asked, noticing that it was just after two. A knot formed in her chest. This could only be bad.

"We've got another one," he said curtly.

"Where?"

"She's in the alley behind Madeline's Hair and Nail Spa."

"I'll be right there," she replied. She hung up the phone and shot into action. She dressed quickly and ran a fast brush through her hair, then grabbed her car keys and headed out.

Damn, she'd hoped there wouldn't be another victim, that she and Nick would be able to capture the killer before a fifth woman was murdered.

The only thing she could hope for at this time was with Nick on the job he would find some clues that had been lacking in all the other murders. They needed something to go on, some clue they could run with.

Night still clung to the skies. At least the moon overhead shot down a silvery light that cut through the darkness.

The streets were deserted until she reached the beauty shop. Parked out front was Nick's car, Gravois's vehicle, another patrol car and several other cars she didn't recognize.

She pulled in next to Nick's car and parked, her heart racing with adrenaline. She walked down the side of the shop and turned into the alley.

Several bright lights had been set up and shone on the body and the surrounding area. She nodded to both Nick and Gravois and then gazed down at the victim. Seeing the women in crime scene photos was much different from seeing one of the victims in person.

Her stomach clenched and she fought against nausea as she saw the poor victim. Even though she wore jeans and a bright yellow blouse, it was obvious she'd been stabbed several times in the stomach, but it was her throat and face that sickened Sarah.

The victim's throat was ripped out and her face was shredded beyond recognition. It was gruesome and horrifying to think that another human being could be responsible for this kind of monstrosity.

"We're just waiting for the coroner," Nick said.

She nodded. They couldn't begin their work until after the coroner arrived and examined the body and the conditions. They all turned at the sound of footsteps approaching. Ed Martin came around the corner.

"Gentlemen… Sarah," he said in greeting.

"I thought you understood it was inappropriate for you to be at a crime scene," Nick said, his anger rife in his tone.

"Gravois called me to let me know another murder had occurred and as a businessman in this town I…"

"I don't give a damn who you are, and what I think is it's damned suspicious of you to show up here," Nick replied.

"Suspicious? Do you really think I have something to do with these murders?" Ed asked incredulously.

"Gentlemen, please stop," Gravois said firmly. "Now isn't the time for any arguments."

"Who called this in?" Sarah asked, hoping to further diffuse the situation.

"Zeke did. Apparently, he and his dopehead friend Dwayne Carter decided to come back here and party, but they found her instead," Gravois said. "I've got Zeke locked up in the back of my car and Dwayne is locked up in the back of Brubaker's car. I'm holding them both for questioning."

"Do we know who she is?" Sarah asked.

"Not yet. Hopefully somebody will come forward to help us with an identification," Gravois replied. "We'll take her fingerprints but if she isn't in the system then that won't help us." Gravois then began to take the crime scene photos.

He had just finished up when the coroner, Dr. Douglas Cartwright, arrived with his assistant, Jimmy Leyton. They all remained silent and let Old Man Cartwright do his work.

Cartwright had been the coroner for as long as Sarah remembered. He had to be in his late seventies or early eighties by now, but she'd never heard of him being interested in retiring.

He immediately took the body's temperature and then bagged her hands. Hopefully she'd fought back and gotten some skin from the attacker beneath her fingernails. They could only get so lucky.

She glanced at Nick, who appeared laser-focused on what was going on. Since this was the first murder scene she'd ever been at, she also watched everything that was being done with apt interest.

She so hoped that with this one they could get a good, solid clue as to who the Honey Island Swamp Monster murderer was. So far, their investigation had been just flying by the seat of their pants. Although James Noman was very high on the suspect list, if the blood and bones in his place turned out to be animal, then they would be back to square one. At least if this woman had to die then Sarah hoped her death yielded the clue that broke the case wide open.

Cartwright finally finished and stood up straight. "Jimmy, go get the gurney," he said to his assistant. "Needless to say, I'm ruling this as a homicide," he said. "Manner of death appears to be knife wounds to the stomach. I'd say she's been dead no longer than two hours. I'll know more after conducting the autopsy."

"Can Officer Beauregard and I be at the autopsy?" Nick asked.

"Of course. However, I don't like to put things off so as soon as you are finished up here, come on to the morgue and we'll immediately do the autopsy," Cartwright replied.

Minutes later the body had been taken away and that was when the real police work began. Ryan Staub was called in by Gravois and when he arrived, he went to interview Zeke and Wayne while the other three of them began processing the scene.

They gathered up anything and everything that had been beneath and around the body. Nick walked between the buildings, hoping to find something on the path the body had been carried in. However, to Sarah's eyes, nothing they collected had anything to do with the murder or murderer. It was mostly just trash.

Almost three hours later they pulled into the morgue's parking lot. The morgue was housed in a small building next to the Black Bayou hospital.

As Sarah got out of her car, a nervous anxiety played in the pit of her stomach. It had been difficult enough to see the Jane Doe dead in person. The autopsy would test her emotional strength in a way she knew it had never been tested before.

Nick joined her at the front of the car. "Are you ready for this?"

"I'm not sure," she replied honestly. "The last time I was here it was to identify the bodies of my parents."

"Oh, Sarah. I'm so sorry," he said. He took a step closer to her and for a brief moment she thought he was going to wrap his arms around her, but he stopped just short of her. "If you want to skip out on this, then I wouldn't have a problem with it."

She smiled up at him. "Thanks, Nick. But I need to do this. I need the experience and I need to hear what her body might tell us."

"Autopsies are pretty brutal. If you need to bow out at any time while it's going on, don't feel bad about it."

She offered him another smile. "I'll keep that in mind."

Together they entered the building where there was a small reception area with a half a dozen chairs.

A woman Sarah didn't recognize greeted them from behind the window. "Dr. Cartwright is waiting for you. Head straight down the hallway and he's in the last room on the right." She buzzed open the door and Nick and Sarah walked through.

The air was much cooler inside. Sarah fought against a shiver, and she didn't know if it was due to the temperature change or for what was to come. She was definitely dreading this.

They passed two doorways and then came to the last one. Nick knocked on the closed door and Cartwright opened the door to allow them inside. This room also had a small reception room with several chairs, a viewing window and an inner door she knew led into the actual autopsy area.

He handed each of them a plastic suit, a hairnet, and booties and gloves to put on. Once they were all suited up, they went into the room where their Jane Doe was on a steel table. She was covered in a sheet with only her ravaged face showing.

"I would estimate our victim to be between twenty and twenty-five years in age. She weighs one hundred and twenty-seven pounds and is five feet three inches tall," he said.

He took off the sheet that had covered the body, which was now naked. "And now we'll begin."

It was a difficult thing to watch, from the first cut to the last. The room filled with the smell of death and several times Sarah was tempted to bow out.

But she didn't. Cartwright talked into a recorder as he worked, memorializing the surgical process. He finished up with the body, finding a total of four stab wounds in the stomach and an injection site in her arm.

"Her last meal consisted of fish," he said.

"Which she probably ate at home or with friends in the swamp," Nick said.

Dr. Cartwright finally moved to her mouth where he discovered a small piece of blue fabric caught in her bottom teeth. He shut off the recorder as he removed the item and placed it on a sterile table next to him.

"Ladies and gentlemen, we have our first solid clue. It appears she tore this from her attacker's clothes," he said.

Nick moved closer to the table and stared down at the small piece of fabric and then gazed up at her. "We'll have to get it tested, but at first look, it appears that it might have come off a police officer's uniform shirt."

A chill raced up her spine. Was it possible one of the men she worked with, a man who had taken an oath to protect and serve the people of Black Bayou, was the Honey Island Swamp Monster murderer?

Chapter Six

"I bet the tox screen will come back the same as the others with a high dose of Xanax in her system," Nick said.

"I would hazard a guess that you're right. It's obvious that's how the killer is knocking them out and then carrying them out of the swamp and to the place where he kills them," Cartwright replied.

"Still, I'm really pleased about that little piece of material. At least she got a bite out of him," Nick said. "And we got a nice clue to follow up on."

"Too bad she didn't get any of his skin along with the material," Sarah said.

Nick looked at his partner. He'd seen the play of emotions on her face during the autopsy and there had been several times when he'd thought she was on the verge of dipping out. But she'd hung in there and he was proud of her for it. Autopsies were definitely rough. He knew some seasoned cops who couldn't make it through one.

"Let me put this beneath my microscope and I can give you a pretty good idea of the blend." Cartwright picked up the small piece of material with his tweezers and placed it beneath a high-powered microscope. "It looks to be about thirty to thirty-five percent cotton and sixty or sixty-five percent polyester." He looked up at them. "That's just my educated guess. I'll send it off to the lab to get it confirmed."

"Then I guess we're finished here," Nick said.

"I uploaded her fingerprints so you can run them through the system and see if you get a hit for an identification."

"Thanks, Dr. Cartwright," Nick replied. He and Sarah took off their protective clothing. As they stepped out of the building, the sun was rising in the sky and painted everything with a soft gold glow.

He heard Sarah's audible sigh of relief. "Are you okay?" he asked.

She flashed that brilliant smile of hers. "I'm fine now that it's over."

"Can I ask you a favor?"

"Sure," she replied.

"Do you mind if I take a look at your shirt label?"

"I don't mind at all." She stepped in front of him, so close he could feel her body heat. The sunlight sparked in her hair and that wonderful floral scent surrounded him.

He was going to have to touch the back of her neck. This was part of the investigation, he told himself. Still, he was reluctant to do this because there was a part of him that wanted to see if her skin was as soft as it looked.

"Nick?"

He realized he'd been standing behind her and doing nothing for too long a time. "Yeah, I'm here," he said and then gently pulled her collar out toward him. He couldn't help that his fingers brushed the skin of her neck.

He quickly looked at the label and then tucked it back in. She turned to gaze at him and her cheeks appeared slightly flushed. "What is it? I've never paid any attention to it before."

He stepped back from her. "It's sixty-five percent polyester and thirty-five percent cotton." Was it really possible a cop was responsible for the murders? Nick wasn't sure what to believe at this point. Noman was still at the top of the suspect list, but this little blue piece of material presented a whole new suspect pool to think about.

"How are you feeling?" he asked. It had already been a long night.

"Energized. Once we get an identification, we'll have a lot more people to interview and hopefully soon we'll have that search warrant in hand." She hesitated a moment and then looked at him somberly. "Nick, surely other people besides police officers wear shirts with the same material makeup."

"Sure," he agreed. "Why don't we head back to the office and see where we need to go from here."

She got into her car and he did the same. There was a sense of urgency inside him, but without an identification of the victim, he couldn't interview her parents or friends.

He was definitely intrigued by the tiny blue piece of fabric that had been found in her teeth. He'd told Sarah that the material could have come from anyone, but he thought it was very possible it had come from an officer's shirt.

How dicey was this going to be? And how dicey was it that he felt such an incredible draw toward his partner? He pulled into the parking lot behind the police station and Sarah parked next to him.

Together they got out of their cars and headed to the

door. "I suggest we both get a tall cup of coffee to fuel us for what's probably going to be a very long day," he said.

"At least at this time of the morning the coffee might be decent," she replied.

They went inside and directly to the small break room. Inside the room was a vending machine holding sodas and snacks, a round table, and a small table holding a coffee maker. Thankfully the coffee carafe was nearly full and the brew smelled nice and fresh.

They each grabbed one of the foam cups provided and once they had their drinks they headed to their little room. As Sarah took a seat, he set his coffee down and then went to the whiteboard, where he added Jane Doe to their list of victims.

"We need to get Staub's and Brubaker's interviews of Zeke and Dwayne," he said.

"Their reports should be done now and they should be at their desks." She got up. "I'll go get them."

She stepped out of the room and he drew a deep breath and stared at the whiteboard. So much carnage done by a man…no, it was definitely a monster. It would take a monster to do what had been done to those women.

How did he move so well under the radar? How could he commit these murders and not leave anything of himself behind? Most serial killers began to make mistakes, but not this guy. Five dead and the killer didn't appear to be getting sloppy or disorganized. He had to be incredibly intelligent.

But somehow the latest victim had gotten a bite of a shirt. He hoped like hell that little blue piece of material led them to the killer.

"Sorry it took so long," Sarah said as she came back

through the door a few minutes later. "Ryan was still typing up his notes, but I've got them both now."

She laid the papers on the table and he sat to go over them. She moved her chair closer to him so she could review them with him.

The interview was much like the one they had conducted with Zeke, and Dwayne's mirrored Zeke's. The two had just been hanging around and had accidentally stumbled on the body.

Nick looked at Sarah in frustration. "I just find it a huge coincidence that these two men have somehow bumbled their way into being around two of the bodies."

"Do you think maybe our killer is two people?" she asked.

Nick considered the question thoughtfully. "No, I believe we're looking for one man. And to be honest, I can't imagine Zeke and Dwayne carrying out these kinds of murders while drugged up or sober. I just don't think they're smart or organized enough."

"I just wonder what they might have seen or heard while they were out on the streets, something that they haven't told us, something they don't even know is important," she replied.

"Who knows," he replied. "All I know for sure is our killer is definitely organized and smart. He's managed to commit these murders without leaving anything behind... no foot or fingerprints...nothing."

"But now we have a little piece of material," she said with obvious hope in her tone.

"She must have fought hard for her life, and now we need to fight just as hard to find this killer for her."

Sarah was silent for several minutes and then released a

deep sigh. She looked toward the room's closed door and then leaned closer to him, so close he could see tiny shards of silver in the depths of her bright blue eyes.

"I keep wondering, who would make those girls feel safe enough to walk out of the swamp with him? And who would have the knowledge to pull off a crime like this and leave absolutely no forensic evidence behind?" Her voice was just a mere whisper.

"A cop," he replied, his voice also a whisper.

"Bingo." She sat back in her chair and her eyes grew dark. "Although I find it very hard to believe that a man I've worked with for years, a man I might have been friends with for years, could be our monster."

"At this point, all we can do is follow the evidence," he replied.

A knock sounded on the door and then it opened. It was Ryan. "Hey, we got a hit on her fingerprints," he said. "Her name is Kristen Ladouix. She was arrested twice for having drug paraphernalia on a public street. I pulled her rap sheet and all the information available on her and printed it off for you." He handed Nick the sheets of paper.

"Thanks, man," Nick replied. Ryan left the room and Nick got up to change the Jane Doe on the whiteboard to Kristen Ladouix.

He returned to his chair and looked at what Ryan had brought him. "She was twenty-four years old and it looks like her parents live here in town. Grab your coffee and let's go."

They stepped back outside where the sun was bright and warm. "Your car or mine?" she asked.

"Mine," he replied.

They took off and headed toward the address given for Kristen's parents. For the next four hours they interviewed not only Kristen's parents but also several of her friends.

They learned that Kristen drifted from house to house in the swamp. She had no boyfriend and she was battling her drug addiction, which meant both Zeke and Dwayne probably knew her.

It was just after five o'clock when they finally called it quits for the day. Given the fact that their day had started at two in the morning, Nick was exhausted and he knew Sarah was, too.

"We'll regroup in the morning," he said as she closed down her computer. "Same place...same time."

"I'll be here," she replied. She smiled at him but her smile wasn't quite as big as usual.

"It's been a long day," he said as they walked out together. He was impressed that she hadn't complained once throughout the day.

"It's been a hell of a long day," she replied. "But at least we're making progress. I'm just sorry we didn't hear anything on our search warrant. I hope Judge Epstein isn't out of town."

"Hopefully we'll hear something on it tomorrow." He walked with her to her car door.

Why was it that every time he told her goodbye, he fought the need to pull her into his arms and kiss her? And why was it she looked at him as if she wanted his kiss? Or was he only imagining that?

There was an awkward silence between them for several moments. "I'll just see you in the morning," she finally said, and quickly slid into her car.

He watched as she drove away and then he got into his car. God, he was exhausted, but that didn't explain his growing feelings for Sarah.

He liked her. He liked her a lot. She was bright and had a sharp sense of humor that matched his own. Even though they were working together, he enjoyed his time spent with her. When they were just resting for a moment their conversations about other things came easily.

Still, he was afraid to make any kind of a move on her because if it all went wrong it could potentially make their working relationship very difficult, and that's the last thing he wanted to happen.

He was so tired he decided to skip dinner and just head straight up to bed. Even then it took him a while to fall asleep as his brain churned with visions of the murder victims, the interviews they had conducted that day and the possibility that the little piece of blue fabric had come from a police officer's uniform.

He must have finally drifted off to sleep, for he awakened suddenly with fight-or-flight adrenaline flooding through his veins. He bolted upright, grabbed his gun from his nightstand and then quickly turned on the lamp.

It illuminated the room in a soft glow. Nothing. There was nobody. There was absolutely nothing in the room to warrant his explosive reaction. He drew in a couple of deep breaths and slowly relaxed. It must have been a dream that had jerked him out of his sleep.

He placed his gun back on his nightstand, turned off the lamp and settled back in. Then he heard it…a strange rattling noise coming from under his bed. In fact, there was more than one rattling sound.

What the hell?

He turned the lamp on once again and then grabbed his phone and turned on the flashlight feature. He bent over and looked beneath his bed. He froze as his blood ran cold.

Snakes...rattlesnakes. They coiled and churned together in a mass of deadliness.

SARAH'S PHONE AWAKENED HER. It was just after two in the morning and as she grabbed the phone, she stifled a groan. Surely there couldn't be another body already.

The caller ID read Brubaker. She frowned. Why would Ian be calling her at this time of the night? "Ian?" she answered.

"Hey, Sarah, I thought you might want to know that I just took a call from your partner. Apparently, he's trapped in his room at Irene's because there's a bunch of rattlesnakes under his bed."

"What?" She bolted upright. Rattlesnakes under his bed? Icy chills rushed through her body. Was she having some sort of a nightmare? How could this even be real?

"Uh... Sarah, are you there?"

"Yeah, thanks, Ian," she replied.

She disconnected quickly and dressed as fast as she could in a pair of jeans and a T-shirt that had a Black Bayou Police Department logo on the front. She buckled on her holster, grabbed her gun and then flew out of her house.

Rattlesnakes under his bed? How on earth had something like that even happened? Had he been bitten? God, if he didn't get the antivenin in time, he could potentially die. What paramedic would be willing to get him out of a room full of poisonous snakes?

Her head spun with all kinds of bad scenarios as fear tightened her chest and made it difficult to breathe. The back of her throat closed off after she released a gasp of fear.

She couldn't lose Nick. The whole town needed him. She needed him. Oh God, who could have done such a heinous thing as to put snakes in his room? How had something like that even been accomplished?

The streets were dark until she turned down the street where Irene Tompkin's house was located. There she saw the swirling red and blue lights of Gravois's vehicle and another patrol car. She pulled up along the curb, as Nick's car and another one was in the driveway.

She jumped out of her car and ran toward the front door, her heart banging an anxious rhythm in her chest. The first person she saw in the entryway was Nick.

He was clad only in a pair of black boxers. Seeing him alive and seemingly okay caused a burst of deep emotion to explode inside her. She ran to him and leaped into his arms, sobs of relief coursing through her.

"Sarah, it's okay," he said softly. "I'm all right."

She looked up at him. "Oh, Nick, I was so scared for you."

She barely got the words out of her mouth when his lips suddenly took hers. It was a fiery kiss that instantly sliced through her fear with steaming desire.

It was as quick as it was hot. He instantly drew back from her. "I'm sorry, Sarah…that…that shouldn't have happened."

"I… I've wanted it to happen," she replied.

At that moment heavy footsteps came down the staircase. Gravois came into view as he walked down to where they stood. He was followed by Colby Shanks. Gravois looked both tired and angry. "Gator bagged five so far and he's got a couple more left to get."

"How did this even happen? H-how on earth did they get in Nick's room?" Sarah asked. This was only one of the many questions she had among others. Gravois looked pointedly at Nick.

She glanced at Nick and tried to focus on what he might say instead of how very hot he looked clad just in his underwear. His body was amazing. His shoulders were so broad and his hips were slim. His arms were well-muscled, as were his long legs. She hadn't even had the time to process the very quick, very good kiss they had just shared.

"I made a very big mistake when I moved into the room," Nick said and a muscle ticked in his jaw. "I didn't check to see if the back door was locked or not. It was a stupid mistake that could have been a deadly error."

He raked a hand through his dark hair. "I didn't think that old fire escape would actually hold anyone, but it must because somebody must have sneaked up those stairs while I was sleeping and put those snakes in my room." His eyes were darker than she'd ever seen them. "Thank God I heard their rattles before I stepped a foot out of bed."

"As soon as I got the call, I sent Officer Lynons to the swamp to get hold of Gator, who is up there now getting all the snakes into a bag," Gravois said. Officer Judd Lynons was a thirty-five-year-old man who had spent the first ten years or so of his life in the swamp.

"Once Gator has all of them wrangled, we'll go in and fingerprint the door and the fire escape. Hopefully we can lift a couple of prints that will give us the identity of who is responsible for this," Gravois said.

"This was attempted murder," Sarah said, once again fighting a chill that tried to race up her spine.

"That's what it appears to be and we'll investigate it as such," Gravois replied. "It was definitely a devious way to try to hurt Nick."

"Where is Nene?" Sarah asked, suddenly thinking about the older woman. She must have been terrified to wake up to the news that there were rattlesnakes in her home.

"She's in the kitchen with Ralph, her other boarder," Nick explained.

"Is she okay?"

"She's surprisingly fine," Nick replied. "She seems to be taking it all very well."

"She's a strong woman," Gravois said.

Gator came down the stairs with Judd following behind him. Gator carried over his shoulder a large burlap bag that writhed with movement. He also had a pair of jeans and a T-shirt which he tossed to Nick. "Thought you might need these," he said.

"Thanks," Nick replied. "So, what was the grand total?" He gestured to the bag.

"Eight big ones," Gator replied. "I'd say somebody doesn't like you too much, Mr. Nick."

"Yeah, I got the message loud and clear," Nick replied. "If you all will excuse me for just a minute, I'll just get dressed."

He walked over to a doorway that she assumed led to a guest bathroom and closed the door behind him. It was a shame for him to cover up his hunky body. And that kiss, it had momentarily taken her breath away. She was just disappointed it hadn't lasted longer. She had a feeling they would definitely need to talk about it later.

"We checked out the entire upstairs, but the snakes were confined to Nick's room," Judd said.

"If Mr. Judd would take me back home now, I'll release these snakes back into the wild," Gator said.

Nick came back into the room, now clad in the jeans and a gray T-shirt. Gravois said, "Judd, go ahead and take Gator home. Shanks and I will go back up there and start processing the scene. Nick, as the victim in all this, you realize you can't be part of the investigation. This is going to take us a while."

"Nick, you want to come to my place to hang out until this is all squared away?" Sarah asked, hoping her invitation sounded casual.

"That's a good idea, Nick. We're still going to be a couple of hours here," Gravois said.

Nick looked at Sarah. "Are you sure you don't mind? You could just go home now and go back to bed."

"I'm far too wired up to go back to sleep and no, I don't mind at all, otherwise I wouldn't have offered," she replied.

Nick frowned. "My car keys are upstairs."

"That's okay. I'll drive you," Sarah replied. She turned to Gravois. "Is there anything else you need from him?"

"Not at this moment, but I'll need to get an official statement from you, Nick," Gravois replied. "But that's something we can get to later. You're free to go now. I'll just check in with both of you sometime tomorrow."

Nick and Sarah left the house. "What in the hell, Nick," she said once they were in her car.

"Imagine my surprise when I heard the rattling beneath the bed and then saw those snakes," he replied.

"I can't imagine any of it. Just thinking about it sends shivers up and down my spine," she said. "I can't imagine who would do something so vile, so cunning as that." Despite the fact that it was the middle of the night, she still smelled the faint scent of his cologne wafting from him.

"My first question to you would be who have you fought with or had a bad time with in town? Who might hold a grudge against you? But I know you haven't had much of a chance to interact with anyone other than in the investigation," she said.

"You've got that right," he replied. "The only thing I can think of off the top of my head is that we've now somehow officially threatened somebody with our investigation."

She pulled into her driveway and parked and then they both got out of the car. They were silent as she unlocked the door and they went inside. "How about a drink?" she asked. "I've got whiskey and rum. I can't think of a better reason to have one than snakes under your bed."

He released a small, tight laugh. "You're right, and I'd love a whiskey and cola." He sank down on the sofa.

"Coming right up." She went into the kitchen and made the drink for him and then one for herself. She carried them both into the living room, set them on the coffee table and then she collapsed onto the sofa next to him.

"So, what do you think has threatened who?" she asked. She definitely wanted to discuss this, but at some point before she took him home, she intended to talk about the explosive kiss they had shared for far too brief a time.

"Really the only thing I can think of is that little piece of blue material threatened somebody."

"But who would know about that except for us?" She watched as he took a drink before replying.

"Gravois would have known," he replied.

"Surely you don't believe he's our monster," she replied in protest. "There's no way I believe he has anything to do with those murders. I know Gravois and there's absolutely no way."

"But he probably told somebody in the department about the evidence we got and I would guess by noon today almost all of the officers in the department knew about it."

It was her turn to take a big gulp of her drink. "Then you really believe one of the officers is our main suspect." Even the warm burn of the whiskey couldn't take away the chill of thinking that one of her workmates was the monster they sought.

"At this point in time I believe it's more possible than not. Got any idea who might like to wrangle snakes in their spare time?"

"I wouldn't have a clue," she replied. "Although Judd Lynons has a little experience in the swamp, I think it has to be somebody who is well acquainted with it." She took another drink and then placed her hand on Nick's knee.

"Oh, Nick, when I think of what might have happened if you'd been unaware and had stepped out of your bed for anything, it makes me sick to my stomach. You could have been bitten dozens of times. You could have died or at the very least become very, very sick."

His hand covered hers. "Trust me, I'm well aware of that."

"How did you manage to get off the bed with the snakes

still in the room?" She tried to fight against the delicious warmth that flooded through her at his touch.

A dry laugh escaped him. "Very carefully. Actually, Gator distracted the creatures under my bed while I made my escape into the hallway. By the way, how did you even know about all this?"

"Ian called me after getting the call from you," she explained. "He thought I might want to know what was happening to my partner."

As they continued to discuss the night's events and the potential suspect pool, they imbibed in another drink and she found herself seated closer to him on the sofa.

She wasn't sure who leaned in first, but suddenly his lips were on hers in a tender kiss that deepened as he dipped his tongue in to taste hers.

The kiss grew less tender and more hungry. His arms pulled her tighter against him. She wrapped hers around his neck, wanting to get closer...closer still to him. She felt as if she'd wanted his kiss for months...for years and now she couldn't get enough of him.

Their tongues battled together and the kiss continued until she was utterly breathless. His lips left hers and instead trailed nipping kisses down the length of her throat.

His hands moved to cup her breasts and she moaned with pleasure. However, her moan seemed to snap whatever had gripped him. He pulled his hands away from her and then he stopped kissing her.

He stared at her with dark eyes that still held a hunger that fired through her blood. "Sarah, I'm so sorry." He swiped a hand through his hair and released a deep sigh. "I... I can't seem to help myself around you."

"Please don't apologize," she replied, her heart still thundering an accelerated beat in her chest.

"It's obvious I have a very strong physical attraction to you…"

"As I have for you," she interjected.

"But, Sarah, we can't do this. We need to maintain a professional relationship."

"Why can't we have both?" She leaned closer to him. "I'm not looking for forever, Nick. I'm aware that once we solve this crime you'll go back to New Orleans. I just want you, Nick, and it won't change the way we work together."

"Sarah, you're killing me here," he whispered softly.

She got to her feet, her heart still beating a chaotic rhythm as warmth suffused her body. "Instead of me taking you home, why don't you let me take you to my bedroom."

She had never been so forward in her entire life, but she had never felt this kind of desire for a man before. It was raw and rich and surely if they made love just once it would get it out of their systems. She held her hand out to him.

Chapter Seven

Nick felt as if he'd been drugged by his desire for her. At some place in the very back of his mind, he knew this was all a bad idea, but kissing Sarah had flooded his veins with the desire for more, for so very much more. Her hand beckoned him to have more and he couldn't deny his own hunger for her.

He slid his hand over hers and stood and allowed her to lead him down the hallway. He followed her past a bedroom that appeared to be a guest room and on the other side was an office. She turned to the left and into her bedroom.

The room smelled of her, the evocative scent that further dizzied his head. The king-size bed was rumpled, with a spread in bright pink and white yanked back to expose pale pink sheets. A silver lamp created a pool of soft light.

It was obvious she had jumped out of bed and run when she'd heard about the snakes in his room. He was sorry she'd been so frightened for him, but right now all he could think about was how much he wanted her.

He immediately drew her back into his arms and captured her lush lips once again with his. She tasted of a little bit of whiskey and a whole lot of hot passion.

He pulled her closer and she molded her small body to his. He loved how she fit so neatly against him...like their bodies had specifically been made for each other.

The kiss continued until they were both breathless. She finally stepped back from him and swept her T-shirt over her head. She wore a plain white bra and he'd never seen anything that looked sexier. Until she took off the bra.

Her breasts were fairly small and absolute perfection. Her nipples were erect and he wanted nothing more than to taste them. His knees weakened and threatened to buckle with the sweet, hot desire that shot through him.

"Are you sure about this, Sarah?" he asked, wanting to give her an out if she needed one. "I want you to be very sure about this."

"I'm completely sure. I want you, Nick," she replied, her voice husky. "I... I feel like I've wanted you for a very long time."

He yanked his shirt over his head, all caution thrown to the wind. They were two intelligent adults. Surely they could enjoy this night together without letting it interfere with their day-to-day working relationship.

This thought erased the last of his worries and instead unleashed the desire he'd had for Sarah since the first day she'd smiled at him.

They finished undressing until she was just in her panties and he was in his boxers. Together they got into the bed and he pulled her back into his arms.

Her bare breasts against his chest felt warm and right as his mouth plied hers with all the fire that burned inside him. She answered him with a fire of her own as her tongue brushed against his and her hands clutched at his back.

As he began to trail kisses down her throat, he slowly rolled her over on her back. His mouth continued down until he captured one of her nipples.

He licked and sucked, loving the sound of her sweet moans. He licked at the first one and then the other. His blood surged inside him and he was fully aroused.

However, he wasn't ready to take her yet. He wanted to pleasure her as much as possible before that happened. His hand slid from her breast down the flat of her stomach and then back and forth across the top of her panties. She arched her hips and moaned in obvious frustration.

Then he slid his fingers over the top of her panties to the place where she wanted him most. She gasped and moved her hips against him and then stopped and wiggled her panties down to her feet. She kicked them off and then he caressed her again.

This time he felt her damp warmth and the rising tension inside her. He teased her at first, dancing his fingers against her in a light flutter, and then he moved his fingers faster and faster. He felt her release as she shuddered against him and cried out his name. Her climax shot his desire for her even higher.

He kicked his boxers off, his need for her now all-consuming. But before he could take her, her hand encircled him. "Ah, Sarah," he groaned as her hand slid up and down the turgid length of him.

He allowed it for only a moment or two and then pushed her hand away and moved between her legs. He hovered above her for only a moment and then moaned with sheer pleasure as he entered her. She wrapped her legs around his back, pulling him deeper inside her.

He locked gazes with her as he began to pump his hips. Her eyes shone with a wild desire. Slowly at first, he slid in and out of her. Her eyes closed as she hissed a soft "yes" and her hands clung to either side of his hips.

His pace increased as the pressure inside him built. Faster and faster, he moved. She had another orgasm and at the same time he climaxed as well.

He finally rolled over to the side of her, his breaths coming in deep gasps that mirrored hers. They remained that way for several long minutes, until their breathing had returned to some semblance of normal.

She placed her hand on his chest and rose up a bit and smiled at him. "That was way better than I'd imagined."

He grinned. "Have you been imagining this for a long time?"

"Only since the very first day you walked into the office," she replied.

"I started imagining this the first time you smiled at me," he confessed. "But you realize this wasn't the right thing for us to do."

"How could something that felt so right be so wrong?" she replied. "Nick, this doesn't have to interfere at all with our working together. We are two rational adults and we can handle this, right?"

Her blue eyes were so appealing and she was so earnest. "I hope so," he finally replied.

"Now, since it's so late, why don't you just spend the rest of your night here."

It felt ridiculous for him to insist she take him home. It was just after four in the morning and neither of them would be any good unless they got some sleep.

"Okay. Why don't we sleep until about noon and then head into the office."

"Sounds good to me. I'll be right back," she replied as she got out of the bed. "Feel free to use the guest bathroom in the hallway before we go to sleep."

As she disappeared into her bathroom and closed the door, he got up and grabbed his boxers from the floor. He went into the bathroom across the hall, cleaned up and put his boxers back on.

He stared at his reflection in the mirror above the sink. Damn, everything had happened so fast there hadn't been a single thought about birth control. It had been over three years since he'd last had sex. Was that what had made making love to Sarah so amazing? Because it had been utterly amazing.

He sluiced cold water over his face, suddenly exhausted. There was a lot to process…snakes in his room and the possibility that a cop was their killer, but he couldn't think about all that tonight. He definitely couldn't think about the fact that he'd just made love to his partner.

After some sleep he would better be able to handle all the new developments and emotions. He left the bathroom and returned to the bedroom where she was back in the bed and clad in a bright pink spaghetti-strap nightgown. She looked positively charming with the pink of the gown and her hair tousled in disarray.

He slid into the bed and she immediately moved to his side, obviously wanting to cuddle as they fell asleep. He'd almost forgotten that he'd once been a snuggler, too, so he had no problem with her filling his arms.

"Good night, Nick," she said softly, her voice already drowsy with impending sleep.

"Night, Sarah," he replied. The lamp on the nightstand was still on, but it didn't deter either of them from finding sleep.

Nick awakened first. The sun shone bright through the blinds at the bedroom windows, letting him know it was probably time for them both to wake up.

However, he was reluctant to move out of the bed. His body was spooned around hers and she fit neatly against him. She felt small and fragile and he realized even though he hadn't known her for very long, he had developed real, deep feelings for her, feelings that went far beyond their partnership in crime.

But their relationship couldn't go anywhere. He had nothing to offer her for any kind of future. His ex-wife had told him he was a terrible husband, and so he would never try to be a husband again. Why make another woman miserable?

The fact that he was even thinking these thoughts after only one night with Sarah disturbed him. It was definitely time to get up and get to work.

He rolled away from her and she immediately woke. She stretched like a kitten waking up from a nap and offered him a groggy smile. "Good morning...or is it afternoon?"

"It's eleven thirty," he replied as he pulled his T-shirt over his head and then reached for his jeans. At the same time, she slid out of the bed.

"Give me about twenty minutes and I'll be ready to go." She walked over to her closet and grabbed a uniform and then headed to the bathroom.

"I'll be in the living room," he replied. He left her bedroom and sank down on the sofa to wait for her. His head whirled with myriad thoughts that would take time to sort out.

True to her word, about twenty minutes later she walked into the living room, looking and smelling fresh from her shower.

"When we get to my place you can just drop me off and I'll meet you at the station within a half an hour or so," he said as they got in her car.

"Aren't you afraid to go back into that room?" she asked.

"Nah, I have faith that Gator got all the snakes out. Now all we have to do is try to figure out is what snake put them all in my room," he replied darkly.

SARAH SAT IN the small room in the station and stared at the whiteboard. She should be thinking about all the criminal activity that had taken place recently, but all she could think about at the moment was the night she'd shared with Nick.

Making love with him had been magical. He'd been both tender and masterful, taking her to heights of pleasure she'd never known before.

Almost as magical had been falling asleep in his arms. She'd felt so safe in his embrace as she'd drifted off to sleep. His arms had felt big and strong as they'd enfolded her and his familiar scent had enveloped her.

She knew she shouldn't be developing any real feelings for him, but she couldn't rein in her heart. The truth was she was more than half crazy about him.

She admired his professionalism. He challenged her to think deeper, to analyze everything. More than that, he made her feel like a breathless teenager when she was around him. She didn't remember feeling this way about her ex-fiancé and at the time she'd believed she had loved him with all her heart. But things felt different with Nick.

And who had tried to kill him last night? It had been a particularly cunning way to try to commit murder. One step off his bed and he could have been bitten dozens of times.

Again, chills raced up and down her spine at the very thought. Thank God he'd heard the rattles before he'd made a move. Who could have gotten those snakes from the swamp, carried them up that old fire escape and then released them into Nick's room?

She jerked around as the door flew open. She stifled a groan as Ryan walked in. "Good morning, Short-Stuff," he said as he threw himself into the chair next to her.

"What do you want, Ryan?" she asked, unable to keep her irritation out of her voice.

He gave her a hurt expression. "Gee, I never get a chance to talk to you anymore. You and Mr. Hot Stuff are always together."

"We're working," she replied pointedly.

"I think you're doing more than that together. I see the way you look at him. You've got the hots for him."

"Don't be ridiculous. I look at him like he's my partner and my friend." The last thing she would want was for her and Nick to become the subject of office gossip. The last thing she wanted was for anything to undermine her professionalism to her coworkers. Nobody had to know what was going on between her and Nick. It was their private, personal business.

"What have you two come up with so far? You have a suspect in mind?"

"We don't have anyone in particular, but we're definitely narrowing it down," she said, careful to not give anything away.

"I heard you got a nice piece of evidence from the last victim," he replied.

"I guess news travels fast around here," she replied.

"But it's a big deal," he said. "We got nothing from all the other victims. At least you now have something to work with," he said.

"Yeah, we'll just have to see where the evidence takes us," she replied.

Before she could say anything else, the door opened and Nick walked in. Ryan immediately jumped up out of the chair and smiled at Nick. "Hey, man, I was just visiting a little bit with Sarah."

"No problem," Nick replied.

"I just haven't had a chance to talk to her lately. But I'll just get out of here now and let you two do your thing."

He didn't wait for Nick to say anything, as he quickly left the room. Nick sat in the chair opposite her and grinned with amusement. "Anything important come up in your conversation with him?"

She smiled. "There's never anything important in my conversations with him, although he did ask about where we were at in the investigation. I didn't tell him anything other than we were narrowing down on suspects."

As usual, Nick smelled fresh and clean and of the spicy cologne she found so attractive. He was clad in navy slacks and a light blue shirt and as always, her heart beat a little faster at the mere sight of him.

"Uh…before we get down to work, I think we need to talk for a minute about last night."

Her heart seemed to stop beating as she stared at him. "Please don't take it back. Nick, please don't tell me you regret it," she replied softly.

He smiled, that soft smile of his that warmed her heart like a fiery furnace. "How could I take back something that was so wonderful?"

She continued to breathe again. "It was wonderful. So what do we need to talk about?"

"I wanted you to know that it has been years since I've been with anyone, but things happened so fast last night I didn't think about birth control."

"It's also been years for me," she admitted. "And I'm on the pill, so we're safe." It was a slightly awkward conversation and she felt the faint blush that warned her cheeks. She supposed these kinds of conversations happened a lot in the dating world today, although she had to remind herself that they were definitely not dating.

All they'd shared was a very hot night together, one that she'd be eager to repeat again and again. However, the ball was in his court on that issue.

"So, let's talk about last night and what happened in my room," he said. "Let's talk about the fact that I was a damned fool not to check to make sure the back door in my room wasn't locked." He grimaced. "I only looked at it once on the day that I moved in and I guess in my mind once I saw the terrible condition of the fire escape, I dismissed the idea of anyone coming in that way. It was a very stupid mistake on my part."

"Don't beat yourself up, Nick. Who would have guessed

somebody would use those stairs to dump nearly a dozen snakes in your room?" she replied.

"I spoke to Gravois on my way in. They didn't get any prints off the door or the railing," he said. "I didn't think they would. Whoever did this was smart…smart enough not to leave any prints behind."

A tight pressure built up in her chest. "Do you think it was our killer?"

"I believe it was definitely somebody who wanted to take me out of the investigation," he replied, his eyes the color of stormy skies. "So yeah, I think it was our killer."

"Why didn't he just burst in and try to kill you?"

"Probably he didn't because he knew I'd have a gun within my reach," he replied.

She opened up her computer and turned it on. "If we believe a cop is behind this, then maybe I should pull up the schedules for this week, especially for the night of this last murder. At least it will show us who was on duty both that night and last night and we can eliminate them from our suspect pool," she said.

"It's a good place to start," he agreed.

"Wait…there's a notification that I have a message waiting." She clicked on the message and then looked up at him in excitement. "We just got our search warrant for James Noman's place."

"There's a lot of blood in that shanty, and I imagine living in the swamp he would be quite adept at snake-handling, so let's go."

She printed the search warrant off using the printer in the little office area down the hall and then together they took off in Nick's car.

She didn't know how the fabric caught in Jane Doe's teeth might relate to James Noman, but Nick was definitely right about the blood in his shanty and the fact that the man probably knew all about snakes.

Even though solving these murders would mean the end of Nick's time here, more than anything she wanted this vicious killer off the streets and behind bars.

ADRENALINE PUMPED THROUGH Nick as he parked in Vincent's lot. At the moment James Noman was as much a suspect as anyone. He would have access to the women who lived in the swamp, although he had no idea if the man had a vehicle or not to transport the bodies into town.

However, James could probably move like a shadow on the streets, getting in and out of the dump of the women without being seen by anyone, and there was no question in Nick's mind that the man was capable of catching snakes.

In the back of his mind, Nick still held the possibility of the killer being a cop, but right now he had Noman in his sights and he couldn't wait to explore that shanty in greater detail.

He had to stay focused on solving this crime as soon as possible. He needed to get away from Sarah as quickly as possible, before things between them got too deep. He'd already developed feelings for her he'd never expected to happen. The last thing he wanted to do was hurt her in any way.

As always, as they entered the swamp, his heart beat faster and he fought against the dark memories of his childhood trauma that sometimes haunted his dreams in the form of nightmares.

He thought it would get easier, but each time he had to

enter the marshlands, his anxiety went through the ceiling. His throat threatened to close off and his mouth became unusually dry. The last thing he wanted was for Sarah to see his anxiousness. He didn't want her to realize that the big, bad homicide cop was nothing more than a ball of nervous angst.

Even now he was acutely aware of her as they moved through the swamp. Despite the pungent odors surrounding him, he could still smell the scent of her perfume. He imagined he could feel her body heat even though she trailed behind him by several feet.

He clutched his evidence kit harder in an attempt to stay focused on the matter at hand. He intended to take samples of the blood and take photos of all the bones on the walls. He was hoping Dr. Cartwright would be able to give them some quick answers without him having to send it all to a lab where it would take weeks or even months to get results back.

If the blood came back as human, then a lot more would have to be done to process what all was there and he would probably need to call in more officers to help.

As the trail narrowed, he turned around to face his partner. "Are you okay?" She nodded in response.

He turned back around and continued walking, trying to make as little noise was possible as they got closer to Noman's shanty. He'd definitely like to find the man at home and be able to question him.

They finally reached the bridge that led to Noman's shanty. He paused at the foot of it and looked all around. Like last time they'd been here, the place appeared deserted from the outside.

His heart raced fast in his chest. They had no idea if Noman had a gun or not. There was no way to even know if he was inside the structure.

"Mr. Noman," he yelled, and waited for a reply. When there was none, he shouted one more time and then carefully maneuvered over the rickety bridge. Once he was on the other side, he drew his gun and watched as Sarah came across.

When they were together on the porch, he immediately went to the broken window and looked inside. There was nobody there. He holstered his gun and went to the front door. It easily opened and the two of them stepped inside.

The stench inside was horrendous and the place looked just like it had before. He glanced at the old quilt on the cot. It was multicolored and had shades of blue in it. Was that where the blue fabric that had been in Jane Doe's mouth had come from? Perhaps he had wrapped the victim up in the quilt before he'd killed her or as he'd carried her out of the swamp.

"Why don't you take the photos of the bones and I'll get busy taking some blood samples," he said.

"Sounds like a plan," she agreed. "The sooner we get out of here the better as far as I'm concerned. This place definitely creeps me out."

It creeped him out as well. As she began snapping photos, he got busy scraping off blood samples from various places in the large pool of dried blood and storing them in his evidence kit.

They were just about finished when the door flew open and James Noman came inside. "Who are you people and why are you in my home?" he asked, with anger flaring his nostrils and a definite edge in his deep tone.

Nick slowly rose from where he'd been crouched down and Sarah inched closer to his side. James Noman was rail thin with dark hair that spilled down past his shoulders. He wore only a pair of nasty-looking gray shorts and his eyes were dark and wild.

He also brought with him a sick energy that instantly put Nick on edge. "Mr. Noman, I'm Nick Cain and this is my partner, Sarah Beauregard," he replied in a soft, hopefully calming voice. "We're here with a search warrant to take some samples of this blood. We're almost finished here and then we'll leave." Nick attempted to hand him the search warrant, but James waved it away.

"Mr. Noman, can I ask you a few questions?" Sarah asked, and gave him her brightest smile.

He stared at her for a long moment. "You're real pretty. I never get any pretty girls here."

"Thank you, so can I ask you a few things?" Sarah kept her tone light and easy.

He slowly nodded. "Okay. Only you, not him." He pointed to Nick with a frown.

"Is James Noman your real name?" she asked.

He frowned. "I don't know my real name. I picked James and then decided to call myself Noman because I am no man to anyone. I've been alone here for as long as I can remember."

"What happened to your parents?" she asked curiously.

"I don't know. I don't remember them," he replied.

"I'm sorry to hear that, James. So, you've always been alone here?" Her voice held a touch of sympathy. While she continued to ask him questions, Nick returned to collecting the last of the blood samples.

"Why are you here? Why is he doing that?" James asked, a thick tension back in his voice as he divided his gaze between her and Nick.

"Have you heard about the swamp women who have been murdered?" she asked.

He frowned. "No, but nobody ever talks to me. People don't much like me and I don't much like people. I talk to the trees and the plants and the animals and that's all I need."

"What are all these bones?" she asked.

"They're the bones of the animals that I've eaten. I put them on the wall to honor them because they gave their lives for me. Sometimes they talk to me, 'specially in the middle of the night."

"And what do they say to you?" she asked.

A smile curved his lips. It wasn't a pleasant smile. "Nothing you need to know." The smile snapped off his face. "So, why are you here? It's not against the law to kill animals for food."

Nick joined Sarah's side, having gotten what he needed of the blood samples and feeling a definite shift in James's demeanor and energy. "We're finished in here, Mr. Noman, so we'll just leave now."

"Don't come back. Do you hear me? Don't come back here. It ain't right. It ain't right at all to just walk into a man's home and do stuff," he said, suddenly angrily. "You had no right to come in here."

Nick took Sarah's arm to guide her out the door as James's temper seemed to be growing with each minute that passed.

Once they were outside, he had her go over the bridge first and then he quickly followed her.

James stood on his porch, watching them go with narrowed eyes and bunched shoulders. Thank God apparently the man didn't own a gun because Nick wasn't convinced James wouldn't have shot to kill them.

Chapter Eight

The next three days flew by. They continued to interview as many people as possible from any and all the murders. They interviewed family members and friends, all pretty much with the same results.

They'd dropped the blood samples and photos off to Dr. Cartwright, but there had been a deadly car accident on the same day with four dead, so he'd been too busy to get back to them with any results.

It was about seven o'clock in the evening of the third night and they were seated at the table, after having updated their notes.

He leaned back in his chair and released a tired sigh. "You know what I'm thinking about right now?"

She looked up from her computer and smiled at him. As usual that smile of hers tightened all the muscles in his stomach and caused a wave of warmth to sweep over him. "What?" she asked.

"A nice juicy steak and a good, stiff drink."

"Sounds good to me," she replied.

"So, where do two tired cops go to get those things in this town?" he asked.

"The café has a decent steak, but if you want a really good steak and a nice stiff drink, then the place to go is Tremont's."

"Are you up for it?" he asked, and stood.

She immediately jumped up from her chair. "Your car or mine?"

He laughed. "Now that's a woman I don't have to ask twice."

Minutes later they were in his car and headed to the high-end restaurant. "So, are you hungry?" he asked and glanced at her. Even after a ten-hour day, she still looked fresh and pretty.

"I'm starving," she replied.

He focused back on the road, as always fighting his desire for her. Since the last time they'd made love, all he'd been able to think about was being in bed with her once again.

However, he kept telling himself he had to remain strong and not go there again. At least they were spending the rest of this evening out in public because if they were in a private place, he wasn't so sure he could remain so strong.

He pulled up to the sleek-looking restaurant where he had to go around the building to park in the back as the places in front were all full.

He fought the impulse to grab her hand in his as they walked around to the front door. Only then did he touch her and that was by placing his hand on the small of her back as he ushered her inside.

They were greeted by a hostess who led them past a long bar filled with well-dressed drinking men and to a booth toward the back of the busy place. They slid in on either side of the seats with red upholstered bench backs and then the hostess handed each of them a large glossy menu.

"Your server should be with you shortly," she said with a friendly smile and then left their booth.

Both of them immediately began to peruse the menus. "Have you eaten in here often?" he asked.

"Not too often, but occasionally. I can tell you I've never had a bad meal here." She closed the menu and grinned at him. "You made me hungry for a nice, juicy steak."

"Ah, the power of suggestion," he replied with a small laugh. He sobered then. "Before the waitress gets here, let's get one thing straight… I'm paying and I don't want any arguments from you."

"That doesn't mean you aren't going to get one from me." She leaned forward, her eyes sparkling brightly. "We're partners and that means we each pay our own way," she protested.

"But I have an expense account and can ultimately write this off as a business dinner. Besides, Sarah, I really want to pay for your meal tonight. Please let me do that."

She held his gaze for a long moment. "Okay," she finally relented.

"Good, now that we have that settled, we can move on to other topics of conversation." At that moment their waitress appeared at their booth.

There were two sizes of the ribeye steak. He got the big one with mashed potatoes and corn and she ordered the smaller size with a baked potato and corn. He ordered a whiskey and Coke and she got an iced tea.

Once their orders were taken and the waitress had scurried away, Nick leaned back in his seat and gazed at Sarah.

"Tell me why a pretty, intelligent and charming woman like you isn't married or have a boyfriend?"

She blushed and averted her gaze from his. "I came really close to getting married about three years ago."

"So, what happened? Did you get cold feet?"

She looked back at him and released a small, dry laugh. "No. I was all in on it. I was engaged to a man who I adored and we were getting married in three months' time. I was spending all my time planning the wedding. I got us a venue and we went cake-tasting together and I thought he was all in as well."

She let go of a deep sigh. "One night we partied with some friends and he got pretty smashed. I put him to bed and as I took his phone out of his pocket, something told me to look at it. I really didn't expect to find anything bad." Her eyes deepened in hue.

"But you did." He fought the desire to reach out and take her hand in his, if nothing else for support as she spoke of what was an obviously hurtful time.

"Oh, I definitely did. I found a recording he'd made of him and one of my best friends having sex and the date stamp on it was for the night before we'd gone to order flowers for the wedding."

Her eyes suddenly snapped with a fiery anger. "The creep was carrying on a full-blown affair with her while planning to marry me. I wasn't sure who I was angrier with, him or the woman who was supposed to be my friend. Anyway, I kicked them both to the curb. Since then, I haven't really been looking for a man to add to my life."

"I'm so sorry that happened to you," he replied. "You deserved so much better than that."

"Thanks, Nick," she replied.

At that moment the waitress arrived with both their drinks and their food. "What about you?" she asked once they had been served and were alone again. "I could certainly ask the same of you. Why isn't a good-looking, intelligent and charming man like you not married or with a girlfriend?"

"Actually, I was married for four years. It's funny, it was about three years ago that like yours, my life fell apart," he said. "My wife sat me down one night and told me I was a lousy husband. I thought everything was fine and that we were trying to start a family and that night she told me she would never have kids with a worthless man like me."

She held his gaze for a long moment. "I can't imagine this, but were you really a lousy husband?" she asked.

"I didn't think I was, but I know through our four-year marriage I was working a lot of hours. According to what she told me, I guess I didn't see her needs. I wasn't available to her the way I should have been so I guess ultimately, I probably was a lousy husband. That's made me realize I should probably never marry again."

"Have you ever considered that maybe she wasn't as patient with you as she should have been? Did she communicate her needs to you? Did she tell you she was unhappy before that night?"

He appreciated that Sarah seemed to be trying to rehabilitate him, but he knew the truth and the truth was he hadn't been and wasn't now great husband material. "No, she really didn't tell me anything until the day she walked out on me."

In fact, she'd never asked him about his work. When he'd tried to talk with her about it, she'd made it clear she wasn't interested in what he did for a living. When he'd ask her how her day had gone, she'd just say okay and that was it.

"Did she work or was she a stay-at-home housewife?" Sarah reached for the bottle of steak sauce on the table.

"Are you really going to do that?" he asked.

"Do what?" she asked.

"Are you really going to smother the goodness of that steak with that stuff?" he asked teasingly.

She laughed. "Yes, I am. I'm a saucy kind of woman." She shook the sauce out in a large pool next to her steak and then put the bottle back where it belonged. "And you never answered my question about your ex."

"She worked as a teller at a bank."

"You realize there's really nobody outside this business that understands the long hours and the dedication it takes in getting bad guys off the streets," Sarah said.

He cut into his steak and nodded in agreement with her. "So your next boyfriend should be another cop. Ryan seems to have a definite thing for you." He'd noticed Staub sniffing around Sarah whenever he got a chance.

"Bite your tongue. That man would be the last one on earth that I would ever want to date," she replied.

Nick was ridiculously happy to hear that even though he shouldn't be. As they ate, they talked about how difficult it was to maintain a relationship with a cop.

"In a perfect world, people in law enforcement should just marry each other," she said. "Except there's nobody in my cop world that I'd want to marry."

"I don't have a cop world anymore," he replied.

"Do you miss being on the police force?" she asked.

"Sure, from time to time I miss it. I mostly miss the companionship of my cop friends. I've tried to stay in touch with them but it's been difficult. Right now, as I told you before, I can work as little or as much as I want. I pick and choose the cases that I work and I don't have to worry about red tape," he replied.

"Don't you eventually want children?" she asked.

"When I married Amy, I wanted two, hopefully a boy and a girl, but now I just don't think about it. What about you? Do you want children?" he asked.

"In a perfect world, if I was happily married, then yes, I'd like to have two kids," she replied. He heard a slightly wistful tone in her voice.

As they continued to eat, they talked about his work and about where she saw herself once this case was solved.

"I'm hoping to gain some respect once this is all over. We have had some crime problems in the past that I would have loved to work and hopefully now Gravois will let me do more than sitting on a corner giving tickets or working the dispatch desk," she said.

"You're too good a cop to be wasted that way," he replied.

Her eyes sparkled as she smiled at him. "Thanks, that means a lot coming from you."

"Well, I mean it," he replied. She had the intelligence and the natural instincts to be a really good cop. All she needed was a chance to show those traits.

"Tell me this, did anything in your entire life scare you more than realizing there were snakes under your bed?" she asked as they continued to eat.

He felt so comfortable with her now. In fact, he felt far closer with her than he had ever felt with his ex-wife. "Actually, that wasn't the scariest time of my life," he slowly admitted. "I told you before that my mother would often take me with her into the swamp. I guess I was about five or six when she took me with her to a client's shanty."

She leaned forward, her gaze intent on his. There were times when he felt as if when they locked gazes it was as powerful a connection as them making love. Her beautiful eyes drew him in so deeply.

"The adult conversation quickly bored me," he continued. "And all I wanted to do was go outside to play, so when nobody was paying any attention to me, I slipped outside and went exploring. It wasn't long before I was completely lost and absolutely terrified."

He released a dry, humorless laugh and looked away from her. "Suddenly the trees looked like tall monsters and I thought the Spanish moss was trying to eat me. I believed there were gators all around me just waiting to grab me with their big jaws and I was absolutely scared to death."

"Ah, poor baby." She reached across the table and took his hand in hers. He looked at her once again and her eyes widened slightly and she squeezed his hand harder. He was sure she could feel the clamminess that had taken over his skin as he'd confessed this fear.

"Oh, Nick, I'm so sorry you had that experience." She finally released his hand but held his gaze intently. "So how hard was it for you to go back into the swamp for this case?"

Feeling her unwavering support, he decided to be completely truthful. "To be perfectly honest, it's been very difficult every time we've had to go in." He laughed. "So much for the big, bad macho homicide cop, right?"

"You're human, Nick, and you had a bad experience as a child. Those kinds of experiences sometimes shape our adult life. But you should have told me about this before now," she replied.

"Why? So you could hold my hand in the swamp?"

"I would hold your hand anytime you needed me to." Her gaze was so soft and so accepting it squeezed his heart tight with a depth of emotion.

"We'd better eat up now before our food gets too cold," he finally said, and swallowed hard against the emotions she evoked in him.

They small-talked for the remainder of the meal. The steak was great and the sides were just as good. As always, their conversation flowed easily and he found himself wondering what it would be like to be married to her.

It was easy for him to imagine coming home from work to her. She would ask him questions about the job he'd done that day. She'd want to know what case he was working on and he'd want to know all about her day and she'd share it all with him.

It was crazy how easily he could imagine it with Sarah and how difficult it had been with Amy. Would it be so different with somebody who shared his same passion? Who loved what he did for a living?

He checked himself. What in the hell was he doing even thinking about being married to Sarah? They were just partners and that was it. He'd be leaving here as soon as the case was solved and he'd go back to his solitary…slightly lonely life in New Orleans.

"Coffee and dessert?" he asked.

"Coffee for sure. I'm not sure about dessert, I'm pretty full," she replied.

"At least look at the dessert menu," he urged her.

"Chocolate lava cake with ice cream and a river of chocolate syrup," she read aloud. "I'm not only tempted, but I'm going for it and you are a very bad influence on my girlish figure."

He laughed. "Stick with me, woman, and I'll lead you down the path of decadent desserts. And trust me, there is absolutely nothing wrong with your figure."

"Thank you, sir," she replied, and a soft pink filled her cheeks.

He waved for the waitress and ordered the lava cake for her and for himself he got something called the caramel dream, which involved a special spice cake with caramel syrup and butterscotch chips. He got coffee for them both.

Minutes later they had the desserts in front of them. "Hmm, you've got to taste this," he said after taking his first bite. He got a spoonful and held it out toward her.

She leaned forward and took it into her mouth. Just that quickly his desire for her roared back to life. He remembered exactly how her mouth had felt against his and he wanted to taste her again. But the closest he got was when she offered him a spoonful of her lava cake.

An attractive couple appeared by their booth. The man was handsome and well-dressed and the woman with him was absolutely beautiful. "Sarah," he said in greeting.

"Hi, Jackson, hi, Josie," she replied. "Jackson, this is Nick Cain and, Nick, this is Jackson Fortier and his wife, Josie."

The two men shook hands. "We don't intend to interrupt you for long. I just wanted to meet you, Nick, and let you know you have a lot of people supporting your efforts here."

"Thank you, I appreciate that," Nick replied.

"If you find yourself needing anything at all that you

can't get through the department, then feel free to call me and I might be able to help out," Jackson said.

"Again, I appreciate that," Nick said.

"And now we'll just move along and let you enjoy your desserts," Jackson said, and then he and Josie followed the hostess on to their table.

"Jackson is one of the wealthiest men in town and he's a major reason why you are here," Sarah said once the couple was out of ear reach. She then explained to him how Jackson and several of his fellow businessmen had confronted Gravois and demanded he bring in help to solve the murders.

She also shared with him how Jackson, a man from town, had met the lovely Josie from the swamp and the danger Josie had been in when one of Jackson's friends had tried to kill her. Thankfully there had been a happy ending and the bad guy had been arrested.

They were just finishing up their coffee when Nick's phone rang. With a frown he dug it out of his pocket. "It's Dr. Cartwright," he said to Sarah, and then answered the call.

He listened to what the coroner had to tell him, thanked him and then hung up. He gazed at Sarah for a long moment and then released a deep sigh. "All the blood samples from Noman's place came back as animal. There was no human blood and he was able to identify the bones as animal as well."

She frowned as she held his gaze. "So where does that leave us now?"

"With a small piece of blue fabric that is our only clue," he replied.

Her eyes darkened. "And that means our pool of suspects has now narrowed down to the members of the police department."

THE NEXT MORNING Sara arrived early for work. It was a few minutes before seven when she got a cup of coffee and then went to their little workroom.

She set up her computer and then sipped on her coffee. She'd tossed and turned all night as she considered the possibility that one of the men she worked with could be their Honey Island Swamp Monster murderer.

If that wasn't enough it was thoughts of Nick that had kept her from sleep. Even knowing there was no future with him, she found herself falling hard for him.

She'd seen the depth of emotion inside him as he'd talked about being a lousy husband. No matter what had gone down in his marriage, she suspected he'd been hurt deeply.

Even though she hadn't been married to Brent, they'd dated for three years before he'd betrayed her so badly. She'd not only written Brent out of her life, but also her girlfriend Casey, who had decided it was okay to sleep with Sarah's fiancé. But once her anger had left her, the pain of their betrayal had remained with her. So, just like Nick, she'd been hurt by love before.

Then there was his confession about getting lost in the swamp when he was a little boy and the residual effect it had on his adult life.

She'd wanted to find that lost little boy and comfort him. She'd wanted to gather him into her arms and hold him tightly until he was no longer afraid.

She admired him so much for being able to push through

his fear and go into the very heart of the swamp to find a killer. However, it sounded like the next leg of their investigation wouldn't take place in the swamp.

She and Nick had both been through the fires of loss and knowing that had only made her feel closer to him. She had a feeling heartache and betrayal were in her near future. Nick was going to break her heart and if it was true that one of her brothers in the police department was the killer, then she would feel utterly betrayed by that.

She turned as the door opened and was surprised to see Nick, who was also early. "Morning, partner," she said.

He gave her a smile that made her stomach swirl with warmth. "You're an early bird," he said as he set his cup of coffee on the table.

"I had trouble sleeping last night," she replied.

"Yeah, that makes two of us." He sat across from her. "I imagine we both had the same thoughts keeping us awake."

She seriously doubted he'd lost sleep over her. "The few clues we have point to somebody in the department." She kept her voice low.

"We have the fabric and we also have the fact that all of those women would have trusted a cop who approached them in the swamp." His voice was equally low. "How many officers are there in total?"

"Fourteen, plus Gravois."

He nodded. "First of all, from here on out we write nothing down on the whiteboard. We don't need anyone to walk in here and see what kind of internal investigation we're about to start doing."

"Agreed," she replied.

"We'll document everything on your computer and make sure you take your computer home with you every night."

"Again, agreed," she replied. "So, where do we start?" She dreaded this whole process, but was determined to follow through with it. If the monster was hiding in the department, then he needed to be found.

"We need to pull up the schedules for every officer for as long as they go back."

"That's going to take up most of the day," she replied.

"Then let's go ahead and get started."

For the next four hours or so, Sarah printed off the schedules for all the officers in the past two months, which was all that was available to her online. As she finished with each one, Nick stapled them together and began making a chart of who was where during the nights of the last two murders.

It took them two days to narrow down what they could but there was no way they could know what the officers did on their nights off.

She told him everything she knew about her fellow officers, their personalities and temperaments. They both knew their monster was intelligent and still highly organized. He'd made no mistakes until the last victim, who had gotten that piece of material from someplace on him.

She also told Nick about their living spaces. They were still looking for a killing ground, so they needed to know not only where the officers lived but also if they owned any other property in or just out of town.

On the afternoon of the second day, they went into city hall to research who owned what. By the end of that day, they had more lists to go through and check out.

One of the things Sarah had learned while working with

Nick was that a murder investigation wasn't just about chasing a suspect through the swamp or anywhere else. Good police work was also long hours of research and desk time.

So far, they had managed to keep their investigation close to their chests. However, sooner rather than later they were going to have to start interrogating the cops in the department, and that was going to open up a whole new can of worms.

It was just after seven when they knocked off for the day. She packed up her computer, along with all the paperwork that had been generated.

"Tired?" Nick asked as they walked out of the building together.

"Yeah, I am. I'm ready to zap something in the microwave, eat and then drop into bed," she admitted.

"Looks like we could get a downpour," he said. The night was dark and overcast with storm clouds as he walked her to her car. The forecast was for thunderstorms overnight.

"I just hope whatever storms we get don't keep me awake," she replied.

They reached her car and she put her computer and their paperwork in the passenger seat and then straightened back up and turned to him.

There was a simmering tension between them that had only grown with each day that passed. She felt it and she knew he did, too. There were moments when their gazes would lock and she saw his desire for her in the depths of his beautiful gray eyes.

She saw it now, shining with a hunger that burned in her blood, into her very soul. "Nick…" she whispered softly.

"Ah, Sarah, what are you doing to me?" He gathered her into his arms and kissed her.

She molded her body close against his as she wrapped her arms around his neck. Their tongues danced together in a fiery kiss that drove all other thoughts out of her mind.

The kiss went on for several long, wonderful moments and then he stepped away from her. The hunger was still there in his eyes as he pulled her back against his chest.

"Woman, you drive me crazy," he finally said as he stroked his fingers through her hair.

"You drive me just as crazy," she replied softly.

"You know we can't go there again," he finally said, and released his hold on her.

She didn't know that, but she wasn't going to throw herself at him. He was trying to be as professional as possible and she didn't want to take that away from him. But this was so miserably hard because she wanted him again so badly.

It was a few minutes later when she was driving home that she realized she was in love with Nick. The knowledge filled her heart with joy and happiness. After Brent she hadn't thought she would ever love again. She hadn't believed she would ever be capable of falling in love again.

Nick was not only the man she loved, but he had also become her best friend. She felt as if she could talk to him about anything and everything and in fact, they had shared both serious conversation and silly ones that had made them both laugh.

However, her happiness at realizing she was in love with Nick was short-lived. She had no idea how he felt about her. Oh, she knew he was into her sexually, but how did he feel about her aside from their terrific sexual chemistry?

She released a tired sigh as she pulled into her garage. She parked and then grabbed her things from the passenger seat and got out. She entered the house and put her computer and the paperwork at one end of her kitchen table and then she headed directly to the freezer to see what was for supper.

She grabbed a fried chicken dinner and got it working in the microwave. While it cooked, she grabbed a soda and popped it open. She took off her holster and gun and then sank down at the table.

God, she was so exhausted. The late nights were definitely starting to catch up to her. Hopefully a good night's sleep tonight would remedy that.

The microwave dinged, announcing that her dinner was ready. She ate in record time and then headed for the shower. It was only when she was under the spray of warm water that she thought about Nick once again.

She had a feeling that they were getting very close to catching the killer and then Nick would be gone. He'd already told her he had no intention of becoming a husband again. What more did she need to know to realize her relationship with him was doomed?

By the time she got into bed she was too exhausted to think about anything anymore. She allowed her soft mattress to envelop her and almost immediately she was asleep.

She jerked awake and bolted to a sitting position, her heart pounding a million beats a minute. A flash of lightning was followed by another boom of thunder that rent the silence of the night. The thunder must have been what had awakened her. She relaxed and drew in several deep breaths to calm the rapid beat of her heart.

As the lightning shot off again, her heart suddenly

stopped beating as she let out a small gasp. She could swear that a dark figure just darted past her doorway. Had it only been a figment of her imagination, a trick of the light, or was somebody really in her house?

Her heart resumed a frantic rhythm as she slowly slid out of bed. What should she do? Damn, her gun was in the kitchen on top of the table. Should she call for help? Was there really somebody in her house? Who and why?

For a long moment she stood next to the bed, frozen by fear and yet needing to know if she wasn't alone. She grabbed her cell phone and held it tightly in her hand.

Was it possible she was being robbed? She really didn't have anything worth stealing other than her television. She supposed somebody could pawn that for a little bit of extra money.

She didn't care about her television, what she did care about was that somebody was in her home…in her sanctuary. Was the person dangerous? Oh God, what should she do? The last thing she wanted to do was call for help when she didn't need it.

With a deep breath she stepped into the hallway and turned on the light. Another rumble of thunder sounded, adding to her frantic anxiety. There was nobody in the hallway and she also heard nothing.

Maybe it really had been a figment of her imagination. Maybe there had been no dark figure at all. Maybe it had just been a trick of the lightning. She continued down the hallway, looking carefully in each room she passed and turning on all the lights.

Surely if she were being robbed, the lights would scare the person away. She finally stepped into the living room and gasped as a man in dark clothes and a ski mask rushed toward her from the kitchen.

He shoved her so hard she fell back on the floor, crying out with pain as the back of her head and her body made contact with the carpeting.

Before she could get up, the person flew out her front door and disappeared into the night. She finally got to her feet, her head pounding as she sobbed and closed and locked the door.

Who was the man? Oh God, what had just happened? Who was he and why had he been in her house? She'd scarcely gotten a look at him but with the ski mask on there had been no way for her to identify him.

She still didn't feel safe. With tears falling down her cheeks, she hurried into the kitchen to get her gun.

As she flipped on the kitchen light, she gasped once again. Her gun was still on the table, but her computer and the paperwork were gone.

Chapter Nine

Nick stood next to Sarah and fought the need to pull her into his arms. She looked so small and so vulnerable as she watched Gravois and Officers Judd Lynons and Jason Richards check out the broken window in the bedroom that served as her office.

Apparently, that had been how the thief had gotten into the house. The idea of her being in the house all alone while somebody had come in half terrified Nick for her.

It could have all gone so terribly wrong. It was bad enough that the man had shoved her to the floor. Thank God he hadn't shot her, or fought with her. What would have happened if she'd gotten to her feet and had really confronted him?

"I'm not managing to lift any prints from anywhere on the window," Lynons said in frustration after having tried for several minutes.

"I'm sure he was probably wearing gloves," Nick replied.

"Let's move into the kitchen and see if we can get something pulled off the table," Gravois said.

They all congregated in the kitchen and Lynons got to work fingerprinting the table. Once again Nick wanted to draw Sarah into his arms. What chilled him to the bone was he had a feeling that tonight she had shared her house with the Honey Island Swamp Monster murderer.

The killer had obviously decided that their investigation was hitting too close to home and so he'd stolen the very work notes and the computer that might have pointed to him.

It was the only thing that made sense. And whoever the killer was, he must have a deep enough bond with Sarah that he hadn't wanted to really harm her.

There was no question that the loss of the paperwork and the computer would set the investigation back a bit, but at the moment he was more worried about Sarah's well-being.

She was clad in her pink nightgown and a short white robe. Her face was unusually pale and her entire body appeared to tremble. When she'd called him and told him her house had been broken into, he couldn't get to her fast enough. He'd heard the fear in her voice and all he'd wanted to do was get to her as quickly as possible.

Lynons managed to lift a bunch of fingerprints off the table but they all appeared the same and everyone was sure they probably belonged to Sarah. Her fingerprints were on file with the department so it would be easy to check for certain.

The storm overhead had passed and it was after two thirty when everyone finally left. The moment they all stepped out the front door, Nick closed and locked it and then went to Sarah, who stood still as a statue by the coffee table.

He immediately pulled her into his arms, holding her tight as she trembled against his chest. She began to cry softly. "It's okay," he whispered to her. "You're okay now."

She continued to cry for several more minutes and then

with a deep sigh she stepped back from him. She sank down on the sofa and he sat next to her.

"When I realized somebody was in the house with me, I got so scared," she said, her voice trembling a bit. "And then when I saw him and he pushed me, I was in shock. Then I saw the computer and everything was gone and I realized the man who had come into my house was probably the killer."

"Thank God you weren't seriously hurt," he said as he took one of her hands in his. "Thank God, you didn't jump up and run after him." The idea of her being killed shot an iciness through him.

"Now that it's all over I'm also so damned mad." She gazed at him with sad eyes. "He got all of our work product…everything."

"We can generate all that again," he replied.

"Who is this person? And why steal all our things now?"

"The killer was desperate to see exactly what we were doing," he replied. "I think our killer must have seen that you downloaded all the schedules and that scared him. It let him know that all the cops in the department were suspects."

He squeezed her hand. "He wanted our work notes to see if we had narrowed down anything. If it's any consolation at all, he must have a friendship with you and that's what kept you alive tonight."

"That is no consolation at all," she replied, some of the fire back in her eyes. "I want this bastard behind bars and I don't give a damn if I have a friendship with him or not. He's sick and perverted. The way he kills these women make him a monstrosity."

"I've been trying to work up a psychological profile of

the killer and why he would want to basically erase his victim's faces," he said.

"He obviously hates women," she replied.

"True, but the psychology goes much deeper than that. Maybe he's trying to replace somebody and when he gets them to his kill place, he's angry that they don't look like what he wants...what he needs."

"Mommy issues?" she suggested.

"Maybe," he replied. "Now, do you have something I can use to board up that broken window in your office?" He released his hold on her hand and stood.

"There are some old pieces of plywood in the garage. They were there when I bought the house." She also got up from the sofa. "I'll get you a hammer and some nails."

Thirty minutes later the window was boarded up, but he was still reluctant to leave her and he could tell she didn't want him to go.

"Do you want me to stay for the rest of the night with you?" he asked.

"Would you mind?" Her gaze was soft and faintly needy. She'd been through a frightening ordeal and he could understand her not wanting to be alone right now.

"Of course I wouldn't mind," he replied, and smiled at her. "When my partner needs me, I'm there."

"Thank you, Nick."

Fifteen minutes later they were in bed and she snuggled into his arms. As always, the desire she stoked in him rose to the surface but he fought against it. Thankfully, it didn't take her long to fall asleep and he soon followed.

He awoke at some point later. The room was still dark,

and even though he was still half-asleep, Sarah's body moved against his and he was fully aroused.

Clothes disappeared and warm limbs wound around each other. Her small gasps of pleasure whispered in the room. It was as if he were in a dream as they slowly made love. It was a wonderful dream. He felt as if he belonged here with her and then he was sleeping once again.

When he awakened again it was a few minutes after seven. He was spooned around Sarah and they both were naked, letting him know that what he'd thought was a wonderful dream had really been a reality. They had made love once again.

Damn, his body was a traitorous thing. Apparently even in sleep he wanted her and she wanted him. He slowly moved back from her warm sweetness and slid out of the bed. She stirred, but didn't awaken, which he was grateful for. She needed to sleep.

He stood next to the bed for several moments and simply gazed at her in the golden morning light that flowed in through the window.

The illumination shone in her tousled hair, turning it into a soft halo around her head. Her lips were slightly parted, as if just awaiting his kiss. She was so beautiful even in slumber.

He loved her wide-eyed wonder when he taught her something new and he adored her when she laughed over something funny. He loved talking to her about anything and nothing.

With a frown he grabbed his jeans and T-shirt off the floor and left the room. He dressed quickly in the bathroom and then quietly left the house.

As he drove to Nene's place, he realized with a jolt that he was in love with his partner. He didn't know when he'd fallen for her. He didn't know if it had been when she'd landed in the swamp while enthusiastically chasing James Noman, or if it had been when she'd held his hand after he'd shared his childhood trauma with her.

He didn't know when it had happened, but it had. He was crazy in love with Sarah. The thought brought him no happiness. There was still no future for the two of them. He had no intention of seeking a relationship with her once these murders were solved.

What he'd done last night by making love with her once again was give her hope. He had a feeling she was totally into him. The signs had been there with her...the way she looked at him and how she touched him when it wasn't necessary. Yeah, he knew she had deep feelings for him.

However, the worst thing he could do was plan a life with her. He knew what he was and he would never want Sarah to suffer his flaws. She definitely deserved so much better than him.

When he reached Nene's, the older woman met him at the door. "Is Sarah okay?" she immediately asked, her eyes filled with a wealth of concern.

"She's fine," he replied. "News definitely flies fast in this town."

"The gossips were busy this morning. A break-in must be a frightening thing," Nene said. "Poor Sarah, I'm sure she was scared to death."

"She was definitely frightened, but thank God she was unharmed physically," he replied.

"Thank God for that. Snakes in your bedroom and then

a break-in…you've really shaken somebody up." She shook her head.

"I guess we have," he agreed.

She looked at him slyly. "At least Sarah has you by her side, just like in a good romance novel."

"Unfortunately, this isn't a romance novel," he replied.

She released a deep sigh. "Well, I won't keep you any longer. I know how busy you must be but I just wanted to make sure Sarah was okay. She's a lovely woman and has always been very kind to me."

He smiled at her. "Yeah, I'm just on my way upstairs for a quick shower and then I need to head back into the office again."

"I certainly hope you catch this man," she said.

"We will, Nene," he replied firmly.

"There are some blueberry muffins in the kitchen if you want to grab one to take with you," she said. "In fact, take two and give one to Sarah."

"Thanks, I just might want to do that." He headed for the staircase and she went into the kitchen. It took him only minutes to shower and then dress in a clean pair of navy slacks and a navy polo.

On his way out he detoured into the kitchen where Nene wrapped up two of the huge muffins for him to take and then he was on his way back to the office.

He had no idea when to expect Sarah. He hoped she slept as long as she needed, long enough to feel refreshed and ready to go again. They'd both been working long hours with plenty of nighttime interruptions. He was used to this kind of a schedule when working a case, but he knew she wasn't.

Once he reached the station he went into their little office, grabbed a fresh notepad from the filing cabinet and then sank down at the table.

Whoever the thief was that had stolen the computer and paperwork must have believed that it would stymie the investigation for weeks to come. But they hadn't stolen Nick's mind and his memory.

The notes that had been on the computer were still fairly fresh in his mind. He began to make a list of the men on the force that they hadn't been able to alibi with work for the nights of the murders. As he worked, he ate one of the muffins, which was delicious.

He'd written down several names when the door opened and Sarah came in.

"Sorry I'm late, partner," she said, and took the seat opposite him with her usual beautiful smile.

"You aren't late," he replied. "How are you feeling?"

"Rested and ready to get back to work."

He was relieved that apparently they weren't going to talk about their lovemaking in the middle of the night. What was there to say about it? It had happened and it had been wonderful, but it had also been another mistake. He had a feeling she wouldn't want to hear that.

"I've just been sitting here writing down all the names of the officers who we couldn't find an alibi for on the nights of the murders," he explained. "Thankfully a lot of our work is still fresh in my mind."

"Let me see who you have so far." She moved into the chair next to his and pulled it closer to him. With his love for her burning hot in his chest, everything about her nearness right now was sheer torture.

The soft curve of her cheek…the plump lusciousness of her lips and the scent that belonged to her alone…he had a feeling they would all…that she would haunt him for a very long time to come after he left this little town.

She added a few more names to the list he'd made and then pushed the remaining muffin before her. "A gift for you from Nene," he said.

"That was nice of her, but where's yours?"

"Gee, I don't know what happened to it," he said.

She grinned at him. "That story would be much easier to believe if you didn't wear the evidence in the form of muffin crumbles on your chin."

"Busted." He laughed and quickly brushed off his chin.

Their levity didn't last long as he leaned back in his chair. "You know we can't keep this investigation a secret any longer," he said as she ate her muffin.

"I know," she replied solemnly.

"It's time for us to start interrogating some of these officers."

"I'm not looking forward to it. I still can't believe one of the officers I've worked with here is a suspect," she replied, and shoved the last of the muffin away.

He looked at her equally solemnly. "I truly believe in my gut that a cop is not only our suspect, but one of them is definitely the Honey Island Swamp Monster murderer," he replied.

"I THINK BEFORE we go any further, we need to let Gravois know where our investigation has led us," Nick said.

"Should we go to speak to him now?" Sarah asked. She was torn between the dread of finding out who among them was the monster and wanting to get the monster behind bars as soon as possible.

That wasn't the only thing she was torn about since awakening that morning. She and Nick had made love again last night. It had been slow and sleepy and beyond wonderful.

He had to love her just a little bit. He didn't strike her as the kind of guy who would have sex with absolutely no feelings behind it. In one of their many talks he had told her he had been completely faithful in his marriage and she believed that of him.

He was the man she wanted for the rest of her life. She was drawn to so many qualities about him and she could easily imagine marrying him and living happily ever after. They would share their love of crime stories and she would give him babies. It would be perfect...except it wasn't.

"Yeah, let's head down to Gravois's office now," he replied.

As she followed him down the hallway, she knew there would come a time when she would tell him exactly how she felt about him. She couldn't let him leave Black Bayou without him knowing the depths of her love for him. But before that could happen, they had a killer to catch...a killer that at this very moment might be in the building with them.

Nick rapped on Gravois's door and after Gravois called enter, they both did. "We need to speak with you," Nick said somberly.

"Then come in." Gravois gestured them into the chairs in front of his desk. "What's going on? Is there a break in the case?"

"We're getting very close. We believe that the killer is a cop here in the department," Nick said.

Gravois reeled back in his chair with obvious stunned surprise. His features paled and then filled with a ruddy color. He leaned forward and frowned. "Are you absolutely sure about that?"

"As sure as we can be," Sarah replied grimly.

"A cop would easily be able to get those women to come with him out of the swamp. He would also know the best areas in town to dump the bodies, and he'd know about forensics," Nick said.

"And then we have that piece of material which is the same makeup as the officers' shirts," Sarah added.

"All of our other suspects had been cleared, leaving us to believe one of your officers is our killer," Nick said.

"I'll be a son of a bitch," Gravois said. "Do you have a specific suspect in mind?"

"No, not yet," Nick replied.

"So, what do you need from me?" Gravois asked.

"We have a list of officers we'd like to start interrogating," Nick explained. "I'm trained in interrogation and hopefully I'll get a tell from the guilty party along with some evidence."

"We certainly don't expect anyone to confess, but we need to find out who has solid alibis for the nights of the murders and who doesn't," Sarah said.

"I'll make sure all the officers know they are to fully cooperate with you," Gravois replied.

"We appreciate that, but we'd like to start the interviews immediately with the men who are on duty today," Nick replied.

Gravois nodded. "That's fine with me, but please keep

me in the loop. If you get a solid suspect, then dammit, I want to know."

"By all means, we'll definitely keep you in the loop," Nick said as he rose to his feet. Sarah stood as well and minutes later she and Nick were back in their little room.

The first officer they pulled in for an interrogation was Judd Lynons. He hadn't been working on the nights of the murders but he was working today.

Sarah went into the officers' room where Judd sat at a desk eating a candy bar from the vending machine. "Hey, Judd."

"Hey, Sarah." He smiled at her. Judd was in his mid-thirties and was physically fit with broad shoulders and big arms. He was big and strong enough to carry a victim.

"Could you come with me into our office for a few minutes?"

His smile faded into a look of curiosity. "Uh…sure." He took the last bite of his candy bar, crinkled up the wrapper and threw it away and then got up from the desk and followed her down the hallway.

Nick stood as they entered the room and then he gestured Judd into a chair at the table. "What's going on here?" Judd asked in confusion. "Why do you need to talk to me?"

"We're in the process of narrowing down our pool of suspects," Nick said.

Judd looked at Sarah and then at Nick in astonishment. "Am I a suspect?"

"We're going to be talking to all the officers over the next couple of days," Nick said.

Judd's eyes widened. "You think a cop did those murders? Man, that's messed up." He shook his head and settled back in the chair. "If you have questions for me, then ask away. I don't have anything to hide."

"We understand that you grew up for the first ten years of your life in the swamp," Nick said.

And so, the first interrogation began. Judd appeared to be open and honest and provided an alibi for the night of the fourth murder that they could easily check out. According to him, he'd been in Shreveport for a buddy's wedding and he had the hotel records to prove that fact.

If his alibi checked out, then he wasn't their killer. They knew without a doubt that the same man had killed all the women, so if somebody had a solid alibi for one of the murders that exonerated them from being the person they sought.

"If you get a chance later today or tomorrow, please bring us the receipts you have," Nick said to Judd.

"And the names and phone numbers of some of the people who were with you in Shreveport," Sarah added.

"I definitely will," Judd replied. "Does that mean you're finished with me?"

"For now," Nick replied.

A moment later Judd was gone. Sarah frowned as she saw who they next needed to talk to. "Ryan and I grew up together. I can't imagine him doing something like this. He might be a total jerk, but I can't imagine him being our killer."

Nick reached across the table and covered her hand with his. "You knew this was going to be difficult. I'm so sorry, Sarah, that one of these men you've viewed as your friend and coworker is probably a serial killer." He squeezed her hand and then released it. "But at this point in the investigation, it's important to keep an open mind."

She definitely appreciated the gesture and his support. "So, now I'll go get Ryan." She got out of her chair, left their little space and then went back to the officers' workroom.

Apparently, Judd hadn't returned to the workroom. He might be in the break room or he might have been called out for something. Whatever the case, Ryan was alone reading something on his phone when she went in to get him.

"Hey, Ryan, you want to come with me to speak with Nick?"

"Speak to him about what?" he asked.

"You'll find out when you get there," she replied.

He shrugged his shoulders and turned off his phone. He then rose from the table and grinned at her. "You know I'll follow you anywhere, Short-Stuff."

Sarah sighed, but was grateful he followed her back down the hallway silently. Ryan had worked several of the murders, but they needed to know what he'd done in the hours before the bodies had been found. It would have been easy for him to kill a woman and then show up a couple of hours later on duty. There were two murders that he hadn't been on duty for and hadn't been called in for.

"Hey, man," Ryan said in greeting to Nick.

"Officer Staub…please have a seat. We have some questions to ask you," Nick said.

"And I'm sure I have some answers for you," Ryan said flippantly.

"Where were you in the hours before you showed up to work the Soulange murder?" Nick asked.

Ryan looked first at Nick and then at Sarah in surprise.

He then leaned back in his chair and laughed. "Is this some kind of a joke?" he finally asked.

"It's absolutely no joke," Sarah replied.

"You really think I'm the big, bad killer you're looking for?" He turned his gaze once again on Sarah. "Short-Stuff, you should know better than this."

"Her name is Sarah or Officer Beauregard." Nick's eyes were the color of dark storms. "If I hear you diminish her name or stature again within this department, I'll file a lawsuit on her behalf."

Ryan stopped laughing and met Nick's gaze. "Oh, give it a rest, tough guy. You aren't going to do that."

"Try me. You'll find out that I don't play," Nick said with a deadly calm.

"Sarah doesn't mind if I tease her," Ryan said with a little less assurance in his voice.

"Actually, Ryan, I do mind," she said.

"Duly noted," he replied to her. "I'm sorry if I've hurt you." His mouth said the words, but his blue eyes were a dark shade that she'd never seen there before. He didn't look sorry. He looked angry.

Was it really possible the man who had been asking her out for the past couple of months was the Honey Island Swamp Monster murderer?

Chapter Ten

Ryan was unable to provide a solid alibi for any of the nights of the murders. He thought he was on a date before one of the murders and then he said he was home alone and in bed. He needed to check his planner to see where he might have been and who he might have been with. He'd have to get back with them.

When he left their room, Sarah released a deep sigh. "God, he sounded guilty as hell," she said.

"Maybe…maybe not," Nick said. "A lot of innocent people when put on the spot can't name what they were doing on any particular night."

"But on several of those nights he investigated heinous murders, you would think his activities for those nights would be burned in his brain," she protested.

"We'll see what kind of alibis he can provide once he checks his planner," Nick replied.

"Planner, my butt," she retorted.

Nick laughed. "You don't believe he has a daily planner?"

"He has a daily planner like I have a flying blue dog," she replied, making Nick laugh again.

"We'll see if he can provide us something tomorrow," he said.

Sarah appeared utterly miserable and again Nick recognized how difficult this all must be for her. These were men she'd worked with, fellow officers she'd considered friends.

"I keep going over and over it again in my mind," she said with obvious frustration. "If one of the officers really is our killer then why didn't I get a sense of that kind of darkness in him? Why didn't I feel something off about him?"

"Sarah, honey, hiding in plain sight, that's what these kind of people…that's what these kinds of killers are good at. He's a cool customer and he definitely believes he's much smarter than us."

"Is he? I mean, is it possible we won't ever be able to identify him?" Her eyes simmered with a wealth of worry.

Nick took her hand in his. "We're going to get him, Sarah. He doesn't realize he's up against a partnership better than Batman and Robin, smarter than Sherlock and Dr. Watson and more tenacious than Scooby-Doo and Shaggy."

She immediately laughed at his silliness, which was exactly what he wanted. He loved the sound of her laughter and the fact that the darkness that had been in her eyes was momentarily gone. He squeezed her hand and then released it. "You can't give up now, Sarah. We're so close and when we do get him, think of all the young lives we'll be saving."

She sighed once again. "I only wish you would have been brought in earlier," she replied. "Then maybe he would have been taken off the streets much sooner and some of these women would still be alive."

"Unfortunately, we can't go back in time, but we're here

now and we're getting closer and closer. Now, who should we talk to next?"

He still saw how troubled she was, but he couldn't do anything to make this process easier on her. He wished he could, but the truth was he couldn't. Still, the torment in her eyes hurt him for her.

They did one more interview and then stopped for a quick lunch of burgers from a drive-through called Big Larry's. After eating they interviewed two more officers.

There were no other officers in house to speak with and so for the rest of the afternoon they made phone calls and scheduled interviews for the next day with some of the men who worked nights.

It was just after six when he sent Sarah home. They would have a full day the next day as they tried to get to as many officers as possible.

Once Sarah was gone, the scent of her lingered in the room. She had to know he was more than a little crazy about her. Surely she'd seen his emotions for her shining from his eyes when he gazed at her. Surely she felt it whenever he touched her even in the simplest way.

However, sometimes love just wasn't enough. He had loved Amy when he'd married her, but his love hadn't been enough to keep his marriage intact. When it came to relationships, he was a total loser and Sarah deserved far more than a loser in her life.

His mind shifted to the interviews they had conducted so far that day. He'd been trained in interrogation techniques and how to read body language. So far today none of the men had given him the tells that they were lying in any way.

Ryan had come closest as he'd deflected a lot during

the questioning and his body language had been closed off and defensive. Nick was eager to see what kind of receipts Ryan brought the next day as alibis for any of the nights of the murders.

Unbeknownst to Sarah, Nick had another suspect in mind, one that she'd already firmly rejected as a possibility. Gravois. The name now thundered in his brain.

Was it possible Gravois hadn't worked too hard in solving these murders because he didn't want them solved? As much as Nick had seen a lot of growth in Sarah, why would Gravois partner him with the least experienced officer in the department? Somebody who hadn't worked on any of the previous murder investigations?

Gravois was physically strong enough to carry the women out of the swamp and to a kill place. He would then be strong enough to take them to the places where their bodies had been found. The women would willingly interact with the head lawman without protest.

Still, Nick didn't intend to jump to any conclusions where Gravois was concerned. He would continue to exclude all the other men in the department and only then would he come at Gravois.

He didn't know how long he sat there lost in his thoughts, but he finally got up from the table and headed for the building's back door.

It was another gray evening with dark clouds hiding the sunlight and gloomy shadows taking over the landscape. He had just reached the driver side of his car when a gunshot fired off. He automatically hit the ground, aware that the bullet slammed into the driver door of his car.

He grabbed his gun as adrenaline fired through his entire body. Two cars over he saw some movement. He didn't return fire…at least not yet. Right now, he realized he was a sitting duck where he was and he needed to move around his car for more cover.

He started to rise to a crouch, but another bullet flew mere inches by his head to hit his car door once again. He dropped down and slithered like a snake on the ground to get around his car bumper and only then did he return fire by shooting twice in the direction where he'd seen the movement.

What the hell? Who was shooting at him? He waited, his heart beating frantically. He shot a quick glance around the bumper but saw no more movement.

The shadows were deepening by the minute. Was the shooter still there? Just waiting for him to leave his cover? Had the person moved to a different location where he could get off another shot?

He looked to his left and then his right, unsure where danger might come from next. He tightened his grip on his gun, ready to fire again if necessary.

Seconds turned into long minutes and nothing more happened. There were no more gunshots but still, Nick was reluctant to move from his cover.

At that moment the back door of the building flew open and Officer Colby Shanks stepped out. He was nothing but a kid and the last thing Nick wanted was for him to somehow get hurt.

"Get back inside, Shanks. There's an active shooter in the parking lot," Nick yelled.

Instead of going back inside, the kid dropped into a

crouching position and pulled his gun. "Where is he?" He pointed his weapon first to the left and then to the right.

By that time Nick had a feeling the danger had passed. Slowly he rose to his feet. Somebody had just tried to kill him. There was no doubt in his mind that the Honey Island Swamp Monster murderer was or had been in this parking lot with him and wanted him dead. That was a sure way to stop the investigation.

SARAH HAD USED her evening to try to de-stress. She'd taken a long, hot lilac-scented bath and then had baked a seasoned chicken breast and had added steamed broccoli for dinner.

She'd then sunk down on the sofa and had turned her television to a comedy show she occasionally watched. The show had just begun when Nick called.

Oh God, please not another body, she thought as she hit Pause on the remote and then answered. "Hey, partner, what's up?"

Nick never called her unless something had happened.

"Not much, I just decided to give you a call and make sure you were doing okay," he replied.

She frowned. Something had happened. She felt it in her bones. The phone call was completely out of character for him. "Okay, Nick…what's really going on? You've never called me before just to check on my well-being."

There was a long pause and then she heard him sigh. "I played a part in the gunfight at OK Corral tonight, only it happened in the station parking lot as I got to my car."

"What?" She tightened her fingers around her phone. "Are you okay?"

"Yeah, I'm fine. Thankfully whoever it was wasn't a terrific shot. He fired on me twice and missed and by that time I'd managed to move to some cover. Then Shanks came out of the back door and the shooter disappeared."

"Do you have any idea who it was?" she asked.

"Yeah, it was our killer. Am I certain who he is? No. I didn't get a look at him."

"Did you go in and report it to Gravois?"

"I attempted to, but he'd already left for the day. Ryan was also gone."

Even though his voice held no judgment, the pit of her stomach burned with anxiety. There was still no way she believed Gravois had anything to do with the murders, but she couldn't say that for sure about Ryan.

"Anyway," he continued, "I just wanted to call and make sure you were okay."

"Let's be honest, Nick. The killer wants the investigation to stop and he obviously doesn't see me as any kind of a threat. I'm just Officer Beauregard, who passes out speeding tickets and sits on the desk."

"The biggest mistake the killer can make is to underestimate you," he replied. "But you need to make me a promise, Sarah."

"What?"

"You need to promise me that if anything happens to me, you'll go on fighting to find this killer," he said.

"Nothing is going to happen to you, Nick," she protested. She didn't even want to think about him being hurt or killed. Her heart wouldn't be able to stand it.

"Just promise me, Sarah," he replied pleadingly.

"Okay, okay… I promise," she replied. "Maybe I should be your bodyguard as well as your partner," she said more than half-seriously. "I could pick you up in the mornings and drive you home in the evenings. With the two of us together, it would be far more difficult for somebody to attack you. Please, Nick…let's do that."

"I don't want to place you in any risk," he protested.

"We'll protect each other. So, it's settled, I'll pick you up in the morning at around seven."

His low laughter filled the line. "You are one stubborn woman."

"Yes, I am, when something matters to me, and you matter," she replied. "So I'll see you in the morning at Nene's and in the meantime, stay safe, Nick," she said, fighting against the words she really wanted to say.

She wanted to tell him that she loved him with all her heart and soul and that she couldn't imagine her life without him. But she also knew in her heart and soul that now wasn't the time for him to hear those words from her. He'd just been attacked by the killer, involved in a gunfight. The mood definitely wasn't right now for a romantic confession.

"Okay, partner, I'll see you in the morning," he replied, and with that they hung up.

The relaxation she'd found earlier in the evening was now gone, destroyed by the fact that somebody had tried to kill Nick in the parking lot.

Had it been Ryan? Or had it been another officer, one they had yet to interview? She didn't have the answer. All she knew was somebody had lain in wait for Nick and tried to kill him.

Chills raced down her spine. The stakes had been high to begin with in this case, but with the killer trying to take out Nick, the stakes had now shot through the ceiling.

The next morning, she pulled into Nene's driveway at ten after seven. Nick immediately walked out the front door, letting her know he'd been watching for her.

He got into the passenger side and grinned at her. "I have to say, you're one of the prettiest bodyguards I've ever seen."

She laughed. "Don't let all this prettiness fool you. I'm a mean bitch when it comes to protecting those I love." Realizing what she'd just said, she quickly pulled out of the driveway.

"We're going to have a long day," he said as she turned onto Main Street. "We've got a lot of interviews lined up for today but the good news is we'll only have four left to do tomorrow."

"And then we check out all the alibis and see where we're at," she replied.

"Exactly," he agreed. "I'd say within the next week we'll be able to name our killer."

"I hope so, and I hope there isn't another murder in the meantime," she replied.

If the case ended in a week, then it would be time for him to leave. What she wanted to tell him was how badly she'd miss him. She'd miss their deep conversations and their shared laughter. She would miss his touch and his warm smiles. God, she would miss everything about him.

However, she said none of that. But she was determined that before he left Black Bayou, he would know how much she loved him, how deeply she was in love with him.

They made one stop on the way in at a small bakery where they got tall cups of coffee for themselves and two dozen doughnuts. "We'll offer the officers a doughnut and while they enjoy the sweet, we'll dig deep into their heads," Nick said.

By the time they got to the office, the first officer on their list of interviews had arrived. Bart Kurby worked nights and Sarah didn't know him very well. On the nights of the murders, he'd been off work.

He was a tall, middle-aged man, physically fit and with dark, hooded eyes. He sat at their table and didn't accept their offer of a doughnut.

He appeared tired and impatient as it was past time for him to go home and get some sleep after being on duty all night long. "We'd like to talk to you about the nights of the murders," Nick said.

"Yeah, I heard you were talking to everyone in the department," Bart replied. "I can't believe you two really think one of us is the Honey Island Swamp Monster."

"We're just following where the evidence takes us," Sarah said.

He shot her a quick glance and then looked back at Nick. "So, what do you want to know from me?"

Sarah frowned. The man had dismissed her with that single look and it definitely irritated her. Apparently, Nick had caught it, too, for he looked at her and gave an imperceptible nod of his head.

"Bart, we have seen from scheduling that you weren't working on the nights of the murders. We need to know what you were doing on those nights between the hours of about six and one in the morning," Sarah said with as much authority as she could muster.

Bart looked at her once again, this time with a little more

interest. "I think on most of the nights, I would have been in bed by about nine in the evening."

"Anybody in bed with you?" she asked. She did know that Bart wasn't married.

He raised a dark eyebrow. "I'm really not the type to kiss and tell."

"Better to kiss and tell than wind up in prison for murders you didn't commit," she replied.

He hesitated a long moment. "Fine, on the night of the last murder I was with Paula Kincaid. We were together all evening and she spent the night at my place."

"Speaking of places, we know you live in an apartment here in town, but you also own a property just outside of town. What is that?" she asked.

"That's my parents' old place. I've been working on it and plan to move in there within the next couple of months," he said.

"Okay, I think that's all we need from you right now," she said, and stood to dismiss the man.

"Good work, partner," Nick said as soon as Bart left.

"He definitely ticked me off by dismissing me. Thanks for letting me do the interview," she replied.

"No problem, you did a good job."

"Thanks. You know what's really interesting? Paula Kincaid is supposedly happily married to George Kincaid, who travels for business. I wonder if push comes to shove, she'll substantiate Bart's alibi."

"Time will tell, and speaking of time, our next officer should be ready to be interviewed," Nick replied.

And so, the day passed. It was half past six by the time they were finished. There were two doughnuts left in the box and Sarah's head was filled with all the information they'd garnered that day.

"How about dinner at the café," Nick suggested as they packed up their notes to leave.

"Sounds good to me," she agreed. Together they left the station and got into her car.

"While we eat, we can talk about everything we learned today," he said once they were headed to the café.

"Good, because my brain feels like it's about to explode with all the new information," she replied. "I'm hoping you can help me make sense of it all."

"I'll do my best, but I was hoping you could help me make sense of it all," he replied with a small laugh.

Fifteen minutes later they were seated at the café and had ordered their dinner. He reached across the table and took her hand in his. She loved when he held her hand, and he did it often.

"I'm so proud of you, Sarah," he said. His beautiful gray eyes held her gaze intently as his thumb rubbed back and forth on her hand. "You've come a long way since you took that bath in the swamp."

She laughed. "There was really no other way than up at that point." Warm shivers stole up her spine as he continued to make love to her hand with his.

"Seriously, you've become a formidable officer and I hope that when all this is over, you aren't handing out tickets or stuck on the dispatch desk. You deserve to be working on criminal cases."

He released her hand only when their food arrived. They had both ordered burgers and fries and for the next hour and a half they ate and talked about the suspects they had interviewed that day.

"What I find so interesting about today is that Ryan didn't bring us any alibis," he said.

Sarah dragged a fry through the pool of ketchup on her plate. "Maybe he lost his day planner," she replied drily.

Nick laughed but sobered quickly. "If he doesn't bring us anything tomorrow, then we need to pull him in for a less friendly interview."

"Sounds like a plan," she agreed. "I want this killer caught and if it's Ryan, then he deserves to go to prison."

"Whoever it is, he's going to be spending the rest of his life in prison. You look tired," he said as they finished up the meal.

"I am," she admitted. "I just need a good night's sleep and then I'll be ready to go hard in the morning."

Minutes later they left the café and as they walked to her car, his hand once again sought hers. He had to love her, she thought. He had to love her more than a little bit. He reached to touch her far too often for this relationship to be strictly partners in crime solving.

None of that mattered as they reached her car and he got into the passenger side while she got behind the wheel. "What about you? Are you tired?" she asked.

"Yeah, I am, but like you all I need is a good night's sleep and I'll be ready to go again."

They were quiet on the ride to Nene's and within minutes he was gone, leaving only the scent of his cologne behind. She had no idea where they would go after the investigation was over and the killer was behind bars.

He'd already told her he never wanted to be a husband

again and Sarah was at a place in her life where she didn't want to settle for less. She wanted a husband and children. She wanted a family. Ever since her parents had died, she'd had a desire to build her own family.

She couldn't think about all this right now. They had a killer to catch and then she'd see what happened with Nick. Still, no matter how she twisted things in her head where he was concerned, she just didn't see a happy ending.

Chapter Eleven

Sarah's head now was filled with alibis and questions concerning all the men they'd spoken to that day. Even talking to Nick over dinner hadn't managed to quiet the chaos in her head.

She got home and pulled into her garage, then entered her house. She dropped her car keys on the table but carried her gun back to the bedroom. She didn't intend to make the mistake of being without her gun at night ever again.

After a quick shower, she got into her nightgown and crawled into bed. As always, her mattress embraced her and within minutes, she was sound asleep.

Her phone woke her. She fumbled for it on the nightstand and noted that it was one o'clock. The call could only be bad news.

She was surprised that the caller identification showed that it was Gravois calling her. She answered. "Gravois?"

"Sarah, I just got a hot tip that the killer is going to act tonight, probably within the next hour or so."

"A hot tip?" She frowned. "A hot tip from who?"

"I'll explain everything when you get here," he said.

"Get where?" She sat up and gripped her phone tighter.

"To the swamp," he said with an urgency in his voice. "You know where the old fallen tree trunk is?"

"Yes, I do."

"Meet me there as quickly as possible. I've already called Nick so there's no reason for you to speak to him. Don't waste any time, Sarah. We're going to get the bastard tonight."

"I'll be there as quickly as possible," she replied.

The minute the call ended she flew into action. As she dressed, she wondered what kind of a tip Gravois had gotten and who was the tipster?

Would they really be able to catch the killer tonight? Oh God, she hoped so. It was past time to get him behind bars, especially before another woman died. She was ready to go within ten minutes and then she got into her car and headed to Vincent's.

The night was unusually dark with a heavy layer of clouds hiding the moon and stars. The streets were deserted so she was able to push the speed limit and arrive at Vincent's in record time.

She didn't see Gravois's or Nick's car in the lot, but she knew where to go and hopefully the two men would show up quickly.

She decided to shoot a quick text to Nick. Gravois called me and I'm here just waiting for you and him to show up. Tonight, we get him! She sent the text and then got out of her car.

She hesitated before entering the darkness of the swamp. On the one hand she wanted…no, needed to turn on the flashlight on her phone, but on the other hand she didn't want a killer to see her or know she was out here.

With it being so dark, she finally decided to turn on the flashlight and point it directly toward the ground. She didn't want to trip and hurt herself. She wanted to be an active participant in taking down the killer. She'd worked so hard for this.

A tipster. Obviously, somebody knew something about the killer and had decided to contact Gravois with this important information. Hopefully no other woman would die after tonight.

She kept the light shining on the ground and hoped nobody would see her. It didn't take her long to find the fallen tree trunk. Once there, she sat on the trunk and shut off her light.

She tried to listen for the sounds of the two men approaching but the swamp was filled with noises of its own. Bugs buzzed around her head and someplace in the distance, a fish slapped the water. Wind blew through the tops of the trees and little creatures rustled in the brush nearby.

She nearly screamed out when a hand clamped down on her shoulder. She whirled around to see Gravois. "Jeez, you scared me half to death," she whispered.

"Sorry," he replied. His flashlight was on and he shone it on himself.

"What's going on? Are you going to tell me who your tipster is?" she asked, her voice still in a whisper.

"Not right now. According to what he told me, we don't have much time," he replied, also whispering.

"I wonder where Nick is?" she asked.

"I don't know, but we can't wait for him. We need to get in position."

"Is the killer coming in this way?" she asked, a faint chill trying to walk up her spine.

"That's what I was told," he replied. "We need to crouch behind this trunk and hide and wait to see who shows up. I definitely think it's going to be one of the officers."

"Your tipster didn't tell you specifically who it was?" she asked.

"No. I was lucky to get as much information as I did out of him," Gravois replied. "Now, we need to get into position."

Who would it be? Who was going to come into the swamp with another heinous murder on his mind? She stood to move behind the trunk, but before she could take a step, Gravois slapped her phone out of her hand and then crushed it with his heel.

She stared at him in stunned surprise. "Gravois…wha- what are you doing?"

As she stared at his face, she suddenly realized his eyes were narrowed and his features were tensed in a mask of evil she'd never seen there before. A daze of shock held her in place as her mind grappled to make sense of what was happening.

Danger. Danger. It flashed in her head that she was in trouble. Gravois…it had been him all along. Oh God, he was the Honey Island Swamp Monster murderer.

"Sarah…" he said softly, and then reached out for her. It was then she saw it…a hypodermic needle in his hand. The daze of shock and surprise snapped and she ran. Blindly she raced into the swamp with Gravois on her heels.

She ran for her life. Frantically she sped into the dark- ness, knowing that if he caught her, she would be the next victim of the monster.

NICK'S NOTIFICATION DING awoke him, indicating he had a text. Who on earth would be texting him at this time of the night?

He grabbed his phone and read the message from Sarah. Gravois called me and I'm here just waiting for you and him to show up. Tonight, we get him!

He read the message twice and then, with his heart pounding, he jumped out of bed and got dressed. Gravois. The name thundered over and over again in Nick's head.

He immediately tried to call her, but it rang and rang and then went to voice mail. He quickly dressed and then strapped on his holster and gun. If Gravois had hurt a hair on Sarah's head Nick would kill the man. Sarah had said she was there and waiting for him, but she hadn't told him where she was.

All he knew for sure was that he believed Sarah was in trouble. Her message had implied that Gravois had contacted him, but that hadn't happened. Yes, Sarah was definitely in danger. If what he believed was right then she was alone with the man who might be the killer.

The swamp. That was the only place that made some sort of insane sense. She had to be there. He jumped into his car and headed out. He continued to try to call her, but all his calls continued to go to her voice mail.

Thank God at a few minutes after one in the morning the streets were deserted, allowing him to get to Vincent's in just a few minutes. And thank God he'd guessed right in coming here as Sarah's car was in the parking lot.

He got out of his car and as he gazed into the dark entrance of the marsh the back of his throat closed up and the familiar high anxiety tightened his chest.

Dammit, he wasn't a frightened little boy anymore. He was a grown man and he needed to go into the swamp and find the woman he loved...a woman he feared was in terrible danger.

With that thought in mind, he swallowed against his fear, turned on the flashlight feature on his phone and headed in. The anxiety he now felt wasn't due to him being in the swamp; rather it was because he needed to find Sarah.

It didn't take him long to reach the old fallen tree trunk and as his flashlight swept the area, it landed on a phone... Sarah's phone. The blood seemed to rush out of his body, leaving him light-headed.

If he needed a physical reason to believe Sarah was in danger this was it. He reached down and picked up the broken phone. He pressed the power button, but nothing happened. He slid the phone into his pocket.

This was why she hadn't answered his phone calls. Who had done this? Who was out here with her? Was it Gravois? That seemed to be the only answer given her text message to Nick.

"Sarah!" He yelled her name as loud as he could. His heart ached as all kinds of possibilities raced through his head. Where could she be?

"Sarah," he yelled once again.

"Nick... Nick, help me." Her voice came from someplace deeper in the swamp.

He released a deep gasp of relief. She was alive! But she was definitely in danger. He raced toward the sound of her voice, desperate to get to her.

"Sarah, I'm coming...keep yelling to me," he shouted.

"Nick...hurry." Her voice was filled with a terror that

torched a like emotion inside him. He had to get to her. Oh God, he needed to save her from whoever was after her.

He ran as fast as possible, batting back tree limbs and jumping over pools of water. Any fear he'd had about being in the swamp was gone, replaced by his need to find the woman he loved.

He stopped for a brief moment, panting for air, and then he called her name again. There was no response. "Sarah," he cried, needing to hear her to find her in the vast vegetation.

She screamed, a blood-curdling sound that shot icy chills through him. "Sarah," he cried desperately. There was no reply. "Sarah?" he called her name over and over again as he hurried forward.

Oh God, why wasn't she answering? And what had made her scream like that? Frantically he ran. His biggest fear was that she was now in the clutches of the Honey Island Swamp Monster murderer.

He didn't know how long he continued to search, but without her calling to him it was futile. Was she still here in the swamp? Maybe. He just didn't know what to believe.

Gravois called me and I'm here just waiting for you and him to show up. Tonight, we get him!

He read her text again. Gravois. He had to be the killer and he'd lured Sarah here to make her his next victim. It didn't matter that she didn't fit his usual profile. The proof was in the text she'd sent to him. Gravois had called her and lured her out here.

Gravois. The man's name pounded over and over again

in Nick's head. He needed to find the lawman as quickly as possible.

With this thought in mind, Nick ran to exit the swamp. There was nothing more he could do here by himself. The marshland was simply too big for him to find her by himself.

He finally reached Vincent's parking lot where Sarah's vehicle was still parked. He got into his car and leaned his forehead against the steering wheel, for a moment overwhelmed with emotion. Tears burned hot at his eyes and his chest tightened as a deep sob escaped him.

His love for Sarah ached inside him. He needed his partner. Was it already too late? No, he refused to believe that. It couldn't be too late. With this thought in mind, he swiped the tears out of his eyes, put the car into drive and tore out of the parking lot.

Hell, he didn't even know where Gravois lived. He'd have to go to the station and see if somebody there knew. He drove as fast as possible, aware that time was of the essence.

He pulled to a halt in front of the police station and went in the front door where Judd Lynons was on the front desk. "Hey, man, do you know Gravois's address?" Nick asked.

"Why? What's going on?" Judd asked curiously.

"I just need his address. It's important," Nick replied. He didn't want to waste time by explaining everything.

"I don't know his exact address, but I know he lives on Tupelo Lane. Tupelo Lane is off Main Street by Mike's Grocery store. His house is in the middle of the block. It's a blue two-story and…"

Nick didn't wait to hear anything more. He turned on his heels and then raced back outside to his car. He tore away from the curb and headed down Main Street where he knew the grocery store was located.

He gripped the steering wheel tightly as tears once again blurred his vision. *Please let her still be alive. Please let her still be alive.* The words repeated over and over again in his head. It was a mantra…a prayer that went around and around in his brain.

He reached the grocery store and saw Tupelo Lane. He made the left onto the street. Tall trees encroached on the narrow street as Nick drove slowly, checking the houses on either side of the road.

The neighborhood was old, but the houses appeared well-kept. And then he saw it. The house was a slate blue with a wraparound porch, and Gravois's official car was in the driveway.

He parked along the curb and his heart thundered as he got out of the car and raced to the front door. He knocked. There was no response. He knocked again, this time loud enough to wake the entire neighborhood.

"Hang on," Gravois's voice drifted out. After only a moment he opened the door. The man was without a shirt and was clad only in a pair of sleep pants. His hair was disheveled as if he'd just been pulled from his bed.

"Nick, what in the hell is going on?" he asked.

Nick stared at the man in confusion. This was not the Gravois that he'd expected to find. "Sarah is missing," he said.

Gravois frowned. "Missing? What do you mean she's missing? Isn't she at home? It's the middle of the night."

"No, she isn't home. She said you called her and told her to go to the swamp?"

Gravois's frown deepened and he stepped out of his door onto the porch with Nick. "I didn't call Sarah. The last time I spoke to her was this morning at the station. So what's going on here?"

"I don't know, but this is what I do know. Sarah was in the swamp." Nick went on to explain as quickly as possible everything that had happened when he'd arrived at the swamp.

"Dammit, if somebody has harmed Sarah, there will be hell to pay," Gravois said angrily. "I'll meet you at the station in fifteen minutes. I'll call in all the men and we'll search the swamp until we find her."

"I'll be at the station waiting for you," Nick replied, and then he got back into his car. As he headed back to the station his brain whirled. Did he believe Gravois? Yeah, he tended to believe him. He'd certainly reacted in a way that made Nick want to believe him. If he didn't believe Gravois was responsible, then who was?

Who had called Sarah and impersonated Gravois? Had she been too sleepy when she'd answered the phone to know that it wasn't Gravois? Was the call so short that somebody had fooled her? He supposed that was certainly a possibility.

So, who was it? Who had lured Sarah to the swamp? He believed it was the Honey Island Swamp Monster murderer. Sarah had believed she was too unimportant in the investigation for anyone to come after her, but somebody had definitely seen her as a threat.

By the time he reached the station, he was once again overwhelmed by a wealth of emotion. He went back into the little room he and Sarah had shared and sank down at the table to wait for Gravois to arrive.

Her scent was everywhere, that fresh floral fragrance

that he found so attractive. He thought of her bright smile, the one that always made him feel like the sunshine was in his chest. She couldn't be dead. She had to be still alive. He needed her.

He jumped up out of the chair when he heard Gravois's voice booming down the hallway. He met the lawman in the hall. "I've called in all the men. The only one I couldn't get hold of was Ryan, but I left him a message to meet us at the swamp and that's where all the other men will meet us, so we need to head out."

"I'm right behind you," Nick replied, a new urgency filling his soul.

Twenty minutes later the men were all at Vincent's. All of them carried high-powered flashlights. It was impossible to do a normal grid search so Gravois appointed the men areas to go. Right now, it was a search-and-rescue operation. He hoped like hell it didn't change to become a recover maneuver.

He hurried to the place where he'd last heard her voice. Right now, the swamp was alive with the sounds of all the officers calling out her name.

Her name resonated in his heart, deep in his very soul. They had to find her and they had to find her alive. He continued to crash through the marsh, looking everywhere for her.

"Mr. Nick." Gator stepped out of the brush, nearly scaring Nick half to death. "What's going on here?"

"Gator, Sarah has gone missing and I last heard from her here in the swamp." Nick quickly explained what had happened. "Did you hear anything out here tonight? Did you see anything?"

"Most nights I'm out and about, but tonight I slept until I heard all the commotion, so the answer is no. I'm sorry, but I didn't see or hear anything. I'll help the search now."

"Thanks, Gator," Nick replied.

The old man nodded at him and then disappeared back into the brush and Nick continued moving forward. One more person searching could only help.

They searched until dawn when Gravois called things off because the men needed a break. They all agreed to reconvene at the station in a half an hour for more instructions.

Nick remained in Vincent's parking lot after the others had left. The morning sun was sparking on the trees, turning it all a rich golden color.

She wasn't there. His gut instinct told him she was no longer in the swamp. The search had been far-reaching, but the swamp was vast. But he now believed she'd been taken away from the swamp.

Had she been taken to the killing grounds? Where was that? How long did the killer keep his victims there before killing them? Maybe minutes…hopefully hours.

Once again, a wealth of emotion tightened his chest and tears blurred his vision. Where was Sarah? If what he believed was true, then one of the cops who had helped search for her was the same person who had taken her.

And where was Ryan? He hadn't shown up for the search. Suddenly it was imperative that he find Ryan.

Chapter Twelve

Sarah regained consciousness slowly. The first thing she noticed was the huge headache that stretched painfully across her forehead. She tried to open her eyes, but she was still too groggy and it felt as if her eyelids weighed a thousand pounds.

She remained still and simply breathed, but there was a noxious smell surrounding her. It was horrible and it reminded her of the stench in James Noman's shanty. Oh God, is that where she was?

No...that wasn't right. Her brain began to slowly clear. She'd gotten a call from Gravois and she'd gone to the swamp. Her smashed phone and the race through the swamp...all the events of the night suddenly flashed in her head.

Gravois. Dear God, it had been him all along. He was the Honey Island Swamp Monster killer. She'd run so hard and so fast last night to escape him and the hypodermic needle he'd held in his hand.

When she'd heard Nick, she'd hoped...she'd prayed he would get to her before Gravois did, but that hadn't happened. If she hadn't tripped over a big tuber, she might have escaped him. But the moment she hit the ground he was on her.

She screamed and fought with him, but ultimately, he'd managed to get the needle in her arm. She'd continued to fight for several more moments before darkness had gripped her and she knew no more.

So where was she now? She finally managed to open her eyes. She was tied to a straight-backed chair and appeared to be in a basement. Even though there were few basements in the area, there were some. This wasn't just any basement; she knew she was in the killing ground.

Oh God. Dried blood stained the floor all around her chair. The stench was so horrendous and she knew it came from what was left of the poor victims. This was where Gravois not only stabbed the women, but also where he ripped out their throats and tore off their faces.

She had to get out. She struggled against the ropes that held her arms behind her as gasping cries escaped her. She twisted and turned her wrists. If she could just get one hand out of the ropes, she would be able to untie herself and escape.

There were no sounds from the upstairs and she sensed she was alone in whatever place she was at. Was the basement in Gravois's house? It had been years since she'd been inside his home.

She continued to fight to get free, but there was no give in the ropes. She fought until she was out of breath and gasping with pain and sheer terror. How long would it be before Gravois would come back here?

She finally leaned her head back and sobbed. Nobody

would know that the chief of police was the monster. Except Nick. If he got her text then he should know.

So why wasn't he here? Did her text not go through? You couldn't always depend on technology. If for some reason he hadn't gotten her text then nobody would know she was here. Nobody would ever suspect the chief of police. She'd even assured Nick that there was no way she'd believe that Gravois was responsible for the murders. She'd been wrong...so very wrong.

Right now, she was on her own. Somehow, someway, she had to get out of here. She drew in several deep breaths and then began working her hands once again, twisting and turning them until she was once again crying and her wrists felt raw enough to be bleeding.

It took several minutes for her to calm herself. She had to stay calm so she could think rationally. She did not want to become another victim of the Honey Island Swamp Monster murderer.

For the first time she began to look around the room. In front of her was a small wooden workbench with two deep drawers, but there was nothing on top of it. However hanging above it was a gardening claw. The tool looked dirty with rust-colored stains she believed to be blood.

Was that what he used to tear out his victim's throats? To rake their faces off? She swallowed hard against the new wave of emotions that rose up inside her. It wasn't just terror; it was also abject horror that filled her.

This felt like a scene from a horrible horror film, one of those sick, bloody films that she had always refused to watch. And now she was living it.

To her left was a staircase leading up and to her right...

dear heavens...there was an old red recliner chair and in the chair was an intact human skeleton.

Gravois's missing wife. The one who had supposedly left him years ago. Yvette. She hadn't left at all. She'd been murdered and her body had been here all along.

For the first time since she'd opened her eyes, Sarah screamed.

THANKFULLY GRAVOIS WAS at the station when Nick arrived. Nick immediately went into his office. "We need to check out Ryan. He didn't show up for the search and he could be our man."

"You're right. With all the commotion going on, I didn't miss him being there, but it's very suspicious that he didn't show up at all."

"Where does he live?"

"He has a little house just outside the city limits. I'll gather up a couple of men and we'll head there right now." Gravois got up from his desk and twenty minutes later Nick was following behind his car to Ryan's place.

The man had brought them no alibis for the nights of the murders and he'd been no place to be found when Sarah had disappeared. Nick also hadn't realized the man lived in a house just out of the city limits. A house that might hold the killing grounds. A man who possibly had Sarah right now.

The tiredness from the all-night search disappeared as a new burst of adrenaline filled Nick. This had to be it, and he prayed that they weren't already too late. The last thing he wanted to do was find Sarah's body, her throat torn out and her beautiful face ravaged, behind some random building in town.

At least Gravois drove fast as if filled with the same anxious energy Nick felt. Behind Nick were two more patrol cars, each carrying two officers.

They finally pulled up in Ryan's long driveway. The house was small, probably a two-bedroom. There was also a detached garage. Ryan's vehicle was in the drive, indicating that he was home.

Gravois took the lead, marching up to the front door and knocking. He waited a moment and then knocked again more forcefully.

"Officer Staub," he yelled.

"Yeah…yeah, I'm coming," Ryan yelled. A moment later he opened his door. The man looked like hell. He was clad in a pair of sleep pants and a gray T-shirt. His face was unusually pale and he looked at them all in confusion.

"What's going on? I'm sorry I missed the search but I'm sick as a dog," he said. "I've got a temperature of 102 and I've been throwing up my guts for most of the night and day, so why are you all here?"

"We're still looking for Sarah," Nick said. "Mind if we come in?"

Ryan looked at him in surprise. "You think Sarah is in here? You really think I'm the killer?" He opened his door wide to allow them entry. "It's not me, man. You're all wasting your time here."

"Check out the garage," Gravois said to the other men and then he and Nick stepped into the house.

There was a blue sheet on the sofa and a box of tissues and a bottle of cold medicine on the coffee table. There was no nasty scent to indicate anything nefarious had happened in here.

"Feel free to look around," Ryan said as he sank back down on the sofa. "I can't even believe you all think I'd have anything to do with the murders or whatever happened to Sarah. I would never, ever hurt that woman."

They did look around. Gravois went into the kitchen while Nick looked in each of the two bedrooms. There was nothing suspicious anywhere in the house. The other officers returned from outside and shook their heads, indicating there was nothing in the garage.

Bitter disappointment shot through Nick. She wasn't here, so where was she? They all agreed to meet back at the station in a half an hour or so. Once there, they would try to figure out where to go from here.

Nick returned to the station and sat in their little room, a sickness filling his soul. So much time had passed since he'd heard her cries in the swamp. If she was still alive, he knew time was running out for her.

Frantically, he went over all the notes they'd made that day, looking for something that would jump out at him.

He was so afraid. His childhood trauma, snakes beneath the bed and the gunfire in the parking lot…none of that had prepared him for the kind of fear that torched through him now.

He'd made her promise to carry on if anything happened to him, but he'd never seen the danger that was coming after her. Why in the hell hadn't he realized that she was at risk?

His job had been to come in and solve this case. He'd told her he'd never lost a partner before but she was so much more than his partner.

Now he didn't know where she was and his heart was slowly dying.

SARAH HAD FOUGHT against the ropes for what felt like hours…days, and she still found no give in them. She'd fought as hard as she could and had wept all her tears she had inside her.

She now leaned her head forward and began to feel a weary acceptance. She was going to die at the hands of the man she'd believed had loved her as a daughter. She was going to die here in this chamber of horrors.

Why, in all the years she'd known him, hadn't she seen the darkness that must be in his soul? Why had she never seen the utter evil that resided inside him?

Thank God, she hadn't burdened Nick by telling him how much she loved him. Hopefully he would go on with the investigation and he'd eventually get Gravois behind bars.

That didn't stop her from mourning what might have been. Even if things hadn't worked out with Nick, she'd still wanted to be somebody's wife. She'd wanted babies to fill her arms and to build a real family with some special man. She hadn't realized how badly she'd wanted that, and she had wanted that with Nick. Now she would never get any of those opportunities.

At least with her death she would be reunited with her parents in heaven. She'd once again be with the two people who had loved her unconditionally and had been her best friends.

A vision of Nick filled her head. His handsome features were ingrained in her brain, along with the sound of his deep, wonderful laughter. She loved the way his forehead wrinkled when he was deep in concentration and the way his smile warmed her throughout. She loved everything about him and she just wished she would have had an opportunity to tell him goodbye.

She straightened up as she heard the sound of a door opening and then closing from upstairs. It had to be Gravois and he was probably here for one reason...to stab her and then rip out her throat and tear off her face.

Once again, she began struggling against the ropes, sheer panic coursing through her. The door at the top of the stairs opened and she began to cry.

Gravois's heavy footsteps coming down the stairs sounded like the rhythm of death coming for her. Then he stood before her.

"Ah, Sarah, I'm so sorry it's come to this," he said with pity in his voice. "Unfortunately, your boyfriend seems to have angel wings of protection around him. The snakes didn't kill him nor was I able to shoot him to death. But I'm sure your death will mess with his mind so much he'll have to quit the investigation."

"He'll never stop. He's going to throw you in jail, Gravois," she said angrily. "You'll suffer for the rest of your life in prison. I can't believe you killed all those young women. I can't believe you're such a monster. And...and is that Yvette?"

"It is my lovely Yvette." His features softened as he gazed at the skeleton in the chair. "It's been years now, but we had a fight and I pushed her. She fell over and hit her head on the edge of the coffee table. Unfortunately, it was a fatal blow. My beautiful, loving wife died."

"Why didn't you go to the authorities? If it was an accident then you wouldn't have been in any trouble," she replied. She needed to keep him talking, on the off chance somebody would find her...that somebody could save her.

"For God's sake, Gravois, why not at least give her a proper burial?" she asked.

"I didn't want anyone taking her away from me," he replied, his voice raised and his eyes slightly wild. "I love her more than anyone on the face of the planet and I needed her here with me. I needed to keep her here with me. I'll love her until the day I die."

"So, why kill all the women from the swamp?" Sarah asked softly, trying to calm him.

"Yvette looked like a lot of the women from the swamp. She had the same beautiful features as the swamp women. I just needed to find the right face. If I found the right one, then I would be able to give Yvette a face back."

Sarah stared at him in true revulsion. This was something out of the worst horror movie. "Gravois, you need help." He was obviously horribly mentally ill. To think that he was hunting for a face to give to his dead wife...the thought shuddered inside her.

"I don't need help," he yelled, his face turning red. "I just need to find the right damn face. So far, they've been all wrong. When I got them back here, I realized their faces were all wrong, so I erased them."

He stalked over to the workbench and opened one of the drawers. He withdrew a sharp-looking knife and then turned back to face her.

"Gravois, you don't want to do this," she cried frantically. "Please, you don't have to kill me. Let me go and I won't tell anyone about this. I'll make sure I screw up the investigation so nobody will ever come after you."

"Ah, sweet Sarah, you're just lying to me now."

"I'm not… I'm not lying to you," she replied fervently. She would say anything to him just to get him to let her go unharmed. "Gravois, please, you can trust me."

He shook his head. "I would never trust you. You've become a good cop, Sarah, and good cops want to get the bad guys off the streets. You're definitely a threat to what I'm trying to accomplish here."

"But I have loyalty toward you. You helped me so much after my parents died. You were there for me, Gravois, and I haven't forgotten that. Now I want to be here for you."

He laughed, but there was no humor in the laughter. Instead, it was a sick, twisted sound. "You're good, Sarah. You're very good. But nothing you say is going to stop what's about to happen."

He jabbed the knife forward. "I'm sorry that the first couple of stabs are going to hurt you, but hopefully you won't be conscious when I rip out your throat and tear your face off."

He stabbed the knife into her stomach and she screamed as excruciating pain ripped through her and she realized she was definitely the next victim of the Honey Island Swamp Monster murderer.

NICK SAT IN the room and went over all their notes and picked apart everything that had happened. Somewhere in the minutiae of it all, he had made a mistake or overlooked something important. He thought about everything that had happened since the moment he'd received the notification from Sarah on his phone.

The notification had said that Gravois had called her yet the man had denied that had happened. When Nick had gone to Gravois's house, the man had looked disheveled and as if he'd just climbed out of bed. But how easy would it have been for him to tousle his hair and change into a pair of sleep pants?

He'd stepped outside his house to talk to Nick. Why hadn't he invited Nick inside? A headache pounded in Nick's head. Gravois, the name once again thundered in his head.

Why had he not investigated the cases better? Why had he partnered Nick with somebody who knew nothing about the cases? Where had Gravois been on the nights of the murders? And where was Gravois now? Why would he call for a half an hour break in the search efforts?

God, Nick had been such a fool. He jumped up from the table and ran down the hallway to Gravois's office. He knocked once and then threw open the door. Gravois wasn't there.

A wild panic rose up in him. Gravois, it was the only thing that made sense. Dammit, Nick had suspected the man and now it was imperative that Nick get to his home and see if Sarah was there.

Colby Shanks and Ian Brubaker were standing by the dispatch desk. "Can you two come with me?" he asked urgently.

"Where?" they asked in unison.

"To Gravois's place. I think Sarah is there and I need you two to back me up."

"You think Gravois is the killer?" Shanks asked in shocked surprise.

"I do and I think Sarah is there and in danger. Will you come with me?"

The two officers looked at each other. "I'll go," Shanks said, and looked back at Nick.

"I definitely need to go, too," Brubaker agreed.

"Then let's go." Nick ran outside to his car, got in and tore out of the parking lot. All his nerves were electrified, shooting a fierce alarm through him. A glance in his rearview mirror showed him that the two officers were behind him.

Was it already too late? Oh God, how much of a lead did Gravois have on him? Had the man had enough time to go home and kill Sarah?

Tears of fear and frustration filled Nick's eyes. It couldn't be too late. She couldn't be gone already. His heart beat so fast he felt as if it might explode right out of his chest.

He reached Tupelo Lane and turned left, cutting off another driver who honked at him and gave him the finger. Nick didn't care, he had to get to Gravois's place as quickly as possible.

He pulled into Gravois's driveway behind the lawman's car. He parked and flew out of the car. It was only when he reached the front door that a wave of doubts overcame him.

Was he jumping to conclusions? Was this just all a big mistake? No, it couldn't be. His gut instinct told him that this was right. Shanks and Brubaker joined him on the porch. Nick knocked hard on the door and it creaked open.

He immediately drew his gun. The minute he stepped into the house he knew for certain he was right. The faint odor of human blood and decay filled his nose.

The two officers followed right behind him. "Check the bedrooms," he said to them. While they disappeared down the hallway, Nick checked the living room and kitchen, but found nothing incriminating.

Where was the man? He had to be home. His car was outside. Brubaker and Shanks walked into the living room. "Nothing," Shanks said.

"Gravois," Nick yelled.

"Nick! We're down here," Sarah called.

He nearly fell to his knees at the sound of her voice. She was alive! Down here? There must be a basement. He opened one door and found a closet.

He ran to the kitchen where there were two doors. He'd already checked them once. The first one was a pantry. The second appeared to be a broom closet, but now on closer inspection, Nick saw that it had a false back. He pulled it away and a staircase was revealed.

"Gravois," he shouted. "It's over, man. Don't hurt her." Nick took two steps down and bent over to see the situation. The stench down here was horrendous and as he perused the area, his blood ran cold.

She was tied in a chair and Gravois stood before her with a bloody knife in his hand. "Put the knife down," he yelled. "Put the knife down right now." He raced down the rest of the stairs and pointed his gun at Gravois. "If you don't put it down right now, I'm going to shoot you."

Gravois looked at him and in the man's eyes radiated the evil that was inside him. "Can you really shoot me before I stab her?" he taunted.

Nick fired. The bullet hit Gravois in the thigh and with a scream of pain the lawman went down to the ground. Nick kicked the knife out of his hand and across the floor. "Call for an ambulance and put him in cuffs," Nick said to the others.

He ran to Sarah's side. "It's okay, baby. You're safe now,"

he said. He left her only to look in the workbench drawer for something he could use to cut the ropes that held her. He found another knife there and hurried back to her side.

She was quietly crying as he worked the knife back and forth against the thick rope. As he labored, he gazed around the kill chamber, horrified by the skeleton that sat nearby in a chair.

He didn't know who the skeleton belonged to but eventually he would find out. It appeared it was another murder Gravois would be charged with. He continued to talk soothingly to Sarah as Gravois yelled his rage.

"Why didn't you just shoot me in the heart?" Gravois screamed.

"Because I want you alive to face all the disgust from your officers. I want you alive to waste away in prison," Nick said tersely.

"Damn you," Gravois yelled as Brubaker and Shanks got him in handcuffs.

"Nick…" Sarah said with a gasping breath.

"It's okay, honey. You're almost free now," he replied. He cut through the last of the rope and it fell not only from her hands but from her waist as well.

It was only then he saw it…the blood that covered her stomach. "Sarah, oh God." He pulled up her shirt and saw the two gaping, bloody wounds in her belly.

"Nick," she whispered. Her eyes fluttered several times and then she fell unconscious.

"Get an ambulance here now," Nick cried. Had he been too late after all? Had Gravois mortally wounded Sarah? His heart cried out with anguish.

Chapter Thirteen

Nick sat in the waiting room in the emergency area of the hospital. The ambulance had finally arrived and Sarah was now in emergency surgery. She'd never regained consciousness while she'd been with Nick.

Once again, an abject fear coursed through him. He had no idea how badly she'd been hurt, how deep the stab wounds had been. But he couldn't help but remember the other victims had died from their stab wounds.

He'd been waiting for about an hour now to hear something, anything about her condition but so far nobody had come out to speak with him.

He knew Gravois was also here in the hospital getting surgery for his gunshot wound. He was also being guarded by Officers Kurby and Shanks.

Brubaker was the deputy police chief and he would be taking over the mess that Gravois had left behind until a special election could be held to appoint a new chief.

Brubaker would also be in charge of the crime scene and collecting the evidence that would send Gravois away for the rest of his life. There was no question in Nick's mind that the blood of all the victims was in that basement.

He couldn't believe what a hellhole Sarah had been held in. He couldn't begin to imagine what kind of horror she must have felt when she saw that skeleton sitting in the chair. God, she must have been so afraid.

She had to be all right. Please, she had to survive this. She was a fighter, but could she fight for her life despite those knife wounds?

He leaned forward and dropped his head in his hands. *Please let her survive.* He couldn't imagine a world without her in it. The world needed that beautiful smile of hers.

The outer door whooshed open and he was surprised to see Ryan walk in. He looked better than he had earlier that morning. "My fever broke and I heard the news about Sarah," he said. He sank down two chairs away from Nick. "Have you heard anything?"

"Nothing," Nick replied.

"I can't believe it was Gravois all along," Ryan said.

"He's not only a serious danger, but he's also a disgrace to law enforcement," Nick said with disgust.

"This is certainly going to shake up this entire town," Ryan replied. "I wouldn't be surprised if this doesn't make national news, a police chief who is a serial killer. So, does this mean you'll be leaving soon?"

"Not for a week or so. I want to make sure we get all the evidence we need for the case. Don't worry, I'll be out of your hair soon and then the path will be clear for you with Sarah." Even saying those words shot an arrow of pain through Nick.

Ryan released a dry laugh. "There's no path forward for me with Sarah. In case you haven't noticed, she's totally in love with you."

Nick didn't reply. Ryan's words only made Nick's heart hurt more. "I appreciate you coming here," he finally said.

"Despite what it's looked like, I care about Sarah as a friend and coworker. I would never want this for her."

"You should see Gravois's basement," Nick replied, and then described the utter madness to Ryan.

"I can't imagine how Sarah felt trapped there," Ryan replied.

"I just wonder what's taking so long? Why hasn't the doctor come out to talk to me yet?" Nick said in frustration.

Was it a good sign or a bad sign that it was taking so long? Was she still in surgery or had she succumbed to her wounds?

Fifteen minutes later a tall, dark-haired man came into the room. Both Nick and Ryan jumped to their feet. "Mr. Cain, I'm Dr. Etienne Richards," he said.

"How's Sarah?" Nick asked as his heart pounded with an unsteady rhythm.

"Given no complications, she should be fine. Unfortunately, one of the knife wounds caught her gallbladder so I had to remove it and I also had to do some muscle repair. Her wrists are raw but right now she's in stable condition."

"Can I see her?" Nick asked.

The doctor shook his head negatively. "She's sleeping now and I intend to keep her comfortable with pain medicine for the rest of the day. It would be better to come back and visit with her tomorrow."

Nick was disappointed but wasn't about to argue. "Thank you, Dr. Richards," he said. The doctor nodded at both of them and then went back through the door.

"At least we know she's going to be okay," Ryan said.

"And now I'm dragging myself back to my sofa. See you later, Nick." Ryan left the waiting room.

Nick left as well. It was time to work the crime scene. He got in his car and headed back to Gravois's house. As he drove his heart was filled with wild relief. She had survived her time with a serial killer. Thank God, she was going to be okay.

Now he needed to do his job to ensure that all the evidence was photographed and collected. Everything had to be done by the book so there was no way Gravois would be freed on a technicality.

When he pulled up out front of the blue house on Tupelo Lane there were three patrol cars there plus a hearse, which indicated the coroner was also there.

As Nick reached the front door, Officer Ken Mayfield and the coroner's assistant carried up a stretcher with the skeleton on top. Dr. Cartwright followed after them.

"Hell of a day," he said to Nick. "Is Sarah okay?"

"She had to go through surgery, but at the moment she's stable," Nick replied.

"Good, at least she's better than that poor woman," he said, and pointed to the skeleton that was being carried to the hearse. "Who knew that Gravois was so sick. He had to have been sick to keep that and to kill all those young women." He shook his head. "Hell of a day," he repeated. "I'll talk to you later." He headed toward the hearse.

Nick went into the house and down the stairs where Brubaker appeared to have a good handle on things. There were three other officers with him and two of them were collecting blood samples around the chair while the other officer was standing by.

"Hey, Nick, what's the word on Sarah?" Brubaker asked.

Nick told him the same thing he'd told Dr. Cartwright. "How can I help?"

"I think we've got it covered right now. We've already taken the crime scene photos and collected both the knife and a claw gardening tool. We'll probably be here for the rest of the day collecting the evidence that hopefully will tie him to all the Swamp Monster murders."

Brubaker shook his head. "I can't believe he was responsible for all the carnage. He was a man I looked up to, the man I worked closely with. Damn, but I'm so disgusted right now, both with him and with myself for not seeing the evil in him."

Nick clapped Brubaker on the shoulder. "Don't beat yourself up. Nobody saw him for what he was. A lot of responsibility just fell on your shoulders. I have confidence that when I leave here the department will be in good hands."

"Thanks. I really appreciate that coming from you."

"If you don't mind, I'll just hang out here awhile and if you need me just tell me what to do," Nick replied.

"That would be great," Brubaker replied. "The problem is this is a relatively small space so not many people can work it. Right now, those two are getting what we need." He gestured to the two officers taking blood samples.

Nick took a seat on the stairs and he remained there until dinnertime. He missed Sarah. While he wouldn't want her down here in the stench and the memories of being tied up, he wished she was here by his side.

He missed the scent of her perfume surrounding him, her leaning over to whisper something in his ear. At least he could see her tomorrow, although he didn't know how long she'd be in the hospital.

As much as he missed her today, it wouldn't be long before he would leave Black Bayou and Sarah behind. He'd leave his heart here with her and it would take a very long time to get over her.

But he had to leave her. The worst thing he could do was allow her to continue loving him. She would eventually want marriage and he knew what kind of a husband he was.

She deserved a terrific husband in her life and so the kindest thing he could do was let her go.

SARAH AWOKE AND for a moment didn't know where she was. She started to jerk up but then pain tore through her stomach. She looked around and realized she was in the hospital. Evening light cast in through the window and she was alone in the room.

She relaxed back and tried to process how she had gotten here. The last thing she remembered was being tied up in Gravois's basement as he stabbed her. She reached down and touched her stomach, which had bandages across it.

Then she remembered Nick coming down the stairs. Nick. He'd found her. He'd shot Gravois and saved her very life. Her love for him blossomed in her chest, filling it with a delicious warmth.

Somehow, she'd been brought here and whatever the doctor had done for her, it had obviously saved her life as well. She needed to know what had been done to her. Would she still be able to have children, or had Gravois taken that away from her with his knife wounds?

She looked around until she found a call button and then

she pushed it, hoping whoever answered would be able to give her some information.

Moments later a nurse came in and introduced herself as Kelly. "I know Dr. Richards has been waiting for you to wake up. I'll just go get him now."

"Thank you," Sarah replied, and raised the head of her bed.

"How's my patient?" Dr. Richards asked as he came into the room a few minutes later.

"I'm having some pain, but what I want right now is some information."

As she listened to what the doctor had done, a wave of relief rushed through her. Who needed a gallbladder anyway? At least there had been no other real damage to her.

"Before you go, Dr. Richards, have you seen my partner, Nick?"

"He was here earlier and wanted to see you, but I told him it would be better if he came back tomorrow to visit with you."

"Okay, thank you," she replied.

"I'll see that the nurse gets you some more pain meds and I'll see you in the morning as well." Dr. Richards left and the nurse came in and administered the pain medication.

It wasn't long before Sarah drifted back off to sleep. She awakened with the morning sun streaming brightness into the room. Her stomach was sore but she knew it was going to take some time for her to heal.

She raised the head of her bed and wondered when Nick would be in to see her. The crime was now solved and so there was nothing more keeping him here. He would be leaving her any day now.

Unless…unless her words of love for him would keep him with her. She was running out of time. She had to talk to him today and tell him how much she loved him. Along with the ache in her stomach, her nerves formed a wave of anxiety as she anticipated laying her heart out on the line to him.

She hadn't been awake long when breakfast arrived. Breakfast consisted of coffee, broth and gelatin. She immediately took off the lid to the coffee and sipped on it. She hoped when they dismissed her, she would be armed with information about diet after gallbladder removal. Hopefully it wouldn't be broth and gelatin for the rest of her life.

She wound up drinking all the broth and eating the gelatin, then continued to sip on her coffee as thoughts of Nick swirled around in her head.

Her breakfast tray had just been removed when Dr. Richards came into the room. "Sarah, how are you doing this morning?"

"Better than last time I spoke with you," she replied.

"That's always what a doctor wants to hear."

"I do have more questions for you this morning."

"Hopefully I have answers for you," he replied.

She asked him about recovery time, surprised when he told her six to eight weeks. Then she questioned him about diet and finally she asked when she could be released from the hospital. Without any complications, she could go home in two to three days.

Once the doctor left, she turned on her television to pass the time. She was halfway through a game show when he walked in. As always, Nick looked handsome clad in black slacks and a gray polo that perfectly matched his eyes. His familiar scent smelled like safety…like home.

"Sarah," he said softly as he sat in the chair next to her and reached for her hand.

All the trauma she'd been through suddenly rose up inside her and she began to cry. "Oh, honey…don't do that. It will only make you hurt more."

"Oh, Nick, it…it was so horrible," she choked out amid her tears. "Being in—in that basement wi-with so much death surrounding me. And—and then Gravois there with a knife. I—I was so sure I was going to die down there."

"But you didn't," he replied gently.

"Thanks to you." She managed to get her crying under control as she squeezed his hand tightly. "How did you know it was Gravois?"

She listened as he told her everything that had happened after she'd disappeared from the swamp. "Thank God, you sent me that text, but Gravois was a crafty one and initially fooled me."

They continued to talk about the case for the next half an hour or so. "You look tired," she observed. His features were slightly drawn with what looked like exhaustion.

"I was up most of the night helping the men collect all the evidence at Gravois's house," he replied.

"He needs mental help. He told me the skeleton was his wife and he was taking the swamp women hoping he could somehow take their face to put on her. But each time he got them to his basement he realized their faces were all wrong. He's definitely mentally ill."

"I doubt he'll get much help in prison, and that's where he belongs," Nick replied. "The good thing is it's finally over. The bad guy is behind bars and according to what the doctor told me you're going to be just fine."

"I'm not going to be fine, Nick. I'm so deeply in love with you. I won't be fine without you," she said. She watched him closely and felt the press of tears once again burning in her eyes as his turned a cold dark, slate gray.

"I want to marry you and give you babies. I want to spend the rest of my life with you. Please, Nick. I know you love me, too," she babbled. Why were his eyes so emotionless while she felt herself falling completely apart?

"Sarah." He pulled his hand from hers. "You knew going into this that eventually I'd go home. I never promised you anything. I even told you I'm not husband material."

"But you are," she protested. "Maybe you and your ex-wife weren't right for each other, but we are, Nick. Look into my eyes, Nick, and tell me you don't love me." She held his gaze, looking for a softening, and she gasped with relief as she saw it.

"That doesn't matter, Sarah. Even if I do love you, I don't intend to do anything about it. I'm sorry, Sarah, but in a couple of days I'll be going home and hopefully in time you'll find the perfect man for you here in Black Bayou."

She stared at him as he stood. How could he not see they were perfect for each other? "Have you ever considered that your ex-wife was wrong about you? You couldn't have been a lousy husband, Nick, because you're not a lousy man. You're the man I choose. I don't want anyone else but you."

"I'm so sorry, Sarah. It was never my intention to hurt you. I'll check in with you before I leave town and now, I'll just let you rest." With that, he left her room.

Rest? Her heart had just been ripped out of her very body. A rush of tears overwhelmed her and she began to cry in earnest. She'd been so hopeful, so sure that he loved her as much as she did him.

She'd been filled with such dreams of the two of them together. She'd been so sure they would have a life together and now all those dreams had been destroyed.

She didn't know how long she wept. By the time she pulled herself together Ryan and Judd Lynons walked in carrying a large vase of flowers.

For the rest of the afternoon officers came in carrying flowers and plants and good wishes. There was definitely a new respect in the way they interacted with her. At least she'd gained that, but nothing could warm her heart with the loss of Nick so fresh.

By the end of the day her room looked like a floral shop and all the officers had been in to visit with her. She directed the nurse to disperse some of the flowers to other hospital rooms.

As the darkness of night fell, so did more tears. She wept until she could weep no more. She'd been so excited to tell Nick how she felt and in her heart of hearts, she'd thought he'd sweep her up in his arms and tell her how much he loved her, how much he wanted to spend the rest of his life with her. Now she just felt empty, so achingly empty.

Over the next three days the emptiness was filled with heartache as she continued to mourn the loss of her dreams…the loss of Nick. She kept hoping he would come back in and tell her he couldn't live without her after all, and that he wanted a life with her. But that hadn't happened.

She was finally released from the hospital and Ryan drove her home. She'd been settled in at home for two days when a knock fell on her door. She went to answer and found Nick on her doorstep.

She hadn't heard from or seen him since he'd walked out of her hospital room and taken her heart with him. She opened her door and gestured him in. As he swept past her, she smelled that familiar scent of him, a scent that now only brought her more pain.

"Hi, Sarah." He stopped just inside the door. "I told you I'd stop by on my way out of town."

"So, you're leaving," she replied. Her heart began a new dull ache of loss.

"I am. I'll probably have to come back a couple of times as it relates to the prosecution of Gravois, but for right now I guess this is goodbye." He oozed discomfort as he gazed at her.

She wasn't going to let him off the hook so easily. "You were an excellent partner. You taught me so much and I loved the time we spent together."

"We were good partners," he agreed.

"We could still be good partners in life," she said softly. "Oh, Nick, if you'd just look deep within your heart, I know you'll find the kind of love for me that will last us a lifetime. All you have to do is take a chance on me, take a chance on us."

His eyes darkened. "I'm sorry that I can't give you what you want, Sarah," he replied with regret rife in his tone.

"I hate your ex-wife," she replied suddenly. He looked at her in surprise. "I hate her because I think she made you believe things about yourself that aren't true, things that have destroyed your ability to believe in yourself, to know what kind of a good man you are. Trust me, Nick. Don't trust her."

"Sarah, I just came by to tell you goodbye." He edged back toward the door.

"I love you, Nick," she said one last time, knowing once he walked out of the door, she would never see him again.

He hesitated for a long moment and in that moment, she held her breath, hoping...praying that she'd finally reached him. "Goodbye, Sarah," he finally said, and then walked out the door.

She wanted to run after him and throw her arms around him. She wanted to beg him to reconsider, but she did have a little bit of pride left. She sank down on her sofa, her heart pain too deep for even tears at this moment.

What would be the point of chasing after him? He knew how she felt and he'd rejected her anyway. Twice he'd rejected her. There was no more she could say to him. Now she had to figure out how to live without him.

Three weeks passed and physically she was feeling pretty much back to normal. But there wasn't a minute that went by that she didn't miss Nick. She had so many memories of him burned deep in her heart and she couldn't forget them.

She had been off work on sick leave and the house echoed around her with emptiness. Her loneliness was intense but she knew nobody else would assuage it except the man who had been her partner.

Hopefully, when she did return to work Brubaker would assign her to some serious case or another so she could immerse herself in something other than missing Nick. Hopefully Brubaker would see her for the good police officer she'd become.

It was right after noon on the twenty-third day since she'd

last seen Nick and she'd just made herself a sandwich for lunch when there was a knock on her door.

She left her lunch and went to the door. She gasped in stunned surprise as she saw Nick.

What was he doing back here? Did he need something as far as the case was concerned? Weeks ago, she had given Brubaker her official statement about her time with Gravois. What could Nick need from her?

For a moment she wished she were dressed in something other than a slightly faded pink T-shirt and a pair of gray jogging pants. He looked amazing in a pair of jeans and a white long-sleeved dress shirt.

She put up all her defenses as she opened the door. "Hi, Sarah, can I come in?" he asked.

Silently she ushered him in. He went directly into her living room and sank down on the sofa.

"What are you doing here, Nick?" she asked as her heart beat an unsteady rhythm. She didn't sit, but rather remained standing. She didn't want to be close enough to him to smell his cologne or allow him to touch her in any way.

"How are you feeling?" he asked.

"As good as new," she replied. Did he have any idea what his presence here was doing to her? As much as she wanted to be strong and unaffected by him, her love for him still burned deep inside her heart and soul. "Why are you here? I'm sure you didn't travel here just to ask me how I'm doing."

"Actually, I was hoping you could help me solve a case."

She frowned at him. "What kind of case?" Had he lost his mind? Why would he be back here in Black Bay asking her about a case?

"It's about a missing woman. I've realized over the past three weeks that I need her in my life. She's a woman I want to desperately find because she fulfills me in a way I never expected." He stood, his gaze soft and warm on her. "Oh, Sarah, I've been such a fool."

She took a step toward him, her heart thundering in her chest. Was this for real? Was he really here for her? She was so afraid to believe it.

"But there's more," he said, stopping her in her tracks. "The woman has to be willing to relocate for me. The bad news is she'll need to leave everything here behind, but the good news is the New Orleans Police Department is always looking for good officers and if that's what she wants she'll easily be able to get a job."

He took a step toward her, his gaze so soft…so loving. "Sarah, I love you so much and I can't imagine you not being in my life. The last three weeks without you have been absolute hell. Marry me, Sarah, and I promise I will try to be the very best husband you would ever want. Marry me and make me the happiest man in the world."

"Are you sure, Nick?" she asked, her heart on the verge of exploding with happiness.

"I've never been so sure in my entire life," he replied.

She could stand it no longer. She flew into his arms where he wrapped his arms around her and kissed her long and deep. When the kiss ended, he stared down at her intently.

"Are you sure you're willing to relocate? I mean, you have a house here and ties to your friends," he said.

"I can sell my house and honestly, Nick, this has never really felt like home. I found home with you and yes, I'm more than willing to relocate," she replied.

He laughed. "I guess Nene was right about me after all," he said.

She looked up at him curiously. "Why? What did she say about you?"

"On the first day I arrived here she told me that I was like one of the heroes in the romance books she read. I was the handsome stranger who had come to save the day and, in the process, would find my own true love." He grinned down at her. "Funny how right she was."

"Funny how right you were to come and get me. You are my hero, Nick, and I will always love you," she replied.

"And I will always, always love you," he replied.

He took her lips once again in a kiss that whispered of passion but screamed of love. Even though she hadn't been looking for love, Nick had come into her life and everything had changed for her. She was truly home with him and she knew their partnership was going to last a lifetime.

* * * * *

COMING SOON!

We really hope you enjoyed reading this book
If you're looking for more romance
be sure to head to the shops when
new books are available on

Thursday 14th
March

To see which titles are coming soon, please visit
millsandboon.co.uk/nextmonth

MILLS & BOON

afterglow BOOKS

Introducing our newest series, Afterglow.

From showing up to glowing up, Afterglow characters are on the path to leading their best lives and finding romance along the way – with a dash of sizzling spice!

Follow characters from all walks of life as they chase their dreams and find that true love is only the beginning...

OUT NOW

millsandboon.co.uk

LET'S TALK

Romance

For exclusive extracts, competitions
and special offers, find us online:

f MillsandBoon

X @MillsandBoon

⊙ @MillsandBoonUK

♪ @MillsandBoonUK

Get in touch on 01413 063 232

For all the latest titles coming soon, visit
millsandboon.co.uk/nextmonth